Sally Worboyes was born and grew up in Stepney with four brothers and a sister, and she brings some of the raw history of her own family background to her East End sagas. She now lives in Norfolk with her husband, with whom she has three grown-up children. She has written several plays which have been broadcast on Anglia Television and Radio Four. She also adapted her own play and novel, *Wild Hops*, as a musical, *The Hop-Pickers*.

Praise for Sally Worboyes

'Unbridled passions run riot' *Daily Mail*

'Sizzles with passion' *Guardian*

'It's a rich, vivid, three-dimensional, gutsy and sexy narrative which has you turning the pages into the early hours' *Eastern Daily Press*

'Here is a vivid evocation of a way of life' *East Anglian Daily Times*

SALLY WORBOYES

Wild Hops

HODDER

First published in Great Britain in 1994 by Headline Book Publishing
A division of Hodder Headline

This edition published in 2017 by Hodder & Stoughton
An Hachette UK company

1

A CIP catalogue record for this title is available from the British Library

Paperback ISBN 978 1 473 65955 1
Ebook ISBN 978 1 444 71946 8

Printed and bound by CPI Group (UK) Ltd, Croydon, CR0 4YY

Hodder & Stoughton policy is to use papers that are natural, renewable
and recyclable products and made from wood grown in sustainable forests.
The logging and manufacturing processes are expected to conform to
the environmental regulations of the country of origin.

Hodder & Stoughton Ltd
Carmelite House
50 Victoria Embankment
London EC4Y 0DZ

www.hodder.co.uk

For Lorraine and Luke

This book is also dedicated to Richard,
whose smile will always be remembered.

Acknowledgements

I am indebted to the nurse at West Suffolk Hospital, Bury St Edmunds, for her advice on how to deal with Julia's burns.

One

1959

Throughout the late August night, smoke from small bonfires has swirled across the tiny gardens in Stepney filling the air with a damp, spicy aroma. But now, just after the dawn chorus, in the pink glow of the rising sun, the ashes are cooling and the scent from red-flowering roses and honeysuckle drifts through the fresh morning air.

The distant echo of a milk cart on its rounds and the clicking of stiletto heels can just be heard, as an office cleaner steps out of a block of flats on her way to catch the early-morning bus into the city.

A ginger cat stretches lazily on a low brick wall, basking in the first rays of the sun, and the distant rumbling sound of a steam train breaks through the quiet, as it approaches Bethnal Green railway station on its way to Liverpool Street.

*   *   *

Laura Armstrong had slept so badly that when the alarm finally went off, she slumbered through that and the noise of the steam train as it passed by.

The sound of the high-pitched alarm clock merged into her nightmare. The block of flats where she lived with Jack and their fifteen-year-old daughter, Kay, was alight and the fire-bell was the signal for everyone to get out. Screams of terrified children filled her head, bars on every window and door filled her vision. She was a prisoner. Through the iron bars she could see her daughter running away from the flames. She could hear Jack shouting about the rubbish chute being a fire hazard. No one could see her through the thick black smoke which was forcing its way into her eyes and throat.

Crashing through the door of her bedroom Laura's husband, Jack, stood in the doorway wearing only his pants and vest, his eyes still heavy with sleep. 'It's not even the crack of dawn, Laura!' he grumbled, stumbling forward and slamming one hand down on the alarm clock. 'What's wrong with you – gone mad, or what?'

Trying to focus, Laura rubbed her eyes and on seeing Jack in his underwear turned away, feeling strangely embarrassed. 'There's work to be done,' she said quietly, aware of her husky morning voice.

'What, at this hour?'

'The lorry'll be 'ere at nine!' Trying to shake off the effects of her nightmare, she slipped her long legs from beneath the covers and sat on the edge of the bed with her back to him, gazing at her new lilac chintz curtains. 'Three tea chests, one 'opping box and a suitcase to pack.'

'Couldn't you 'ave done that yesterday?'

'I was at work, Jack, remember?' She slipped on her pale lilac candlewick dressing gown and tied the cord tightly around her small waist. 'Other women get help with their packing.'

'Yeah, well, I wouldn't know what to put in and what to leave out, you know that.' She felt his light blue eyes burning into her back, and knew he would be gazing at her long auburn hair, remembering how much he used to love the way it fell in curls down her back. 'You could put the kettle on,' she snapped, conscious of the sudden awkward moment.

'Call me at eight and I'll do the breakfast.' He was by the door now, reaching for the handle.

'The lorry's coming at nine!'

'Plenty of time. Egg and bacon? Won't take five minutes. You're too anxious, that's your trouble. Can't wait to smell them 'ops – and get away from me.' He pulled at the door handle which was stuck again, gave it a sharp tug and the door flew open. 'You wanna get this thing fixed. Find yourself locked in 'ere one of these days.'

'Forgotten how to use a screwdriver 'ave yer, Jack?'

Grinning, he turned to face her, and showing off his lovely beaming smile and white teeth, gave her a wink. 'Is that an invitation?'

Laura shot him a look from big hazel-speckled green eyes, draining any sign of humour from his face. She wanted to remind him who had moved out of the marital bed in the first place, but thought better of it. Let him go back to his room, where he would sleep until what he considered to be a decent time. She could manage without him.

Now that the picking season had finally arrived Laura wondered if she was ready for it. Another week would have been perfect. She would have liked more time to prepare herself properly for the four or five weeks that lay ahead. It had been hectic during the past months. The decorators had been working on the flats, painting and wallpapering every room, and she had only just got straight.

Fully awake now, she took in the new décor and was glad that she had paid the extra few pounds to the council for her chosen wallpaper. The tiny lavender flowers blended perfectly with the soft furnishings.

Carefully pulling back her curtains, the sun streaming through the new white nets, she wondered if she would have given hop-picking a miss this year if it wasn't for Richard. The thought of his warm brown eyes and gentle smile lifted her. *Not long now*, she thought. It had been a long ten months and until the last few weeks or so, the time had dragged more than she imagined possible.

This time, Laura told herself, she would make the most of every minute she was with Richard. After all, five weeks out of fifty-two each year was hardly a lifetime. Closing her eyes, she imagined his strong arms pulling her close, her face buried in his chest, as he kissed her hair. He always kissed her hair. Remembering the lovemaking which usually followed, she snapped herself out of that dangerous mood and went into the kitchen. She would have a cup of tea and a biscuit before she started to pack her hopping saucepans into a tea chest.

The smell of paint was still in the air and Laura loved it. Not that she was fond of the smell but the way the paint had transformed her home. Every window-frame and door had been painted in white gloss and every wall had been papered, even in the kitchen, which Jack moaned about every morning, saying it felt like he was sitting in a fruit shop. But then Jack liked to have something to moan about. Laura couldn't see what was wrong with having lemons, limes and bananas against a white background. Better than the council's green paint on offer from the Borough.

Taking her tea and biscuit into the front room, she opened the deep red curtains leading to the balcony and sat in the armchair that caught the sun as it shone through the windows. This was the best time of the day for Laura; she loved the quiet when she had time to think, especially in the living-room where it was comfortable. Even Jack had to admit that the decorators had made an excellent job of the wallpaper. The black and red over the fireplace was a good contrast to the other three walls, which were lightly patterned with dashes of grey against a white background.

Sitting there, sipping her tea, she tried to imagine Richard in one of the armchairs smoking his pipe, a glass of brandy on the coffee-table and his slippers on the red carpet. Smiling to herself, she sighed. It was a fantasy, and she wasn't daft enough to think it could be anything else. They came from different worlds and although her flat was her castle, Stepney was hardly the place for Richard. She could imagine him going outside, maybe chastising one of the boys for breaking a window and being told to *piss off* by one of their fathers.

No. He would never fit into her world the way she did into his. Well, she slipped into part of his world, anyway, but always had to slip out again when hop-picking was over.

By ten o'clock, most of the packing had been done and the large hopping box was on its way down the concrete stairs, propped up by Jack and his brother-in-law, Bert. Laura was giving the flowers in her window-boxes on the balcony a last-minute soaking. The marigolds looked glorious, like a golden carpet sweeping through the mass of trailing blue lobelia. She could see a few neighbours in the grounds below, waiting to wave the lorry off. Some of the smaller children were enjoying a game of tin-tan-tommy, some were playing marbles and there was the usual skipping game going on. The sound of children playing, laughing and yelling at each other echoed around the brick buildings.

Jack and Bert could also be heard as they struggled down the flights of stairs. Laura couldn't help smiling, they reminded her of Laurel and Hardy. Creeping forward, she listened to their conversation as they paused on the flight below.

'Jesus, what's Laura packed into this thing, Jack? Your three-piece suite?'

'Don't ask me, Bert. This trunk's like our double bed, I never get a look-in.'

That was Laura's cue to stop eavesdropping as her mother's words came flooding back: 'Those who listen at keyholes only hear bad of themselves!' She was back in the flat like a shot.

Bert, being twenty-odd years older than Jack, was finding the weight of the trunk a bit much to cope with. Pausing for a while, the men took the opportunity to rest between the flights of concrete stairs in order to let Kay pass.

'Aunt Liz wants to know how long you're gonna be, Dad. It's hot on that lorry and she's sick of waiting. They're all gettin' grumpy.'

'Well, go and tell your mother, then. She's the one taking all the time. Right, Bert, you ready?'

'Yep. Up your end.'

'And tell 'er to get a move on! It's your Uncle Bert's lorry we're travelling in. Not the royal bloody coach!'

Kay squeezed her way past the men and took the stairs two at a time, calling back to her dad as she went, 'You tell 'er! I'm sick of being a mouthpiece for you two!'

'That's it Kay, you tell 'im.' The shrill voice of Sarah James the nosiest woman in the block, announced her arrival as she bumped her wheelie bag down the concrete stairs. 'They had a row then?' she continued, hoping to find something she could get her teeth into.

'Why don't you ask my mum,' Kay retorted, knowing full well the woman wouldn't dare. Laura was outspoken in her dealings with people who had nothing better to do than gossip. Kay smiled to herself as the only reply was the bumping of that shopping trolley as she continued down the stairs. 'Good job the lift is out of order,' Kay mumbled to herself as she passed the *No spitting* sign. She could never understand why that black-and white enamel plaque was up there. All it did was encourage the boys to do exactly what it told them not to.

Laura heard Kay coming back and presumed she would still be moving things from the kitchen to the lorry. Standing in front of the full-length mirror, considering the maroon jacket she had recently purchased, she suddenly felt a fool. Why had she let that pushy saleswoman talk her into buying it? She looked good in it, no doubt about that, but it was a mad impulse buy that would hardly look in keeping on the hop fields. Sweeping her slim fingers across the front and lingering for a few seconds on the velvet trim, she imagined herself wearing it for the man she loved. A mixed feeling of excitement and fear swept through her body. What if he no longer felt the same?

The door of her bedroom suddenly flew open and Kay burst in looking pleased with herself, ready to relay her confrontation with the nosy neighbour. Laura recoiled at the unexpected intrusion, feeling her embarrassment rise with the flush of colour creeping into her cheeks. Kay had not only caught her admiring her reflection, she had also seen the wistful look in her eyes, but more importantly perhaps to Laura, she had seen the new expensive jacket.

'How many times have I told you to knock before barging in here, Kay!' she snapped, conscious of feeling like a guilty child, caught with her hand in the biscuit jar. She regretted her words as they spilled out: sometimes she did tend to speak first and think later.

Kay's face fell, and as her smiling eyes clouded over she blushed and looked on the verge of tears. 'You've never told me that,' she said in a quiet, injured voice, 'but I will knock in future, if that's how you feel.'

'Oh, I didn't mean it, Kay.' Laura smiled at her daughter and shrugged, aware of her foolishness. 'Vanity,' she added with a shy smile.

Pleased that everything was OK again, Kay returned

a broad grin which reminded Laura so much of Jack. 'It's really nice, Mum. Suits you.' She walked over to her mother and examined the jacket, feeling the luxury of the soft material between her fingers. 'Bet it cost a few bob.'

A few quiet seconds passed as the two of them gazed into the mirror. 'You don't think the velvet trim's too . . . ?' Laura's voice trailed off.

'Classy? Yeah. But you can get away with it. You'd best not wear it on the lorry though. I can just imagine what Aunt Liz'd say.'

Aunt Liz was the last one to occupy Laura's mind, which was centred around someone else. All she could think of was whether Richard would like her in the jacket. He was like a shadow, forever slipping into her thoughts.

Moving across to Laura's bed, Kay sank down on to the soft mattress, ran her hand over the silky cover, then propped the pillows up behind her. Drawing her knees up and hugging them, she began to giggle quietly. 'I can just ima-gine the pickers when you walk into the White Horse wearing it.' She grinned, stretching her legs so that her cherry-patterned skirt slipped above her knees, enabling her to admire her summer tan. 'They'll be green with envy!' Catching a glimpse of her mother's face in the mirror, she sat up. 'You're not worried about it, are you, Mum?'

Still preoccupied with Richard, her lover, Laura answered vague and slow, a glazed look on her face. 'It was in Hammond's sale. Bought it last week. The saleswoman said it had been made for me, fitted like a glove. Probably says that to every customer . . .' She sighed heavily, not really in tune with what she was saying; the words were gently tumbling out as she tried to push her secret to the back of her mind. 'Reduced from twelve pounds, ten shillings . . .'

Kay loved it when they spoke together like this. Woman to woman, sharing private moments. She wanted to keep it going; she didn't want anyone or anything to disturb their time together, so seldom did it happen. 'To how much?' she urged.

'Seven pounds, fifteen shillings.' There was a touch of guilt in Laura's voice, but it had nothing to do with the cost of the jacket. She had suddenly realized how preoccupied she was and how far from the conversation her mind had wandered. She sighed and smiled at her child. Her child, who was now on the brink of becoming a beautiful young woman. Kay's long straight hair was as fair as Laura's was dark, and she had her father's clear blue eyes; 'Laughing Eyes', as he was nicknamed down the docks.

She wanted to take hold of her daughter and squeeze her close, but the risk of losing control of the tears which she had been on the verge of shedding all morning, stopped her. Kay would have wanted to know why she was crying and that was something which could hardly be answered in a word. After all, the aching pain which gripped Laura's heart was not misery. She had been looking forward to this day since the previous autumn and now that late August had finally arrived, she wanted to shout her joy from the rooftops. Tell everyone about her romance. But how could she? How could she chance hurting Kay? Laura was under no false illusions about the bond between daughter and father and the last thing she wanted was to damage that.

Kay had been working out how many bushels of hops it would take to pay for the jacket. She had her eyes shut and was mumbling under her breath. 'A . . . hundred and forty bushels of hops. Six days' good hop-grabbing. Easy.'

Laughing, Laura picked up her mock tortoiseshell hairbrush and swept it through her long auburn hair. 'Your father'd hit the roof, if he knew how much this cost.'

'Don't tell him, then.' Kay stared into her mother's shame-filled eyes. 'You didn't buy it for *him* to look at anyway!'

13

Sensing her daughter's sudden mood swing, Laura turned her face away and continued brushing her hair. The silence that followed could have been cut with a knife and as she glanced back at Kay's angry face, she was instantly reminded of the guilt locked away in a dark corner of her own mind. She had a feeling that Kay knew about her and Richard but she had always been careful to skate around it.

Kay stood up and made for the door. 'Aunt Liz was doing her nut down there. Why are you taking so long?'

The thought of her sister-in-law's knowing looks and the other families on the lorry brought Laura sharply to. The arduous journey though the Blackwall Tunnel, cramped up in a lorry, was not something she cherished the thought of. 'I've got weeks of that lot to look forward to . . . a few more minutes without them won't hurt.'

'Oh, here we go.' Kay was seeing the other side of her mother again – the side she didn't care for. 'You're gonna get all above yourself again. You change when we go hop-picking!'

Laura stiffened but said nothing. She slowly undid the buttons of her new jacket. Kay hadn't finished her retort and she knew it.

'You've lived in the East End longer than you've lived out of it! You went to schools round 'ere from

Infants through to Seniors, same as everyone else. Just because you were born in *Dagenham*!'

Laura took in a deep breath. 'You are nudging the line again Kay. Don't step over it.'

'Don't worry.' Kay turned away and pulled at the door handle, her expression conveying her mood. 'I won't!'

Desperate to turn those last couple of minutes around, Laura called after her. 'Kay! Did you remember to pack your hot-water bottle?' The answer confirmed it was too late.

'It's in the tea chest, on the lorry. Like everything else I've loaded!' The street door slammed and the loud bang seemed to stir every nerve in Laura's body. She buried her head in her hands and felt like having a good cry. There were times for weeping, but this was not the time. People were waiting. A world full of people, waiting. Yet here she was in her bedroom feeling strange, unreal, as if she was somehow caught in a twilight.

Jack was leaning against the warm brick wall when Kay arrived at the lorry. He was enjoying a smoke. 'Is that the lot, Kay?'

'Just the blankets to come. Mum'll fetch 'em.' With that, Kay made for the back of the lorry and climbed aboard, catching her cotton cherry-printed skirt on a tiny nail, ripping half the hem down. She instinctively slipped the hanging fabric under her knicker elastic. Her Aunt Liz, not one to be slow off the mark, was quick to bring a smile back to her niece's face. 'Good job I've brought some needles and cotton, eh? That'll mend, you'll see.'

'I hope so. This is my best skirt. Mum specially bought this red blouse to go with it as well.'

'I don't know why you're blushing over it.' She looked into Kay's face and smiled. 'Or do I?'

'How should I know?' Kay ignored her aunt's gentle teasing and casually untucked her torn hem. She knew very well what Liz was getting at.

'Couldn't be one of them boys grouped over there that's making your heart flutter, could it?

'No it could not! I owe one of 'em a punch in the face if you must know.'

A woman's voice from deep in the lorry sounded above the excited buzz and chatter of the three families on board. 'It's about time you acted your age, Kay! Must be all of fifteen now.'

'That's right, Mrs Brown. I am fifteen and yes, I am still at school!'

'Oh, yeah? So that's not lipstick I see then? You being a schoolgirl . . .' The woman was teasing Kay and everyone except her and Aunt Liz enjoyed the bit of mockery.

16

'You leave her be! A shadow of lipstick don't make her a woman. Anyway, that's Laura's chair you're sitting on. Pass it up here. I was saving that one for her.' Liz stood up, reached over and grabbed the kitchen chair from the tall skinny woman. 'There's an orange box in the corner. Sit on that!'

'I should have thought Laura would want a throne to perch on,' the woman retorted. 'Queen of the hop fields, or so she likes to think!' Again, laughter followed her words. Liz thought it best to ignore them, they were after all in high spirits and having a bit of fun. And there was a bit of truth in what they were laughing at.

'What's keeping your mother, anyway?'

'Turning off the gas and electric. She'll be down soon.'

Jack appeared, grinning as usual, 'You OK, ladies?' He addressed them as if each one was the only lady he was flirting with. His sister, Liz, just rolled her eyes. She was well used to him.

'Have a word with your Bert, will you, Lizzie. He won't let me help out with the driving!'

'You get your licence back, Jack boy, and you can drive our lorry to Kingdom Come. Until then, keep away from that wheel.' Liz looked at Kay and they both giggled at the way Jack was reacting, like a spoilt kid who wanted sweets.

'I ask you, Kay! Is that any way for a sister to talk to her baby brother?'

'I wouldn't know, Dad, would I?' Those few words from Kay came right out of the blue. Not planned, not even in the forefront of her mind.

'No, I don't suppose you would, babe.' Turning his attention to the bolt and chain attached to the tailboard, he tried not to think about the small brother who should have been sitting at Kay's side. Almost a minute passed without speaking. When the next word did come, at long last, it was from Liz who could see Laura approaching the lorry. She silently thanked her sister-in-law for her timing. Kay's remark had cut deep.

'About time an' all, Laura. What you been playing at? Gawd knows how long we've been sat in this bloody lorry waiting for you. What you been doing up there?'

'Oh, I just quickly papered the front room so it would be nice for Jack while I was away.'

'Cheeky cow. Here, give us your hand.' Liz reached out for Laura but Jack was in before they could link up.

'I'll lift yer, Laura. We don't want you to ladder your nylons, do we now?'

'I can manage, Jack.'

'I'm sure you can. But I'm gonna lift you anyway.

18

We're waiting to go!' In one swoop, Laura was in his arms and swinging through the air. 'It's like carrying you over the threshold again.'

An urgent toot of the horn from Bert stopped any more protest from Laura. Once she had landed squarely on the lorry, she pulled away from Jack and brushed herself down.

Jack gave Liz a cheeky wink. 'Right. Are you all sitting comfortably?'

A chorus of *Yes, Jack!* resounded through the lorry, followed by remarks urging him to get a move on.

As Laura watched Jack secure the tailboard, she was aware of a sudden attack of anguish which she struggled to calm. She felt Jack's eyes on her tanned legs and could tell he had picked up the faint, familiar smell of her perfume, Blue Grass. His eyes slowly followed the slim line of her pale green summer dress that almost matched her eyes, and up to her face, until they were looking at each other. A shy, furtive smile passed across his mouth.

'Let's be on our way then!' His strong voice rang through the quiet morning. 'Hoppin', here we come!'

A cheer went out while Jack made his way to the driver's cabin to keep Bert company. The engine was running and Bert's expression and constant rapping of his fingers on the cab door made it clear that he was bored with waiting. He soon relaxed once his best friend, his brother-in-law, was in the seat next to him. Jack took out his Golden Virginia tobacco tin and began rolling cigarettes for the journey.

'I see the Old Bill are blacking their noses,' Bert mused, 'they've been parked over there in that black Wolseley for as long as we have.'

'Got nothing better to do than watch us load up our sticks of furniture,' Jack grinned. 'Don't know what they think we've got inside them tea chests. It's a good job Laura didn't notice 'em over there. I'd 'ave got the third degree all right.'

'I take it you did get rid of them bangle watches, Jack?'

''Course I did. Georgie Smith took the lot, sale or return. I forgot to ask if you wanted one for Lizzie.'

'Wouldn't mind.'

'Thirty bob is what I told him to charge. Tell him I said you can have one for what I'm asking. Twenty-five. I'll give you a dollar back when he pays me. Thinks I'm not making anything on this lot. Only cost me a nicker each. He won't . . .' A loud thumping from the inside of the lorry stopped him.

'That'll be Liz,' Bert moaned. 'Nag, nag, nag.'

With that he pushed the gears into place and slowly drove through the grounds of the flats.

'Nar, he won't shift that many on the hop field,' Jack continued, 'the money's not about.'

Waving and yelling their goodbyes to the onlookers, the families on board settled themselves for the journey ahead. As they pulled away, Laura noticed that Kay was paying special attention to the fifteen-year-old Tommy Sharp whose name was still scratched in a heart on the lift door, next to Kay's. The caretaker had had Kay for that. He knew every initial, and the lift had just been given a quick coat of council green. Still waving, Kay stood up to get Tommy's attention but he was more interested in his football.

'You been on the stretch rack, Kay?' one of the women on the lorry called out. 'You'll be as tall as your dad you keep growing like that.'

'She's gonna be a model!' Liz yelled back while winking at Kay. Liz knew from previous chats that Kay was shy about her sudden growth. No amount of complimenting, though, would convince her niece that she was a stunner.

There were three families on board the lorry and not one of them complained about being cramped: they had too much to look forward to. The summer had been long and hot and now, in late August, it was rumoured that the hops in Kent were as big as damsons and as plentiful as peas. Hop-picking might well go on for seven weeks this year, right into October.

Once Kay had settled back on her comfortable pillow which had been carefully positioned on an orange box, Laura reached out and swept a few strands of her daughter's long fair hair away from her face. Kay reacted by leaning her head against her mum's shoulder.

They pulled away from the council estate on to the small winding road which led them through the backstreets of Stepney. As they passed a new tower block, Laura wondered what it would be like to live on the sixteenth floor, up in the sky, away from the world. A far cry from the small cottage where she was brought up, in Dellemar Place. She noted the gate as the lorry rumbled past; the green paintwork was in desperate need of a fresh coat to cover the patches of flaking grey undercoat. She remembered how happy her family had been, living in that small corner of London with the lovely old paved pathway under creeper-covered walls. The tiny cottages, gardens fenced with pointed wooden rails, were full of lilac, roses, hydrangeas, wallflowers, lupins and delphiniums. And only a stone's throw from the busy Whitechapel Road.

She remembered how Jack used to hang around

outside the gate, waiting for her. How she played hard to get. He was one of the most sought-after young men in the neighbourhood, good looking and full of fun, with a reputation for breaking a girl's heart. He was known to dump a girl when another lovelier maiden came his way but Laura had decided earlier in life, during their time together in the same classroom at the local Whitehead Street school, that the popular Jack Armstrong would not win her over so easily.

As the lorry travelled along the Mile End Road, Liz slowly began one of her favourite songs:

Pack up your troubles in your old kit bag and
    smile, smile, smile . . .

In no time, everyone on board was singing. They sang their way through the Blackwall Tunnel and didn't stop until the scenery changed from bricks and mortar to trees and fields, 'Bye Bye Blackbird' being the favourite tune. Once in the countryside the song changed to a softer pitch as everyone relaxed. Packing to go hop-picking hadn't been a slight affair, it was almost like moving home. They had to be sure not to forget the essentials: tin-opener, saucepans, kettle, teapot, matches, paraffin can, wellingtons and a thousand other incidentals, all crucial to making life easier for the women who had to turn out substantial meals on an open fire or Primus stove. But now the packing was over and there were good things to look forward to.

While Kay slipped into her imaginary world of rivers and orchards, Laura enjoyed the opportunity to let Richard move back into her thoughts. At first, respect had been all she felt for the landowner, then the sudden pangs of guilty desire, followed by a yearning to be near him, had taken over. She knew he had felt the same even though it was never mentioned. They had danced around it with polite conversation at first until that one evening when they had met in the lane, a chance meeting which was the beginning of a deep and impossible relationship.

Liz saw the dreamy look in her sister-in-law's eyes. She knew where Laura's mind was, all right. Dreaming her life away no doubt. As for Liz? She had no time for it. Life was tricky enough without wasting thoughts on what was, or might be. Today was all she cared about, and getting through it the best way she could. It was her and Bert's lorry they were travelling in and she knew full well that should anything happen to draw the attention of the law, Bert would be for it. The lorry might have looked roadworthy but on close examination it would prove otherwise. Still, they had been lucky so far and once hop-picking was over they would have some cash to get it seen to properly.

Two

Richard sat opposite his wife, Julia, at the gleaming mahogany table, and made a gallant attempt at appearing to enjoy his lunch; yet every morsel seemed as if it would stick in his throat. It might as well have been cardboard and water he was forcing down between the casual exterior smiles as he tried to cover the growing excitement he felt inside.

Food was the furthest thing from his mind, but he kept up the feeble pretence while the only sound made in between the awkward silences was the scraping of silver cutlery on bone china. Neither of them was enjoying the meal and the pretence was painfully obvious to them both.

Richard knew perfectly well that Julia was conscious of the fact that he would rather not be there for lunch, that he had a mountain of incidentals to attend to. She knew the men were out there on the hop fields, waiting for him, yet he still had to go through with the charade. So why was he allowing her to make him a captive like this? Why didn't he simply rush through his soup and get out? And what was causing the tightness in his stomach, anger or guilt? Whatever it was, he decided that the best thing to do was sit tight and try to ease the atmosphere. Julia was in one of her moods, so the last thing he needed was to give her an excuse to quarrel. If the usual quick cold meat salad had been offered he might just have got away with refusing it, but Julia was a clever woman who knew how to play on his conscience.

'Had a terrible dream in the night.' He finally broke the silence.

'I'm not surprised. Falling asleep by the fire hardly guarantees a comfortable time,' she said drily.

'Stanley had ripped most of the fields down.' He spoke in what he hoped was a relaxed, easy manner, attempting to soften her mood. 'Our beautiful crop was full of disease. Every field. Every single bine. I remember screaming, 'The pickers, Stanley! The pickers will be here first thing! Stanley was laughing. Saying it was my own fault.' Richard sighed heavily. 'What a way to spend a night. Dreadful. The bines looked like wet slimy seaweed . . .'

Making a determined effort not to show the least

bit of interest in his little anecdote, Julia started to read the morning paper. 'Don't feel you have to eat on my account,' she said calmly, deliberately ignoring his dream.

Richard could see that a change of tactics would be necessary, as there was no appeasing Julia when she was in this stubborn frame of mind. Carefully he replaced his spoon in the soup-plate. 'I did warn you, Julia. A quick sandwich would have been fine.'

She smiled tauntingly. 'I'm sure those poor hop-pickers wouldn't turn down French onion soup and freshly baked rolls.'

Hating her for that smirky tormenting tone, he glared into her face, but she averted her eyes to the distraction of an old lorry rumbling down the road on the way to the common, to avoid his scathing looks.

'They come thick and fast,' she sighed, 'and no doubt as rowdy as ever.'

Lifting the white damask napkin to his lips, he cursed under his breath, struggling to keep his composure. 'I had better go. There's bound to be confusion over keys.'

'One of the hands left a key in every padlock on every hut,' she said, leaning back, a fixed smile on her face. 'You just can't wait to see your old chums again, can you?'

She was looking at him now, at the nervous tic by his left eye which was flickering rapidly, betraying familiar signs of agitation. The more he tried to control it, the worse it seemed to get.

'It is sweet, though,' she mocked, pushing the bounds of his patience as far as she could. 'Making such a visible effort to identify with people who choose to live in cowsheds and sleep on straw, admiring their poverty and tolerance.'

'And of course that would never do!' he spat out with rage. The blood was rushing to his face and his hazel eyes blazed with fury. He was being forced to play right into her hands and he knew it. His temper was rising while she glowed with excitement and self-satisfaction. Determined to have some of his way, he tried to relax by leaning back casually in his chair and smiling benignly at her. He watched as she slowly pushed her slim manicured hand through her short brown curls.

'I shall never understand your attitude towards those people, Richard. What is it about the low working class that attracts you?'

'I wonder?' he said, giving her a half-smile and lighting his pipe. At last she had revealed the real reason for her cutting remarks, and had finally cast the first stone. If only she would come out and ask if he was in love with another woman, he could tell her once and for all. Julia could be a clever bitch at times, but very shallow.

Bringing himself back to reality, he casually stood up and eased the dining-chair back under the table. There was still quite a bit of work to get through before evening.

'Yes, well, I'm sorry I couldn't stay for lunch. Not quite enough hours. All work . . .'

'Makes Richard a very excited boy,' she drooled sarcastically.

Tired of her persistence, he sighed heavily. 'For goodness' sake, Julia. What is the matter with you?'

'Oh, please!' Losing her composure, Julia stood up and threw her napkin down, catching the cut-glass sugar-bowl and knocking it over, sending it spinning across the table, to end up on the Persian rug with grains of sugar flying everywhere. 'I suppose it could be your eagerness to see one or two of them again!'

He dug his fingers against his forehead and then through his hair, silently swearing and feeling desperate to get away.

'Thank God the twins are spending some time with my mother before going away to school. I'm sure the whole lot of the pickers are full of fleas and bugs.'

Richard could see no end to this. 'You should try talking to some of the women. You might find you're not so many miles apart!' he snapped back, regretting his words almost before they were out. Julia's brown eyes were glinting and looked more alive than ever. He turned towards the door hoping to escape but she had not finished, and her words followed him in a torrent of fury.

'Do you honestly believe those ruffians are just as eager to see you again?' She was almost screaming now. 'Do you imagine them, lying on beds of straw, knowing it's in order to feather yours, and thinking, "Isn't it wonderful! The way Mr Wright admires our spirit and our tolerance!"' Julia shook with rage, angrily pushing a few strands of hair from her eyes. She was in full swing now, and if he wasn't careful she could easily start smashing a plate or two – it wouldn't be the first time.

Her voice went through and around Richard's head. She had no time for the working class, and was glad their days were numbered. Glad that soon she would see an end to them trampling all over her property. Her property? It wasn't even his, not entirely. The farm had been left to Richard and his two brothers. He just happened to live in the family home with the family heirlooms. Apart from the few bits of modern furniture here and there, the rest was still the property of his mother, who was spending the last of her years in a nursing home near Maidstone. Sensing that Julia was at the end of her attack, he glared into her face, daring her to utter another word. He had had enough and his mood clearly showed it.

'I hope you've told the men to keep their mouths shut,' he said at last, speaking in low, tired tones, 'I want to tell the pickers myself, when I feel the time is right.'

Julia's ability to change her tune at a moment's notice was at its height, her angry voice suddenly full of elation as she slipped into her *I told you so* routine.

'They're not going to like it; you should have let them know before now. You should have written and told them this would be the last season.' She made a display of folding the napkins. 'Why didn't you tell them?'

He spoke slowly, pacing himself, controlling the frustration he began to feel building up again. 'Because if I had, they would now be in the wrong mood for picking.'

Raising her chin, she looked accusingly into his eyes. 'Are you sure that's the reason, Richard?'

Passing the farmhouse, Bert's lorry was alive with

the sound of the hop-pickers' song, with Liz's voice booming above the rest of them:

> They say that 'oppin's lousy,
> We don't believe it's true,
> We only come down 'oppin
> To earn a bob or two,
> With a tee-aye-oh,
> a tee-aye-oh,
> a tee-aye-ee-aye-oh!

The lorry with its high-spirited, melodious travellers made its way down the gravel lane, alongside the orchard where Cox's pippins grew and where several hungry stomachs had been satisfied by the fresh juicy apples which hung ripe and low.

Spotting a baby rabbit in his path, Bert swerved to avoid it, causing Jack to grab the door handle and push both feet hard against the footrest.

'Sod you, Bert!' he yelled. 'What yer been drinking?'

'I couldn't kill the poor thing, could I!'

'No. Mustn't do that,' he snapped wryly. 'Save a rabbit and finish three families in one go. You worry me sometimes!'

The song of the three families aboard changed to laughter and then mirth on seeing the bewildered face of young Jimmy as he awoke to find himself on the wooden floor. It was Liz who swept him up into her rough golden-brown arms. She sat him square on her lap, her happy ageing face smiling into his sorry one, and tousled his thick curly hair. Wiping his tears away with the hem of her new green-and-orange summer frock, she tried to comfort the child.

'Come on, cheer up, Jimmy. Big boys don't cry.'

'I think I've broke my neck.' Moving his head from one side to the other to see if it was still attached, he made the others roar with laughter.

'Well now,' Liz chuckled, 'we'll just have to mend it with vinegar and brown paper, won't we?' Pointing to the apple trees, she said, 'Look, there's our favourite orchard and Richard Wright still hasn't got round to fixing that gate back on.'

That seemed to do the trick. Jimmy's mind was suddenly full of scrumping. 'Mr Wright should take more care of his gates. People could just go in and out, in and out.' The boy was well away now, gesturing with his hands, mimicking his own father. 'How would people know they're not supposed to be in there if there's no gate?'

'There's nothing wrong with your brain is there, Sparrow? Eh?' Laughing, she added: 'And you can nip in there later and scrump a few. Then Liz will make some nice toffee to go round 'em. Yeah?'

Young Jimmy liked that idea and according to the cheer that went around the lorry, so did the others.

Laura eyed her sister-in-law disapprovingly. 'It's bad enough the bigger ones go in there and spoil the trees without you encouraging tots.'

'Oh, shut up, Laura. Julia Wright charges too much for her lousy windfalls anyway.' Liz pulled a face at young Jimmy as if to say *She's put me in my place again*. The boy grinned up at Liz, enjoying the mickey-taking. Liz started to tickle him then, keeping her thoughts to herself. Where was the harm in the kids scrumping a few apples? Sixpence for twenty is what they charged, and most were half eaten by the birds or so badly bruised you could hardly see green flesh. In her eyes, millionaires like the Wrights could afford to lose a couple of dozen apples. Anyway, he wasn't such a bad bloke, he turned a blind eye all right. It was his miserable wife, Julia, you had to keep away from, and those stuck-up little brats of hers.

Liz stopped tickling the boy and reached into her pocket for the little blue snuff tin. She sprinkled a bit of her favourite powder on to the back of her hand and waited for Laura to have a go at her.

Kay was the first to notice. She looked from her Aunt Liz to her mum, waiting for a reaction: she knew full well that Laura hated to see Liz taking the stuff, especially in front of the children. But Laura was not going to take the bait. How well those two women knew each other. Instead, she ignored the whole thing and stared out of the back of the lorry.

Not satisfied, Liz carried on provoking her. 'This is special powder, Sparrow, for my blocked nose!' This was said in a nice loud clear voice. Young Jimmy stared at Liz's nose and quickly moved his head out of the way when she prepared herself for a really good sneeze. When that was done, he went back to examining her nostrils.

'My nose is quite blocked,' he said hopefully.

'You don't want any of this, cock. It's for silly old women, like me. Ain't that right, Laura?'

Pushing his face up close to Liz, Jimmy examined her face. 'You've got a brown nose now!' Not liking the look of it he couldn't understand why the others found it funny. Even Laura couldn't help smiling, not that she would let Liz see, she kept her face turned away, but she needn't have bothered, Liz had her eyes on Laura's feet. When she was annoyed, Laura always had her legs crossed and swung one foot to and fro in quick, short movements and when she was amused, she pushed her toes into the floor. And right then, Laura's toes risked getting splinters from the rough boards of Liz and Bert's lorry.

While Laura was engaged in playfully hiding one emotion, another swept through her body. Richard's Land-Rover had suddenly appeared from around a bend and, as it drew up close, she could see his face clearly as he looked up at her. Her heart began to beat so fast and loud she felt sure Liz and Kay would hear it. Her head suddenly felt light and dizzy as if she had drunk ten Babychams. Carefully eyeing her sister-in-law she was relieved to see that Liz was more interested in the dirty plaster on young Jimmy's knee and as for Kay, she seemed to be miles away, lost in her own dreams.

Gripping a nearby tea chest, Laura did her utmost to cover her feelings. Her heartbeat wasn't going to slow down, that was obvious, and other parts of her body seemed as if they were waking after a long sleep. Trying to control her emotions and take heed of the voice inside warning her to take care, she felt faintly ashamed of the tingling sensation in her breasts and loins. The voice inside was lost in the sizzling body heat that had taken over. She longed to lean forward, reach out and smother his strong handsome face with kisses.

The expression on Richard's face, and the way he was deliberately slowing down the Land-Rover and pulling back, told her that he was sending her a message of caution. Once she lost sight of him as the lorry turned a corner, she leaned back in her chair and began to calm down.

'All right, Laura?' Liz said in her mock-innocent, knowing way. All that Laura could do was gaze back, motionless, not caring whether there was any trace of love in her eyes for Liz and the world to witness. It had been a long ten months of making do with memories.

Steering the lorry through the gateway on to the common, Bert remarked that it looked as if they were one of the last to arrive, since the place was full of vans, lorries, cars and people.

'Don't think so; the pink huts are only half full, so are the black ones. Must be a good three-quarters here though.'

Grinning, Bert shook his head slowly. 'How can they be half full with three-quarters here at the same time,' he chuckled. 'You should have been a mathematician, Jack.'

Paying special attention to the standpipe by the gateway, Liz shook her head despairingly. 'Look at that! Still only one tap between the lot of us!'

'What did you expect, then, running hot and cold?' Laura was smiling now, almost laughing. Knowing from past experience that happiness was short-lived, she was making the most of the euphoria which swept through her body. Seeing Richard again was the best tonic she could have wished for.

Liz glanced sideways at her, that mischievous look back in her eyes. 'If we'd made more of a fuss a couple of years ago, when Jack had Richard Wright listening, we might well have a few mod cons by now!' Then pushing her face up close to her sister-in-law, she spoke in a quiet tone: ''Course, if you'd had a word with him, he might have done a bit more.' Folding her arms, she looked innocently up at the sky and grinned.

There wasn't really much Laura could say to that; she still wasn't sure whether Liz knew about her and Richard, and if she did, why hadn't she said anything? After all, Laura was still married to Liz's brother.

Pulling slowly to a halt, Bert's lorry stopped in front of the row of brick huts and before Bert had turned the engine off old friends who had arrived earlier were waving and calling out to the three families on board.

Milly Smith, a vivacious thirty-five-year-old, was the first to show her face. 'How are your corns,

Liz?' she called out playfully. 'You had 'em done
yet?'

'I've got the prettiest feet for miles around, Milly!
You wait till I get off this lorry and I'll show you.
How's Georgie's leg?'

'Nothing wrong with his bloody leg, you know
that. Crafty bastard uses it as an excuse for not
moving out of bed! Not that I mind, if you know
what I mean,' she said, giving Liz a crafty wink.
Milly started to walk away towards the water-tap.
'Come and see me soon as you've settled, I've got
loads to tell yer!'

Standing and stretching, Laura smiled to herself.
'Don't change, do she? Good old Milly, she's a sight
for sore eyes all right.' A quick glance around the
common told Laura that most of the pickers had
already arrived.

Buzzing with activity the common was alive with
men, children and women as holes were being dug
beneath iron frames, ready for the camp-fires which
would soon be alight and whose flames would be
licking the sides of stew-pots, as they hung on
crosspoles. Faggots were being dragged over, two
and three at a time, and stacked up ready for the
weekend. Women were sitting outside their huts,
enjoying the sun, while stuffing their ticks with

straw to form comfortable mattresses and there were already a couple of women in the cookhouse tending the hot bubbling family meal. The smell of boiled bacon drifted through the air.

A buzzing, welcoming mood spread over the common; everyone looked happy, meeting up with old friends and exchanging the gossip of the past year.

Leaning out of the lorry to get a glimpse of the hop fields, Laura was moved to see the familiar forest of thick green bines, the orchard in the background and the River Medway. The gypsy wagons added brilliant splashes of colour to the merging green surroundings.

Pushing the passenger door open, Jack jumped down from the cab and, stretching, took in a deep breath of fresh, clean country air before going to the back of the lorry to unbolt the tailboard.

Liz was impatient, though, and had already started to stamp one foot, a message for Bert to move himself and let her out.

Undoing the bolts, Jack told his sister to lay off nagging Bert, because one of these days the man might just give her a right-hander.

'Mind I don't give you one for not respecting your elders.'

Laughing, Jack undid the bolts and let the tailboard crash to the ground. Kay couldn't wait to touch the soil. She had already seen her old friend Terry across the common, struggling with two white enamel buckets of water. She screamed out his name and was off the lorry in a flash, jumping down and just missing a stale cow-pat.

Laura eyed her daughter disapprovingly. How many times had she told her not to shout out like a fishwife?

'I don't want you to skive off, Kay! There's a lot to do before dusk.'

Kay backed slowly away, smiling at Laura and holding up one hand, splaying her fingers. 'Five minutes, and I'll be back. Promise!'

'You always say that and then I don't see you for hours.'

Liz slipped up behind Laura and spoke quietly. 'Let her go, Laura. She's been cramped up too long in that lorry for the likes of her.'

'Yeah, I suppose you're right. Go on then, Kay! But not for too long!'

'She's a good kid, Mog. You should be proud of 'er.'

'I know. But she's not such a child now is she, Liz?'

'Can say that again. How's she coping with her new shape?'

'Tries to hide it.'

'She'll be all right in a year or two. Won't be able to keep the young men away. Drive 'em mad with them blue eyes.'

They watched as Kay half ran, half walked towards Terry. Liz started to chuckle. 'Tell you what, though. Young Terry wants to get his hair cut.'

'Love his drainpipes and luminous pink socks,' Laura laughed.

'Come on, Lizzie! Get that kettle filled up and on someone's fire! I'm gasping for a cup of tea!' Jack's voice rang through the air and the two women rolled their eyes. His tone changed from jovial to indifferent as he turned to Laura: 'What d'yer want off the lorry first? Tea chests or 'opping box?'

Sensing the change in atmosphere, she felt herself sink a little, but quickly tossed her hair back and in her best aloof manner gave her instructions. 'The hopping box, please, Jack.'

Young Brianny Smith passed by then, the proud owner of a portable radio. Of course it was too loud, Chuck Berry belting out 'Sweet Little Sixteen'.

'Oh, Gawd, whatever happened to Johnny Ray?' Liz moaned, but Laura's attention was elsewhere. Richard's Land-Rover was pulling on to the common. Turning away, Liz broke into one of her favourite songs, 'Just a-walking in the rain', and sang purposely, while strolling to her hut.

Laura watched as the Land-Rover slowly drove past the black tin huts on the opposite side of the common, stopping once or twice while Richard got out and spoke to his pickers. She couldn't take her eyes off him: he looked tall and broad beside the other men, and his thick dark hair was curling around the nape of his neck, making him look more handsome than ever. She wondered if this was his new style, or if he had been too busy to get it cut. Whatever the reason, it suited him; it looked right with his square jaw and roman nose. He was still wearing his old green Barbour jacket, and would until the day he died, according to Richard. He joked that he wanted to make absolutely certain it was on his back when he reached heaven, so that any of his friends who were already there would recognize him – and get a pint in.

Laura wasn't sure whether she should risk speaking to him once he got round to her, or keep out of the way in case Jack or any of the others sensed what was between them. After all, she had waited this long to be near him, another day wouldn't hurt. Another day and Jack would be returning to London with Bert.

Common sense won as she forced herself to begin

unloading the hopping box which was now parked in front of her hut, ignoring the rapid heartbeats which resounded through her like the beating of a drum.

Knowing Richard was close by, and the thought of five or six weeks in the country with the promise of an Indian summer, caused Laura to glow with an inner excitement, which did not go unnoticed by Jack. He had no idea that his wife had a lover, and quite a catch at that. As far as he was concerned she was celibate and had been for a few years now. The reason for it was too painful for him to think about, so he never did. Always looking on the bright side, was Jack – always living for the day in hand. He put her radiance down to the fact that she was looking forward to her picking holiday.

Liz arrived from her hut and stood next to Jack, shaking her head. 'Look around you, Jack. Not a lick of paint to be seen. Wright's slipping, you know. Letting the place run down like this. Think we should have a word when he gets round to our side?'

'Bit late for that, Lizzie. He's just going.'

'Would you believe it! What does he think, we're not worth driving round for, or what?'

'Never mind him, where's Kay got to? I'm out of tobacco.'

'Oh, Gawd . . . what with you and Laura finding

her jobs to do. Why don't you leave her be? She's
not a ten-year-old!'

'All right, all right, keep your hair on. Where is
she, anyway?'

'Over there, with Terry.'

'Oh, yeah. Look at him. Right little Jennifer he's
turning out.'

Pleased to see her friend again, Kay gave Terry
a slap on the back. 'See you've got rid of your
pimples, then!'

'Sod you! Now look what you've made me do.
Water spilled into both my wellingtons.'

''Scuse me for breathing. Anyway, give your feet
a wash.'

'Don't know what my mum's gonna say. Takes
ages to dry out.'

Remembering what a worrier he was, her voice
took on a gentler tone. 'Give us one of your
buckets then.'

Keeping one step ahead of her, he blew his hair
away from his eyes. 'No, it's easier with two. I'm
balanced.'

'Suit yerself. I had to plead with Mum to let me
off, you know. Anyone'd think you weren't pleased
to see me.' She walked beside him on their way to
his hut. 'How long you been here anyway?'

'Couple of hours.'

'Is Marian 'ere yet?'

'She's not coming this year. Her mum died in July. Gassed herself. Her dad's sent her off to live with her aunt in Wales.'

'Terry! You wouldn't joke about a thing like that?'

''Course not!'

They carried on walking in silence until they reached the hut. Terry's mother, Nell, was busy sewing up a pillowcase which she had just finished stuffing with a mixture of straw, hay and a few stolen hops. She glanced up at Kay and then went back to her needlework.

'Hallo Kay. Terry, go and help your friend fetch the bales of straw. I want to get the beds made up while the sun's out.' She looked across at the bundles of faggots which had been allocated to her. 'Them faggots have got to be laid out on the hut floor and the oil-lamps need filling.'

Kay suddenly felt in the way, with all that talk of work to be done. It hadn't been like that last year or any of the years before. Terry's mum usually asked her to muck in. She toyed with the idea of offering to lay the faggots out; she knew how to do it even though her own hut had special wooden platforms for the mattresses to lie on.

'You've shot up since last year, miss. Quite the young lady now. No more climbing trees for you, I shouldn't think.'

Kay watched as Terry joined his friend and helped him carry a large bale of straw and hay mix. 'Who's Terry's new friend?'

'Oh, that's young Raymond. Nice boy. Should have brought him last year as well.' She snapped the cotton thread between her teeth, and slipped the needle and remaining yarn through her blue-and-white spotted blouse. 'It's not good for a boy of my Terry's age, always mixing with girls.' She shook the pillow and plumped it up. 'Should have been out there kicking a ball about with the others.' Picking up a second pillowcase, and grabbing a handful of straw, she began stuffing again. 'Should have been learning to swim, instead of picking blackberries . . . still, I expect you've got other things to think about now.'

Realizing that Terry's mum was giving her the cold shoulder, Kay thought it best that she left. From the way the conversation was going, and Terry's cool reception, she could only surmise that she must have done something the previous year to make them go off her.

'What are you, Kay, fifteen? Must have left school by now. Suppose your mother's fixed you up with a posh office job. Can't see her settling for you working in a factory.' She began stitching the top ends of another pillowcase together.

Trying desperately to hide her hurt feelings, Kay picked up a twig and scratched at a patch of dry earth. 'I don't leave school till next year. I'm taking a Commerce course when I go back.'

'Commerce course? All right for some,' Terry's mother tutted.

Wondering whether to stay or leave, Kay noticed that Terry and his friend were on their way back. She took an instant dislike to the other boy, who looked to be about sixteen and too cocky for his own good. The type that looked and made you feel as if your clothes were transparent.

Giving Kay the once-over, he grinned approvingly. 'Someone gonna introduce me, or what?'

Standing up and deliberately blocking Kay from the boys, Terry's mum peered at her wrist-watch. 'I expect your mother'll be wanting a hand with the unpacking, Kay.' The expression on her face made it abundantly clear that she did not want Kay there.

Tossing her twig into the small fire, she just missed the pot of boiling water. 'Yeah. I expect she will be needing me by now.' Kay swallowed hard and held her breath for a couple of seconds. No way would she let them see the tears which were welling up behind her eyes. 'See yer.' She forced herself to smile, gave a quick wave and turned away.

'I'll come round later and give you Marian's address in Wales!' Terry called after her.

Standing there with folded arms, staring at Kay as she walked away and licking the inside of his bottom lip, Terry's friend tapped out a popular tune on his elbow and called out, 'You're named after my favourite film star, Kay Kendall. Hope I'll be seeing more of you! I'm Ray, Kay!' he laughed with an oily sense of fun. Then, turning to Terry, he let out a low whistle. 'Wouldn't mind some of that, Terry my old son. Would not mind a quick swim there. That's what I call form!'

Pushing his hands deep into his pockets and avoiding his mother's disapproving eyes, Terry pretended to be checking the sky for any storm clouds that might be on their way. 'Kay's all right. Bit immature though.'

'Whoa . . . ! Hark at Mr Experience talking! You'd best watch him, Mrs Button, he'll be taking married women to the pictures next!'

Sighing, Terry's mum went back to her bedmaking. She didn't like Ray any more than Kay did.

Laura was searching through a tea chest when Kay

arrived. With everything unloaded from the lorry and stacked in neat piles, Jack was now busy slapping some white distemper on the inside walls of Laura's hut. Having cadged someone's portable he listened happily to the racing-results and whistled while he worked.

Leaning against the hut wall and making the most of the sun, Milly, the bleached blonde, pulled down the elasticated neckline of her turquoise blouse to reveal small white shoulders. 'Gonna take you ages to sort this lot out, Laura,' she said, flicking ash from her cigarette on to the grass.

'Jack! The water-jugs are not in either of these tea chests! Have you moved 'em?'

'They're in the 'oppin box, for the third time!' he yelled back.

'You had no business moving them. I knew exactly where everything was!'

Jack looked a comical sight as he came out of the hut, holding his dripping paint-roller and smelling of paint, distemper smeared across his cheek. 'Never listens to her old man, Milly. I might as well not be here.'

'I don't know why you didn't come down a few days earlier. I've scrubbed our huts from top to bottom, put new wallpaper up and laid lino. Gone contemporary this year. White paper with red, black and gold stars on two walls and red embossed on the other. Got a nice new bit of net curtain for the doorway an' all. Stop the bees coming in.'

'I think we might have more trouble with flies this year, Milly. What with this heat.' Laura carefully lifted the hem of her calf-length dress to her forehead and patted away the perspiration. Her white petticoat could just be seen between the folds of pale green linen. She felt Jack's wandering eyes on her legs so let go of the hem and made for the hopping box.

Milly gave a gentle tug at Jack's shirt to get his attention. He spun around and looked deliberately into her face. 'Milly, you're a little cracker, but I haven't got the time,' he joked.

'Tell me something, Jack.' She spoke quietly with an unusual touch of sincerity in her voice. 'What on earth have you done to deserve the cold shoulder she gives you?'

'Search me, Milly.'

'Any woman on this common would give her right arm . . .'

'It's not the right arm I'm interested in though, is it?' he grinned. 'Anyway, don't you worry your pretty little head about me and Laura, OK? We're still together, ain't we? Ours is what you might call a . . . stormy relationship. Now how about lighting up one of your fags for me and popping it between my lips?'

'You're a sexy fella, Jack, you know that?'

'Milly,' he said, 'if it wasn't for the fact that I'm holding this paint brush . . . and what with all this straw about . . .'

Striking a match and lighting one of her Woodbines, she giggled nervously. 'You sod, Jack, you're making my knees go all weak.' She offered the cigarette to his mouth and parted her own red lips. 'Catch me when you can,' she whispered, giving him a promising wink.

Laughing at her cheek, Jack strolled back into the hut to finish his work of art. Enjoying the scented taste of lipstick on the end of the cigarette and catching Milly's Lily of the Valley cologne made Jack fancy a pint.

Moving closer to Laura, Milly dropped her cigarette-end to the floor and stubbed it out with the heel of her white wedge sandals. 'I see Richard Wright followed your lorry in, Laura. Jack staying is he?'

'No, Milly. He's got to get back.'

'Yeah? I didn't think there was much work down the docks. My George's been bomping on and off for the last fortnight. Still, your Jack's got the muscle. Little skinny ones like my old man don't stand a chance in lean times. Wright looked well, didn't he?'

Searching through the hopping box, Laura fought to keep Richard out of her mind. 'George's a good picker, Milly. He'll earn you a few bob, and no doubt he'll have a few goods to sell. Ah! Found them at last.' Pulling the jugs from the trunk she looked up and smiled at Milly. 'Best get to the tap before there's a mile-long queue.'

'What paper you gonna put up this year, then?'

Turning away with an enamel jug in each hand Laura blew some strands of hair out of her eyes. 'I don't wallpaper, Milly. I prefer white distemper.'

'Oh, yeah, I forgot,' she giggled, 'you go in for all that bohemian lark. Had a rug on the wall last year, didn't yer? My George couldn't believe it when I told him.'

Walking away, Laura raised her eyebrows at Kay who had just arrived. 'She's on form,' she said, quietly amused.

'Hallo, Kay, mate! Look as if you've lost a tanner and found a penny.'

'Do I?'

'Won't be seeing your friend Marian this year. Her mother . . .'

'I know!' Kay interrupted, hoping to stop Milly from going on.

'Fancy gassing herself! Should be ashamed . . .'

'I just saw your George showing the Blakes around your hut. Sounding off about his flair for decorating. They were saying how he had an artistic . . .'

'His flair?' she screeched, almost amused. 'The man's colour blind! Always has been.' Turning quickly away and passing Laura's hut, she couldn't resist a quick peep at Jack. 'See yer!' she called out, and then threw a backward glance at Kay. 'And you wanna put a smile on it! Else you'll drag everyone else down in the dumps with yer!'

From where she was standing, Kay could see her Aunt Liz enjoying a mug of tea with one of the other women. She walked slowly up to them.

'What was Milly spouting off about this time, Mog?'

Preoccupied with her own thoughts about her friend Marian, Kay was miles away. 'Do things seem different to you, Aunt Liz? Around the common?'

Eyeing her niece, she tipped her tea grouts on to the grass. 'No . . . same old place all right, same old people. Why?'

'Oh, I dunno.'

'Come on. Your Uncle Bert's cadged a kettle of boiling water. A nice fresh mug of tea's what you want.' She put her arm around Kay's shoulder, gently lifted her chin and looked into her watery eyes. 'Then you could start sweeping out the huts!' She knew how to raise her niece's spirits when she was low.

'Oh, you know I hate spiders, Aunt Liz!'

'That's why we have to sweep them away,' she smiled.

Three

Standing in a small queue on the gravel lane by the water-tap, waiting her turn, Laura admired the tunnels of rich green hop bines which spread out into several acres of fields. Lifting her face to the sun, she closed her eyes and wished she could take some time to sit in the shade of the hop garden, as the midday heat was now touching ninety degrees.

Listening to the refreshing sound of running water as someone filled an enamel bucket, she let her thoughts wander, remembering the time when she and Richard walked hand in hand along that lane when no one was around to see them. Smiling, she relived the memory; it had been Richard who had shyly brushed his hand against her own before gently cupping it and then easing and locking their fingers together, and it was Laura who took it one tiny step further, gently rubbing his hand with the tip of her thumb.

That was several years back, before they had even kissed. Who would have believed then that their time was spent walking and talking? His learning about Laura's interest in the history of fashion, and her wanting to know about his life in Kent, apart from growing hops.

No matter how hard she tried, Laura could find nothing interesting about him sitting by the river for hours on end, fishing. She tried not to let on, but she had a feeling he knew and told his angling yarns to tease her.

The voice of Fran, her closest friend among the pickers she met only yearly, broke into Laura's thoughts. 'Hallo, Laura. All right?'

Resenting the intrusion, Laura did well to cover it. 'Not too bad, Fran. You?'

'Oh, up and down, up and down. Pleased to be back here though. I suppose you've heard?' She looked at Laura questioningly, grinned and slowly shook her head. 'You 'aven't, 'ave yer? Well, here's one to take the stardust from your eyes. Wright's going mechanized! Sodding machines to do the work of man! After decades of coming down 'ere to pick for 'im! What we s'posed to do next year, eh? Find a blade of grass to sit on in the middle of bloody London?'

'Don't be daft, Fran!' Laura laughed. 'We would have been told when we were sent our tickets.'

'We should have been, but we weren't. Wright must have sensed it was out. He left quicker than he soddin' well arrived!'

Feeling the blood drain from her face, Laura could do nothing but stand there, her sixth sense telling her that this was no rumour. Her mind was suddenly blank, as if someone had swept a hand across and wiped every thought away. In a trance, she lowered her body and picked up the two jugs, inching her way forward to be next in line at the tap.

Dragging the full jug from under the running water and scraping it on the concrete plinth, another woman enjoyed a throaty laugh. Sidling away, she threw Laura a sideways glance. 'I shouldn't think *you* need to be told, Laura. If anyone should know.'

Turning quickly around, ready to give the woman a piece of her mind, Laura felt Fran's hand grip her own arm. 'Let it go, Laura, she's not worth it.' Then, lifting the jug for her friend and placing it under the running water, Fran searched for the right words to say, but none came to mind.

'It's all right, Fran. I know you've known for ages and we were stupid enough to be seen by that horrible old cow a few years back. I wouldn't mind, we were only talking . . .'

'Yeah, but it's the mood you would have been in,

Laura. What you would have been talking about. Even if she couldn't hear, she's got eyes and it don't take an intelligent person to see when two people are falling in love . . . well, you know . . .'

'Funny thing is, I don't even care that she might blab it now. Not much to lose, is there? Don't matter what the likes of Mrs Brown think; if it's over, it's over.'

'Your jug's overflowing, mate.'

'Yeah . . . you could say that.' Laura smiled, covering the overwhelming pangs of bitter disappointment and pulling the full jug away, replacing it with the empty one. 'Fran, you couldn't do me a big favour, could you?'

'If I can, Laura, I will, you know that.'

'You couldn't take my jugs back to the hut for me, could yer? I fancy a walk.'

Giving Laura a warning look, Fran chewed on the side of her cheek. 'Won't your Jack wonder where you've got to?'

'No, Fran, he won't. Jack's got other flowers to pick.'

'OK then, if you're sure . . .'

'I'll only be gone an hour. I wanna walk up to the church, have a roam around the grounds and then go inside for while.'

'Sounds a bit morbid, Laura.'

'No. I often go. It's lovely inside. Thirteenth century.'

Pulling Laura's second jug away and replacing it with her bucket, Fran slowly shook her head. 'Shouldn't think there were many people about then. Gawd knows why they took the trouble, in a tiny village like this, building a church like that. Morbid places if you ask me.'

'Oh, Fran,' Laura smiled, 'you've never been in there!'

'No, I 'aven't. Why, should I 'ave done?'

'It's worth it just to see the old coloured glass in the windows. It's really lovely when the sun shines through.'

'Tch. You always was a dreamer. Go on, get going.'

Feeling the tears well up in her eyes, Laura bit her bottom lip and forced a smile. Fran was no idiot though, she knew how her friend was feeling. Pushing her hands deep into her side pockets, Laura nodded and thanked her, then turned and walked slowly along the lane, holding her head up high.

Easing open the lovely old church doors, relieved to find the place empty, she gazed at the stone seat in the sanctuary where priests had sat 700 years ago and felt a desire to rest on it herself, but knew better. Hearing her own footsteps echoing around the church was strangely comforting. She knew where she would sit for a few quiet moments before leaving: her favourite place by the altar. Turning to the huge alabaster tomb on which Sir Thomas Fane and his wife lay as they had from the sixteenth century, he in his armour and she in her unusual head-dress, she trailed her fingers across the face of their daughter, and then touching the cold head of her baby lying in a tiny altar tomb at the side, she realized why she came back to the church time and time again. Not just to collect her thoughts and enjoy the solitude but to gaze at that family scene, frozen in time. Suddenly, Kay filled her mind and she was struck with remorse. Turning quickly away she walked smartly out of the building to make her way back to the common, saturated with a mixture of shame and stupidity for behaving like a lovesick schoolgirl.

Kay sat on the gate which led into the hop field and gazed at the huts and orchard beyond, enjoying the late afternoon sun. Her eyes wandered from the Londoners to the gypsy camp and to Zacchi, who was grooming Old Grey. She had seen him many times before but they had never spoken. In fact the only time she had a chance to speak to any of the travellers was when the women went round the huts, selling their lace and peg boxes. Zacchi seemed to be in a world of his own, paying attention only to his pony, as if no one else was around. His white baggy shirt with sleeves rolled up to the elbow showed off his chestnut tan. Kay remembered being struck a few years back by his deep blue eyes, when she and Zacchi were queueing up at the baker's van. In contrast, Terry seemed pale and skinny as he made his way towards her.

'Been looking everywhere for you, Kay. What you sitting all on your own for?'

Not wanting to change the scene she felt part of, Kay tried to draw him into it. 'See the way the sun shines on the roof of the pink huts . . . and just catches the corner of the black tin ones. Looks like a painting. I'd love to be able to paint a picture like that.'

'Yeah, right . . . here, Marian's address in Wales.' He tried to follow her line of vision to see what was so interesting about rows of hopping huts. 'What's up with you, Kay? You all right?'

'You wasn't so talkative earlier!'

'Why are you sitting by yourself?'

'Where's your new friend?' she asked with a touch of distaste.

'Waiting to go for a swim. We would ask you, but we forgot our swimming cossies.'

Jumping down from the gate she felt resentful that he had spoilt her evening now as well as her afternoon. 'I don't like him, Terry, so as long as he's around, I won't be, right?'

Backing slowly away, he shrugged. 'Suit yerself.'

'Don't worry, I will,' she said indifferently, noticing her mum walking through the gateway. She gave a wave and Laura waved back, asking in sign language if Kay fancied a cup of tea. Kay showed two hands, fingers spread, to indicate ten minutes and Laura returned with a smile and a thumbs-up sign.

Scrubbing her small pine table outside her hut, Liz greeted Laura with a searching frown. 'Where the bloody 'ell 'ave you been? You go off to fetch some water and we don't see you for an hour!'

'Fran offered to carry my jugs back for me.'

'What kind of an answer's that?'

'I'm sorry, Liz, I shouldn't have wandered off like that, I know.'

'Well you're gonna have to get a move on now if your beds are to be made up before night draws in. Kay's sloped off an' all. It's a good job the fish-and-chip van's coming round later, that's all I can say. Left to you, we'd all starve!' She stopped scrubbing, picked up a bucket of water and tipped it over the table to wash away the soap and bleach. 'Ain't seen Bert for the last half-hour neither, you wait till he shows 'is face!'

'I'd best sweep out our huts before I do anything else. Shall I do yours while I'm at it?' Leaning her head to one side she looked into Liz's fuming face. 'I will get in all four corners,' she said, trying to win her over, 'and I'll scrub the floor . . .'

'You're too late. I've already done it. Yours as well. You can make a fresh pot of tea if you want to make amends. And later on, you can tell me where you've been!'

Rolling his left shoulder and then his right to ease the pain in his neck, Jack appeared, covered in white distemper. 'Oh, you're back then?' he said, throwing Laura a suspicious look and letting everyone know by his groans how much pain he was in. Dropping down on to the grass, he let go of his paintbrush and closed his eyes. 'I'll have to get you to rub some of your lotion into my shoulders later, Lizzie. This pain's killing me.'

Covering her pine table with a new dark green oilcloth, Liz began laying the table for tea. 'A couple of hours' work and look at him, dead on his feet.'

'I give that hut two coats of paint without stopping for a bite to eat!' he protested.

'You managed a couple of pints though, didn't yer?' Lizzie teased.

'That I did, Lizzie, that I did. And that is why, apart from all that work, my bad back and this sweltering heat, I need to sleep. Wake me up when you've got the tea ready.' With that, Jack closed his eyes and before anyone could object to him taking time off, he was snoring.

Liz rolled her eyes and then pulled a kitchen chair over to the camp-fire and sat down next to Laura, pulling out her little blue tin from her apron pocket. Leaning towards Laura, and speaking in a low voice, she offered a few words of advice. 'Don't walk around with your 'eart on your sleeve, Mog. It's not good for Kay and it gets me down as well.'

'I don't know what you're talking about, Liz.'

'Suit yerself,' she said with a sigh.

Standing up, Laura brushed down her skirt and turned her face away from Liz's searching eyes. 'Pour the tea out once it's stood, I'm gonna lay my bit of lino and put the curtains up. Kay should be 'ere soon, she can make up the mattresses for me.' With that Laura disappeared into her hut to inspect Jack's paintwork.

Returning from her short inspection of the hop field,

Kay made her way back to the common where she knew she would be needed. Not wishing to pass Zacchi, she took the longer route round by the row of black corrugated makeshift lavatories, knowing she would blush like mad and be lost for words if he spoke to her.

Kay thought she was hearing things when her uncle's dispirited voice sounded from one of the small tin constructions. She moved closer and listened, hoping no one would appear and wonder what she was up to. The look of concern quickly faded from her face and was overtaken by one of her smiles. Obviously in distress, Bert was talking aloud. 'Oh, Gawd! Some God you are! Hiding as usual whenever you're needed!'

Keeping her voice down and trying not to laugh, Kay put her mouth to the slim gap beside the door hinge. 'Uncle Bert? Is that you in there?'

'Kay? Oh thank Gawd for that. I'm stuck on the khazi! I was reading me paper, studying form, forgot where I was and leaned back. Then I slipped down. I'm wedged, Kay!'

Pressing her fingers hard on her lips she managed not to laugh. 'But there's no bookie's runner around. How you gonna lay a bet?'

'It's an old 'abit! I was hiding from your Aunt Liz. Now kick the door in, there's a good girl!'

Composing herself and trying to take him seriously, she cleared her throat, started to giggle, then cleared it again.

'I'm slipping farther down! Someone's christened this bloody thing as well! I'll be sitting in it soon!'

'All right, all right! Hang on!' Taking a few steps back, she rubbed her hands down the side of her jeans, took a deep breath and kicked out with her right leg. The door stayed firmly shut but the corrugated tin lavatory shook. She took aim again and was taken aback when a deep voice whispered in her ear.

'I hope you don't make a habit of that.'

Kay spun round to stand face to face with Zacchi. Feeling the blood rush to her cheeks she blurted out her words. 'My uncle's in there and he's wedged! He can't get up!' Zacchi's throaty chuckle and flashing smile made her see red. 'It's not funny! He might be hurt!'

'He might be a lot of things. Well, stand back then.'

Worried that her Uncle Bert might be embarrassed when he saw Zacchi, she warned him, 'Someone's gonna kick the door in for me, OK?'

Taking up his position, Zacchi drew up one leg and aimed his polished brown leather boot at the door. One good kick and it crashed open.

70

'Don't look! Don't look!' Bert screamed.

Once they had pulled him free and he was on his way back to the huts, running and buttoning his flies at the same time, Zacchi threw back his head and rocked with laughter.

'It's a good job you came along when you did,' Kay murmured.

'Well, I've been watching you for the past hour. While I was grooming Old Grey. Watching you, watching me,' he said knowingly.

'I wasn't watching yer!' Kay protested, more out of embarrassment than anything else. She took one step back and he moved in closer.

'I'm glad we won't have to pussyfoot around all this season as well. I nearly made a move last year. Wish I had now, you're even better close up.'

Trying not to show how thrilled she was that he had noticed her, she started to walk slowly back to the common, pushing her long, white-blonde hair back as she went. 'You do know that we're not really allowed to . . .'

'Mix with Romanies?' Unable to take his eyes off her lightly freckled face and lovely blue eyes he bent down to pick up a long twig. ''Course I know. I've seen the signs on pub doors. "No dogs, no gypsies." It rubs off on your lot who're no better than us.'

'I think those signs should be taken down.'

'Dead right. But then, a dog'd look pretty silly leaning on the bar and enjoying a pint, wouldn't he?' Zacchi was playing with her but she didn't mind one bit. 'I'll tell you all about us "gypsies" if you like, when we're out walking the country lanes.'

'You're pretty sure of yourself.'

'I'll be around, when you're ready. I'll be here. I'm not going anywhere and neither are you. We've got five long weeks to look forward to.' Turning away and walking back to his camp, he gave a backward show of his hand and then sauntered off, hands deep in his pockets, with a confident, happy manner that Kay liked.

Kay stayed for a few minutes, leaning against the back of the pink huts, gazing over at the gypsy camp. The travellers were busy organizing their colourful wagons to form a small train. Feeling very happy and wanting to hold on to the moment, she wondered if the warm feeling inside would fade away once she was back with her own people. She also wondered what it must be like, wandering around England, relying on seasonal work and fortune-telling. A far cry from the concrete and brick jungle she had left behind.

Liz looked at her sister-in-law and smiled. 'Never mind Laura, you've got your memories. Your mother'll always be remembered. Even though she was a snob.'

'She wasn't a snob, Liz. Just liked to keep at arm's length, that's all.'

Laura felt Kay gazing into her face. 'Your remember her, don't you love? Used to give you a silver sixpence for the money box you pretended to keep. She knew you used to go straight round to the Jews' sweetshop and treat yourself to a bar of Cadbury's Milk.'

'Yeah. I can still see her, always sweeping the path behind that green gate while Granddad fussed around his roses and tomato plants.' Laughingly, Kay told of the way her grandparents used to sit by the coal fire in the tiny living-room eating cooking apples, Cheddar cheese and raw onion, encouraging her to try some.

Laura laughed at the memory. Her mum and dad had seemed old-fashioned compared to her friends' parents, but she wouldn't have wanted them any different. 'And Dad still swears that sucking a raw egg from its shell keeps him young!'

'It must be hard for the poor sod, carrying on without 'er. Thick as thieves, they were.'

Clearing her throat, Laura tried to look on the bright side. 'He's all right, Liz. So long as he can have his pint every day with his old cronies down the Golden Eagle, he's happy enough.' Secretly she was wishing she could have her mother back again; there had been several times during the past eleven years when she needed her good sensible advice and a reassuring hug. At least her death had been quick. A massive heart attack had killed her in one clean swoop. The doctor had said it was owing to her 'weight problem'. Laura had never considered her fat. She just had a bit too much flesh on her small-framed body, that was all.

'Your dad's strong, Laura,' Liz chuckled, 'he'll outlive us with all that raw onion and raw egg in his blood.'

Laura swallowed hard and pressed her dry lips together. A settled calm was now spreading through the common as everyone finished sweeping, unpacking and setting up home. Large kettles full of boiling water bubbled away over camp-fires and the smell of sizzling bacon and sausages was in the air as the women stood in pairs, sipping hot tea and enjoying a gossip.

Four

Sitting at his desk in his office, a small room in the tiny cottage some five hundred yards down the lane from the common, Richard crossed from his list the pickers who had already arrived. When he came to Laura Armstrong, he stopped and poured himself some coffee from the large blue and white flask, toying with the idea of adding a slug of brandy, but deciding that since it was only just after five in the afternoon it might not be such a good idea.

Settling himself on the small comfortable sofa, he stretched his long legs and let his head sink back into the feather cushion, remembering the first time Laura came into his office almost nine years ago, to complain that she had been given the wrong hut. She had explained how she needed her usual brick one because of the raised platform – she couldn't possibly lie on the floor, no matter how comfortable the mattress – and as she was seven months pregnant, who could blame her?

The vision of her face became clearer by the second: pregnancy had not diminished her good looks, if anything it had made her more attractive, a glowing picture of health. He remembered her faded green-and-white linen maternity frock, her freshly washed wavy chestnut hair, which tumbled freely past her shoulders, and those soft, hazel-flecked green eyes.

He had felt an immediate rapport with her because at that time his own wife, Julia, had been expecting the twins. But unlike Julia, the lovely young woman who had stood before him demanded no more than a half-decent place to sleep, while his wife had all the comforts an expectant mother could want.

His mind raced on to the following autumn, when he had met Laura in the lane while walking his dogs. He had asked her about her new baby and whether she'd had a boy or a girl. It had been more than pity he felt when she told him the baby had died two months after he had been born, a seemingly perfect, healthy boy.

Richard should have realized then, when he had had the strong desire to let go of the dogs' leads and hold her close. He wanted to hold and comfort someone else's wife. He never dreamed in a million years that it could happen to him.

A sudden ring on the doorbell brought him back sharply from the past. He guessed it would be another picker with a complaint, so he made his way to his desk and sat behind it. 'Come in!'

The woman who stood before him was the one Laura had encountered earlier by the water-tap.

'Mrs Brown . . . of course,' he grimaced. 'I should have been expecting you.'

Pulling up a chair and sitting herself down opposite him, she slapped her small worn handbag on to his desk, almost as if it was his fault that she had to carry it around with her. 'It's 'appened again Mr Wright. Thirteen years I've been picking for your father . . .'

'My father's no longer with us, Mrs Brown,' he reminded her pointedly, with a smile, 'he died three years ago.'

'You've given me someone else's hut again! I can't sleep in them tin things, not with my chest.' A short bout of coughing followed.

'Not to worry, I'm sure you've something in mind.'

'It happened last year if you remember rightly. You know I always used to have number six, a pink hut with a window that opened.'

'Yes,' he said, drumming his fingers on the desk, 'it's coming back to me . . . this must be the . . . third time in fact? And I think, if my memory serves me right, that you'll be happy to stay in the allocated hut to . . . help us out, and we compensate you by . . .' He tried desperately to remember, knowing this woman would otherwise make the very most of his bad memory.

'Eight pounds!'

'I think it was five?'

'Five at first, three later. I'd like ten this year. Three pairs of wellingtons for the children and a pair of strong boots for myself . . . apart from anything else.'

Resigning himself to her pushy manner, he drew open the left-hand drawer of his writing-desk and took out the small grey petty-cash tin.

'We'll say five, Mrs Brown, and see how we go. If it got out that I gave you extra cash for . . .'

'Discomforts,' she grinned.

'. . . I would have a lot of pickers queueing outside the door, complaining about their huts.'

Shedding a few crocodile tears and hiding her sham behind an off-white handkerchief, she slowly shook her head. 'If my children had a father around to look after them, I wouldn't be reduced to asking for charity.'

Amused with her amateur display he pressed his lips together and smiled inwardly. 'Er . . . forgive me if I was mistaken, but I was on the common earlier . . . and I thought I saw – Mr Brown?'

'Well, someone had to fetch me down!' she snapped back.

'Of course. I er . . . I take it he's been . . . behaving himself . . . ?' Richard's voice trailed off as he realized he had just stepped over the borderline.

'Behaving himself, Mr Wright? I'm not sure how to take that?'

'No. Don't know what I could have been thinking . . . It's been a long day.' He fidgeted uncomfortably in his chair. 'Now, where were we . . . ?'

'What's he supposed to have done then?' she persisted, determined to get an answer.

It was obvious to Richard that this tiresome woman was not going to let him off the hook. 'Well, he has been known to hit out at you and the children from time to time.' Gritting his teeth he crossed his fingers. He really was very tired and not able to cope with any more melodrama.

Sitting bolt upright, the woman stared into his face and narrowed her eyes. 'How do you know about that?' Then, as it dawned on her, the expression on her face changed. Smugly sitting back in her chair, she folded her arms and smiled knowingly. 'Laura

Armstrong. I knew I shouldn't have told her. You want to be careful what you accuse people of, Mr Wright . . . after all, I've managed to keep my mouth shut where your business is concerned. If it had been anyone else who had seen you and that tart, Laura Arms—'

'Yes, all right, Mrs Brown!' he cut in, wishing he could strangle her and do everyone a favour. 'I take your point,' he said, being a sensible law-abiding man.

'Good. So I'll come for that other three pounds next week . . . shall I?'

Later that day, Laura relaxed on a chair outside her hut and gazed at the darkening landscape, the camp-fires and setting sun. The sinking orange glow was casting rays of warm pink light in the sky.

In a comfortable mood, she took in the things that made up her surroundings; reflections of the sunset on the roofs of the corrugated tin huts, the smell of smoke from camp-fires and the echo of children's voices. It was a welcome return after the long ten months in London.

'A farthing for 'em, Laura,' Bert teased as he passed by on his way to join Jack by the fire.

'Cost you more than that to know what dark thoughts are going on in my mind, Bert!' Lifting her chair, she carried it over to sit with the men while they waited for Liz to return from the fish-and-chip van.

Shifting his chair to make room for her, Jack flicked his cigarette-end into the glowing embers. 'Economics, my arse,' he said sharply. 'Greed more like.' He was picking up on a conversation he'd had with Bert before he went into the hut to fetch some beer-glasses. 'Wright can't bear to think there might be a quicker way to make money if he's not in on it.'

'You don't know that, Jack,' Bert argued, 'the man might not have any choice!'

'You reckon? Well, he'll get 'is comeuppance. Machines might strip the bines quicker than we could but they won't clean out the leaves.' Frowning at the thought of it, he pulled the top off a bottle of stout with his penknife. 'Gawd 'elp the beer, that's all I can say!'

Arriving with their evening meal, Liz sat herself firmly down on the chair closest to the fire. 'Bit of a nip in the air now that the sun's going down,' she said, and, pulling her cardigan round close, she started to hand out the newspaper-wrapped parcels. 'That's . . . skate for you, Jack . . . haddock for Laura and cod for me and Bert. Kay's took hers to eat by the river.'

Unwrapping the paper and sprinkling the piping-hot fish and chips with salt and vinegar, the four of them were in their element. Blowing on a hot chip before popping it into his mouth, Bert said, ''Course, it might only be a rumour.'

'Oh, leave it be, Bert,' Laura pleaded, 'haven't we heard enough for one day?'

'It wouldn't be on everyone's lips if there was nothing in it, Bert. He's probably leaked it himself. Hasn't got the guts to tell us face to face. Frightened we might not pick as fast for 'im,' Jack said with his mouth full.

'You could be right there, Jack, boy,' his sister agreed. 'Anyway, some of us women have had enough of this life. Pick your fingers to the bone and for what? Lousy one-and-fourpence a bushel. It's all right for you men coming down at weekends, waited on 'and and foot.'

'Leave off, Lizzie! You can't tell me you ain't gonna miss hoppin'. You start packing in June,' Jack laughed.

Eyeing her carefully, Bert added, 'You didn't 'ave to come, love.'

'Bending over fires, trying to turn out a decent meal,' she went on, not appeased.

Licking his fingers, Bert picked up his glass of beer. 'This is a lovely bit of fish and chips, that I do know. And he said he'd be round again on Wednesday, so you needn't cook then, need yer?'

'Where d'yer reckon you'll go next year, Lizzie? French Riviera?' Jack joked.

'We'll 'ave a week in my David's caravan, that's what we'll do. First proper 'oliday me and Bert will have had.'

Shaking his head and laughing, Jack picked up his beer-glass. 'Gypsy Liz,' he teased.

'Could do worse,' she said, breaking off a piece of steaming, crisply battered fish. 'Anyway, the youngsters have got it right if you ask me. Different attitude. It's the age of change all right, and not before time.'

Picking up a bundle of faggots with his left hand and setting them on the fire, Jack shook his head slowly. 'Things you say. It'll always be the same, workers scratching a bloody living while them up there are having Christmas every day. Change? Do me a favour.'

'We'll see, Jack, we'll see.'

'You come into this life with a silver spoon at your lips, like Richard Wright, or a docker's hook in your hand, like us.' Jack couldn't keep the scorn out of his voice.

'Well, one thing's for certain,' Laura chipped in,

'these huts'll be flattened. It'll be just another field for grazing. As if we'd never been.'

Jack downed his beer in one go. The one word that did bother him was *change*, but for other reasons than those Liz was talking about. There would be some in his life and soon, he could feel it in the air, and he still wasn't sure it was what he wanted. He didn't want to decide. If he had his way, he would leave well alone.

Tilting his head slightly to look at Laura, he admitted to himself that she was still a good-looker, especially with the flames from the fire reflecting across her face like that. Theirs hadn't turned out to be the ideal marriage, but it was better than some. He remembered how they used to be together, always laughing. He never did know quite where to lay the blame for the way they were now, but one thing was for sure, it had gone wrong well before he had taken up with Patsy.

Almost instinctively, Laura raised her eyes and looked back at him with only the roaring, crackling fire between them.

'Well, Bert,' Jack suddenly said, 'I think it's time we paid our friendly publican a visit.' With that, he rolled his fish-and-chip wrappings into a ball and tossed them on to the fire.

'You'll have to ask the boss. You know I don't go anywhere unless she's happy about it.'

'Oh, piss off, silly git!' Liz smiled; she was pleased he had asked.

The two women were happy to see the back of them for half an hour. They were quite content to sit round the fire and chat about nothing of much importance, enjoying the background sound of old familiar songs being sung around other camp-fires, knowing that before very long they too would join in. 'I wonder where Kay could have got to,' Laura murmured.

'I told yer, she made her way to the river, "to be alone",' Liz joked.

'I hope she's all right.'

Laura needn't have worried; having left the river, Kay was now sitting on the ground, leaning on the end wall of the huts and watching the activities around the gypsy camp, which seemed like another world.

She hadn't seen Terry since the afternoon and although others close to her age had arrived throughout the day, none of them were friends that she had struck up with in the past.

Sighing, she leaned her head back, clenching the muscles in her neck to stop herself crying. She didn't know why she felt low, especially since she had been so happy that morning when she climbed on to the back of her Uncle Bert's lorry.

The gypsy camp was quietening as the dim glow of lights shone out from each wagon. She wondered what Zacchi would be doing right now. Whatever it was, she had no part in it. Standing and brushing down the back of her jeans, she made her way to the hut, passing a courting couple who saw no one but each other as they strolled arm in arm, she resting her head on his shoulder and carrying their portable radio with a singer's voice drifting over and then fading, as the lovers walked away into the night.

Lifting the iron latch, Kay pushed the hut door open and went inside, thinking about Zacchi, wondering if he had meant it when he said, 'I'll be there . . . waiting.' She eased off her new white sandals and stretched her toes before turning up the oil-lamp. Then, climbing up on to the straw mattress, she pulled her paperback from under the pillow and started to read her new love story. The low voices of her mum and Aunt Liz as they talked around the camp-fire was a comforting sound which made her feel drowsy. Five minutes later, Kay was fast asleep.

Five

The Sunday-morning smell of sizzling bacon coming from Laura's hut drew Jack from the isolation of his own sleeping-quarters. Pulling the door shut behind him so no one could see the mess – full ashtray, dirty mug and yesterday's clothes – he wandered lazily into Laura's hut.

'Smells nice,' he said, sitting himself down on a small kitchen chair. 'Looks like today's gonna be another scorcher,' he added, trying to make conversation. Then, lifting a corner of the familiar floral curtain which separated the sleeping-quarters from the living-area, he nudged the drowsing Kay on the shoulder. 'Lazy cow. You should be out there making a pot of tea for your poor old dad!'

'Get off, Dad . . .' she mumbled and turned away, pulling the silky pale primrose quilt over her head.

'How long d'yer reckon breakfast'll be, Laura?'

'Five minutes.'

'Yeah?' Then looking at his watch he stood up. 'Just enough time to go and have a cup of tea with Lizzie and Bert. 'Spect he's been out for the Sunday papers by now. Call me when it's ready.' With that he whistled his way out and along by the row of huts, calling out to Milly as he went. 'You're looking as fresh as a daisy in winter, Milly!'

'Yeah,' she giggled back, 'well you can pick me whenever you want, Jack!'

Standing over the Primus stove, turning the bacon and hearing the banter going on outside, Laura couldn't help wishing the day away.

'You awake, Kay? This is nearly ready.'

Snuggling further down between the white sheets which had just a faint smell of soap powder on them, Kay dug herself deeper into her comfy straw bed and remembered the day before, and the way Zacchi had looked at her with those deep blue eyes beneath curled black lashes.

It was just before three in the afternoon, after a delicious meal of potroast beef, potatoes and two veg, followed by baked apples, compliments of the Wrights' orchard, that Jack and Bert were ready to climb into the cab of the lorry and make their way back to London.

Liz and Laura were sharing the heavy load of

washing-up. With their arms up to the elbow in suds, they both sang 'Catch a Falling Star' along to Perry Como as his voice floated across from someone's portable.

'Whoever invented portable wirelesses should be shot! Bloody rubbish! Call those songs?' Watching Jack striding out towards the cab of Bert's lorry carrying two bags of apples, the women couldn't help smiling at him; raising her voice, Liz joined in with the song again:

And put it in your po-cket, save it for a rainy
    day!
For love may come and tap you on the shoulder,
    some star-less night.
And just in case you feel you want to hold
    her . . .

'*Oi!* Turn that down!' Jack's voice boomed across the common. Chuckling, Liz gave Laura a quick wink. 'What's up Jack, don't you wanna go back to London?' she called out in her most sincere voice.

'Can't bear to leave us?' Laura chimed in.

Arriving and not looking his happiest, Jack lit a roll-up. 'Yeah, something like that. Anyway, where's Kay got to?'

'Right behind yer.'

Turning swiftly around he grinned, 'Oh, yeah, here, half a crown. Don't spend it all at once.' He flicked the coin towards her and she caught it in one hand.

'What's there to spend it on?'

'Oh, here, I'll 'ave it back in that case.'

'Up to you,' she said sulkily.

'Getting as touchy as your mum. Come on, give us a hug.' Offering his stretched arms to her, his eyes filled with tears, as she threw herself around him.

'I wish you wasn't going, Dad.'

'Yeah, well, I'll be back next weekend.' He managed to force the tears back but anyone could tell by his cracked voice that he was choked.

'I hate to think of you in that flat all by yerself.'

Impatient to get on the road, Bert gave Liz and Laura a quick kiss on the cheek and climbed into his cab. 'Come on, Jack! Let's be 'aving yer!'

Letting go of Kay, Jack turned to Liz and gave her a hug, the usual saucy banter going on between them. Then turning to Laura, who stood awkwardly, drying her hands on a tea towel, he stiffened. 'Right then. Drop us a note if you've forgot anything, and, er, I'll fetch it down with me next week. Right?'

'Right.'

Making his way towards the front of the lorry, he turned back to his sister. 'Liz!'

'Hallo?'

'Get them hops picked! You'll need the cash for when you tow that caravan to the French Riviera!' Laughing, he climbed up next to Bert and with a toot on the horn they were away, shouting more goodbyes from the open window.

Picking up a tea towel and wiping the clean plates dry, Laura fell into a pensive mood.

'Penny for 'em,' Liz coaxed.

'You'd be wasting your money.'

Sighing, Liz shook her head slowly. 'One of you 'as got to break this daft rift, you know.'

'Yeah? Well why don't you try telling that to Jack?' Feeling Kay's arm coming across her shoulders, Laura dropped the tea towel on to the back of a chair and stroked Kay's hair. 'I'll finish this when I get back.'

Kay watched her mum go, knowing she was on her way to the river, wanting very much to run up and walk beside her, but something warned her, as it had so many many times, that she wasn't wanted right then.

'Fetch us a couple of chairs from in the hut, Kay. The kettle's just boiled.' Liz knew that her fifteen-year-old niece was desperate for a bit of company, not friends at that moment, just family. And for now, as on many other occasions, she would have to make do with Liz.

Staring into the flames, Liz wondered how things would turn out in the end. Her biggest fear was that Laura and Jack would split up once they felt Kay was old enough to take the blow.

'Won't you really be sorry, Aunt Liz,' Kay asked, 'not to be coming back here any more?'

'Oh, I'll be sorry, Mog,' she said dreamily, 'I'll be more than sorry. Don't forget, 'opping has been part of my life for as far back as I can remember. I was a babe in arms on breast milk when I made my first trip to the hop fields, over at Paddock Wood.'

'Was it much different in them days?' Kay asked, as if the question had never been raised before. The truth was she loved hearing her aunt tell stories about the old days, when they would arrive on the early train which had been put on especially for hop-pickers.

'Did I ever tell you about the time your grandfather fell in a ditch on his way back from the pub?' Drawn back in time, Liz didn't even hear Kay tell her that she had heard it but had forgotten what happened. 'Slept in that ditch all night he did. Poor chap, first time he'd ever come down 'opping as well. Wasn't used to the heavy Saturday-night drinking. The first and last weekend he ever paid us a visit. I think we were all a bit too rough for your mum's side of the family. If ever you want to see the old man go white, just ask him about that night.' With that Liz roared with laughter and slapped her knee several times.

It wasn't long before others joined Liz and Kay round the fire, bringing their own chairs with them. Liz was like a magnet on the common, they were all fond of her. They knew they could always rely on her for a favour if they had troubles; they also knew she would give the edge of her tongue if any of them put a foot wrong.

Driving through the backstreets of London, the two men were quiet, tired after their journey. Jack had two roll-ups between his lips and, after lighting them both, he offered one to Bert.

'Oh, ta. Next turning, innit?'

'Yeah, then straight up and on the left.'

Taking a good drag of his cigarette, Bert spoke in his quiet, serious tone. 'I don't agree with what you're doing, you know.'

'I'm not asking you to, Bert.'

'Can't love more than one woman at a time.'

'Yeah, well, like I said yesterday, I never get a look-in on Laura's bed, and a man's gotta do what a man's gotta do. This'll do me. Pull up by that lamppost.'

Slowing down to a stop, Bert pulled on the brake but left the engine running. 'I'll tell you something,

Jack. I'm a darn sight happier with one woman than you'll ever be with two, or even three.'

'Four, as it 'appens. All right if I leave my docker's hook down there? You'll pick me up in the morning, won't yer?'

'Right bloody nuisance you are,' Bert sighed. 'Go on, get out, and say hallo to Patsy for me.'

Searching through his inside pocket, Jack looked worried. 'Don't call her that, Bert.'

'Why not? It's her name, innit?'

'Yeah, but I don't know . . . calling 'er by 'er name, makes me feel uncomfortable. Don't seem right on Laura.' Feeling pleased with himself because he had found what he was looking for, he slipped the packet of three back into his pocket.

'I'll never fathom you, Jack, not in a million bloody years.'

'Good!' Jumping down from the lorry, he slammed the door shut. 'Fire away!'

Bert gave a couple of toots on his hooter, then pulled away and drove through the backstreets of Bethnal Green towards his terraced house in Columbia Road. He didn't cherish the thought of being alone all week but it would give him time to do up the front room, a little surprise for Liz when she got back.

Pushing his street-door key into the lock, he thought about Jack and Laura again and the way they used to be. Then, letting himself in, he slammed the door behind him, shutting out the world.

Jack hadn't got the greeting from Patsy that he expected. He imagined she'd be in high spirits with Laura out of the way for a few weeks, but he was wrong. She was in a foul mood, enough, Jack thought, to make anyone turn around and go back to Kent. There had been no kiss hallo, no cuddle. Settling himself down on the sofa while she messed about in the kitchen, he pulled the Sunday papers from under a cushion to catch up on a bit of news about the forthcoming general election, and ignored her. He knew how to melt the ice.

Patsy stayed in the kitchen for as long as possible, banging pots and pans in the vain hope, Jack reasoned, of keeping up her mood. When she finally came in with two cups of tea, he looked wistfully at her.

Taking his tea, he dropped the newspaper to the floor. 'What's up, then?' He used his childlike voice which usually won her over. 'Ain't you pleased to see me?'

Sipping her tea, she gazed at the floor. 'I'm pregnant, Jack.'

Silence hung in the air and stayed there. Jack was shell-shocked. He couldn't understand it. He nearly always had something with him when he paid her a visit. Nearly always.

'Do you still love Laura?' she asked casually.

'Oh, leave off, Patsy. Fancy asking a thing like that at a time like this. Give me a while to take it in, for Christ's sake!'

'I need to know!'

'Well, I don't know so I can't tell yer, can I?'

'All right, fair enough. But there's one thing you can tell me, and I won't be fobbed off. I want an answer. I want to know if you've spent the past six years wishing your marriage could work.'

Dropping his head back into the armchair, he sighed.

'You have, haven't you?'

'Patsy, I haven't spent the past years wishing anything! Wishing 'as never worked for me yet. I found that out years ago. Things 'appen and you get on with 'em the best you can.'

'I have to be a wife now, Jack. There's no way I'm gonna settle for being an unmarried mother.'

'I've already got a wife.' He was beginning to get upset, his voice had that tell-tale crack in it.

'There are such things as divorce courts.'

96

'I know that.'

Knowing she was pushing him into a corner, she tried to control her breathing. 'So?'

There was a quiet pause, while he stared into her gas fire before saying, with a heavy heart, 'I can't give you an answer, Patsy. I just can't.'

Peering into her hand-mirror, Laura wondered which shade of lipstick to apply. 'You asleep behind there, Kay?'

'No, I'm reading my book.'

'You should pull the curtain back, then. It's not good for your eyes, reading without proper light.'

'I'm using my torch,' she said, wishing her mum wouldn't disturb her when she was at a good bit. 'What you doing?' she asked, trying to show she wasn't that involved in her romance novel.

'Just brightening up my face a bit.'

Pulling the curtain back, Kay narrowed her eyes. 'Lipstick?'

'Yeah.'

'Going out for one of your "little walks", I suppose.'

Pressing her lips together, Laura dabbed the corner of her mouth with her new handkerchief, using the embroidered corner so it wouldn't show. 'I thought you were going to see Terry?'

'I don't like his new friend. Anyway, they're going for a swim, and it's getting dark.'

Sweeping one side of her hair back and slipping a tortoiseshell comb in, Laura considered the new look. 'Thought that would've been right down your street.'

'They swim in the nude!'

'Oh?'

'Dad left me half a crown. I thought we could play cards.'

'Ask Aunt Liz,' she said, while checking first one side of her face, then the other.

'She's having her tea-leaves read.'

Annoyed with Kay's persistence, Laura dropped her lipstick and powder into her small bag and snapped it shut. 'Well, it won't hurt you to have an early night then, will it?'

Kay pulled the curtain back, climbed down from the bed and pushed her feet into her wellingtons.

'Where do you go on your "little walks" anyway?'

Lifting and unfolding her favourite dark rose-pink cardigan from the suitcase and putting it up to her face, Laura was pleased that the lipstick she had chosen was a perfect match. 'Nowhere special. Blow a few cobwebs away, that's all.'

'I'm sure!' Pushing the hut door open with so

much force that it crashed against the wall and bounded back, Kay marched off across the common.

Laura dropped into her chair and took a deep breath. She was going to see Richard and no one would stop her. If someone didn't show her some affection soon, she felt she would go mad. Sick of Jack's cold shoulder, she knew he was carrying guilt. He hadn't touched her in years and knowing Jack the way she did, he wouldn't choose to live without sex. He had always been demonstrative, wanting her all the time, until things went wrong. Well, if one could play that game, why not two? If he had been enjoying another woman all these years, why shouldn't she love another man?

Grabbing her cardigan and purse she walked out, gently pulling the door shut behind her. Holding her head high, she walked brazenly across the common towards the gate, heading for the cottage where she knew Richard would be waiting. Let the others see her. Let them talk! Sod the lot of them!

Kay had made her way to her aunt's hut, but she was sitting around someone else's fire telling them all about the palm-reading and what her life was supposed to hold in store. Not interested in that, Kay sat alone by Liz's smouldering fire, wondering

how the boys were getting on. Now that night
had fallen, the temperature had dropped and the
river must be freezing. She couldn't resist going
to see.

The boys were having a wild time; they had pulled
their clothes off and scattered them everywhere
before lowering themselves into the river.

Looking forward to a good swim, Terry's friend
Ray pushed his way through the dark water. 'This is
barmy! It don't go no higher than my belly button.
What d'yer wanna go and pick this part of the
river for?'

'You know why!' Terry shivered.

'Mud and sludge oozing between my toes. God
knows what's on the bottom of this bed. There must
be deeper parts than this?'

Unable to stop his teeth from chattering, Terry
wrapped his thin white arms around his ribs. ''Course
there is. It gets deeper as you get nearer the bridge.'

'What we messing about here for, then? Come
on, you prat! Keep walking till it's up to your neck.
You'll be all right.'

'I'll go in as far as my chest, and that's it!'

Swimming and enjoying himself, Ray turned on
to his back and floated, staring up at the full moon.
'If I had known you were this yellow, Terry Button,
I wouldn't have bothered to come! You wanna

toughen up a bit if you wanna impress the girls. Oi, Terry! What's better than a moonlight swim?'

Wishing he hadn't let Ray talk him into being there, Terry toyed with the idea of climbing back on to the river-bank. 'A warm straw bed,' he grumbled.

'A moonlight swim . . . with the lovely KAY! What d'yer reckon? I bet you a tanner she'd come, if you went and fetched her! Well? What d'yer reckon? Terry!'

With the very last of the sunset behind her and the full moon shining across her shapely body, Kay piled her hair up on top of her head and pushed in a couple of grips to secure it. 'I reckon,' she whispered, 'that he must need glasses.'

Shocked at the sight of the naked Kay, Terry felt the blood rush to his face. 'How long've you been there, you silly cow! Frightened the life out of me.'

'You shouldn't be in there, Terry, it's not clever.'

'No, and you shouldn't be standing there like that either. What if someone sees yer?'

'I checked first. There's no one about.'

'What if Ray sees yer?'

Lowering herself into the river, she had to catch her breath. 'God almighty! It's freezing!' Wasting no more energy fighting off the cold she plunged in and began swimming. 'Can you see me that well, Terry?'

'No but . . .'

'Well, then. Stop worrying about your precious friend. If he puts a toe out of line, he'll be for it.'

'Who you rabbiting to, Button?' Ray called out.

'No one! Talking to myself, that's all.'

'I'm gonna swim up to the second bridge,' he yelled, 'don't sneak off before I get back! Right?'

Making his way to the bank and his nice big towel, Terry shouted back, ''Course I won't!'

While he sat on the grass wrapped up like a baby, Kay swam to and fro across the river, enjoying the tingling sensation in her breasts. This was the first time she had swum in the nude, and she liked the feeling of excitement that shot through her body. If either of her parents could see her now, they would go berserk.

'Shouldn't you get out now, Kay, before Ray comes back?' Terry said anxiously.

Swimming towards him until it was shallow enough to walk, she reached out and grabbed a good tuft of grass and pulled herself on to the bank. 'I am gonna get out now, Terry, but only because I'm ready to.' Wrapping her towel around her, she sat down next to him and started to dry herself. 'Have I done something to upset your mum, Terry?'

Staring out across the river, he sighed. 'What makes you say that?'

'She didn't exactly make me welcome, did she?'

'What did you expect her to do, get up and kiss you?'

Turning away from him, she eased on her white cotton knickers and pulled on her bra. 'No, I didn't expect that.'

'You have to understand,' he said in a low, sad voice, 'my mum's been on her own for a long time, without my dad, I mean. I'm all she's got.'

Pulling her big baggy dark green jumper over her head she stretched the neckline so it wasn't too close to her sensitive skin. 'So why turn against me?'

'She hasn't turned against yer. She's just trying to do the right thing by me. It worries 'er that I mix more with girls than boys.'

'Never used to bother 'er,' Kay said, lying down and lifting her face to the moon.

'No. But I was younger then.'

The two of them sat for a while in silence. Just two friends and the river, or so they thought, but Zacchi had happened across them when Kay first walked into the river and had watched from a distance, not hiding, just quietly watching. And now, as she sat there, fully clothed again, he felt his pulse gradually slow to a normal pace and the blood stop pumping at speed through his body. His breathing became easier as he leaned on the trunk of an old tree. Not only had he spoken to her for the first time the day before, he had now seen her completely naked, and couldn't understand why he felt no guilt at watching her like that.

Sipping cognac and turning her enamel pillbox in her hand, Julia sat in the study listening to her favourite piece from *The Marriage of Figaro* and decided that she would not take her tranquillizer tonight.

Richard was at the cottage as usual and would be there until late, making the excuse that he had a mass of paperwork to catch up on, but she knew otherwise.

Julia had chosen this evening to discover the truth finally for two reasons; first, she needed to know at the beginning of the season if Richard was seeing someone, so that she could execute her plan of action sooner. Secondly, she was afraid that as this was the last time his lover would find the opportunity to *poach*, she might persuade him to arrange a secret rendezvous in London. As the grandfather clock in the library struck eight, she felt her stomach tighten. Only fifteen minutes and the maid would be in to light the fire.

Feeling awkward and cheap, leaning against the small sofa in Richard's office, Laura wished she had stayed in the hut. Twice she had got as far as his gate and only on the third attempt had she managed to pluck up the courage and knock on the cottage door.

'I was just thinking about you,' he said as he turned the key in the door.

He had his back to her, and she wondered what she would say to him after all this time. There were so many things she wanted to say but the words wouldn't come, her mind was blank.

Turning to face her, he shook his head slowly. 'You look beautiful.'

'Thank you,' she smiled.

'I was just sitting there . . . praying you would come. Terrified you might not want to see me. That you'd—'

'I wasn't sure whether I should,' she broke in; 'I was getting some fresh air; I saw the light was on . . .'

Gently cupping her face, he lifted it slightly and kissed her softly on the cheek. 'Welcome back,' he murmured, his familiar husky voice sending waves of delirious longing through her body. Forcing herself back to reality, she drew away. Half smiling, she pulled nervously at strands of her wavy auburn hair and twisted them round her finger. 'I've written you endless letters.' She laughed superficially. Seeing the look of concern on his face, she added quickly, 'It's all right. I didn't post any of them.'

'You should look in the secret compartment of my bureau. I've written you the longest letters in the world.' Then reaching out again he pulled her to him and kissed her hair, nestling his face into her neck. 'I'll wake up in a second and find this is just another of those dreams, that it's really only the spring and there are months to go . . .'

Pulling away from him a second time, she placed her hand gently but firmly on his broad shoulders, looked him in the eye, braced herself and drew breath. 'We need to talk.'

'I've been talking to people all day,' he said, pulling her back to him and holding her tighter.

'I'm really sorry, Richard, but I have to know.'

'Well, before you ask,' he murmured, his breath hot on her neck, 'Yes. I do. Very much.'

Swallowing hard and blinking back her tears, Laura was determined to find out the truth. 'Picking-machines, Richard. Is it true?'

Letting out a painful low groan, he relaxed, let go of her and shrugged. 'I think it's time for a brandy.'

'Going to need it, am I?'

'We're both going to need one.' He unscrewed the bottle and poured the amber liquid into two glasses.

'I was hoping it wouldn't get out just yet. I didn't want you to hear it from someone else.' Handing a glass to her, he raised his own. 'One thing I do know – I'm not giving you up.'

Julia waited patiently while her maid set and finally lit the fire in the library, planning the best way to deliver her request. The girl had been with her for three years now, and they had shared the occasional brief moments, talking over coffee, when Julia felt the need for a working-class view of things. Standing and brushing some ash from her hands the maid turned to her employer. 'I'll be off, then, ma'am.'

Taken aback by the casual announcement, Julia smiled at her. 'Really?'

'I'm meeting my boyfriend. You said I could change my night off.'

'Ah. Oh dear . . . I'm awfully sorry . . . it slipped my mind.'

'You . . . won't be needing me?'

Julia lifted the lid of the silver box on the coffee-table and withdrew a Balkan Sobranie. 'I was rather hoping you'd walk the dogs for me,' she suggested, with a mere hint of persuasion.

'But I promised my young man,' the girl pleaded.

'Well, isn't that too bad!' Lighting her cigarette,

she pulled the ruby glass ashtray towards her. 'I'm afraid you'll have to let him down, Janet.'

'That's not fair!'

'Oh, do stop whining!' Then, changing her tactics and with a haughty gesture of the hand, she lowered her voice. 'Don't stand there as if you're on parade, Janet. Why not sit down and join me?' Seeing that the girl had no intention of crossing the barrier at that precise moment, she stood up, walked across to the marble fireplace and braced herself. 'I wanted to talk to you, Janet. I'm worried about Mr Richard. I think one of the hop-pickers! . . . one of the women, is pestering him; it's not unheard of. The rich handsome landowner. A sitting target.'

Janet shifted nervously from one foot to the other. She felt embarrassed that Julia Wright should be speaking to her like that, and about the master too.

'I don't see what that's got to do with me, ma'am?' She spoke in a whisper, but Julia was off on her own track and wasn't listening.

'I just thought, if you were walking the dogs, past the cottage, then . . .'

'I'm sorry. I couldn't do that. My young man is expecting me.'

'Oh, for goodness' sake, Janet! I'm talking about my husband! Don't you care? Doesn't it bother you that some wretched cockney's taking advantage?'

Once again she decided to soften her tone. 'Look, if you find out who it is, we can see her off. Mr Richard doesn't have to know about it. No one need know. And to show my appreciation, I could always slip a couple of extra pounds into your envelope on Friday.'

Lowering her head to hide the fear in her eyes, Janet cleared her throat. 'I couldn't do it. And I'm sorry to be so bold, but I don't think it would be right.'

Filled with resentment towards the pathetic figure standing before her, Julia strode across the room towards the door. 'Get the dogs ready, I'll take them myself!' Turning round to face her maid, she glared at her. 'And not a word of this to anyone. If it should get out – I'll know where to lay the blame.'

Having moved from the office into the snug at the back of the cottage and settling themselves on the sofa in front of the coal fire, Laura felt as if she was being swallowed up in one of her dreams, as she curled up closer to Richard. Easing off her shoes and kicking them to the floor, she pushed her toes into a soft cushion.

Happy to be back in his arms again after all those months, she looked up into his serious face and wondered what might be going through his mind. His fiery passion had died as quickly as it came and it crossed her mind that he would rather she went back to the common, but couldn't bring himself to say so.

Just as if he had read her thoughts, Richard turned his eyes from the fire and smiled teasingly, 'I thought you'd fallen asleep on me.' Then, trailing one finger across her forehead, he cupped Laura's face and kissed her, making up for all the nights they had spent wishing they were together. Her flesh tingled as his strong hands moved slowly to her breasts and down over the silky blue material. Longing to feel him inside her again, she began to unfasten the neck of her dress, but his masculine hand stopped her, a look of mischief on his face. 'That's my pleasure,' he said earnestly. 'I've thought of nothing else for the past weeks.' Standing, he gently pulled Laura to her feet. 'I want you in that dress,' he smiled, 'and I want you out of it.'

'You can't do both,' she said shyly.

'Why not?' He placed his hands on her narrow hips and slowly lifted the soft material. Not taking his eyes off her face, he began to caress her body until every part of her was throbbing. When he brought his mouth down hotly on hers, Laura felt herself slip into that paradisiacal world away from all things real.

*   *   *

Bringing the hounds to heel, Julia tied their leads to a nearby tree and, in a hushed voice, firmly ordered them to be quiet. They were obedient dogs and she trusted them to stay until she returned from the back garden of the cottage.

Now that she was actually carrying out her mission, she began to feel the old power charging through her veins. The apprehension she had felt when she started out had gone, and she was enjoying the thrill of the challenge.

Driving her hands deep into the pockets of her brown sheepskin coat, she listened for other footsteps crunching on the gravel. Relieved that there were none, she took a deep breath and made her way along the dark lane, hoping that, since it was a Sunday night, the women would not be on their way to or from the White Horse. Even they, she thought, must have some sense of morality.

She arrived at the wooden gate leading into the back garden, which was almost hidden in the overgrown hedge, and stopped again to listen for footsteps. Then, making attempts to push the gate open, she realized that the nettles and weeds had rooted themselves firmly in and around it and that she would have to climb over.

Placing one foot on the bottom support of the

gate, she swung her other leg over. She crushed some nettles down, landing with a soft thud in the tangle of the garden. Surprised at the sound of her own rapid heartbeats she leaned on the rickety gate and waited for her breathing to return to normal.

It had been a hot day but now that the sun had gone down, with the harvest moon taking its place, the air was chilling and apart from the call of owls and bats the shadowy night was silent – almost too quiet.

Turning to look at the back of the cottage, Julia could see that the only light coming from it was the soft glow through the snug window, a sign that Richard was not in his office but sitting by the coal fire. She was instantly filled with doubt. What if she was wrong? What if he had simply fallen asleep by the fire? What if he caught her stealing through the back garden like a thief?

Now that she had come this far it would, she decided, be cowardly to turn back. Besides which, she knew he was guilty; had known for a couple of years, but she had been biding her time, waiting until she felt sure her instincts were right. Had she confronted him before now, she would have risked his denying it all and being one step ahead of her, free to weave his web of deceit and to continue his nasty little affair.

A comforting smile crossed Julia's face, and she

felt quite suddenly elated. This being their final season and the end of Laura meant that, once she had unearthed the truth, she could pay Laura back for degrading their marriage; humiliate her while she still had the chance, before the woman slipped from her grasp, back to the gutters of London where she belonged.

Driving herself on, treading down the thick undergrowth, Julia moved slowly towards the lighted window. The dread which had lived in her mind for so long had turned into something else. She felt as if she had the power to do anything she wanted. There was nothing and no one to stop her mounting this witch-hunt, and keeping her find to herself until she was ready to use it.

She looked up at the moon and then back at the cottage, and a sizzling mixture of thrill, power and revenge ran through her when she saw the gap in the curtain. That, she told herself, was fate stepping in to lend a hand. With great caution, treading carefully on safe patches of earth, she moved forward.

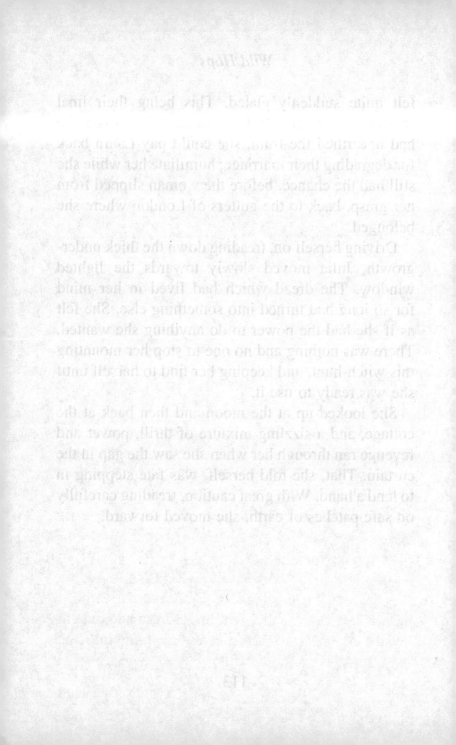

Six

Laura woke early the next morning before dawn and knew that it was useless trying go back to sleep when all she could think about was Richard. Even though he had told her over and over again that he wouldn't give her up, she was filled with a sickening fear that she might never see him again, once the season came to an end.

It had been a strange mixture of guilt and being in love which made her wake time after time during the night. Her mother's face and voice seemed to drift in and out of her dreams, warning her to take care and to give herself to Jack instead of this other man. *Love him, Laura*, she had said, in her soft, disciplinarian way.

After boiling a large saucepan of water and adding it to the cold in the small enamel bath, she slipped off her pale blue Winceyette nightdress and caught a waft of Richard's aftershave. Stepping into the lukewarm water she sponged the frothy suds over her, carefully avoiding her neck where his smell was strong. The spicy aroma began to arouse her until Laura's entire body flushed with a tantalizing glow, a warmth that swept through her whenever he was in her thoughts.

Enjoying the tightening, tingling sensation in her nipples she lowered her body and splashed water over her breasts, wondering if Richard might be awake and thinking about her. Sinking her shoulders down into the water and stretching her legs, she rested her feet on a small stool and closed her eyes, filling her thoughts with the way he had lovingly brought her to a climax the night before.

From behind the curtain, Laura could hear Kay mumbling in her sleep, which quickly brought her back into the real world. Feeling the need for some fresh air, Laura eased herself out of the tub, turned to the tiny window and quietly opened it. There was hardly a murmur on the common, other than birdsong and the distant sound of cattle lowing. The calm morning with the sun shining through the mist, she told herself, made a perfect start to an early September day.

She pulled the thick soft towel from a rail fixed to the door and wrapped it around her shoulders, and sliding it down her back, she gave herself a brisk rub-down and began to dress.

The sound of a van pulling up and the short blasts of a hooter caused Laura to smile – it was the baker. He had been delighting them with his array of freshly baked cakes and bread for as long as she could remember.

Slamming his van door shut, he made his presence felt, yelling that the baker had arrived and it was time for them to get out of their beds. He was obviously pleased to be back on the common again, enjoying his role as the town crier. 'Rise and shine!' he yelled playfully, while making his way along a row of huts, thumping his fist on the doors as he went.

'Warm bread! Fresh buns!'

Laura chuckled as she lifted the enamel jug from the floor. The baker was in good form and right on time. Pouring water into the cream and blue kettle, she remembered how much Kay enjoyed a warm Bakewell tart, covered in soft white icing, with her early-morning cup of tea.

'Oh, does he have to?' Kay groaned, as she turned in her bed.

Eyeing the curtain which separated the sleeping-compartment from the living-space, Laura chuckled. 'Everyone'd soon moan if he didn't wake 'em.'

'There's one 'ere who wouldn't,' Kay murmured from beneath the covers.

Deciding to leave her tucked up for a while, as it was the first day of picking, Laura turned up the Primus stove until its blue flame licked the side of the kettle just enough to bring it slowly to the boil, giving her time to buy warm bread and cakes.

'Do I 'ave to get up today?' Kay mumbled from behind the curtain. 'Can't bear the thought of cold, wet hop-bines dripping down my neck.'

'Dew's very good for your skin, Kay. Anyway . . .' Laura teased, 'a nice refreshing cold shower like that'll soon 'ave you in the mood for picking!'

The sound of the baker's call gradually died away and the unbolting of doors could be heard outside, as the pickers made their way towards the green van.

Pulling her baggy lilac mohair cardigan around her shoulders, Laura kicked off her slippers and pushed her feet into her wellingtons.

'Turn the Primus off and fill the teapot once the kettle boils, there's a good girl.' She pushed the door open and dropped the hook into the iron staple on the outside wall, enabling the sun to stream into the damp hut.

She joined the small queue and was relieved that at that time in the morning no one was in the mood

118

for chat. Idly scanning her surroundings, she enjoyed her euphoric mood. 'If paradise is better than this,' she thought, 'only angels should live there.'

Laura stood soaking up the atmosphere of the busy common and gazing at the timeless scenery. The hop gardens, orchards and barley fields; the winding river, with people toing and froing from the rows of huts, lighting fires and boiling large black kettles, created a focal point reminiscent of a medieval village square.

She looked across at the hop gardens and the gypsy camp, the colourful wagons adding splashes of colour to the shades of green and yellow. She watched as two of the gypsy women arrived with their long brightly coloured skirts swishing around worn leather boots, black lustrous hair swept back from their tanned faces and soft penetrating eyes.

Moving slowly forward in the queue, Laura's respectful, unimposing smile of recognition was rewarded with a beaming grin from Gypsy Rose.

'It's good to see you again, Laura.' She detected a wistful expression on her friend's face. 'I'll be round after picking, with my peg boxes.'

'Good. You can give my palm a quick once-over.'

'That's right.' Nudging Laura's arm gently, she whispered in her ear, 'You may be surprised who I see in your tea-leaves this year.'

'Then again, I might not be,' Laura laughed, thinking it was Richard that her gypsy friend was referring to.

'How's that lovely girl of yours?' she asked with a glint in her eye.

Placing her order with the baker, Laura looked towards her hut. 'Knowing Kay, she's probably gone back to sleep while the kettle boils itself dry.'

The buxom Romany let out a short burst of hearty laughter. 'Something like her father, you mean?'

Laura sighed, wishing Jack didn't have to be dragged into nearly every conversation she had. Rose was right though, Jack could be a lazy devil at times.

Once back in the hut, Laura pulled up a corner of the curtain and looped it through a hook in the wall. Giving Kay a gentle nudge, she rustled the white bag of cakes under her nose.

'You don't have to do that,' Kay murmured, turning over. 'The smell of that warm bread's enough to wake anyone up.'

'You can stay where you are. I'll wait on you this morning, then you can do the same for me tomorrow,' Laura said playfully, knowing full well it would take a lot to see Kay up first.

Sitting on a kitchen chair by the open doorway, Laura broke off a small piece of her cake and washed it down with a sip of freshly made tea. Seeing Terry saunter by she was tempted to invite him in for a chat but knew that Kay would still be snuggled into her plump pillows, relishing her Bakewell tart and mug of tea, enjoying her seclusion behind the curtain.

'What's it like out there, Mum?' Kay asked lazily.

'Mmmmm . . . bit nippy. But I reckon we're in for another hot one,' Laura said, checking the sky.

'I hope so,' Kay answered, with a mouth full of cake.

Moving from one thought to another Laura added: 'It's so good to see those gypsy wagons again . . . and Gypsy Rose.' Wiping a bit of icing from the corner of her mouth, she took another sip of tea. 'There's something special about the Romanies. Dark and mysterious. Why don't we wear long colourful clothes like them, eh?'

'I was talking to one of the boys yesterday,' Kay said carefully. 'Zacchi. He's got incredible eyes.'

'Oh, yeah? You was late in last night as well. Wasn't curled up with him I hope?'

'No I was not! I was swimming in the river with Terry and his friend if you must know. I did come back by ten but you were still out on one of your "little walks".'

'You shouldn't swim in that river at night,' Laura

said swiftly, turning the conversation away from her rendezvous.

'What's the difference?'

'It's freezing cold for a start!'

'You were soon fast asleep when you did get back. Must have been a long stroll to tire you out like that.'

Sensing another of Kay's mood swings, Laura decided to give in to her daughter's probing. 'Does it bother you that I go out alone in the dark, then?'

'Does it bother yer that I do?'

A moody silence fell between them. Laura knew that Kay had something on her mind and knowing her the way she did, whatever it was would be presented any second.

'Last night was 'ardly the first time!' Kay suddenly blurted out. 'I do it a lot back in Stepney! When the atmosphere between you and Dad gets too much. I walk under the dark railway arch, along by the deserted garages, past the bombed-out pub . . . was even propositioned last week. He offered me half a crown.'

'Kay! That's not clever! Don't you think I fret enough without having to worry about that sort of thing as well?'

Kay's hand clutching the empty mug suddenly appeared from under the curtain. Snatching it from

122

her, Laura slammed it down on the table. Surely it wasn't true. Kay was just letting her wild imagination take over again? Half a crown?

Feeling a short burst of laughter coming on, Laura squeezed her lips together and pressed her fingers against her mouth, trying in vain to stop herself giggling.

'I'm glad you think it's funny!' Kay snapped from behind the curtain.

Doubled over with laughter, Laura just managed to apologize. 'I'm sorry, Kay . . . but half a crown's not very much is it?'

'That's exactly what I told him. I said I usually charge three and six; and that was to my mates!'

Lifting the curtain back Laura playfully pulled Kay's pillows from under her. 'You lying cow!' she giggled.

'That tea still warm?' Liz shouted from the doorway.

Slapping Kay gently on the leg, Laura turned to her sister-in-law. 'Yes, Liz, it is. Sit yerself down. I don't s'pose you want a Bakewell?' she teased.

Pulling up a kitchen chair, Liz dropped into it. 'That crafty bleeder's put the bread up again. Gawd knows 'ow much he charges for a tart!'

'Half a crown . . .' Kay giggled from behind the curtain, 'plus sixpence commission!'

Pouring Liz a cup of tea, Laura burst into another fit of giggles.

'Well, you're not gonna share the sodding joke with me, so I'll 'ave a nice tart instead!' Liz snapped.

Composing herself, Kay threw the curtain back, fixed it to the wall, then swung her legs around and sat on the edge of the bed, facing her aunt. 'Tell me the truth, Aunt Liz,' she said with a mock-serious tone, 'if a bloke offered you half a crown, would you take it?'

Pursing her lips and thinking about it for a few seconds, Liz narrowed her eyes and looked up at the ceiling pensively. 'Well, I would – but for that kind of money he wouldn't get much more than a quick flash of my drawers on the washing-line. Why?'

Falling back on to her bedding, Kay screamed into her pillow while Laura wiped away her own tears of laughter.

'What's up with you two, anyway? You bin on the cider or what?'

'Don't ask, Liz,' Laura chuckled, 'don't ask.'

A few minutes before seven, the women were drifting away from the huts towards the hop gardens. Small family groups strode out, their wellingtons leaving imprints on the plush dewy grass. Everyone was wrapped in thick jumpers and coats with colourful scarves on their heads, tied around and knotted on top to protect their hair from the rough hop-bines and flying insects. Some had their packed lunches with them, cheese sandwiches wrapped in waxed paper from the sliced bread. Hopping stools and folding chairs were nestled underarm and at least one member in every family carried the familiar large brown teapot, the mainstay of the morning picking session.

In just a few hours, after the whistle went for the lunch-break, it would be a different scene. Warm clothing would have been peeled off and sun-dresses of all colours revealed, looking out of keeping with the wellington boots that most people wore to cope with the heavy clay and mud of the hop gardens.

As Laura, Kay and Liz walked towards the fields, Zacchi leaned on the back of Old Grey and gave a nod and a smile to Kay. Lowering her eyes and grinning, she could feel herself blushing again. Once past him, she looked around for the boys, remembering the river, but they were nowhere to be seen. Stepping up her pace, she walked ahead of Laura and Liz.

'Fanny Adams was giving that gypsy the once-over, and he couldn't take his eyes off her, neither,' Liz said with a touch of concern.

'Oh, Liz, that's young Zacchi. You talk as if he's some stranger. He's Gypsy Rose's boy!'

'Must be all of seventeen, Laura.'

'So?'

Letting out a deliberate sigh she pulled her coat collar up around her neck. 'Suit yerself.'

'They were only looking at each other!'

Liz chuckled knowingly. 'Yeah. It all starts with a look, don't it?'

Rushing up from behind and somewhat out of breath, Milly called out: 'Slow down, you two, for Gawd's sake!'

Turning around, Liz and Laura couldn't help smiling. Even in her long mac and heavy boots, Milly still managed to look as if she was ready for the camera.

'I've bin trying to catch up since I saw you leaving your 'uts.'

'Where's your old man, Milly, in bed?' Liz asked with a saucy sparkle in her eye.

'His leg's playing up again, actually. He'll be on the hop fields later, don't worry. Pick more in an hour than some can in four.' Turning her attention to Laura, she tucked a blonde curl back under her pink and pale green turban. 'What d'yer think about this rumour then, Laura? Is it true, or what?'

Laura didn't answer straight away but caught

126

Liz looking at her sideways with a raised eye-brow.

'Won't we be coming back down 'ere to pick no more?' Again Milly directed the question at Laura.

'How should I know?'

'Well,' she shrugged, 'my George saw you coming out of Wright's office, so we assumed . . . that's why you went in. To ask. Mind you, it was late at night.'

There was an awkward silence while Milly waited but it was Liz who answered for Laura. 'You wanna get that silly bleeder some glasses, or a brain-job. Laura was playing cards with me and Kay last night!'

'Oh, right . . .' The smug look on Milly's face caused Laura's anger to rise, but a warning look from Liz stopped her reacting.

Stepping ahead of them, Milly looked back over her shoulder. 'I'll tell George! Must rush . . . I'm aiming to pick thirty bushels today.'

Walking slowly on, keeping in step with Liz, Laura wondered why some people wasted their time probing into other peoples' business. A sick worried feeling was creeping in now and for no other reason than a few selected words from a flirt like Milly.

'You needn't have lied, Liz,' Laura said suddenly, looking at her sister-in-law.

'No?'

Wondering if this was the time to explain a few home truths to Liz about herself and Jack, Laura thumbed her wedding ring nervously. There was so much to tell, it was difficult to know where to start.

Arriving at the two bins in the hop garden on field number one, which had been earmarked for Laura and Liz, they settled themselves and wondered where Kay could have nipped off to. Unscrewing her flask of tea, Liz, in her usual forthright manner, spoke out.

'So what did Wright 'ave to say for 'imself then?' She tried to sound casual while pulling her little blue tin from her pocket. 'Stop scowling, I'm only making sure I've got it with me. It's a bit too early in the day for snuff.' Slipping it back into her pocket, she glanced swiftly at Laura's face. 'Surprised I've twigged it? Ha! You should watch your step. Others have noticed how friendly the pair of you are.'

Grasping each side of her hop bin with both hands, Laura pulled it apart and took hold of the sacking, giving it a good shake. 'Grab that trestle, Liz, while I take this end. That whistle'll be blown for us to pull the first bine any second now.'

Taking hold of each end, Laura and Liz lifted and stretched the long poles attached to the sacking and pulled them as far apart as possible, making a roomy bag for the hops, and then pushed hard so that the legs of the trestle were firmly planted into the ground.

Sitting on the wooden edge of the bin, Laura pulled off her scarf, pushed her hands through her hair and shook her head. Unlike most of the women picking, she preferred her hair to be hanging loose and free. 'If you're so sure about me and Richard, why haven't you said anything before now?' The question came right out of the blue and she could see that Liz was relieved that Laura had not simply ignored her.

'And risk it all coming out?' Liz snapped back; 'Jack would 'ave torn Wright limb from limb.'

'I wouldn't bank on it, Liz.'

Moving in close, Liz spoke in a low voice. 'Listen, you dozy cow, Jack might 'ave bin playing the field . . .'

Interrupting, with eyes blazing and her temper rising, Laura threw her scarf into her holdall. 'There's no might about it! He has and still does. If you've got any lecturing to do, aim it at your brother, not me!'

'You're too old to be lectured, Laura,' Liz argued.

'If you haven't learnt by now – you never will! For Gawd's sake, act your age!'

'Oh, fuck off, Liz. I don't need you to bring me down. There's enough people around 'ere who can't wait to put the boot in.'

Realizing that she had gone too far and had upset her best friend, Liz backed down. 'Yeah, you're right there, Mog. If families can't stick together in this crazy world, what 'ope is there?'

The shrill ringing of the telephone in Richard's office brought him sharply back to earth. He had been recalling the night before.

'Richard Wright.' He spoke in a low flat tone, hoping this would fool the caller into thinking he was busy and had no time for anyone who simply wanted to chat.

'Good morning, Richard!' came the cheery voice of his brother.

'David! Well, you sound bright enough. I'm glad someone's happy.'

'Bad news, old man?'

'Noooo . . . I just have to go out on to the fields and face everyone, that's all.'

'I'm not with you?'

'Exactly! If you were with me, I could send you out there to do the bloody talking.'

The penny finally dropped. 'Ah. Word is out,' David said resentfully, with a hint of blame in his voice.

'Yes, unfortunately it is. If I hear "picking-machines" one more time . . .' He stopped short as the door of the cottage suddenly flew open. Looking up, Richard couldn't help noticing that Julia had a certain look of achievement on her face. 'I'll have to go old man, Julia's just turned up.' He was just about to replace the receiver when a thought struck him. 'David, I don't suppose you could come and explain—'

'Sorry, Richard; not the time. Ask me next week, once the pigs have been sold.'

Slamming the receiver down, he looked up at Julia. 'My brother knows exactly when to lie low,' he fumed.

'What else would you expect?' She smiled contentedly, like a cat who has been given cream. 'You Wrights are all the same.'

'Thanks – you're all I need.'

'I know.'

Clasping his hands and locking his fingers together, Richard slowly inhaled and studied a dirty mark on the wall. Julia was obviously in a sarcastic mood and he could expect the worst.

Placing a white plastic lunch-box on his desk,

she pulled a flask of tea from a carrier bag. 'I've brought you some sandwiches. I shan't be home for lunch. Just off to Maidstone. They forecast eighty degrees again.'

Staring up at her with a bemused expression he gave a quick shake of the head. 'What's so compelling about Maidstone, all of a sudden?'

'Ice-creams, Richard, and ice lollies.' She spoke slowly and deliberately as if she were dealing with a cretin.

Richard couldn't believe his ears. 'For the pickers?'

'Oh, well done. We are on the ball today.'

He was flabbergasted. 'Ices, and lollies? You haven't done that in years. Not since you fell out with the Women's Voluntary Group.'

'I just thought,' she was now in philanthropist guise, 'that since this is to be the last time we'll be seeing these people, it's the least I can do.' Smiling beningly, she added: 'Of course, I shall only charge them cost price with a bit on top for petrol.'

'Well, what can I say? I think it's a marvellous gesture. I'm sure they'll be delighted.'

'I've also booked myself in for a trim. Might even find time to shop for a new ballgown. The season will be upon us before we know it.'

Feeling comfortable in her company for the first

132

time in ages, he picked up his pipe and tapped it into the large ashtray, smiling. 'What's brought all this on?'

'Who knows?' There was the merest hint of malice in her tone. 'I found myself looking in the mirror this morning and thinking, "Julia, it's time for a change."'

Richard felt a sudden wave of suspicion enter his mind, and could tell by her face that she had detected it.

With a swift change of body language, taking on a flirtatious pose, she softened her tone. 'Time for a new look,' she said.

Lighting his pipe, Richard felt decidedly unsure about her behaviour. 'I thought you had a bad night? You called out once or twice.'

With her hand on the door, ready to leave, she turned to him. 'Yes, I did have a bad night. Awake for most of it. But the saving grace was that it gave me time to take stock and formulate new ideas.'

'But – there's nothing wrong?' he asked cautiously, a feeling of dread creeping in.

'Oh, well now, that's rather a searching question; but one thing I can say . . . in all honesty,' she hesitated, and looking straight into his face, spoke in a low, positive tone: 'I haven't felt this good in years.' With that, she turned and glided out of the cottage, slamming the door and leaving him to ponder.

By eleven-thirty that morning, the pickers were well under way. Small children were either playing by their mothers' bins or picking the hops into a bushel-basket, earning their sweet money. The sun blazed in the clear blue sky and the temperature was nearing sixty degrees.

Laura sat on the edge of her bin. She had already picked six bushels of hops with the help of Kay, who had now slipped off to the lavatory. Enjoying the warm air and the shade from the thick hop-bines, Laura was content to let her mind wander, remembering the past and wondering what the future might hold. Maybe Gypsy Rose would tell her later?

'Fanny Adams sloped off already?' Liz said, poking her head through the bines.

'Liz! I wish you wouldn't do that!' Laura complained half-heartedly, 'You made me jump.' She dragged her half-picked bine across the bin and pulled off a thick branch, plucking the soft, plump cone-shaped hops with her usual speed and rhythm. 'Kay's gone to the lavatory. Thinks she's too grown-up to hide in the tunnel.'

Sitting herself down on the opposite side of

Laura's bin, Liz pulled out her blue tin, eased off the lid and sprinkled a little of her favourite brand on to the back of her hand. 'So what *did* Wright 'ave to say for himself then?'

'God! You're like a dog with a rag doll, won't let go. Why ain't you picking them 'ops?'

'It takes me a while to get into the swing of things, you know it does.' She sniffed the brown powder from her hand. After a short burst of sneezing, she eyed Laura again. 'Well? Out with it.'

Taking a minute to collect her thoughts, Laura wondered how much to tell Liz. She couldn't put it off for ever and, besides, her canny sister-in-law knew enough already, so a bit more could do no harm.

'You've been a really good friend to me over the years, Liz. You know that, don't yer?' she said genuinely.

'What's that supposed to mean?'

From Liz's tone, Laura could tell her mate was already on the defence. 'I hardly slept last night. Kept tossing and turning. My mind was spinning. Still is.'

'Oh, yeah?' Liz folded her arms and waited.

'Richard said he couldn't get through the year knowing I wouldn't be here next harvest. Didn't actually put it into words . . .'

135

'Oh, well no, he wouldn't, would he?' Liz laughed. 'That's asking for too much.'

Ignoring her sister-in-law's jibes, she continued. 'I've got some serious thinking to do, Liz. Got to think about my future.'

The speed at which Laura was snatching the hops from the branch was a clear indication that she was building up to something. 'Haven't we all, my dear!' Liz said in her mock posh voice.

'This being the last season.' Laura was beginning to lose patience with Liz and wondered why she was bothering to explain.

'And this being the last you'll see of Mr Richard Wright!'

'Well, that's just it!' Laura said gravely, 'I don't think it will be.' Then, lowering her voice, she let out a deep sigh. 'But it might be the last I'll see of Jack.'

Pulling the bine away from Laura's bin so she could get nearer to her, Liz spoke in a low whisper. 'What is that crafty bastard Wright up to? If he wants you so badly, how come he never got 'imself down to London now and then?' Unable to control her temper, she practically spat her words into Laura's face. 'Or is that something I did miss?'

Turning away, Laura cast her eyes down and then closed them, forcing the tears back.

'No, I thought not! A bit of rough – that's all he was after!'

'Oh Liz, how can you say that?' Laura cried. 'I'm not like that, you know I'm not!'

Moving up close and keeping her own voice down, Liz hoped Laura would follow suit. 'He's using you, Laura. And that's all he's been doing. It's all 'is kind ever do to the likes of us. Use!'

'Oh, and you're an expert I suppose?'

Deliberately changing the subject when she saw Terry approaching, Liz shot Laura a warning look. 'Hallo Terry, love. If you've come looking for Kay, she's gone to the lav.'

'Should be back any minute,' Laura murmured, keeping her head down and blowing her nose.

'You gonna give us a song, Terry? Get everyone going,' Liz suggested.

'I'm just going back to the 'uts to make our sandwiches.'

'Pity. We could all do with hearing your lovely voice again. P'raps later, yeah?'

'Might do. Could bring my guitar back with me. I got it for my sixteenth.'

'Guitar, eh? You'll be in one of them pop groups soon. Star of the show!' Liz laughed, trying to hide her true feelings. 'Well,' she suddenly announced, 'I can't sit 'ere all day yacking. There's 'ops to be picked.' With that, she walked away back to her own bin. Laura wasn't sorry to see her go.

'I don't know if Kay'll wanna go back with you, Terry. We brought our lunch with us. Save trudging over the hop fields. I had a feeling today was gonna be a scorcher,' Laura said, undoing a second button of her white poplin blouse and catching sight of Kay approaching. 'Here she is now, strolling along as if she's got all the time in the world.'

Making no effort to move any faster, Kay sauntered up and threw Terry a sulky look.

'I'm just going back to our 'ut to make the lunch. You coming?' Terry asked.

Kay ignored him and began pulling the hop-bine back across the bin, nonchalantly snatching off the cones.

'Well?' Terry urged.

Laura eyed her daughter disapprovingly; she was in a sulk for some reason and poor Terry was taking the brunt of it.

'I like your hair that way, Terry. It suits yer,' Laura said, hoping to bring about some conversation.

'Thanks,' Terry said, shyly.

How long Kay would go on having her mood swings was beyond Laura. Liz had told her to look out for it and not to react too harshly. It was to be expected, apparently, while Kay was going through this adolescent phase. But there were times when Laura felt as if she could strangle her own daughter.

Kay finally broke her silence. 'Where's your friend, then?' The withering look she gave Terry was enough to put anyone down.

'He went 'ome this morning. Got a lift in someone's van. Hates spiders,' Terry said disappointedly.

'God put them on this earth to catch flies, love, not people,' Laura teased.

Terry's news was the best Kay had heard for a long time: her face lit up and she slipped her arm through Terry's. 'Come on then, slowcoach, move yerself.' Glad to learn that Ray had gone, she dragged Terry away. 'Be all right if I 'ave a paddle in the river first, Mum?' she called back over her shoulder.

'Yeah, but not for too long, Kay! And fetch me a fresh pot of tea back with yer. I'm parched!' She said this knowing that her second flask was still full, but she was looking for a reason for Kay to come back. She felt the need of her daughter's company.

Watching the pair of them go off together, giggling like kids, Laura pulled a packet of five Weights from her skirt pocket. She wasn't a real smoker but enjoyed an occasional cigarette. This was the first time she had smoked out in the open. It wasn't something she admired, especially in a woman.

She sat on the edge of her bin, leaning on the wooden crossends, feeling confused. Was she being stupid? Had Richard been using her, as Liz liked to put it? Her thoughts turned to the evening before, to that small room where they had made love. There hadn't been anything sordid about their meeting. She did love Richard and felt sure he felt the same, and there was probably a good sound reason why he had never arranged to see her out of season.

Liz had certainly given her something to think about. The question of them meeting in London had never arisen. She had just accepted that those blissful weeks, once a year, were all they were entitled to. Even then, they weren't really entitled, him being a married man and Laura having commitments. She'd had her day-dreams to keep her going, reliving every second of their times together, during the lonely winter months. But now of course it would be different. No more trips at the end of August. The calendar would just go on from one year to the next with nothing in between to look forward to.

'Are you honestly telling me,' Liz snapped suddenly, causing Laura to jump, 'that you're stupid enough to be bloody hoodwinked by one of *them*?'

Laura felt as if her privacy had been stamped on. She wished Liz wouldn't creep up on her like that. 'Oh, do me a favour! One of them? What d'yer think they're made of?' Raising her voice and not caring who heard, she rolled up the sleeves of her blouse, full of anger. 'And don't forget that when you're throwing your insults at "one of them", and you know which one I mean, you're sticking the knife right into my stomach!'

'Just don't forget about the class gap, and who put it there, and who do their best to keep it that way.' Pulling and straightening her long cardigan, Liz drew a deep breath. 'Jack worships the ground you walk on! Silly long sod don't know how to show it, that's all!'

For Laura that was enough. That was it. Liz telling her how Jack felt! 'Yeah? Well let me tell you, that silly long sod hasn't slept in my bed for nigh on four years! And it wasn't me who fixed up the spare room, neither!'

'Keep your voice down, Laura!' Liz hissed.

'Oh, yeah. Now that your precious brother's manhood's at risk? Mustn't let anyone know about that, must we?' Unable to control her breathing or her temper, Laura slowly shook her head, the tears welling up behind her eyes. 'Well I'll tell you something, Liz,' her voice was getting louder as she spoke, 'and I don't give a toss who hears me! Our marriage was over years ago! Can you hear that everyone? My marriage was over years ago. All right? OK! Satisfied?'

'Stop it, Laura. You'll only regret it later.' Liz could hardly speak, her words were choking her.

Then, at the top of her voice, Laura cried out: 'Jack hasn't been near me since our baby died!' A terrible silence followed, and Laura sat on the edge of the bin, twisting her handkerchief in her trembling hands. 'It was like a nightmare,' she cried quietly, 'a nightmare that wouldn't go away. A dark heavy cloud moved in, always there, night and day.' Wiping her tears away with both hands, she dropped her head back and swallowed hard. 'When I saw that tiny lifeless body lying in the cot . . .'

'Yeah, all right, Mog. Don't remind me,' Liz said, choking on her words and wincing, as a sharp needle-like pain gripped her chest.

'It was as if I 'ad no right to be loved, or to love. I think Jack must 'ave felt the same.' She lowered her head and stared out at nothing. 'It shouldn't have pushed us apart like that, I know.' Laura's tears were not from anger now, but bottled-up emotion. 'God knows what it must have been like for Kay,' she whispered.

142

'Neither of you was to blame, Laura,' Liz said, still in pain.

Laura felt wretched because there was her sister-in-law trying to comfort her when she herself looked on the verge of tears. 'I know that, Liz. But no amount of being told then, or now, helps. You keep asking yourself over and over – why? Why did it happen? Why was he so full of life when I put him down and dead still the next morning?'

She looked up at Liz and smiled through her tears. 'I'm sorry,' she murmured, reaching one arm across and placing it around Liz's shoulder. 'I don't know why I dragged all that up.' The two of them hugged, and held on to each other while a lovely voice from somewhere near by began to sing softly, 'Smile', with the other pickers around the hop gardens gradually joining in. Laughing and crying at the same time, Laura began to sing too, coaxing Liz to join in, but she gave a show of her hand to show she wasn't in the mood. In truth Liz, for the first time she could remember, felt drained, even though the pain in her chest had eased.

Once at the river, Kay and Terry kicked their wellingtons off, at each other. Laughing, they rolled up their jeans and waded into the shallow part of the cool river.

'I 'ope you're not gonna strip off again,' Terry said, pulling off his red sloppy joe and tossing it on to the river-bank.

'Unlikely, Terry.'

'Not after last night, it's not. You wouldn't 'ave done that last year.'

'And neither would you!' she snapped back. 'Seems we've both changed. I'll tell you something, though,' she said, grinning broadly, 'it might 'ave been the first time but it won't be the last.' Cupping her hands in the water and gently splashing her face, she pushed her head back to enjoy the sun. 'I might well creep away at night to have a secret swim in the moonlight.' Then turning to Terry she saw the despondent look on his face. 'Why don't you let me teach you? It's daft someone of your age not being able to swim.'

Ignoring the question, as he had done so many times before, Terry pretended to be more interested in a frog sitting on a muddy patch by the edge of the river. 'If you do go in the nude again,' he said, 'you'd best make sure that gypsy's not lurking in a dark corner.'

'What's that supposed to mean?'

'He was there last night, leaning on that tree.'

'Don't lie!'

'I saw 'im once you were dressed, but he could

have been there longer for all I know. You'd best watch your step there. He'll soon have you rolling about in the hay!'

Laughing and kicking water over him, she soaked his jeans. 'You've got a disgusting mind, Terry Button!'

'All right, all right! Leave off, Kay,' he laughed. 'Silly cow!'

'Can't you be a bit more quiet?' an angler yelled from further down the river. 'Scaring all the bloody fish away!'

Pulling herself up on to the river-bank, Kay wiped her feet on the grass. 'Come on Terry, we'd best get back. Leave 'im in peace. Bet he hasn't had a bite all day. Miserable old sod.' Grabbing Terry's sloppy joe, she sat down and used it to dry her feet. 'He's one person I won't miss when this is all over.'

'Don't s'pose he'll lose any sleep over us, either,' Terry said, snatching back his jumper from Kay.

'Sod machines! And sod Wright!' Kay suddenly snapped.

Drying between his toes, Terry sighed. 'You can't blame 'im! Most of the other farms have laid the pickers off. All this 'ad to finish sometime. We live like animals down 'ere.'

'Yeah, well,' she answered lazily, pulling on her socks. 'Living like this is more natural than being shut up in those concrete flats, with all that smog and not a blade of grass to sit on.'

'Can you imagine the Wrights sitting side by side in one of them lavatories,' he laughed, 'with pegs on their noses?'

'Yeah,' Kay giggled, 'and silk drawers round her ankles.'

Standing up, Kay realized for the first time that she had grown a couple of inches taller than Terry. Admiring his soft curls which fell below the collar of his red and green check shirt, she suddenly felt an impulse to kiss him on the cheek.

His baby face flushed with embarrassment and made his light brown eyes stand out even more. 'What was that for?' he said shyly.

'Dunno. Just felt like it.' Then reaching out to wave a dragonfly away from his head, she sighed. 'I'm gonna miss you, you know.'

'Come on,' he said, walking away. 'I've got the sandwiches to make yet.'

Catching up with him, she linked arms in their usual manner. 'Will you miss not being here with me every year, Tel?'

Frowning, he turned his face away. 'Shut up, Kay,' he said in a gruff voice.

The sweet-sounding song from the pickers filled the

hop gardens as they harmoniously crooned another favourite song, 'Around the World in Eighty Days'. Humming quietly to herself and enjoying her solitude, Laura was thinking about her dad, reminding herself to send him a postcard. She had given up asking him to come hop-picking with her; it wasn't his cup of tea.

She thought about him in his small, cosy gaslit room, looking forward to the following month when the landlords would send in the London Electricity Board to convert his cottage.

She imagined Richard in the front room with him, and wondered how her father would react to a change of man in her life if things did go that way. Her mind filled with a vision of Richard being shown around the tiny two-up-two-down, and she imagined him going into her own bedroom which was still the same as the day she had left.

In her mind's eye, she could see herself and Richard sitting on her pale pink quilt, her showing him a photograph album from her school-days, when she had been captain of the netball team.

The sharp blast of a hooter suddenly penetrated Laura's head, pushing any further thoughts of Richard from her mind as she caught sight of Julia Wright pulling up in the Land-Rover.

Feeling the blood drain from her face, she watched

Julia climb out of the Land-Rover and prop a large sign bearing the words *Ice Cream* against a hop-pole. The few men that were around had stripped to the waist and a couple were on their way towards Julia, who seemed happy to be there even though a look of distaste passed across her face as one of the bare-chested men approached her.

Laura's mind was racing. What was Julia doing selling ice-creams again? And why hadn't Richard warned her that his wife would be back in the hop gardens? Was this a one-off visit or would Laura have to avoid facing her lover's wife every day?

Arriving by Laura's bin with a flask of tea, Liz nodded towards the Land-Rover. 'That's a turn-up for the books, her coming on the fields again selling ice-creams.' Unscrewing the red and white flask, Liz chuckled mischievously. 'Why don't you go and buy us a lolly each? See what kind of a greeting you get?'

'No thanks,' Laura answered curtly.

'Seems odd to me that she should choose today of all days. Perhaps lover-boy's told her all about yer,' Liz purred, pouring herself a steaming cup of tea.

'He wouldn't have done that.' Laura turned her back on Julia and began picking the hops again.

'Only one way to find out.'

'If you're so interested, Liz, why don't you go?'

148

✳

'Do what?' Liz exclaimed indignantly. 'We lock 'orns, the minute we get within a mile. Never could stand the woman.' Resting her cup on the soft clay, Liz poured another out for Laura. 'Her mother used to run a corner shop over at Paddock Wood. The prices they used to charge us pickers!'

Taking the cup of tea from Liz, Laura narrowed her eyes. 'How come you never told me?' she said disbelievingly.

'I just did, didn't I?' Liz sniffed and grinned cheekily.

Laura couldn't help smiling. Liz was a saucy cow, but a real tonic. Sipping her tea, but keeping one eye on Julia, Laura couldn't help thinking how attractive she looked, in a countrified sort of way. She liked the look of riding-boots with jodhpurs, but wasn't taken with the sweetheart neckline of her green blouse.

'She's tarted herself up a bit, ain't she? Got a new hairstyle.'

'Has she?' Laura answered in a throw-away tone.

'I reckon she's up to something,' Liz said, eyeing her sister-in-law; then seeing the look of concern on her face, decided to hold her tongue.

Making herself comfortable on Terry's straw-filled mattress, Kay lay with her arms behind her, staring

149

up at the black tin roof and enjoying the warmth of the sun as it streamed in through the open upper half of the stable-type door. Trailing her fingers along the faded floral curtain that separated Terry's part from his mother's sleeping-quarters, Kay idly scanned the room while Terry prepared lunch for himself and his mother.

The sparkling white sheets on his bed had a slight sweet smell of washing powder and starch. That, together with the smell of furniture polish, created a feeling of a real home rather than a hut. There were a couple of painted kitchen chairs, a small scrubbed pine table and a tiny matching cupboard nailed to one wall. Two small oil-lamps hung from nails which had been banged into a wooden support next to a long shelf, where Terry's mother kept her soap powder, disinfectant and other cleansers.

Sitting up, Kay caught a glimpse of herself in the small mirror which hung on the back wall of Terry's sleeping-compartment. Moving up close she examined her face and wished her blue eyes weren't so pale, and that she could look more like her mother, with dark eyelashes instead of blonde.

'What d'yer reckon on me dying my hair black?' she said, more to herself than Terry.

'Silly cow,' he answered in his usual soft tone,

'haven't you heard what they say about young Kay?'

'No, what?' She turned away from the mirror.

Mimicking one of the adults he said, '"Young Kay is turning into a true English rose! The face of innocence" – until you open your mouth.'

'Yeah, well,' she retorted, 'we all know what they say about you!'

Ignoring the remark, Terry removed the whistling kettle from the Primus stove and filled the large enamel teapot.

'They reckon,' Kay said teasingly, 'that young Terry sings just like a girl.' Then she carefully added, 'They've been saying other things too.'

'I know,' Terry answered sadly. Placing the lid on the teapot he threw himself down next to her on the mattress, stretched out and gazed up at the tin roof.

The pair of them lay there enjoying the silence. 'I love it in here,' Kay said. 'Can't bear to think I won't be seeing these old familiar curtains no more.' Receiving no reply from Terry, she turned on her side and looked into his face. 'What's up now?'

Waving a bee away, he sighed heavily. 'There's not much I can do to stop people saying things about me, is there? Can't help the way I feel.'

'And how do you feel?'

'More comfortable with girls for a start. Always 'ave done. I should 'ave been born a girl. Dunno why I've bin given a boy's body. I don't really know what to do about it. I've tried 'aving girlfriends . . .'

'Terry,' Kay cut in.

'What?'

'Shut up!' Grabbing the pillow from under his head she started a pillow-fight and he wasn't slow in retaliating. Laughing and giggling, they bashed each other until they had to stop from exhaustion. As Terry fell back, out of breath, Kay pinned him down. 'So, Terry Button; I know your innermost secret!'

'Yeah,' he said, 'and don't go spreading it. Now get off!'

Allowing him to use his strength to push her off, Kay rolled back over to her side. 'You know what I fancy? A thick slice of that bread with some of your mum's blackberry jam.'

'So you won't say anything, then?'

'Terry! What are friends for?'

'They won't all be as loyal as you though, will they?' he said wistfully. 'It wasn't really spiders that made Ray go back. He asked me if I fancied you, and when I told 'im I didn't feel like that about girls, his face turned red and he threatened me with a bunch of five. I won't tell yer what he called me.'

'Shouldn't take any notice of people like 'im, Terry. They're not worth it. Now give us your 'and.' Stretching her arm out across his stomach, she grinned broadly as she grabbed his fingers and locked them in hers.

'Promise me,' she said earnestly, 'if you ever feel low, you'll come and talk to me.'

'Silly cow,' he murmured, ''course I will.'

Julia Wright did not enjoy role-playing on the hop fields. The women who queued up for ice-creams wore sun-dresses which in her opinion revealed too much flesh, and the men with their sweat-beaded hairy chests filled her with disgust. The thought of any woman climbing into the same bed with such loathsome bodies made her shudder. But serve ice-creams to them she would: that she could manage. It was all part of her plan. Relieved that most of the pickers had been served, she sat in the doorway of the Land-Rover and waited for the one person she wanted to see.

'Four penny-lollies, miss.' The face of a snotty-nosed boy was peering up at her.

She looked with distaste at the grubby child with his mop of unruly hair. 'No penny-lollies this year,' she grimaced, hoping he would go away. 'They've gone up to tuppence.'

'Wot about misshapes?'

'I've none of those, either.'

'I s'pose I could 'ave two tuppennies and share them . . .' he said thoughtfully, 'but I'd 'ave to ask me mum first and our bin's right back on field two. It'll take me ages to walk there and back 'cos me boots are too small an' I've got blisters.'

Making a display of the nuisance he was making of himself, she climbed into the back of the Land-Rover and spoke to him through the open window. 'Here you are. Take four and owe me for the other two.'

'Oh, I could never do that! Me mum'd kill me!' Then, wrinkling his nose and closing one eye, he recited as if from the Bible, 'Niever a borrowa or a lender be.'

'Oh, just take them! But remember next time!'

Grinning broadly, the boy dropped his sweaty pennies into her Oxo tin. 'Fanks, Mrs Wright. I'll tell all me friends 'ow gen'rus you are!' Laughing at her slow wit, he ran off, calling to his mates as he went.

Making a quick sharp turn he crashed into Laura.

'Sorry, Mrs Armstrong,' he said shakily, 'I couldn't 'elp it.'

'Go on,' she smiled, seeing that he had taken the

154

brunt of the collision and was trying to put on a brave face, 'but slow down a bit!'

Picking up one of the lollies that had gone flying, he wiped the wrapping with the sleeve of his worn grey jumper and curled his lip in disappointment because some grit and mud had got on to the ice. 'Want this one for Kay? You can 'ave it at the old price.'

Laura turned away laughing. 'You should wait till Mrs Wright's sold out – then make a killing!'

Feeling a bit disgruntled, he scratched his ear. 'Where is Kay, anyway?'

'Down by the huts with Terry.'

'Ah, right!' His face suddenly lit up. 'Yeah, Terry Button'll buy one. He's as soft as they come.' With that, the scruffy seven-year-old turned on his heels and ran off.

As Laura turned to go, she heard a woman yelling at the top of her voice, 'Bloody tearaway! You've knocked my pot of tea over! End up in Borstal, you will! Ruffian!'

Smiling to herself, Laura wondered if she would ever have another child. She had always wanted a son. Her mind filled then with the beautiful baby boy she had loved so tragically – he would have just turned nine years old.

Deep in thought, Laura suddenly realized that she had arrived at Julia's Land-Rover, and the last customer was paying for her ice-creams. It was just Laura and Richard's wife, face to face for the first time.

She had always done her best to avoid this situation and wondered why she had let Liz talk her into going for those ice-creams. Panic suddenly rose inside her and she froze. Feeling like an idiot, she stood and stared blankly into Julia's half-smiling face, and no matter how hard she tried, she could not manage to say a word.

'It's Mrs Armstrong, isn't it?' Julia smirked, staring accusingly into her rival's face.

Laura tried to avoid the spiteful eyes; swallowing hard she forced herself to speak. 'Two ice-cream bricks, please,' she murmured, feeling the muscles in her throat tighten and beads of sweat break out on the palms of her hands.

'Just two?' Julia asked, feigning an interest. Then, as if the thought had only just crossed her mind, added, 'Oh, of course! Your husband will have gone back to London. It's just you and that provocative beauty.'

There was a pause while Laura tried to take in what Julia was getting at. Narrowing her eyes, she glared at her tormentor, her anger rising. Why should she let this smug bitch look down on her in that regal way?

Julia was obviously enjoying herself. Her eyes were glinting and the smirk on her face looked as if it would last for ever. 'I was referring to your daughter.' She deliberately chose a tone to suggest that Laura was a halfwit. 'I expect she gets that blonde hair and those blue eyes from her father? Must be a constant worry. *Elle fait venir l'eau à la bouche.*'

Composing herself, Laura took a deep breath. 'I'm not sure what you mean, but if you are referring to Kay – she's only fifteen!'

'Of course she is. But then . . . Lolita?' Satisfied that she had taken that particular snipe as far as she could, Julia placed two ice-cream bricks on the makeshift counter and, avoiding Laura's flaming eyes, looked idly at the sky. 'One shilling, please.'

A few seconds ticked by as Laura fought against unwrapping both ice-creams and squashing them into Julia's face.

'Of course if you're embarrassed,' Julia ran her hand through her short hair and sighed with boredom, 'we could always put your name in the little red book.'

'That won't be necessary,' Laura snapped, offering the coin. 'I'm not poverty-stricken, if that's what you think!'

'No,' she smiled, 'of course you're not.' Staring at Laura's green-black fingertips, she grimaced. 'If you could drop the shilling into the tin. Hops do tend to stain the hands.'

Clenching her teeth, Laura hurled the coin into the tin, sending it crashing to the floor, and was just about to give Julia a mouthful when the other woman got in first.

'I wonder how you've put up with picking hops all these years? I shouldn't think you mind one bit, now that it's coming to an end. My husband's certainly had a load taken from his shoulders. Machines will be far easier to deal with than people. No more dreading the autumn.'

Flicking her hair back, Laura stretched herself up to her full height and managed a smile. 'Dreading the autumn? Well I can't say I ever did. And before you say anything else,' she snapped, 'if you ever suggest again that my Kay is a Lolita I'll—'

'Sue me for slander?' Julia smiled.

'I wouldn't bother with the courts, you silly bitch! I'd drag you in front of the pickers and give you the biggest hiding you can imagine.' Not caring now about anything or anyone, she pointed a finger and pushed it very close to Julia's face. 'Say what you like about me, but don't you ever cast a slur on my daughter's good name again!'

Pulling back, Julia looked sheepish, her expression showing that she had seen the light. The woman who stood before her would not be as easily crushed as she had imagined.

Relieved that she had parked her Land-Rover away from the pickers and that none had overheard those few heated words, Julia slid shut the small window between herself and Laura, climbed into the driver's seat and roared away.

Furious with herself for not hitting out at Julia, Laura stomped back to her bin, ready to kill the first person who crossed her.

She handed Liz her ice-cream without a word and perched herself on the edge of the bin, avoiding her eyes.

'Mmmm . . .' Liz smacked her lips, 'Ain't 'ad an ice-cream in ages.' Carefully peeling back the paper, she eyed Laura. 'What yer got to tell me, then?'

'Nothing!'

'Can't see any scratches round your eyes.'

'Leave it, Liz.'

'That bad?'

'I said, leave it. I'm not in the mood!'

'So Wright did tell 'er?'

'I don't know!' Laura scowled at Liz, daring her

to continue with her line of questioning. 'I'll find out tonight,' she said sullenly, 'when I go to the cottage.'

A smile of satisfaction spread across Julia's face as she drove along the gravel lane. She felt exhilarated. She had rattled Laura Armstrong, and this was only the beginning. The cockney woman had been left wondering if she and Richard had been found out. This was Julia's reward, her due. Laura's coarse threats had fired the fight within her and she felt confident that during the next few weeks she would push the whore to breaking point.

There was a screech of brakes as Julia turned into the farmhouse. She was ready for a stiff drink and a cigarette. Slamming the Land-Rover door behind her she marched into the house, ordering the excited dogs to be quiet.

'Janet!' she shouted, throwing her keys on to the hall side-table.

'I'm right here, ma'am.' Janet's quiet voice came from just behind Julia.

'So you are. Tell cook the pheasants are ready. There'll be eight for dinner; the Sparks's, the Goodwins and the Bradys. Cook's to choose the vegetables, the sweet and the hors-d'œuvres. We'll be dining at eight!'

'Will Mr Richard be in for dinner, ma'am?' she asked carefully.

'Yes, Janet; why on earth shouldn't he be?' Throwing Janet a scornful look, she turned away and disappeared up the wide oak staircase, leaving her maid to look down at the champagne-coloured carpet in dismay. She had spent hours vacuuming up dogs' hairs that morning and now there were muddy footprints instead. Her eyes went from the floor to the staircase as she pondered her mistress's behaviour. She hadn't known her to walk into the house wearing her riding-boots before; she couldn't understand why she was wearing them at all, since she hadn't been out that morning and as far as Janet knew she wasn't riding that afternoon.

Stretched out on her colourful quilted silk eiderdown, Julia revelled in her success. She hadn't dreamed for one minute that she would receive such marvellous results from her first trip to the hop garden. Yes indeed, the cockney slut had been well and truly put in her place.

Lying there in the quiet, Julia allowed herself to be carried away by her thoughts. Maybe Laura Armstrong really did have her sights set high? Perhaps she imagined herself in Julia's place, lying on that very bed, ordering Janet to fetch and carry.

A sudden thought struck her: what if Janet was in

161

cahoots with the woman? She had, after all, refused to help Julia find out the truth, without giving a reasonable excuse. She had heard that their kind stuck together.

Determined to leave no stone unturned, she swiftly left the bedroom; stood defiantly at the top of the staircase and shouted the girl's name. After a few seconds Janet arrived from the kitchen and gazed up at Julia.

'I don't want you mixing with those hop-pickers ever again! Is that clear?'

'I don't think I ever have mixed with them, ma'am,' she said sheepishly.

'Well just see that you don't!' Returning to her room, Julia left Janet standing in the hall, wondering about the state of the woman's mind.

Once alone at her bin, Laura had, for the first time since her mother's death, shivered from top to toe, tears rolling down her cheeks. Although she pulled herself together by the time Kay arrived, she still felt low and hardly said a word while they both picked. Sensing her mother's mood, Kay was decidedly forthright in her manner, and she began to ask questions.

'What's up, then?' she said with a touch of impatience.

The last thing Laura wanted was to explain anything to anyone, especially not to her fifteen-year-old child.

'Nothing.' Her tone was deliberately intended to end the conversation right there.

'Can't kid me.' Kay smiled.

'I don't know what you're on about, Kay.'

'Lady of the Manor. Found out, 'as she? About you and the bossman?'

Astonished at the words dropping from her daughter's lips, Laura stopped picking and looked back at her, her face blank.

'I've known for ages, Mum,' she said, in a matter-of-fact tone. 'So what did she say to yer? When you went for the ice-creams?'

'You've known *what* for ages?' Laura was surprised at her own reaction to this sudden revelation. She should feel alarmed, guilty, shocked, but she didn't. The tiny wave of emotion that did pass through her was relief. She had done her utmost to keep the knowledge of her affair from Kay, too ashamed to let her see that side of her life. Yet here was her daughter casually unfolding the secret as if it were nothing to fret about.

'I don't think Dad knows.' Kay began to pull the tiny pale-green petal-like leaves from a hop. 'He's too wrapped up in his own affair. I've seen them

163

together. Didn't see me though.' Unable to cover her feelings, Kay sounded choked. 'It's all right,' she said, blushing, 'I gave up years ago, wishing you and Dad would just love each other.'

Laura threw the branch of hops into the bin, lowered her head and closed her eyes tight. 'Kay, please . . . please don't talk like that.'

'Why not? It's the truth. You can't stand each other.'

Wringing her hands, Laura spoke carefully, not wanting to hurt her daughter any more than she had to. 'No, Kay, we just . . .' Then taking a deep breath she forced her words out, 'You're too young for all this!'

'I'm not too young!' Kay screamed back, 'And I don't have to spy on you to know what's going on! I hate Richard Wright! And I hate Dad's other woman! I don't want our family to break up!' She was sobbing now. 'I don't want you, or Dad, to leave me!'

Laura watched as Kay turned and ran away, stumbling over the sun-dried clay lumps as she went. Feeling faint, Laura gripped the crosspole at the end of the bin and took in long, slow breaths of air, trying to clear the nausea from her stomach.

A comforting hand on her shoulder caused her

to look up. 'Oh, Liz,' she cried, 'did you hear what she just said?'

'Every word,' Liz whispered, 'every word.'

Pushing her head back, Laura closed her eyes for a few seconds and then sighed loudly. 'D'yer think she was telling the truth? About seeing Jack with someone?'

Sudden, unexpected belly-laughter filled Laura's ears. She stared at Liz, hardly believing her eyes. How could she laugh at a time like this?

'Is that all,' Liz chortled, 'you can think of to say?' Pulling out her little blue tin, she slowly shook her head. 'Laura, if you ain't the craziest mixed-up woman on the hop field, this powder in my tin is sherbert.'

Laura reached out and casually lifted the branch of hops from inside the bin. As usual, Liz was right. The thought of Kay actually seeing Jack with someone else and referring to her as 'Dad's other woman', had hit home. She knew he was a terrible flirt and that he had probably given women lifts home before he lost his licence, but the way Kay had spoken, it hardly sounded like a casual one-off.

'You're gonna 'ave to sort this mess out, Laura. It's time the pair of you sat down and talked.' Slowly running her hand through Laura's hair as if she were a small child, Liz added, 'Jack cares about yer, you must know that. I think you're just as crazy about 'im as well. Sort it out, Mog, before it's too late.'

'It is too late, Liz,' Laura said quietly. 'Believe me, that part of our life is over.' Looking up at her sister-in-law she swallowed hard. 'I don't want you saying anything to him. And I do mean that. Especially not . . .' Her words began to trail off. 'Especially not about me and Richard.'

Scattering some snuff on to the back of her hand, Liz's tone swiftly changed when she heard Richard mentioned. 'If Jack 'ad any idea that I knew what'd been going on it would push us apart – and I wouldn't risk that, not for anyone.' Lifting the back of her hand to her nostril she added, 'I still think of him as my baby brother.'

While Liz enjoyed her snuff, Laura could feel her own temper rising. Why was it that her private affairs couldn't be kept that way? Why did her secret have to be dragged out for an airing every other minute?

'It's all right for the men,' she said angrily; 'when the men go astray it's one notch up! But if a woman dares to fall in love with another man . . .'

'That's because,' Liz cut in, 'women should have more sense! We've been put in this world to set an example . . . to the weaker sex! As well as bear babies. They might have the muscle, but when it comes to a bit of logic – they're way behind!' Grinning and nudging Laura, she added: 'That's what makes 'em so endearing.' Liz enjoyed her joke and chuckled. Before long Laura was joining her and their belly-laughter could be heard above the pickers' singing.

Seven

Jack and Bert were quiet for most of the journey through London, each of them deep in thought. Jack was trying to imagine life without Laura and Kay. No matter how bad things had been at home, he still couldn't convince himself that moving in with Patsy would make him a happier man.

Laura deserved better than him, he knew that. Patsy hadn't been the first woman he had jumped into bed with. He had played the field, and felt sure Laura must have known and had her own reasons for turning a blind eye.

He looked across at Bert and studied his round friendly face. He was a good bloke who hardly ever complained. He drove Jack backwards and forwards to the docks in his lorry, and would never take a penny for petrol. But Jack found ways of making it up to him, a crate of Jersey spuds in the spring, Canary tomatoes throughout the year and the best oranges from Spain at Christmas. All courtesy of the London docks. The promotion he had got when he lost his driving licence was the best thing that could have happened to Jack. Pen pusher! Signed out a hundred crates of fruit and out went one hundred and four. Perks – a man's livelihood.

The traffic was always thick on Saturday afternoons, but the small winding roads to the Blackwall Tunnel were worse than ever. During a scorching summer like this one, Londoners got out of the city whenever they could.

Slowly rolling up his shirtsleeves, Jack pushed his head out of the open window of the lorry and strained his neck to see if there had been an accident further along the queue.

'I dunno, Bert,' he moaned, 'they're gonna 'ave to do something about the approach-roads into the Tunnel. Bloody hour to get this far!' He reached out for one of the cream soda bottles Patsy had filled with water, and removed the stone stopper. 'Want some of this?'

Expressionless, Bert shook his head and kept his mouth tightly shut.

'Well, let me know when you do.' Raising the bottle above his head Jack poured the water first down the back of his neck and then over his face, before placing the mouth of the bottle between his lips and drinking another third of the warm contents. 'I've got another two down 'ere. Should keep us going till we stop at the Half-Way for a pint.' He ran his tongue across his teeth and sucked at a grinder. ''Ow much do I owe yer for petrol?'

'Nothing.' Bert made no effort to hide his bitter feelings. He was seething inside and Jack knew it.

'Oh, dear . . .' Jack chuckled, 'you're not gonna sulk all the way to Kent are yer?'

'I'm not sulking, Jack, I'm fuming! For two pins I'd stop this effin' lorry and chuck you out!'

'You wouldn't have to stop, Bert. We're hardly moving.' Jack quietly laughed, his blue eyes standing out more than ever against his tanned face. 'It's at times like this a bloke needs someone to talk to, you know?'

'If I'd 'ave thought . . .' Bert slowly shook his head. 'If I'd 'ave thought things were gonna turn out like this . . . It's my own fault. Trusting you knew what you were doing!' Changing up to second gear and catching sight of the entrance to the Blackwall Tunnel, Bert accelerated a little too hard and only just pulled up in time to avoid hitting the car in front of him. 'You wait till Liz finds out! She'll do 'er nut!'

'Yeah, all right, Bert . . .'

'And guess who'll be tarred with the same brush?'

Sighing, Jack rolled his eyes. 'You worry too much.'

'Yeah? Who's your best mate, Jack? Eh? Who's your drinking partner? And who's covered for you in the past? Had a drink more than once with your Patsy and her mate, who just so 'appens to be a right little cracker!' Pulling into the long tunnel, Bert reached forward and flicked on his lights. 'Yep,' he said, 'it'll all come out now and I'll be in it, right up to my effin' neck.'

The journey through the Blackwall was slow and hot. The fumes from the traffic added to the nightmare and when the lorry finally pulled out of the darkness into the blinding sunshine, there was a sigh of relief from both men.

Remembering the chocolate he had bought for Kay and Laura, Jack reached out and moved the white paper bag away from the windscreen and slipped it under the dashboard, out of the sunlight.

They continued their journey in silence, passing pubs at which they would usually have stopped to drink. Even though Jack was gasping for a beer, he wasn't going to give Bert the satisfaction of refusing to stop. He would sit it out until his brother-in-law got over his mood and suggested they pulled in for a pint.

Jack made himself comfortable with one arm

across his waist and the other resting on top. That way he could cover his face with his hand and keep an eye on Bert's expression through the tiny gap between his fingers.

Liz spoke in harsh whispers that night, as she sat propped up in her bed with two large pillows behind her and her special hop pillow, which she used only when her mind was troubled and she couldn't sleep.

'You can't tell me you didn't know what was going on! I knew the silly sod 'ad bin messing about, 'course I did. But to let it go this far . . . I'd like to strangle 'im!'

'Shush, Liz,' Bert urged, 'you know how thin these walls are.'

Not listening to Bert, Liz ranted on, her temper rising with every fresh thought. 'A common bloody tart!'

'She's not a tart, Liz! You'd like 'er.'

'And how would you know?'

Bert turned over, keeping his back to Liz. 'Talk to me about it in the morning. I've 'ad a long hot drive and I'm tired.'

'I said, how would you know?' Liz had no intention of letting it drop. 'Well?'

'Because I've met 'er,' he said quietly, waiting for the explosion.

For a while there was a silence. It had come as quite a blow to Liz, discovering that her man moved in a world she knew nothing about. Her anger drained away and she was left with a sickening fear. Maybe there were other things to emerge? Things that included Bert and that she would rather not know about. She could feel herself shiver and tremble and had to clasp her hands together to stop them shaking. Her chest felt tight and there was sharp pain which felt as if she'd swallowed a boiled sweet.

'If you've got anything to tell me, you'd best say so now,' she murmured.

'There's nothing to tell. I met her in a pub once . . .' His voice trailed off.

'And she was on 'er own?' Fearing the worst, Liz drew a deep breath, trying to ease the strange pain.

'No,' he murmured, 'she was with a friend.'

'And you made a nice little foursome.'

'I bought them both a drink, that's all.'

'Yeah?' Liz said disbelievingly.

Bert inhaled slowly; he had no choice but to tell her. 'I walked 'er friend 'ome because it was dark. That's all!'

That was enough. Liz could take no more. She slid down under the covers, pulled her hop pillow into her face and, turning her back on Bert, tried to sleep.

When morning finally broke, Liz opened her red,

swollen eyes and looked across at Bert, who was fast asleep. He looked as innocent as a baby lying there and she couldn't imagine him with another woman, not her Bert. He was too tired for all that. Sixty-two next birthday and going bald. She began to feel sorry for him. Sorry that she had turned her back after she had looked forward all week to his visit. It was all Jack's fault. Her no-good womanizing brother had dragged Bert into his sordid life!

Liz smiled at the way Bert moaned in his sleep, opened his eyes and then closed them again, not wanting to face the world. She could forgive him for buying the women a drink. No crime in that. But then she thought about that other snippet of information. He had walked one of them home in the dark after a night of drinking! She forced back her tears. This was going to be a day for taking stock of her own life, never mind Laura and Jack.

She climbed down from her straw bed and pulled her red dressing gown around her. Then sun, streaming through the tiny window, gave her enough light to see her reflection in the cracked mirror hanging on the back of the hut door. She looked terrible. Too old for her age by far.

At least she hadn't gone completely grey, she told herself while lighting the Primus stove. There were still a few strands of copper hair to be seen. Sitting on her kitchen chair, waiting for her kettle to boil, she wondered if Jack had said anything to Laura yet. And if he had, would that have prompted Laura to tell Jack about Richard Wright? She shook her head; it didn't bear thinking about.

Liz wasn't the only one to wake at the crack of dawn. Jack was lying on his bed wondering if he should wait a few more weeks before breaking the news to Laura that Patsy was pregnant. He prayed that Bert hadn't said anything to Liz yet. It would be wrong if she found out first.

Making a snap decision to go in and talk to Laura before Kay woke up, Jack dragged his clothes on and lit a cigarette. It was only just gone six but he could hear noises from either side of his hut which meant that both Laura and Liz were up and about.

Once outside in the morning sun, instead of tapping on Laura's hut door Jack found himself lifting his sister's latch. Liz gazed at her brother, more surprised at herself for not bolting the door the night before than at Jack paying her an early visit.

Sitting himself down, he whispered that he wouldn't mind a cup of tea. Then, stretching out his long legs, he chuckled to himself at the sound of Bert snoring behind the thick red curtain.

'Sounds like a bloody foghorn,' Jack joked. He could tell from his sister's long face that she was in no mood for their usual banter. 'You all right, Liz?' he asked tenderly.

Pouring boiling water into two tin mugs, she sluiced them around and tipped the water into her washing-up bowl. 'No, Jack. I'm not all right: far from it!' She poured a little sterilized milk into each mug, topped it up with fresh tea and gave him a look that would kill, recognizing that hangdog expression of his – he knew he was in the wrong.

'I s'pose Bert's told yer?'

Liz raised an eyebrow, passed Jack his tea and sat down without saying a word – she knew how he hated long silences.

'No point in my trying to explain, is there?' Jack spoke as if he were an innocent victim.

'Please yerself. But it won't alter what I think of yer.'

'Don't be like that, Lizzie,' he murmured. 'I'm upset as it is. I didn't want things to turn out like this.'

Knowing how easily her brother could win her round, Liz reminded herself how irresponsible Jack had been and how he had led Bert astray. 'Someone put a knife to yer throat did they? Someone told you to treat Laura as if she's not worth a light?' She kept her voice down even though she felt like screaming at him. No sense in waking Bert, not yet. She wanted some time alone with him, so they could talk, before this mess became a family discussion.

'She 'asn't exactly been all that loving to me, you know,' Jack said, sipping his tea. 'Anyone would think it was my fault that baby John died like that.'

'Don't you dare bring that poor innocent child into this!' Liz hissed, her eyes blazing. 'Don't you blame that baby for your womanizing!'

Lowering his head, shamefaced, Jack sighed. 'I 'aven't treated Laura badly, Liz.' He looked sheepishly up at her. 'I've never let on about Patsy.'

Gripping the handle of her tin mug Liz pushed it close to her brother's face. 'You mention that woman's name again and I'll chuck this tea all over yer!'

Slowly shaking his head, Jack pulled his tobacco tin out of his shirt pocket. 'You don't know what she's like, Liz. You 'aven't met 'er. If you had—'

'I wasn't joking, Jack,' Liz warned, her tin mug dangerously close to his face.

'All right, all right.' He spoke slowly and deliberately, 'I don't want you telling Laura either. I'll break the news when I'm ready.'

Disturbed by the possible outcome of his confession and what it might lead to, Liz pursed her lips. 'You dozy sod, Jack! You mention this to Laura and you can kiss her goodbye. Don't think she 'asn't got admirers.'

Leaning back in his chair, he gave Liz a searching look. 'What's that supposed to mean?'

'Work it out for yerself.' Before she could say any more, a low moan came from behind the red curtain, then a rustling sound as Bert turned over on the straw mattress.

By eight-thirty most families were at their bins. The men were enjoying a bit of picking; it was a novelty for them, and a relief for the women who could afford to go at a slower pace. It was expected that each bin would produce somewhere around forty bushels of hops a day, twenty on a Saturday morning. The measuremen had keen eyes, and had been known to reject a bin if it had more than its fair share of leaves. Tractors stacked high with bulging sacks of hops ready for the oast-house were the daily requirement.

Jack was a good picker; his strong hands mastered the tough bines while his long fingers plucked with speed. His mind was working equally fast; the same thoughts going round his brain time and time again, and never reaching an answer. He wondered if there was anyone who could simplify his life for him in one sentence.

He raised his eyes from the hop-bine and glanced

at Laura; she looked miles away. He wondered where her mind wandered to, and decided she was probably thinking about work. As far as Jack could tell, she loved her little office job in the brewery, keeping all those men in order. He'd often thought she should have been a career woman, though she used to be home-loving, back in the old days, when things were OK.

'I see Richard Wright's slumming again.' Liz's smiling face appeared through the bines.

Turning his head, Jack peered at Richard as he approached and dropped the half-picked branch of hops to the ground. 'Just the man,' he murmured to himself. His long legs strode out and away from Laura and Liz.

'Did you 'ave to, Liz?'

'What?' She looked innocent.

'You can be a right stirrer at times.'

'Don't know what you're talking about, Laura,' she said serenely.

They watched as Jack approached Richard and the pair of them stood talking, man to man, Jack waving his arms about and Richard slowly shaking his head. There wasn't much between them for height, and they were a similar build. The only real difference was their colouring; Jack the blond, blue-eyed one and Richard with his thick, dark wavy hair and hazel eyes. While Liz focused on her brother, watching proudly as he crashed through the class barrier, Laura had eyes only for Richard. She could just make out his expression; Jack was giving him a hard time, she could see that. There was a split second when Richard looked her way and their eyes met, which instantly set her heart pounding.

'You'll be sorry in years to come, you know. Machines might clear these fields quicker than we could but will they clean the leaves out?'

'Possibly not.' The last thing Richard wanted was to strike up an argument with Laura's husband, his good-looking rival. 'I can't really afford not to follow the trend. We've put it off for as long as we possibly could.' Richard gave a short nod to end the conversation but he hadn't realized how persistent Jack could be.

'Your machines'll whizz through these fields like lightning but you won't end up with any more hops, will yer? All you'll 'ave is more time on your 'ands – to sit around regretting the passing of old ways.'

'That's true.' Richard did his best to sound as if Jack were telling him something he hadn't considered himself. 'I'll mention it to my brothers when we next meet.' He nodded, trying to get it across that he had no more to say.

'You think there's a chance you might get them

to put if off for a year? Let everyone come back one more time? Give 'em a chance to get used to the idea that there won't be no more hop-picking? You'll be ending a way of life yer know, changing the future. Changing history. That's a lot of burden on one man's shoulders,' Jack advised.

'Three. You forget about my brothers. They finalized this, not me.'

'Yeah?' Jack suddenly warmed to Richard. 'So you agree with me, then? You'll be in the White Horse tonight, won't yer? Come into the Public an' I'll buy you a drink – we can talk about it.'

'I'm afraid I shan't be in tonight. We, er, we're entertaining. But I have to tell you, there really is no chance of our changing our minds. The new machines are due to arrive in six or seven weeks' time.'

'Oh, yeah,' Jack grinned, 'once we're nicely out of the way.'

Sensing that Jack's temper was rising, Liz started to sing, willing Laura to join in, if only to break up what could be an ugly scene.

> Oh we ain't got a barrel of money,
> Maybe we're ragged and funny,
> But we travel along . . .

She glared at Laura, urging her to help get the others joining in too.

Singing our song, side by side . . .

Laura sang along, hating every minute of it, embarrassed with the entire scenario.

Before long the melody had spread its way through the hop tunnels and across the field until the chorus reached its peak. Men, women and children joined in, enjoying their favourite song. Richard walked slowly away, feeling out of it and sorry that very soon the happy sound of the pickers' ballad would no longer fill the air.

The atmosphere between Jack and Laura had been tense, but now, in the early afternoon with the sound of children laughing and playing around the common, the mood was more relaxed. The men had enjoyed their brief spell of picking hops; it made a refreshing change from the tough, heavy work that most of them were used to on the London dockside or in Spitalfields or Smithfield markets.

Everyone seemed relaxed around the common; an afternoon off from picking was a welcome escape for the women, even though they were busy with their laundry, scrubbing clothes in tin baths, boiling the whites and hanging them out on trees and makeshift washing-lines.

Most of them were looking forward to dressing up in their best for their evening out at the White Horse before rounding off the day, when they would be tucked up in their cosy huts wrapped in the strong arms of their men, having been deprived of love all week.

Sitting on a chair outside her hut, Liz had her face to the sun and enjoyed drifting in and out of a light sleep against the background noises of someone's transistor and the general buzz of the common. The gentle swishing of water, as Laura washed her smalls in an enamel bowl next to where Liz was sitting, was like music to her ears. Liz's washing was already dry and ready for a spit and press.

Jack lazed around in his usual fashion, spread out on the grass, soaking up the sun and watching the world go by, enjoying his pint. The delicious taste of beef stew was still on his mind. Laura was a good cook, he told himself, but it was the fresh air and burning wood that gave the food that extra smoky flavour.

Normally the familiar distant sound of crocks and cutlery clinking in washing-up bowls made a nice background noise against which Jack could drift off into welcomed sleep, but no matter how much he tried, his present dilemma with Patsy kept his brain active. He had made up his mind not to tell Laura yet, and hoped that Liz and Bert would keep it to themselves. Pulling himself up from the warm grass, he eased the lid off his tobacco tin and smiled at the sight of Liz dozing with her head back and mouth wide open.

'Oi, Lizzie!' he called out mischievously. 'You'd best exercise them fingers, gel. You'll be plucking a nice fat chicken tonight!'

'Arse-'oles!' Her instant retort made Jack rock with laughter. 'We'll be 'aving pot-roast beef tomorrow,' she yelled, 'and Bert's stopping right by my side when you go out chicken-thieving tonight!'

Strolling over to Laura, Jack was still laughing. 'She says the same thing every year.' He directed this remark at his wife, but as usual spoke as if it was for anyone's ears.

'Maybe,' Laura said, squeezing the soapsuds from her powder-blue underwear, 'this time she means it. Something's put her in a mood.'

'Don't look at me, Laura,' Jack said, turning his attention to young Brianny Smith, who was strolling across the common, the proud owner of a red-and-cream portable radio which was turned up full. The song boomed out as if all the world were desperate to hear Paul Evans singing 'Seven Little Girls Sitting In The Back Seat'.

'Brianny!' Jack called, in a loud cheerful voice.

Holding her white enamel bowl of washing in one hand and resting it on her hip, Laura picked up her box of wooden pegs and walked away. 'If Kay turns up, tell her I'll be round at Fran's hut once I've rinsed this washing and hung it out.'

Watching her go, Jack couldn't help the old feelings stirring inside again. Her pink and white candystriped pedal-pushers hugged her bum perfectly and he liked the way she had pinned up her long auburn hair on top of her head, with just a few wispy strands falling down the V-shaped back of her white cotton top. She looked different somehow, younger . . .

'Hallo Jack, mate,' Brianny grinned, 'all right?'

Jack turned his attention from Laura and looked up at the seventeen-year-old with the carrot-coloured hair and mass of freckles, and tried to keep a straight face. 'What you done to your 'air, Brianny?'

''Ad it cut, ain't I,' he sniffed. 'Gotta keep abreast, Jack. This is mod, innit!' He laughed with a touch of embarrassment, stroking the top of his head.

'Turn that bloody thing down!' came Liz's shrill voice.

Rolling his eyes, Brianny did as he was told.

'Tch. What's up with Liz? She got the 'ump, or what?'

'You off to do a bit of pinching, are yer?' Jack asked, ignoring the fact that Brian was showing a little bit of disrespect this year. He reckoned it was all down to his new image and age.

'Nothing round 'ere worth 'aving, is there?' Brianny said, pushing one shoulder back – a habit copied from his dad.

'The old man got anything for me to look at?' Jack asked, amused by the boy's style.

'Might 'ave, Jack. Then again, he might not.'

'Depends if I'm gonna treat yer for telling me, you mean?'

Pulling in his stomach muscles and forcing out a belch of wind, Brianny narrowed his eyes. 'We've got a few solid gold bangle watches you might be int'rested in.'

'Solid gold, eh?' Jack pressed his lips together and rubbed his nose, hiding his laughter.

Sucking at his teeth, Brianny pulled a packet of five Weights out of his pocket. 'Well,' he shrugged, pushing his grinning face up close to his senior, 'who's to know, Jack, eh? Who's to know?'

'Me for a start,' Jack said, gently waving the boy away from his face. The fish and-chip van had been round earlier and Brianny had had more than one pickled onion. 'I passed 'em to your dad. What else he got?'

'Ladies' knitwear. Pure . . . cashmere.'

Unable to control himself any longer, Jack threw his head back and rocked with hysterical laughter, his blue eyes filling with tears.

'Straight up!' Brianny sounded hurt but there was no fooling Jack with those sham tactics.

'Says so on the label, does it?' Jack wiped his eyes with his large white handkerchief and then blew his nose.

'Don't be silly, Jack boy. Had to cut the labels out, didn't we?'

Jack pointed a finger at Brianny. 'Not so much of the "Jack boy".'

Ignoring the gentle chastisement from his elder, Brianny searched in his trouser pockets and found a screwed-up label. ''Ere you are,' he said, feeling chuffed with himself. '"Pure cashmere"! Anyway,' he added cunningly, 'there'd be no fooling your Laura. Got class, ain't she? Not like this lot round 'ere. She'd know the difference between good stuff an' rubbish. So, 'ow many d'yer want then?'

'How much?' Jack said, expecting an inflated price.

Brianny leaned forward, checking either side of him for a grass who just might be listening. 'We've only got a coupla dozen. Best quality. Keeping it quiet 'cos there was a bit in the paper about 'em.'

Sucking in the air and making a whistling sound of disapproval, Jack shook his head. 'Sounds a bit too hot for me, Brianny boy.'

'Naah . . . 'course not. Tiny little bit in a corner of the *East End Advertiser* – who's gonna take any notice of that, eh? You're gettin' old, Jack – turning into an old woman.' Before Jack could give him a mouthful, Brianny was rolling out his spiel again. 'Anyway, the 'otter they are, the cheaper the price, right?'

'Go on then,' Jack said impatiently, rubbing one eye, 'how much?'

'Two quid to the others; thirty five bob to you. Can't say fairer than that.'

Pulling a wad of one-pound notes from his pocket, Jack began to peel them off. 'I'll take four; thirty bob each.' His tone made it clear that he had no intention of haggling.

'Tch. You drive an 'ard bargain, Jack.'

Jack rolled the notes together and popped them into Brianny's shirt pocket. 'Get Lizzie to sort out the right sizes. One for 'er, one for Laura and one for our Kay.' Then looking Brian in the eye he shot him a trusting look. 'Slip the other one to me on the quiet. Large size'll do.'

Turning his portable up, Brian winked at Jack. 'Some blokes 'ave all the luck.' He grinned and walked away, leaving Jack to lean back and do a bit more sunbathing.

Jack knew that from her chair just three huts along, Liz had watched the little scenario and would be wondering what he was spending his cash on. She was probably thinking that as far as she was concerned he was going to need every penny, whichever way things went. He could read his sister with his eyes shut and from a mile off.

Dragging her chair along the concrete plinth she placed it next to Jack and settled herself. 'What's he 'ave to sell, then?' She kept up her cool manner from earlier on.

'Tried to pass me one of my own watches.' Jack kept his eyes shut. 'Did Bert treat you to one? He said he was gonna.'

'Yes, he did,' she snapped coldly.

Jack couldn't help smiling; the present would have really thrown Liz. She still wasn't talking to Bert but wouldn't have been able to turn down the watch – it was a nice gesture and she would respect that, but accepting it couldn't have been easy for her. She had pride enough for ten people.

'Best gold plate that is, Liz. Lovely little rubies . . .'

'As long as it tells the time I couldn't care less.'

'Don't gimme that!' Jack laughed. 'You've always wanted one of them bangle watches – you know you 'ave!' He opened one eye and checked her face; she immediately turned away. 'At least you've decided to talk to me again. You've bin sticking pins in all day.'

'I know where I would like to stick a pin,' she said drily.

Jack knew that this was an opening for Liz. She was waiting to have another go at him and he wasn't sure he was ready for it. The questions would come one after the other and he didn't have the answers. Tired now of going over it time and time again, day and night, he just wanted to leave it be. But it was fresh news to Liz and she would need to talk it through, leaving no stone unturned, the way she had done when he had been in trouble at school.

When Jack's parents had died within a year of each other, he was just approaching ten years old and Liz, being his elder sister by twenty years, took him under her wing, bringing him up as if he were her and Bert's son. It was only natural that she would want to question him, especially about Bert's involvement with Patsy's friend, which amounted to nothing. The girl had seen him as a kindly father-figure who was more concerned with her safety than what might have been on offer.

'I wish Bert would learn that he don't 'ave to tell you everything, Liz,' Jack said, rubbing his shoe on a worn patch of grass. 'So what's he told yer, then?'

'Enough. I dunno what Mother would 'ave done about this, God rest her soul. I s'pose the old man would have grinned proudly.'

'Oh, come on Lizzie! Gimme a break!' Bending over, Jack leaned both elbows on his knees and spread his hands over his face, wishing he had whatever it took to get up and walk away from his sister.

'She gonna 'ave it?' Liz's voice, full of compassion, caused Jack to feel even more choked. He cleared his throat and swallowed hard.

'If I leave Laura and move in with 'er, she will, yeah. Other than that' – he sat up and looked into Liz's concerned face – 'she'll 'ave to have an abortion.'

'So it's all down to you, then?'

'Seems like it.'

'How far gone?' Liz asked, ignoring the first option of Jack leaving Laura.

'Three and a 'alf . . .'

'At least she's caught it in time,' she cut in with a sigh of relief.

'Months.'

'Do what?'

Jack looked away from her, praying she would keep her voice down. He knew there was no point in asking her to.

'Fancy lettin' it go that long! What's the woman got between 'er ears, sawdust?'

'She was frightened to tell me.'

'Oh, do me a favour! Frightened? She knew what she was doing all right. She's trapped yer, Jack. You've walked straight in with your eyes wide open!'

There wasn't much Jack could say to that. Liz might not know it, but she was right, not that he would let on. He had worked out the exact time when he and Patsy had taken the risk and remembered it well. A Saturday night after a few drinks at her local; they could hardly wait to get back home. She had been teasing the life out of him all evening and when they finally shut the street door behind them, no matter how many times Jack searched his pockets he couldn't find his packet of three. Having been to the barber's that day he remembered slipping the packet of Durex Featherlight into his inside pocket. It stayed in his mind because he was looking forward to trying out a different brand.

With a few drinks inside him and Patsy slowly peeling off her clothes in that seductive way, he had taken the chance of what he considered to be a million-to-one that she would get pregnant. And Patsy being a fastidious diarist and timekeeper, would have known exactly when it was her time of the month to conceive.

Jack didn't blame her. She had said from the beginning of their relationship, six years ago, how much she wanted to give up her position in the Accounts office at the local umbrella factory and start a family. Although he had never said he would leave Laura, Jack often told Patsy how futile it seemed for them to carry on, not even sharing the same bedroom. From that she had deduced that he would one day, given a good reason, leave his wife.

'Well,' Liz said after a long silence, 'I can't help yer. No one I know'll touch 'er. Not at fourteen weeks. Be like killing a child. She'll 'ave to 'ave it. Give it over to the Welfare.'

'What, and let it be brought up in an 'ome?'

'You should 'ave thought of that, Jack, when you was giving 'er one.'

'Yeah, well, it's not exactly the first thing that comes into your head, is it?'

'What does the tart wanna do about it?'

Inhaling slowly, Jack locked his fingers and cracked his knuckles. 'Her name is Patsy.' His tone warned Liz to treat his girlfriend with a bit of respect. 'And she thinks she knows someone who knows someone who'll do it – should it come to that.'

'And you'd stand by and let 'er kill off an Armstrong?'

Looking into her face again, he sighed. 'What am I s'posed to do, Liz? What *am* I supposed to do? You tell me.'

Liz thought about it and then shrugged as if the answer was obvious. 'Where do 'er family come from?'

'Leicester.'

'Her mother still there, is she?'

'Yes, and Patsy's told 'er about me and she knows I'm married. She's not too 'appy about it, neither.'

'Well.' Liz stood up and grabbed the back of her chair ready to drag it back to her hut. 'It seems pretty obvious to me what you should do.' She grinned at him. 'Send 'er back to Leicester.'

Shaking his head and pressing his lips together so she wouldn't see him smiling, he pulled his tobacco tin out of his pocket. 'You can be 'ard at times, Lizzie, you know that?'

'Tell me something, Jack. D'you know where your Kay is? Right now, I mean. Right at this minute?'

''Course I don't – talk sense. She could be anywhere.'

'That's right, she could.' Pushing her face close

up to his she raised her eyebrows. 'She might be fifteen, but she's still a baby. A baby who needs a bit of love and affection from her DAD! Stop mooning over what you could 'ave and take a bit more care of what you've got!'

Jack stared after Liz as she dragged her chair away and disappeared into her hut. He couldn't fathom why he felt a bit lighter than he had earlier on because nothing had changed. His problems had hardly gone away. He wondered if something she had said had gone in but not registered. Casting an eye around the common he focused on the kids who were playing on top of the black corrugated cookhouse, remembering the previous year when Kay was up there with them.

Terry came into his vision then, on his way to the greengrocer's van. If Kay wasn't with him – where was she? As he stood up, Jack realized that sitting in the sun like that had made him sweat; his white shirt was drenched already. He pulled it over his head, not bothering to undo the buttons, and threw it on to the bed in his hut. Catching sight of himself in the mirror hanging on a nail behind the door, he admired his tanned body and could see why the women couldn't keep away from him. Splashing some cold water under his arms he caught sight of Milly through the open door; she was wearing lovely little peach-coloured shorts and a boat-necked blouse to match.

Jack stood in the doorway and gave her a good wolf-whistle. He loved the way she blew him a kiss in return. Laughing, he pulled on his new red Fred Perry, tucked it into his stone-coloured cotton slacks and walked away from the hut, hands deep in his pockets. He began to hum a little tune. Maybe Kay was enjoying a swim in the river? If so, he would go back for his trunks and join her. The thought of cool water on his body brought a smile to his face.

Laura was enjoying a cup of tea in Fran's hut when Jack sauntered by. 'I never know whether Jack's got a rotten memory or if he just never listens to me. I told 'im I would be in 'ere with you and he just strolls past as if . . .' Her words trailed off. What should she care anyway?

'D'yer reckon Jack knows about you and . . . you know?'

'Richard. You can call him by his name, Fran. Frogs and toads won't drop from your mouth.' Laura smiled at her friend.

'I know; it just seems, well, him being the boss an' all that. I s'pose I'm used to referring to 'im as . . . Wright. Can't 'elp it.'

Suddenly pensive, Laura gazed out at nothing. 'I honestly can't tell any more what Jack does or doesn't know, what he feels, or what he wants. It's like living with a stranger in a way. Every now and then you remember the way it used to be.' She turned her watery eyes towards Fran. 'I'll tell you one thing though, I despise him at times . . .' She dropped her head back, closed her eyes and bit her lip.

'Come on, Laura. You don't mean that.'

'Oh, but I do, Fran. I don't know why I do, but I do.' She pulled her embroidered handkerchief out and blew her nose. 'Nothing I can put my finger on. Just . . .'

'He doesn't knock you about, surely?'

'No, of course not. He doesn't do anything. That's the trouble. I never know what he's thinking. We don't love each other any more, that's obvious, but at least we could talk, or something. You know, sometimes when I'm back in London and we're sitting in that front room, I'm desperate to talk to someone about Richard. I miss him so much it hurts. And I think, why can't I tell 'im? Why can't I tell Jack?'

'Bloody hell, Laura!' Fran looked as if she wanted to give her a good shaking. 'What's wrong with you? Tell your old man about your lover?' She looked into Laura's hazel-green eyes – they seemed full of anguish – 'You are in a state, gel.'

'You don't think I should, then?'

Fran's look of dismay said everything. She slowly shook her head and topped up Laura's cup with hot tea. 'You wanna get 'is permission? Don't even think about it. Unless . . . you're ready to leave 'im?'

Laura composed herself. 'Well, that might be on the cards, Fran. I think Richard's building up to asking me to leave Jack and live down here.'

'You're kidding me?' Fran grinned.

'No. I'm serious.'

'Well! There's a turn-up for the books! So why the long face then? It's what you want, it's what most of us would want. God, Laura; you living in that lovely house? Lucky cow!'

'It's not gonna be that easy, Fran.'

'Well, of course it's not! You'll get opposition all round. What d'yer want – jam on it? You've got a bloody fight on your hands, gel, and they'll be gunning for you from both sides. Unless of course you're planning on bringing Kay, Liz, Bert, and your dad down with yer?' She sat back in her chair and grinned. 'Rather you than me, mate. I wouldn't fancy taking on Julia Wright.'

'No, I know what you mean. She's a funny woman.'

'Funny? Glad you think so – split personality . . . ?'

'She can't be that bad . . .'

'You don't do yer 'omework, do yer Laura. She

used to be up and down like a yo-yo, till they put her on medication.'

'You are having me on, Fran . . . ?' Laura felt herself go cold.

'We went hop-picking one year over at Paddock Wood – that's where I heard about it. Her mother—'

'Used to own a corner shop,' Laura cut in.

'That's right. One of the yokels told me . . . reckoned she could be as sweet as apple pie one minute and pepper-'ot the next.' Fran bit her bottom lip and leaned back in her chair. 'I thought you knew.'

'Richard never said a word . . .' Laura said pensively.

'Well, he wouldn't, would he, you dozy cow. They've got 'er on medication now and she's all right for most of the time. Probably all right all of the time, I dunno. I shouldn't like her as an enemy though, especially not with Halloween coming up!'

'Fran! You've been 'aving me on!'

'No, I 'aven't, Laura,' she chuckled, 'but I just couldn't resist that last bit.'

Kay had achieved what she wanted when she strolled past the gypsy wagons. Zacchi had seen her and managed to slip away, catching her up once she had got as far as the third meadow, away from the common and closer to their favourite quiet spot by the river.

They wandered lazily hand in hand through the hop gardens and into the orchards, where purple Victoria plums grew in abundance. Pulling a branch down, Kay picked a few and carefully placed them on the grass while Zacchi leaned on another tree and watched as the blazing sun shone on her pale gold hair.

'The best ones are at the top,' she said, hoping he would climb the tree. 'My Aunt Liz makes the best plum pudding in the world.'

Moving forward, Zacchi reached his arm up and plucked the plum she had her eye on and offered the fruit to her mouth. She bit into the soft flesh and the juice ran down the side of her mouth. Zacchi gazed into her beautiful soft blue eyes, threw the plum away and pulled her against his hard body. Licking the juice from her lips, he pressed his mouth on hers.

This kind of kissing was a new experience for Kay; she enjoyed it as much as he did but wasn't quite sure how to respond. Zacchi wasn't looking for a response: it was enough to hold her soft body close to his. She offered no resistance as he pushed against her and brushed his hand slowly across her breasts, his body fitting itself into hers, his breath hot on her mouth.

While one part of Kay was throbbing with pleasure, another seemed to be melting. She loved the way he made her feel, but from somewhere deep inside came a cry of warning. She pulled away from his strong but gentle hold and tried to control her breathing. She looked into his deep blue eyes and smiled, slightly embarrassed. 'I think we should go back now.' Her voice held no conviction.

'I won't go too far, I promise.' He smiled at her, knowing she wanted them to make love every bit as much as he did. Seeing the wistful look on her face, he pulled back, leaned on a tree and composed himself. He could wait, would wait, until she screamed out for him to take her. He knew he would be the first so it had to be taken slowly, carefully.

Not really wanting it to end, Kay leaned forward and gently kissed his lips, allowing him to draw her in and kiss her full on the mouth again. This time she responded instinctively and as he pushed himself against her she allowed her legs to move in time with his. The longing he felt was almost unbearable, but he kept control. It wouldn't be long now; soon she would be ready.

Easing himself away from Kay, he waved away a dragonfly from her hair. 'Come on, enough of this,' he said with determination. As he pulled her through the orchard she found herself laughing out loud, running beside him, wild and free.

Just before they reached a clearing he swung her round and kissed her again. 'A man has to be careful with someone like you,' he said, his voice gruff and serious. 'We don't want to go falling in love.'

'I think it might be a bit too late for that advice, Zacchi.'

The sound of a Land-Rover approaching caused them both to freeze.

'Oh, God . . .' moaned Kay, 'that was Julia Wright!'

'Don't worry,' he said, slipping his arm around her waist, 'she couldn't have seen us. Too many trees.' Together they strolled out of the orchard, without a care in the world.

Eight

Richard was stretched out on a deck-chair soaking up the last of the afternoon sun, when the sound of wheels on gravel woke him from his light sleep. He pulled himself up, ready to help Julia in with the supplies.

There was to be another dinner party that evening and he hadn't quite recovered from the one that had gone on far too late the night before. Julia had been in fine fettle and had positively glowed when they talked about the new Rostabuff picking-machines which would be arriving in a few weeks' time.

Two of the other hop-growers around the table, Rodney Brady and Michael Sparks, had given their pickers the sack the previous year, keeping on some of their best workers, inviting them to return to work the machines. Both men had chosen the Brett machines and had already changed to oil-fired fan furnaces for the kilns. When Richard had said how sorry he was that the old way of life was over, they had, with Julia and the other women, pulled his leg about the lack of lovely ladies in his life being more important than social history. But Jeremy Goodwin, a man slightly older than the other two, had sided with Richard and insisted he would change from hand-picking only when he was forced to do so. He had aroused a feeling of weakness in Richard, for not sticking to his guns as a traditionalist the way Jeremy had.

Struggling with a large box of groceries, he followed Julia into the farmhouse and gave Janet the maid a sympathetic look when his wife barked at her to bring the rest of the shopping in from the Land-Rover.

Kicking off her shoes and dropping into a soft armchair, Julia looked pleased with herself. 'I saw something just now,' she said casually, pushing her fingers through her newly coloured red hair, 'that we have been lucky to avoid all these years.' She allowed a few seconds to tick by, hoping suspense might add to the blow she was about to deliver.

'I just saw the Armstrong girl,' she purred, 'in one of the orchards, with a traveller. I shan't say what they were doing.' She quickly turned her head away so he would not see the smile on her face. As she could have predicted, the mere mention of the name Armstrong shook Richard and stunned him into silence. Biding her time, she waited for him to return from the kitchen.

'I shouldn't think that matters now.' He appeared uninterested as he crossed the room to the fireplace and tapped his pipe on the edge of the grate. 'A few more weeks and they can do what they bloody well like.'

'If the men from either camp get to know about it, all hell will break loose. You know how clannish gypsies and cockneys are.' She watched as he turned his back to her, lighting his pipe, avoiding eye contact. 'She can't be a day over fifteen – and he no less than twenty.'

'There's only one lad amongst the Romanies and that's young Zacchi. And I happen to know he's only just seventeen.'

'I always thought her kind did their utmost to scramble up the ladder. Not crawl from one pit to another. Those men might tolerate picking on the same field, even singing together, but when it comes to mixing the blood—'

'It's none of our bloody business!' Richard snapped, walking to the window and gazing out. Julia had hit home. The thought of Laura's daughter with a traveller did make his blood run cold. He wondered why Julia had been so eager to give him this piece of news about a girl that should mean nothing to her.

That evening, around six-thirty, most of the men on the common were either by the water-tap, stripped to the waist, giving their hair and body a good wash before splashing on some Old Spice, or outside their huts peering into small mirrors nailed to the back of hut doors, shaving. None of them would be seen dead with a six o'clock shadow, not on a Saturday evening.

Sitting on a kitchen chair, gazing up at her dad, Kay remembered something she had heard that day. She wondered if it was worth mentioning.

Slapping lather on to his face with his favourite brush, Jack eyed his daughter. 'What you staring at?' he asked, striking up a conversation to keep her there.

'Mr Wright's looking for a pole-puller, you know. Why don't you pretend you've hurt your back, go on the Panel and take the job?' she asked hopefully.

'*Was* looking,' Jack said, rinsing his brush in the small bowl of water. 'He's given both jobs to them scraps of kids, Billy and Johnny Lipka. Neither of them are fifteen if they're a day older. The man's asking for trouble, letting 'em jump the queue like that.'

208

'Oh, right.' Kay sounded disappointed. 'They are tall though, Dad, and strong. An' that family's bin coming down 'ere as long as we 'ave.'

'Yeah, I know. Wouldn't wanna fall out with their dad either. Wright knows 'ow to keep the peace.' With his face covered in white lather, Jack searched on a small wooden shelf for a razor-blade. 'Oh, Gawd,' he moaned, 'go and ask yer Uncle Bert if he can spare a Blue Gillette, will yer, babe?'

'Uncle Bert!' Kay yelled, 'Dad wants to know if you've got a razor-blade to spare?'

'Go on then,' Jack snapped, 'tell the whole bloody common!'

Kay had no intention of moving from her chair, it wasn't often she and Jack were together like that. 'Would you have asked for the pole-puller's job, Dad, if Billy Lipka hadn't got in first?'

'Probably, yeah. Coupla weeks down 'ere – do me good.'

With his shirt off and braces dangling, Bert made an appearance. 'Here – one blade. Right bloody nuisance you are. I'm gonna 'ave to use mine again in the morning. It's your fault if I scratch my face to bits!'

'You sound in good nick.' Jack laughed.

'Yeah. 'Course I am. Looking forward to a nice night out.' Bert rubbed his smooth chin and stared thoughtfully out. 'Don't know what's come over Liz, but she can't do enough for me. I get a little squeeze whenever she sees me.'

Moving in on the family threesome, Brianny Smith arrived and gave Kay the once-over before turning his attention to Bert. 'Hallo, mate! How's Liz gettin' on with her watch?' He addressed the men as if he were their equal.

Turning to Jack, Brianny shook his head and grinned. 'You look a right picture all soaped up like that. Santa Claus, without 'is hat.' Laughing at his own joke, Brianny moved in and spoke into Jack's ear. 'Listen, if ever you find you're without again . . . razor-blades, or anything else in the barber's line . . . give us a nod – know what I mean?'

'Brianny boy, you are giving it a bit too much lip lately. Watch yerself.' It was a friendly warning. 'Anyway,' Jack continued, not wishing to dampen too much of the boy's spirit, 'what you looking so pleased about?'

'Got m'self a little rendezvous down at the manor. Wright's place.'

'You've not bin sniffing around that pretty little maid agen, 'ave yer?' Bert grinned.

'Not sniffin', Bert, not sniffing. The gel can't keep 'er eyes off me. Every time I walk past the place . . . still, there you are; if you've got it, use it, eh, Jack?'

he said, giving him a friendly punch on the shoulder before walking away.

'And he wanted to take Kay to the pictures . . .'

'You didn't tell me!' Kay said indignantly.

'Would you 'ave gone?'

'No.'

'Well, then.' Jack shrugged.

Laughing, Bert walked back to his hut, admiring the way Jack got round the tricky insinuations that Brianny was throwing at him in front of his daughter.

Slipping the blade into his razor, Jack looked sideways at Kay. 'Coming up the White Horse, tonight?'

'Might do,' she said with an air of indifference.

''Course,' he added while carefully pulling the razor down one side of his cheek, 'you'll 'ave to check with your mother. She might 'ave other plans for yer. Like an early night.'

'Dad! I'm not a kid, y'know.'

'All right. Just thought you'd best check it, that's all. Don't wanna upset 'er, do we?'

Thinking fast, Kay made up one of her stories, hoping to pull her mum and dad together. 'She has been crying quite a lot lately,' she lied.

'Has she, now?' Jack asked, showing concern. 'And why d'yer think that is?'

'Well, because of our baby dying, for one thing.'

As she had hoped, the remark had the desired effect. It was the first time Jack could remember Kay ever mentioning it. He lost concentration for a second and nicked himself. 'Sod it! Pass me a fag-paper will yer, Kay? I don't wanna get blood on this new shirt.'

She pulled a thin tissue from the flat red packet and passed it to her dad. 'She was holding one of Marsha's twins. He must be about . . .' Kay thought back to how old her brother had been when he died; 'eight weeks.'

Jack tore a small corner of the paper and laid it on the tiny scratch just below his cheek-bone and stared down at his girl. She even knew how old baby John was when it happened. Trying to push it out of his mind, he went back to his shave. There was something different about his daughter, the way she was talking to him, more like a woman than a kid.

'I don't think she really wanted to hold the baby. You know what she's like, won't go near a pram . . .'

This was too much for Jack to take. He turned away from Kay's searching eyes, doing his best to control his emotions.

'Aunt Liz told Mum it was the best thing she'd done in years, crying over that baby.' Kay was

212

getting in deeper by the minute, one lie following another, but she couldn't stop.

Half shaven, Jack dropped down on to a wooden chair and lowered his head. 'Your Aunt Liz's not always right, Kay. Some things are best left alone.'

She knew it was hurting him to bring back the sad memories but something was willing her to go on. Something from deep inside. 'Who did my brother look like, Dad?'

With the familiar tell-tale crack in his voice, Jack tried to speak. At first he couldn't manage it but then, after clearing his throat, he swallowed hard. 'He was the image of your mother. Had a mass of thick dark 'air and lovely green eyes.' His voice gave way and the tears streamed down his face. 'And he smiled the minute I looked at him.'

Wiping away her own tears with the back of her hand, Kay forced a smile. 'Yeah, I remember now, his little blue cot; you painted it, didn't yer?'

'Yeah.' Jack caught his breath. 'And you climbed in it two days before he was born. Found yer there, fast asleep, 'appy as a sandboy.'

There was a silence then, as they shared a few moments of mourning.

'Do Daddy a favour, Kay,' Jack murmured, wiping his eyes. 'Go and see if Georgie Smith's coming out with us after the pub shuts. They reckon that farm over the bridge's got too many chickens roaming about . . . nothing like sizzling golden chicken with crispy pot-roast spuds.'

His cheery smile and wink lifted Kay. She was pleased they had talked about her brother and wondered why she had left it so long before asking about him.

After delivering her message to Georgie Smith, Kay made her way to her favourite spot by the river. Other than the lone fisherman across the bridge, there was no one around. She settled herself and stared into the quiet water. Tossing a stone in, she watched the disturbance it caused. Life was a bit like the river, she thought, flowing quietly until someone comes along, interferes, making ripples and waves.

Enjoying her solitude, she wondered what her life would be like a year from then, when she would have left school. She wondered if she would ever see Zacchi again after this season.

'Bin looking everywhere for you.' Terry sat down beside her. 'Might 'ave known you would be 'ere.'

Kay looked at her friend and smiled. 'I was gonna call round for yer but . . .'

'You wanted "to be alone",' he teased. 'At least you're not with the gypsy again.' He tried not to sound hurt.

'I'll 'ave to introduce you one of these days,' Kay

said, realizing that she had neglected her best friend all week.

'Introduce me? Silly cow. Anyone'd think you'd swallowed a dictionary.'

'Come on.' She stood up. 'Best get back.'

'Why? Is he waiting for you, then?' He slipped his arm into hers and enjoyed walking by her side.

'No, he's not. I won't be seeing him till tomorrow, *actually*.'

Laughing and joking, they made their way back. 'I daren't take that risk again, slipping off with him while Dad's around.'

'Oh, so that's where you went earlier, then?'

'Yeah,' she said dreamily, 'that's where I went. And that's where I want to be all the time, with Zacchi.'

'Well just make sure no one sees yer, that's all.'

'That's just it. Someone did see us.'

'Who?' Terry sounded more worried than Kay.

'Julia Wright.'

'Oh, Gawd,' he sighed, 'I s'pose we'll 'ave to pretend it was me if it comes out!'

'Terry! That's the best thing you've ever thought of. You clever sod!'

'Come on then, we'll walk through and round the camp until they've all seen us. I'll give you a kiss now and then and you can hug me. That'll give 'em food for thought.'

Laughing and enjoying their play-acting, Kay and Terry returned to the huts to collect his guitar. He would play and sing a love song to her round the fire.

Wandering back to her hut to collect a warm cardigan, Kay saw that her dad had finished shaving and was groomed ready for his night out. Jack glanced at Kay and a certain smile passed between them: for the first time ever, they felt as if they were sharing something special and she knew that she could talk to him about her brother whenever she felt the need. Whether she would ever manage to get her mum and dad together again was another thing. But she felt certain that, if she failed, it wouldn't be for want of trying.

Julia's temper rose by the second as she banged about in the kitchen, turning out her cupboards. She couldn't remember how many times she had told Janet about organization and method. Life would be far easier for her if Mrs Hillditch, the cook, didn't have to search for utensils every time she came in to prepare a four-course meal when Julia threw a dinner party. And since she had decided to entertain more guests in the future, organizing at least two social gatherings a week with the occasional soirée thrown in, the kitchen would need to be more than just functional – it must be in tiptop order.

Telling herself she could expect no help from Richard when it came to the running of the household, she dragged the copper fish-kettle from a cupboard and slammed it down on the large pine kitchen table. Janet could give that a polish, too. Of course, if her husband showed a little more interest instead of skulking off to his study, the staff wouldn't need Julia to keep them in order. But what could she expect when he was so deeply immersed in his own private, sordid world? Well, God help him, she fumed, if he sulked his way through this dinner party, making Julia feel as if it were her fault that he had a mistress.

As she opened the door to the larder to see what kind of a mess that was in, she noticed the clock just above the door. It was approaching seven and cook hadn't yet arrived. Dragging a tray of eggs from a shelf, she turned too quickly and crashed her elbow against the door support. As the pain shot through her arm she let go of the tray and watched in horror as it landed upside down on the floor, causing every egg to smash. Hitting out in temper, she kicked the tray and stamped the eggshells into an orange-yellow mess, screaming for Janet.

Standing in the kitchen doorway, Janet stared forlornly at the state of the room. Every surface was covered with pots, pans, china and supplies. She looked from the pine table to the messy floor and then up to Julia's flushed face; lost for words, she felt herself begin to tremble. The worst of it was that upstairs, in Janet's room, Brianny was waiting; she had sneaked him in through the side-door.

'Don't you think it's time you set the dinner table?' Julia bullied.

'I have, ma'am,' came the small voice in defence. 'I've finished everything.'

'Flowers?' She dared the girl to have forgotten anything.

'Arranged along the centre of the table in the cut-glass dishes as you asked, and in the tall vases on either side of the window.' Janet tried not to let her mind wander away from the questions being fired at her. Somehow, with the help of cook, she would have to clean up the kitchen in record time. Brianny would have to wait.

'And why isn't Mrs Hillditch here yet?' Julia demanded.

'Because she was in earlier, ma'am. You remember you asked her to prepare everything ahead of time. All she has to do is grill the fillet steak.'

'Well, I don't see any food prepared, Janet.' She

was beginning to climb down, but had no intention of showing it. Her eyes bore into the girl's face fit to kill.

Swallowing hard, Janet tried to give her mistress a reassuring smile. 'It's in the pantry. Everything is ready to be served, apart from the steak . . .' Her voice trailed off. She would have to mention the state of the kitchen soon. Time was marching on. 'If you want to get ready, ma'am, I'll soon have this mess cleaned up,' she said tactfully. 'I've pressed the creases out of your new silk dress. It looks beautiful.'

'Yes.' Julia stared thoughtfully back at her. 'Yes, thank you, Janet. I am rather looking forward to wearing it.' Without another thought about the task of organizing the kitchen, Julia left the room.

'That's all right your highness,' Janet mumbled to herself, 'think nothing of it. I'll just wave my magic wand over this lot.'

Before climbing the stairs, Julia looked in on Richard who was standing by the window in his study, admiring the flaming red and orange berries on the cotoneaster, and the pyracantha bushes in the garden. He wished he hadn't got to go through the ordeal of another dinner party and that he could be out walking with Laura instead. He had got to know her more during the past week than during all the years they had been seeing each other. He had no idea she was a museum-goer and that costume and fashion through the ages was her biggest interest. He was wondering how he could arrange things so that they could both be at the antiques fair in Maidstone the following Tuesday afternoon, where he knew there was be a display of fine period costume.

'Wishing you were somewhere else again, Richard?' Julia sounded very smug, very sure of herself.

'Actually I was admiring the garden.' At least it was half true.

'Were you really? Well let me tell you now, so you can think about it while you are looking at the flowers. I have come to a decision.'

He smiled at her, wondering what was going through her mind now. 'Spit it out, then,' he said, barely controlling his cynical thoughts.

She closed the door and leaned on it in a casual, relaxed manner. 'I'm not prepared' – she spoke in a matter-of-fact tone – 'to stand by and watch you stare out of windows wishing you were with someone else. If you want our sham of a marriage to continue, you had better accept the fact that you will never see that whore, Laura Armstrong, again.'

Richard could not believe his ears. In one clean

sweep, his wife had gathered everything together in one neat package. 'You can't be serious?'

'Can't I?' she grinned, enjoying every minute as a new energy charged through her veins. 'I think you'll be surprised to know that I can be whatever I choose. And right now, I choose to be serious. Think yourself lucky I'm not in one of my angry moods.'

'You're telling me,' he said, trying to consolidate his own interpretation of her statement, 'that you think I have been seeing someone and unless I stop, our marriage is over?'

'No Richard. I *know* you have been with a woman and I know who she is. But you were right about our marriage.'

'How do you know?' He tried to sound angry when he was actually quite worried. Julia was definitely feeling on top of things – that was obvious.

'You were seen together, with most of your clothes off, making love in the cottage.'

'What rubbish. And whoever it was that saw us – was there as spectator?'

Julia threw her head back and laughed, overjoyed with his reaction. He was lying. She was making him tell lies. She was forcing him to lie, and the wonderful, euphoric buzz sweeping through her like lightning was her pay-off for having to creep about at night, spying on her own husband.

He was lying to her now, and the magic of it was that she knew.

'I'm not leaving this room and neither are you, until I hear you admit that you've been having an affair with Laura Armstrong.'

'Fair enough.' He narrowed his bright hazel eyes, sucked at his pipe and shrugged his shoulders. He felt quite relieved, she was making things easier for him. 'I'm in love with Laura – will that do?'

'That's not what I said!' Julia could feel her anger rise again.

'No. It's what I said. I love her. Have done for some time. And I have no intention of giving her up. What you choose to do about our marriage is up to you.' His voice began to crack. 'I'll do whatever you want.'

Easing the study door open, Julia smiled sweetly back at Richard's grave face. 'Try to be ready in time for our guests; I'm expecting them around eight-thirty. I shall be wearing pale apricot – do try to blend in.' She slipped quickly out of the room, calling for Janet to fetch her new shoes which were still in their box in the back of the Land-Rover.

Stretched out on Janet's bed, Brianny was feeling very pleased with himself. Roses on every wall. A nice little country love-nest, he told himself. A clean firm bed, wall-to-wall carpet and to top it all, he had heard the heated conversation below. This had turned out to be his lucky night.

Pulling the last curler from her hair, Liz dropped it into a small plastic bag and sprinkled on some Amami setting lotion.

''Ere, Lizzie.' Solemn-faced, Jack appeared in the doorway. 'Has Kay ever asked you about baby John?'

Taken aback, she gazed at his ashen face. 'No! Why?'

'Just wondered,' he said gravely.

'She throws out little teasers now an' then, though.' Liz brushed her hair. 'And I know what she's up to, an' she knows I know what she's up to, yet I still can't bring myself to talk about it. There are some things, Jack, that words can't do justice to.'

'You're telling me.' Jack peered at the small wooden shelf, 'Where does Bert keep 'is after-shave?'

'There's some Imperial Leather in that cupboard.' She gave the small green door a gentle kick. 'In there. I'm glad you came in. I've been thinking about this new baby.'

Jack crouched on the floor and searched for the aftershave. 'Give it a rest, Liz! You can talk some things to death, y'know.'

She admired herself in the small mirror and tweaked her new, springy curls. 'Do Laura good to nurse a little one,' she said, in a matter-of-fact tone.

Jack dropped down on to his backside and closed his eyes. 'Are you suggesting what I think you are?'

'Adopt your own son – what's so terrible about that?'

Shaking his head he quietly laughed at the nerve of his sister and the way she so often got the wrong end of the stick. 'You're miles out, Liz. Miles out. I'm just about ready to ask Laura if she'll give me a divorce.'

Nine

'So you are telling me you've spent the last few years wishing you were with someone else?' Julia fumed.

Dropping down into an easy chair in his study, Richard leaned his head back and closed his eyes, wishing he had the guts to walk away and leave her to receive their guests by herself. 'I think our marriage might have been a mistake, if that's what you mean.' He spoke in a low voice. 'I've kept it going for the sake of the twins. Maybe once they've grown into their teens . . .'

Julia poured herself another gin and tonic. 'I meant what I said.' Her tone was low and tight. 'If we are to go on, you've got to promise me you'll never see that woman again.'

There seemed no point in his saying anything. She wasn't taking it in. 'And you accuse me of never listening.' He smiled wryly. 'It's not that I don't care

about you; you've been a good companion. And I am
still fond of you . . .'

'I'm a woman, for Christ's sake! Not the family
dog!'

He looked up at her, still preoccupied. 'The daft
thing is, if you knew Laura as I do, you'd really like
her. I'm sure you'd get on.'

Julia's temper rose by the second. Her eyes were
alive and angry and her hand shook as she cupped
her glass. 'Oh, well,' she smirked, 'let's invite her
round for tea. We'll have to chip a few cups first
though; wouldn't want her to feel uncomfortable!'

Strangely undisturbed by her performance, he
stared out thoughtfully. 'You're quite alike, funnily
enough.'

Swallowing the remains of her drink, Julia slammed
the glass down on to the side-table and pushed her
head close to his. 'To use a word with which I am
sure Laura Armstrong is familiar – bollocks!'

Having enjoyed a quick cuddle with Brianny before
she changed into her afternoon uniform, Janet was
trying to quieten him. On hearing most of the heated
argument from below, he doubled up with laughter.
Janet was beginning to regret smuggling him in.
She had no idea that raised voices from the study
below could be so clearly heard. Afraid that Brianny

226

would be discovered, she pushed a pillow into his face. 'Shut up, will you! You'll get me the sack!'

Quietening down, he gestured to indicate he would behave, even though he was still laughing. 'Is this how they always carry on?' he whispered.

'No, they hardly ever speak to each other during hop-picking. She went out the other night though and spied on him. Must have caught them at it.'

Brianny sank back down into the pillow and pushed his hands behind his head. 'Who'd 'ave believed it, eh? Richard Wright and Laura Armstrong!'

'Yeah, and you make sure you keep it to yourself.' She sounded worried but Brianny was off on his own track.

'Bit of inside information like that . . . never know when it might come in 'andy.'

The sound of Mrs Hillditch the cook calling for her quickly brought Janet to her feet. Brushing herself down she made for her bedroom door. 'I'll pop back once they're on the main course. She always serves the dessert – likes to pretend she's concocted it herself.'

'Yeah, go on then. And don't forget to bring me up a bit of the fillet steak like yer promised. Gotta keep me strength up,' he grinned.

Cook was not in the best frame of mind when

Julia waltzed into the kitchen, her pale apricot silk chiffon dress drifting gracefully over a large bowl of half-eaten dog food. Had Julia realized the hem of her new creation was absorbing brown gravy it would be cook or Janet who would have taken the brunt of her temper. Praying that Julia would not lower her eyes, cook forced a smile while she received instructions that wild mushroom soup was to be served instead of consommé as planned. She was still angry at having had to rearrange her kitchen back the way it had always been and had suited her since she had been coming in on a regular basis for the past eight years.

'I take it you still want to follow with the prawn cocktail?' she asked with a touch of sarcasm in her voice.

'Now then, cook,' Julia smiled, 'don't be like that. You know we love your consommé, it's just that I wanted to prepare something for Mr Richard myself. He works so hard at this time of the year, poor darling.'

Lifting the enamel pan from the larder, Julia placed it on the largest ring on the electric stove. 'Try not to bring it to the boil. We don't want to spoil it.'

Passing Janet on her way out of the kitchen, Julia scrutinized the maid's face. 'You're looking

228

decidedly peaky, Janet. Give your cheeks a rub before you serve the guests.'

Janet inhaled slowly and waited until Julia was out of earshot before she let out a low growl, causing cook to smile.

'It's all right for you. You don't live in. She's been driving me round the bloody bend!'

'Tip of the iceberg.' Cook chuckled.

'You wouldn't say that if you'd been here earlier when she was pulling everything out of the cupboards.'

'I've seen worse. Now then,' she added, unscrewing the top from a bottle of brandy, 'you won't like the taste of this, but it'll put some colour back into your cheeks and help you cope with madam's mood.'

'Could have done with that earlier.' She looked anxiously at cook. 'She can be so bossy sometimes, she scares me . . .'

'Be there, but keep a distance, Janet,' the friendly face warned, 'and agree with anything she says, no matter how contrary . . .'

Julia had to admit her table looked magnificent with the splendid array of cut flowers, sparkling crystal glasses, best lace-edged linen and the beautiful Rockingham dinner service. Her guests were chatting happily and Richard looked very much at ease.

'You're looking very slim, Julia,' an attractive female guest murmured. 'And a new hairstyle?' Leaning forward, Sylvia whispered jokingly, 'What's his name?'

'That would be telling,' Julia beamed. 'Could be any one of the men sitting around this table,' she teased.

'You wouldn't have slimmed for any of this lot.'

'Oh, I don't know. I've always had a hot spot for your man,' she purred in her kittenish way.

'Have you, now? Well, I'm not averse to a little swapping.'

Sylvia had no idea how close to a rebuke she came, and if Janet had not entered the room at that moment, carrying a steaming tureen of wild mushroom soup, and taken her attention, Sylvia might have picked up on the flash of anger in Julia's eyes the second the word 'swapping' escaped from her full red lips.

'Wild mushroom soup, everyone! Picked them myself today!' Julia's eyes sparkled with enthusiasm and pride. Sounds of delight filled the room as Janet carefully spooned the piping-hot liquid into the china plates. When she arrived at Julia's place, a hand quickly covered the empty bowl. 'Aren't you forgetting, Janet? It's melon, melon, melon and melon!' She shot Janet a look and then relaxed into a beautiful smile. 'I've thrown so many dinner parties

230

that I am now forced to diet for one day each week!'
She deliberately lied, hoping to unnerve Richard.

'Well, you're certainly looking good on it, Julia!'
one of the men chimed in. 'Stunning, if I may be
allowed to say so?'

'You may indeed,' she said coquettishly, 'any
time!'

Waiting for her melon to arrive, Julia admired her
pale, soft hands. There was not a blemish to be seen
on the deep red gloss nail varnish.

'Delicious, Julia; wonderful!' 'Mmmmmm!' The
compliments flew around the table and made Julia's
head spin. Knowing that Richard was looking at
her, a slight frown on his brow, a touch of worry
in his eyes, she tilted her face and threw a quick
half smile at him as he slowly brought the spoonful of soup to his lips. A more nervous man she
had not seen, not in a long time. Did he really
believe she would spike the soup, just for the hell
of it?

The White Horse was alive with laughter, music and
song as the pickers sang along to Milly's brother
Frank, who played 'Don't Laugh at Me 'cos I'm a
Fool' on the piano.

'Jack?' Liz spoke into her brother's ear. 'Jack,
listen . . .'

He stopped singing and peered at his sister who looked more than a bit tipsy. 'What?'

'You're not really gonna say anything to Laura, are yer? About a divorce?'

'Oh, leave off Lizzie! I'm trying to enjoy myself.'

'I just don't think you should say anything. Not yet anyway.'

'We'll see. Don't make a song and dance about it though, eh?'

Jack turned away and joined in again with the song, but Liz hadn't finished. She tugged at his jacket sleeve. 'She's not short on admirers you know.'

Laughing aloud, Jack picked up his beer-glass and finished the contents. 'You don't give up, do yer? Laura's not interested in all that. She's . . . well . . . what's the word for it . . . celibate! Yeah, that's it. See, I'm like a drunken dictionary. Celibate. That's what Laura's gone. And I should know.'

'Should know, yeah.'

Even though Jack had enjoyed more than his normal two pints, his mind was alert enough to know that Liz was giving him a message. He thought about it for a while. He wasn't sure he wanted to hear what she had to say. One thing he did know, she had something on her mind. Maybe Laura was the dark horse he sometimes thought she might be. Maybe she had a boyfriend. 'Is there something

232

you're trying to tell me, sister dear?' he finally asked.

'Yeah.' She grinned into his face. 'Get me a rum and black while you're up!'

'But I'm not up, am I?'

Slipping her hand beneath his buttocks she gave him a good pinch which got him to his feet in a flash. 'You are now.'

Howling exaggeratedly in pain Jack turned to the others. 'Did you see that? What d'yer reckon – is that fair or what?'

'And not too much black in the rum!' She rocked with laughter.

Making his way to the bar, moaning and holding his rear end, Jack stole a quick glance at Laura. She was chatting away in the corner to her friend, Fran. The way Jack saw it, they were involved in a serious conversation. 'D'yer wanna another drink, Laura? Fran?' he yelled.

The women looked up and nodded. Jack noticed that Laura was looking over his shoulder at someone else. He turned quickly to see the lovely Milly standing as close to him as possible. Without thinking, he lifted her until that pretty face was level with his and then he kissed her on the cheek. He might have kissed her twice, but Georgie Smith had his good eye on the pair of them.

Witnessing the scene, Fran shook her head and smiled at Jack's behaviour. 'You 'ave to admit it Laura, your old man's got charisma. Sure you wanna leave 'im?'

'He stopped turning his charisma on for me years ago.'

Julia had cleverly managed to get rid of her guests early, pleading a headache, and she could tell from Richard's expression that he had no objection to them going. Leaving the table for Janet to clear, Julia went straight to the bedroom and emptied the cupboard which contained all their photograph albums.

Richard was in his study, sulking. When he asked why she had chosen to make wild mushroom soup she had simply grinned at him, and asked, why not? She had been very careful, she said, in choosing the right kind of fungi growing in the wooded part of the garden. She also told him that she wasn't so far gone that she would dare to poison all her guests. Him maybe, but not her friends.

That was followed by a flaming row. Richard had lost his temper, yelling at her that she was a hard bitch, and she had retorted that he was no better than a cheap womanizer. It had all got ridiculously out of hand and Julia knew it, but, as sometimes happened, she could not control her temper. He really had believed she might have spiked the soup with a special mushroom or two. She smiled to herself. It was certainly an idea to toy with, perhaps when she was in need of a little fun . . .

To one side of Julia, spread out across the silk eiderdown, were photographs of her and Richard before they had the twins. On the other side were the photographs she had torn into pieces. She would continue until every one had been destroyed. Then she would go to work on the wedding album.

Just as she was about to rip another photo in half, there came a soft tapping on the bedroom door. As it slowly opened, she stared into Richard's solemn face and felt a sudden wave of self-reproach.

'I'm sure you won't mind my doing this,' she said. 'After all, we don't want to be reminded of how happy we used to be before the harlot tore our marriage to bits.' She knew her actions would hit the mark, Richard was perfectly aware how much those pictures meant to her.

'I wish you would come downstairs so we could talk.' He sounded as miserable as he looked.

'We have nothing to discuss. Save it for her. I'm sure you have plans to make, if you haven't already made them?' She looked back at the pathetic figure standing in the doorway and forced herself not to give in. Using every bit of her will-power, she clenched her fists and stopped herself calling him back, as he slowly shut the door behind him.

She reasoned that, given enough time alone, Richard might begin to think about the damage he was causing and regret his misdemeanours. He obviously hadn't been prepared for the confrontation. Now that the moment of truth had arrived maybe he realized the last thing he wanted was for their marriage to end. As far as Julia was concerned, he could suffer a bit longer; it would serve him right for dancing too close to the edge.

It crossed Julia's mind as she lay in the quiet room that Richard might have heard about some of *her* quick flings. None of them had meant anything, she had simply followed her moods and could see no harm in that. After all, when she was sad she cried and when happy, she laughed. It seemed perfectly in order to her that should she ever feel sexually aroused and the man who was causing her to feel that way was in the same mood . . .

Suddenly the door to the bedroom flew open and crashed against the wall. Richard stood in the doorway, his face full of anger. 'Why are you doing this?' he demanded. 'Why must you torment yourself?'

'You've been tormenting me for the last three

236

years.' She slowly brought herself to her knees and sat back on her heels. 'I'm sure it must have been going on for much longer than that, but I was too naïve to realize before.'

Slamming the door shut behind him, he moved closer to Julia. 'If you knew, why didn't you say something?'

Pushing her face closer to his, forcing him to back off, she narrowed her eyes. 'If you don't know the answer to that, then I am certainly not going to tell you! Think about it, Richard! Think about it!'

Richard shook his head. 'I don't understand. You've brought it into the open now – why couldn't you have done that earlier on?' He covered his face with his hands. 'I don't understand the way your mind works.' His voice sounded different, broken.

'You can stop worrying,' she snapped. 'I'm not going to confront her. Not yet. I want to see you squirm. I want you to wake each morning wondering if today will be the day that Julia tells the family about the little cockney that's to take her place'

'Please, Julia!' He swallowed hard. 'Please don't talk like that.'

'You've never been one for facing the truth.' She spoke contemptuously. 'I don't know how long it'll take before I'm satisfied. But when I am, I shall ask you to leave this house. You can live with your little dreams, in your little cottage, which has her fingerprints all over it!'

Richard could think of nothing to say. Julia was right. He had turned the cottage into a sordid secret place and all the times when he had lied about his reasons for being there late at night, she had known the truth. She had probably been lying in their bed, knowing he was making love to another woman. Another woman! He shook his head. Why was he suddenly thinking about Laura in that way? Why was he filled with regret now, and not overwhelming love for the woman he had almost promised himself to? The woman he loved. There, he was thinking it again, thinking of Laura as the other woman. He spun around to avoid Julia's accusing eyes and gripped the oak window-sill as his legs began to feel light and a sickly feeling swept up from his stomach.

Brianny walked away from the Wrights' farmhouse grinning like a Cheshire cat. 'Who would 'ave thought it?' he murmured to himself, 'the snooty hop-grower's no different from us lot in the East End.' Making his way to the White Horse to grab a drink before time was called, he mused on everything he'd heard. He couldn't help laughing, especially as he held a nice little silver pocket watch in his hand. There must have been at least twenty in that collection, and they all looked the same – as far as he could tell. He'd never seen so much silver. That little room he'd slipped into was full of it. Good thing he wasn't greedy.

There was a good atmosphere in the White Horse when Brianny walked in. The piano-player was in full swing, most were singing and a few women were dancing and jigging around to the hoppers' song:

> They say that hoppin's lousy,
> We don't believe it's true,
> We only come down hoppin'
> To earn a bob or two . . .'

'All right! All right!' Jack's voice thundered above the noise as he called everyone to attention. 'Stop the racket, you lot! Get off that bleeding joanna, Frank!'

Leaning on the bar, Brianny ordered himself a beer and smiled as Jack took over. He wouldn't be so full of himself if he knew what Brianny knew.

'Right! You listening? Shut up in that corner, if you please!' The public bar gradually quietened down as he gained their attention. 'We've bin 'aving a little chat over this side, and we 'ave decided that it's time to confront Mr Richard Wright!' Swaying slightly, Jack was pleased with the rowdy cheering that filled the room. He raised his right arm, fist clenched, and yelled at the top of his voice, 'WHAT DO WE WANT?'

'A LABOUR GOVERNMENT!' came a drunken voice from a smoky corner, causing a burst of laughter all round.

'Yer silly bastard,' Jack laughed, 'we're not talking politics now! We want to be back 'ere, picking them 'ops, next year. Right?' Another collective cheer went up. 'We should 'ave been given proper notice before we came. And that's what we're gonna demand! We want one more go at it before he wipes us off his land!' Everyone shouted their agreement. 'We're not putting up with this leaking bloody rumours lark, then telling us officially to fuck off on the day of departure!' None of them could have agreed any louder. 'So,' Jack continued, 'who's gonna volunteer to walk the women back to the 'uts?'

Making themselves heard, the women banged their glasses on the tables, stamped their feet and threw mild abuse at the men who were agreeing with Jack.

'No . . . sorry girls! No. A woman's place is in the home, or outside, round the fire – you please yerself . . . but a protest march has to be led by the men and followed by the boys.' More shouts of protest, and this time the young lads joined in. 'And that,' Jack lowered his voice, 'is an end to it! We love our women and we'll do what we can for you ladies . . .'

'Yeah, all right Jack!' Liz cut in. 'Get off your soapbox! We don't wanna join in your silly games!' Some of the women agreed with Liz, the others moaned among themselves. Most of them were too merry or drunk to care much one way or the other. 'We've got better things to do, eh, girls?'

'Who woke Lizzie up?' Jack laughed. 'Last time I looked, she was snoring!'

Bulrushes gathered from the nearby brook had been dipped into a can of methylated spirits and set alight. The landlord of the White Horse had supplied the fuel; he wanted to see the pickers back the next year, too. Their trade was the best he could hope for.

Against the navy sky and full moon, the silent army moved forward, each man carrying a flaming torch. Some were too drunk to make conversation and others were caught up in the comradeship and memories of wartime emotions that came flooding back.

The sound of boots marching along the gravel lane reminded Jack of when he was a youth and had marched with the Blackshirts to a meeting at the York Hall. He remembered stopping to listen to Mosley on Speakers' Corner when a gang of local Jewish men appeared and set about them, giving Jack a punch on the nose for looking like a Kraut. Outraged, Jack had gone to the meeting with the intention of joining up, until he heard the speech and realised they were condemning the people he lived amongst, families he knew and liked. He had walked out of the meeting in a temper, wanting no part of it.

It was the thrill of the Blackshirts' march that had excited him, and nothing else. He got that out of his system once the war broke out when he had no choice but to be a soldier, expected to kill other human beings. It wasn't his cup of tea and had he had the nerve, he would have legged it in Calais, like some of his mates.

Leading the men, Jack told himself that this collection of the male species was quite different. These men, he reasoned, were justified in confronting Wright to ask for more time. Hardly any of them would be able to afford a holiday next year, never mind the hopping money they would have to do without. He supposed that it never occurred to Richard Wright that some of the families with five and six kids would go without a Christmas tree and a decent bird on the table, if they didn't have that bit of spare cash. Jack had always closed his front door with no more than a glare when a Communist speaker was doing his rounds on the council estate. He had no time for all that. But the present situation was unfair, and the gap between the rich and poor was wrong. Something had to be done about it, and soon. Young people today should have a better chance than his generation had.

Jack could feel his temper rising and his step quickening. He was in a strange mood tonight. Liz going on about Laura having admirers, hinting she might have a fancy man, hadn't helped matters. As if he didn't have enough to think about.

'Keep up, men!' he yelled as his long legs strode out. 'No falling behind!' Jack was flattered that the men obeyed his orders and offered no complaints.

The silent men marched on, their footsteps echoing through the quiet countryside, their flaming torches lighting the way.

Richard downed the remains of his brandy and placed the glass on the coffee-table, determined to go upstairs and stop Julia destroying all their family photographs. He knew she would only regret it later and blame him. After searching his bureau and finding a small reel of Sellotape, he went upstairs and into their bedroom.

'I've brought some Sellotape, Julia. I think we should stick the pieces back together again.'

She looked up at him questioningly. Was he just talking about the photographs, or their marriage? 'There's one here of our honeymoon,' she sighed. 'The Isle of Man.'

Sitting down on the edge of the bed, he looked into her tear-stained face. 'I'm really sorry. I didn't mean to hurt you.'

'I want more than that, Richard,' she said coolly, avoiding his eyes, 'much more.'

'I'm not sure I can give it. I'm too confused.'

'Well then, go away until you can. I'm not interested in your mixed emotions. Act like a man, for God's sake.' She ripped another photograph.

'What do you want me to say?'

'That it's over, for a start. Then we'll see.'

He sat for a moment, trying to pluck up courage to go one way or the other. He wasn't in love with Julia, he knew that, but it was rapidly dawning on him that her moods were becoming more irrational and without him to see that she took her medication there was no saying what she might get up to. The thought of them splitting up and the effect it would have on the twins gave him a hollow feeling inside. But the idea of never seeing Laura again was just as bad. He realized then just how much he missed his boys. They were always into mischief on the farm when they were home, but all the same . . .

He glanced at Julia, wondering if he dare ask if she had taken her pills, but he could tell from her expression that her attention was elsewhere. He watched as she slowly rose and went to the window which looked out from the front of the house. Turning her head, she looked back at him, a strange glazed look in her eyes.

'It's the pickers,' she said, 'they're carrying flaming torches and heading this way.'

They could hear the sound of marching feet as the men approached. Moving cautiously towards the window, Richard stood by her side, sensing trouble. 'Oh, Lord. This looks like a protest march.'

'After a night's drinking,' Julia warned.

The men were very quiet, which to Richard was more disturbing than if they had been rowdy. He watched as they slowly came to a halt and waited while their leader moved forward and knocked very loudly on the front door.

'I had better answer it.' Richard sounded unsure of himself.

'No. Speak to them from up here.' She reached forward for the handle but he pulled her away.

'They want a confrontation. I'll have to face them properly. You stay up here and if it gets out of hand, call the police.' He made his way towards the bedroom door.

'Richard!' Julia called. 'You do realize who their spokesman is?'

'I can guess.'

'Does he know?'

'I have no idea. I can't imagine Laura would have said anything.'

For a moment they stood in silence. A second loud banging sent a shiver down Richard's spine.

'Don't lose your temper.' Julia knew from experience that, unlike herself, Richard was a placid person but on the rare occasion when he was pushed too far, he could fly off the handle.

'I'm sure Mr Armstrong is a reasonable man.' He smiled and left the room.

As Richard turned on the hall light a harmonious song from the men at once surprised and moved him. He stood still, listening as the chorus filled the air.

There'll al-ways be an Eng-land, while there's
    a coun-try lane;
Where-ever there's a cot-tage small be-side a
    field of grain;
There'll al-ways be an Eng-land, while there's . . .

*   *   *

Richard opened the door and the singing stopped. Seeing the men grouped together, swaying slightly, with tear-filled eyes, hanging on to their flaming bulrushes, Richard was wary.

'One more year,' Jack pleaded, 'that's all we're asking.'

Richard nodded and smiled with embarrassment at this show of genuine feeling. He couldn't think how best to handle the situation. He had expected angry threats to be hurled at him.

'I'll do what I can . . .' he finally managed to say.

'We've been faithful.' Jack was sincere. 'We've picked for you all these years . . . never caused you any real problems, a bit of scrumping now and then . . .'

'I know, I know.' Richard felt a certain sympathy for them. He drew a deep breath and was ready to say he would talk to his brothers and try to persuade them once again to cancel the arrival of the machines when Julia appeared next to him.

'When will you get it through your thick skulls that it's over?' She stared straight into Jack's eyes. 'You might scare my husband with your cheap threats but to me – you're pathetic.' She turned to the others. 'Go back to the common and sleep off the gallons of beer you must have consumed! And if you ever trespass on our property again with your threats of burning our house down, I'll call the police!'

'Threats of burning your 'ouse down? You silly bitch. Who said anything about that? Eh?' Jack was furious.

'Wouldn't be a bad idea!' one of the men yelled.

'We told yer it was a waste of time trying to reason with the upper classes! Selfish bastards!'

'Burn their fucking 'op fields down!' another roared.

Jack turned and raised his hand to the men, signalling for them to calm down. 'So, Mr Wright. I can tell my men that we will be back next year? Is that right?'

Julia moved forward again and stood in front of Richard. She smiled smugly at Jack. Obviously this man knew nothing about his wife's affair with her husband or he wouldn't be insisting she come back the next year.

'It doesn't really matter what my husband agrees to; it won't happen. I will die before I let him change our plans. And if you want to know why I am so adamant – ask your wife.' She spoke in low tones so the others couldn't hear. Looking up at Richard, she grimaced. 'Or would you like to explain?'

Before Richard could say anything, Jack said: 'It's all right, thanks. If my wife's got anything to tell me, she can tell me herself. I don't need the likes of you to—'

'Goodnight, Mr Armstrong,' Julia grinned at him. 'I wish you luck. They'll want to know why you've climbed down and whose fault it is that the purchasing of machines has been brought forward a year.'

She slammed the door in Jack's face.

Bracing himself, Jack turned to face the men. 'D'yer know what? I don't think I want to come back and pick their fucking 'ops!' He eyed the men; they looked a sorry bunch, tired, drunk and disappointed that nothing had really happened.

'Now then, why don't we live up to our names as the riff-raff from London and pinch a few chickens for tomorrow's dinner!'

A cheer went up and the crowd moved away from the farmhouse feeling relaxed and in a better mood.

Richard leaned on the front door and looked at Julia. He felt nothing for her but contempt and wondered how he would manage to spend the rest of his life with someone he despised. She ignored him and walked into the dining-room to pour herself a large brandy.

Fearing that his love affair with Laura would have to end, Richard leaned back on the closed door and resigned himself to his circumstances as he listened

to the song of the men as they walked away into the
distance singing,

Pack up your troubles in your old kit bag and
smile, smile, smile . . .

Ten

Kay had given the White Horse a miss, using the time to practise applying her new make-up. She had been on a shopping expedition with her friend, Lorraine, the day before she left the East End. All of it was new to her, the pan-stick foundation, the liquid eye-liner and pale blue shadow, and the grey-black mascara. The corn-silk lipstick, a pale apricot, was something she had tried before and was pleased with. It had taken a while to get to grips with painting a fine, clean line above her eyelashes but it had worked. She even used her lash-curlers before brushing on the mascara. All of this had taken almost an hour and a half, but she was thrilled with the effect.

Once the women were back from the pub, Kay passed the hut key to her mum and went for a stroll to the river, where she was to meet Zacchi for just ten minutes. He had hoped to get away earlier but had been asked to look after his younger sister and cousins while the adults were at a party given by gypsies on another hop farm.

'You might 'ave told me you was coming over to the river,' Terry moaned as he sat down next to her. He shone his torch into her face. 'Let's 'ave a look, then.'

She pushed his arm away. 'Don't be stupid, Terry. You'll make me go light-blind!' She was embarrassed about her make-up.

'You look really different!'

'Come on then – let's get the insults over with.' She was begging her friend for compliments and he knew it.

'Looks OK,' he said in a bored tone.

'Don't mess about, Terry! Zacchi'll be 'ere any minute. If I look stupid, say so!'

'You don't look stupid, yer silly cow,' he murmured, 'you look like Brigitte Bardot.'

'Very funny!'

'You do. Honest. You'd best watch yerself with Romeo, he'll be all over yer.'

'He's not like that. Anyway, he might not even come. He's bin babysitting. He promised to meet me 'ere ten minutes ago.'

'Oh, right . . . I'll go when he turns up.'

'You don't 'ave to.' She looked sideways at him. 'You still depressed?'

'No. Bit fed up, that's all.'

'You're gonna 'ave to put a smile on it, Tel.'

'Why? Think anyone cares?'

She began to recite, 'No one feels sorry for those . . .'

'Who feel sorry for themselves!' he cut in. 'Trouble is, I don't feel sorry. I don't feel anything. It's as if I'm missing out on something and I don't know what it is.'

Offering him her hand, Kay smiled into his face. 'You need a boyfriend.'

He quickly pulled his hand away and stiffened. 'Thanks!' He was offended and hurt. 'I get enough of that back in Stepney. I don't expect it from you.'

'You're too sensitive, Terry. I didn't mean it the way you think. I meant . . . a friend, a real friend, someone who feels the same as you, so you can talk to him. You're not the only one with the problem!'

'Join a club for queers, you mean?'

'No! Oh, I don't know. There must be someone you can talk to. Get advice?'

'You must be dreaming. You saw how quickly Ray went, once he knew. And he's bin my mate for years. There's no one else, only you.'

'And I'll always be 'ere, but I just thought . . .'

'Yeah, I know.' He wanted to end it.

'Hope I'm not disturbing anything?' Zacchi

appeared out of the darkness wearing a black baggy shirt tucked into his jeans.

'Zacchi! I wish you wouldn't creep up like that.'

'I don't creep. Just move around quietly.' His deep husky voice sent a shiver though Kay and when he sat down close to her she picked up a scent of the aromatic soap he used.

'Anyway,' Kay pushed her hands through her long hair, 'it's time you two met. This is Terry, my best friend. We were just trying to sort life out.' She spoke differently from her usual way, slightly more adult and worldly.

Zacchi had noticed her make-up and new image and smiled inwardly. He preferred her face clean and without that sickly smell of perfumed greasepaint. 'You'll have a job,' he smiled, 'life's not unlike the river – it'll flow the way it wants to.'

'Zacchi writes poetry,' Kay said proudly.

'So do I,' Terry said with a touch of jealousy in his voice. 'Well, songs anyway. Same thing in a way, words with music instead of silence.'

'You must 'ave 'eard Terry playing his guitar?'

''Course I have. Always listen to the singing that goes on. Where will your people gather once this is over? No more camp-fires.' Zacchi directed his question at her almost as if Terry wasn't there.

Kay couldn't help smiling to herself. Life had a

funny way of repeating itself. She was in the middle again, just like at home, when her mum and dad spoke to each other through her, after one of their rows which were always followed by long silences. But these two boys were her closest friends – she would get them talking before long.

Laura, Liz and a few of the other women sat around a fire outside Laura's hut and sang, together with other small groups gathered around other camp-fires. This time it was Johnny Ray's 'The Little White Cloud'.

'I think we should 'ave stopped 'em, Liz,' Milly said with a touch of worry. 'A couple of whiskies and my George suffers from a personality clash – with 'imself.'

'Ha!' Liz chuckled, 'have you ever managed to stop that lot doing what they want? Anyway, it's about time Wright 'eard what the men think.'

'But he won't hear that, will he,' Laura chimed in, 'he'll hear what they've got to say after a night's boozing. Time they've finished, he'll thank 'is lucky stars it *is* the last time. They should 'ave left things be.'

'If we all felt like that, Laura, you know who'd be ruling Britain now, don't yer?'

'Oh, Liz!' Laura laughed. 'You're not honestly

comparing that beery lot with the king's army and government?'

'Queen's army, Laura. Coronation? We've got a queen now,' she said, proudly.

'And don't forget' – Liz was off on her own track – 'who the king's army consisted of! Most if not all of our men wore the uniform!'

A sudden cry from the Browns' hut took the women's attention. First Mrs Brown and then the children. It was obvious by the cries that Brown was lashing out at them.

'Oh, not agen!' Liz waited for a few seconds hoping it might stop, but it seemed to get worse. Standing up, she passed her glass of stout to Laura. 'I've 'ad just about enough of listening to them poor kids' cries.'

'Liz . . . wait till the men get back, let them sort it out.' Laura knew it was useless; Liz had that determined look in her eye. She sighed as Liz walked over to the Browns' hut. 'We'll give her a couple of minutes, then go over.' The other women nodded in agreement.

Standing outside the closed door, Liz braced herself: she could hear Brown's voice booming out.

'Lazy cow! I told you I wanted that button sewn on!'

She pushed the door open and glared at Brown,

who had his wife's arm twisted behind her back and was gripping her jaw. 'All right Brown, that's enough!'

Letting go of his wife and throwing her down on to the straw mattress, Brown moved closer to Liz. 'Do what?' he growled. 'Who the bloody hell do yer think you are, eh? This is my hut and you are not welcome, lady! Right? Now get out!'

Liz pointed her finger right into his face, and her eyes bore into his. 'You listen to me, you bag of bones. We've had to listen to your kids' cries for long enough.'

'My kids?' he grinned. 'Their cries?' He put one hand to his ear. 'I can't hear anyone crying. You must 'ave bin 'earing things, gal.'

Liz looked down at the four children huddled together on a bed, their eyes swollen from crying, their noses running. Each one was doing their best to keep quiet, but an uncontrollable sob escaped now and then. 'I stopped my brother from coming over and giving you the hiding of your life, but I swear blind, if you raise your hands to them kids or your missus one more time . . . I'll set the bloody lot of them on to yer; and I'll inform the Welfare when I get back to London!'

Taking Liz by complete surprise, Mrs Brown stood up and pushed her face up close. 'You do, and I'll set light to yer! He's got a temper, that's all. It's not his fault! When we want your help, we'll ask for it!'

'You don't 'ave to put up with this.' Liz was filled with compassion for the woman who, as far as she could tell, had to defend the swine for her own safety. She was probably too scared to speak out in case he set about her once Liz had gone. 'Look at your kids, they're terrified of 'im.'

'Sling your 'ook! And keep your nose out of our business.' The woman sounded convincing but Liz wasn't easily fooled.

'Throw 'im out. The men'll look after yer.' Liz knew she was treading on thin ice but she had to try.

'Out,' Mrs Brown almost spat at her. 'Out, out, out!' she chanted with her husband and children joining in, 'out, out, out!'

Once she was back round the fire, Liz wished she hadn't interfered. The pain in her chest was there again, the same as before. It made her feel as if she had swallowed a boiled sweet whole.

'You did your best, Liz.' Laura squeezed her hand.

The sound of the men returning lightened the mood. They were singing at the tops of their voices:

Six men went to mow,
Went to mow a meadow,
Six men, five men,
Four men, three men,
Two men, one man and his dog and a bottle
   of beer,
Went to mow a meadow . . .

'They sound 'appy enough. P'raps they did get their way and we'll all be back next year.' Laura was hopeful.

'That'd please you, Laura, wouldn't it?' Milly smiled knowingly.

''Course it would. Queen of the hop fields, me. Liz's gonna weave me a crown of red berries and Kent cobs tomorrow.' There was a carefree tone to her voice that came dangerously close to admitting she was the boss's lover. She could feel Liz's eyes boring into her, warning her not to let the night's drinking loosen her tongue.

As the men arrived, singing to their hearts' content, so they left, without stopping *en route*.

'Now where they goin'? Bert? Bert!' Liz screamed out.

'Hallo?'

'Come over 'ere, you dozy sod!'

'One of these days, Liz . . .' Laura warned.

259

'Beats me 'ow she gets away with it. Call my old man that and I'd get a black eye.'

Swaying from side to side, Bert staggered across and pushed his beery face forward. 'What now?'

'Well?' Liz waited for a report, but he just looked out through bleary eyes. 'What happened?'

'Eh?'

'Wright. Did you sort him out?'

'Er . . . yes and no.'

'What d'yer mean, yes and no?' Liz was trying not to laugh while the others were enjoying Bert's drunken state.

'What you bin giving 'er to drink, Laura? Keeps asking me questions.'

'I would leave now, Bert, if I was you, while you're still in one piece,' Laura teased.

Liz took a deep breath, then spoke very slowly so he would understand. 'When we left you in the pub, you were hollering about sorting Richard Wright out. Right?'

'Was we?' He thought about it for a second or two. 'Oh, yeah. But now . . . we're goin' over the bridge to get tomorrow's dinner.' He chuckled and winked at Liz. 'And . . . I'll find you a nice new-laid egg for your breakfast as well, Liz. Yeah?' He started to back away – he had to catch up with the others. 'And . . . I'll . . . chuck the plicken;

No! I'll . . . p-pluck the chicken!' Pleased with himself that he had consoled Lizzie and that she hadn't stopped him from joining up with the men again, he strolled away singing, 'Roll out the barrel'.

While Terry played his guitar and sang 'Summertime Blues', Kay and Zacchi lay on the grass, holding hands and gazing up at the stars. It was a clear night and Kay found herself wishing over and over again for time to stand still; Zacchi would be leaving her any second, he had to get back to check his charges. Almost as if he had read her thoughts, he turned to look at her. Sensing him admiring her face Kay felt herself blush.

'How long will you be here for?' Zacchi asked, his deep voice brushing against every nerve in her body. 'I might be able to slip away again.' He moved closer and lightly kissed her neck.

'As long as it takes,' she answered without thinking. She would have to go back to the huts soon – her Dad would be angry if she stayed out after midnight and it was already eleven-fifteen.

Kissing her lightly on the lips, Zacchi cupped her face. 'I'll stay for another ten minutes and then we'll have to say goodnight.' She loved it when he laid down the rules like that, especially since they were good, sensible rules. Left to herself, Kay knew deep down that she would be far more reckless and stay out later than she should.

'As much as I want to come back, I don't think I should.' His eyes were full of passion and love.

Finishing his song, Terry placed his guitar next to him and pulled his navy sweater over his head. 'I wonder 'ow the chicken stealers are getting on?' he giggled. 'I've never seen such a rowdy drunken bunch.'

'Oh, don't remind me. It's so embarrassing. Seeing your own dad creeping across the bridge like that, followed by his beery troop.'

'Jack! Jack – where the fuck are yer?' There was panic in Bert's voice – he had lost his way in the dark.

'Oh, Gawd,' Kay laughed, 'it's my uncle.' She stood up and waved her arms. 'They've gone across the bridge!' she yelled.

'Oh, right!' he shouted. 'What you doing out at this time of night, Kay?' Bert tried to sound sober and responsible. 'Should be in your cot.'

Zacchi and Terry fell back on the grass rocking with laughter. 'He did actually say *cot*, didn't he?' Zacchi asked.

'Yeah. He's well over the top.' Kay was worried he might fall into the river. She was aware

262

that his footsteps were unsteady as he crossed the wooden bridge.

'Rotten lot,' he mumbled aloud, 'they could 'ave waited.'

'I won't be a sec. I just wanna make sure he gets over that bridge in one piece.' Kay moved slowly towards her uncle.

'I s'pose I 'ad best get back,' Terry said. 'Unless you wanna hear another song.'

'Not unless it's one you've written yourself,' Zacchi answered, knowing full well that Terry was too shy to sing one of his own.

'No. Maybe tomorrow.'

'You should get used to singing your own words, if you want to make it as a songwriter.'

'I'm not exactly Gene Vincent. And I'm not aiming to be famous. I use words and music to release . . .' His words trailed off.

'You don't have to be ashamed. We don't choose the way we are.'

Taken aback by the revelation that Zacchi knew, and was OK about it, Terry was lost for words. 'Kay told you, then?' he said at last.

'Didn't have to. You should accept what you are.'

'You try telling that to the boys back in the East End.'

'Keep it to yourself then. Don't broadcast. No one really cares that much. They've got their own problems.' Zacchi turned on to his stomach and pulled at some grass. 'You could change the way you dress,' he said carefully. 'Try wearing black instead of bright colours.'

'Why should I?' Terry was indignant.

'Can't have it both ways. Either show people what you are and be proud of it, or stay anonymous. I could be like you for all you know.'

'It's just as well you're not,' he said. 'I think Kay's in love.'

'I know. And before you ask – yes, I am too.'

'She's only fifteen, you know.'

'You can stop worrying. I've no intention of seducing her.'

Terry stood up ready to go. 'You've only got a few weeks, then she'll be gone.'

'We'll see.' Zacchi was irritated by the obvious remark.

As Terry turned to go, Kay arrived, still amused at the antics of her uncle. 'Listen to that,' she giggled.

Bert was peeing into the river from the bridge and it seemed as if it would go on for ever. They could hear him mumbling to himself. 'Rotten lot. Can't wait for a man to 'ave a quick slash.'

'See you tomorrow,' Terry called back as he disappeared into the shadows.

Not wasting another second, Zacchi reached out and pulled Kay down on to the grassy bank, squeezing her soft body close to his.

'Fucking 'ell!' Bert's cry was followed by loud groaning.

Kay sat bolt upright, listening to his shouts and urgent footsteps as he ran across the bridge calling out for Jack.

'What's 'appened, Zacchi?'

'I've got a good idea,' he smiled, 'but there's nothing we can do about it.' He sat up and slowly shook his head. 'Come on, I'll walk you back to the huts.'

The drunken gaggle of men were creeping along by an overgrown hedge, by the side of the river, closing in on the farmyard, when Bert's distant calls stopped them.

'Shouldn't we wait for Bert?' one of the men asked.

More shouts from Bert could be heard as he approached. 'Wait! Don't go! Jack!'

'What's the silly bastard done now?' Jack grinned, shining his torch in Bert's direction.

'What's up, mate?'

'Give us your torch, Jack. Quick!' Bert said, writhing in pain.

Before Jack could think, Bert snatched the small silver-coloured torch from his hand and shone it on to his crotch. A couple of seconds passed while the men grasped the reason for the spotlight on Bert's dick. He'd caught it in his zip. A low chuckle from one of the men started the others off and before long they were howling with laughter.

'You'd best take the torch and go back, mate.' Jack tried to compose himself. 'That looks serious.' Then, unable to resist, added: 'Get Lizzie to rub a bit of marge on it.' Another outburst from the men.

'You can flippin' well laugh. It's swelling by the minute!' Bert limped slowly away. 'You and your sodding zips, Jack. I knew I should 'ave stuck to buttons!'

To Bert, the short distance back across the bridge and over the meadow to the common seemed to go on for ever. When he finally reached the huts and realized how many people he would have to pass, he pulled his jacket down with both hands and received some strange looks as he hobbled through towards his hut.

Laura, Liz and some of the other women were enjoying a cosy time by the fire singing 'We'll meet again' when one of them noticed Bert. 'Looks like your old man's hurt himself, Liz.'

Swivelling her head, Liz frowned. 'Oh, what now?'

'You'd best go and see, Liz. He's having trouble walking.'

'Liz! The hut! Now!' came the urgent request from Bert.

'I'll kill our Jack for this! I told 'im to go without Bert!' She stood up, knocking her chair over, and marched towards the hut.

'How come your Jack's always to blame, Laura?' Milly asked.

'Need you ask?' She was ready to blame him too.

'At least he's got a bit of spirit.' Milly defended the man she had always had a soft spot for. 'More than I can say for most of that lot. He's a bloody good laugh – and don't we all need it?'

Peals of laughter suddenly erupted from Liz while screams of pain escaped from Bert.

'You'd best go and see what's 'appened, Laura.'

'I'm not sure I want to.'

They waited a few seconds, watching the hut door for any sign of action. When Liz emerged, doubled over with laughter, there was a sigh of relief all round.

'At least Bert's quietened down.' Laura picked up Liz's chair and pushed it firmly into the ground.

'God works in mysterious ways all right,' Liz chuckled. 'Got his dick caught in 'is zip.' The women winced at the thought of his pain. 'When I told 'im' – she could hardly speak for laughing – 'that it was punishment for buying a tart a drink, he' – she could hardly get her words out – 'he held his soft, bruised little willy' – another burst of laughter – 'and said: "This 'as only ever been for you, Lizzie."' The uproar from the women could be heard throughout the common.

Later that night there were sounds of a shotgun piercing the silence, as Jack and his thieving friends ran for all they were worth, carrying a squawking chicken each. The sound of their footsteps racing across the wooden bridge echoed through the quiet night.

'Shouldn't we break their necks, Jack?' A panic-stricken voice came from the back of the race.

'No way I'm stopping now! Just keep going!' Jack yelled.

Once back at the huts and having regained their breath, one of the men made a quick, clean job of breaking the necks of the five chickens while Jack waved his arms in protest. 'That's a cruel way of doing it!' he cried. 'There must be a kinder way!' Jack had trouble with people killing spiders as well.

'If you know another way, Jack, do yours yerself!' The man had no time for sentiment. He had worked in the meat market since he was thirteen and knew what was best for the fowls. 'But get on with it! Bloody squawking'll bring the farmer right to our doorsteps!'

Jack had a firm grip on the bird but when it worked a wing free and flapped around his face, he screamed out and let it go. 'Someone give me an axe!' he yelled, chasing the chicken around the common, desperate to put an end to its loud harsh cries.

When the implement finally arrived, Jack took seven swings at the chicken before he lopped its head off with one clean blow. Dropping the axe to the floor he stood rooted to the spot as the fowl carried on running – in his direction. His long legs strode out as he ran around pursued by the chicken with no head. Jack's terrified screams brought people out of their huts and gave them the best show they had seen in years.

Julia awoke at the crack of dawn to find Richard asleep on an armchair in the lounge, a half-empty bottle of brandy by his side. His usually tanned face looked ashen. She gazed sadly down at him as it dawned on her that she still loved him, and that the last thing she wanted was to lose her man.

She walked into the kitchen and filled the electric kettle, remembering that she had smoked the last of her cigarettes after the mob had left the night before. She berated herself for being so absent-minded as to forget to add them to her shopping list. She poured a little hot water into the teapot and swirled it until her hands could feel the china warming. She stood motionless, caught up in her thoughts.

It had been a strange week and, thinking back to the many events that had taken place, she wondered if she had been wise to spy on Richard. Maybe she should have just waited for the affair to come to a natural end. Tipping the water into the sink she reached out for the packet of tea.

'I'm sorry, Julia.' Richard's quiet voice coming out of the blue would normally have startled her but she was in a very calm non-reactive mood.

'I didn't want to hurt you.' His words encircled her, almost as if they needed permission to enter her mind. She poured boiling water on to the tea-leaves. The fight which had been in her the previous night seemed to have ebbed away. Everything seemed distant.

'Why did you do it?' Julia could hear the words, yet it seemed as if someone else inside her mind had posed the question. She didn't care. It was easier that way. She didn't have to think.

'I don't know,' he said softly.

Slowly she turned to face him as he lowered his head, avoiding her eyes.

'There's no excuse for what I've done and you gave me no reason to stray, not really,' he continued.

Julia thought he looked a sorry sight in his crumpled clothes.

'My only excuse is that I do remember feeling out of it when the twins came along.'

She watched as he searched his pockets in vain for a handkerchief. Pulling open a drawer she handed him a small white cotton napkin. She smiled at the way he opened it and covered his face, dabbing at his tears. He looked like a child that had been punished. Without glancing at her, he reached out and pulled her close and kissed the top of her head. She had seen him do the same to his favourite dog. Maybe he would give her a bone?

'You and the children are what matters most,' he murmured.

She thought that was rather a nice thing to say. She thought about the twins and wondered if they were enjoying school. She could feel Richard stroke her and pat her back. Her mind flashed to the ham bone in the larder.

'I'll make it up to you, I promise.' He gripped her by her shoulders and looked gravely into her face. 'Things will work out, you'll see.'

She felt he needed comforting. She would tell him not to worry, that she would love him and take care of him. 'There's a ham bone in the larder,' she heard herself say, 'with quite a bit of ham on it.'

She watched as the expression on his face changed. It reminded her of when she used to make Plasticine people. She could, in seconds, change a smiling face into a sad one, or an angry boy into a silly girl. Richard was now sporting an expression of worry and fear. This puzzled her; he should be smiling. She was being good. She was making him a pot of tea. Yes; that's what she had been doing . . .

She looked at the teapot. She must put some tea in and then some boiling water. She lifted the lid; it was already three-quarters full of hot liquid but that didn't matter. She shovelled in another spoonful of tea, poured in boiling water and watched as the steaming liquid spilled over and on to the kitchen surface and down to the floor, soaking her silk dressing-gown and making her legs feel numb.

Richard started to shout; all kinds of unstrung words were floating out of his mouth and around the room, finally forming a diagonal sentence which seemed to be asking her something. Some of the words were louder than others.

'Don't bother with all that, Richard,' she could hear herself saying, 'don't be bothering with it.'

She felt like a rag doll, the way he was suddenly throwing her about, pulling off her dressing-gown . . . why was he in such a hurry? Why had he shoved her down on to a kitchen chair like that?

She watched him as if she were watching a film. He was filling and refilling a jug with cold water. One jugful after another of freezing cold water, and throwing it over her very hot body. Was this a punishment? Had she been bad? Richard didn't look angry.

She would shout at him, try to snap him out of it. 'Don't be bothering with all that, Richard,' she murmured, 'it isn't worth it.'

He swept her up into his strong arms and laid her naked body gently down on the cool silky sofa in the lounge. Then he rushed up the stairs and came down again carrying a wet cotton sheet and a big soft pillow. He reminded her of a doctor, the way he wrapped the sheet around her legs, draped her winter shawl around her shoulders and placed the pillow under her head. It made her feel very sleepy. She began to drift off as Richard dialled a number. He sounded terribly urgent about something. He was asking for a doctor or an ambulance. Someone had scalded herself with boiling water and quite badly, by the sound of it. Julia felt an electric buzz sweep through her body . . . her skin felt strange. The cold electric feeling reminded her of something. It reminded her of pain.

'Will you promise me one thing, Richard? Will you promise me you won't ever speak to that woman again?'

Replacing the receiver, Richard looked sadly down at her. 'An ambulance is on its way. You'll need to have those burns looked at.'

'I said will you promise me?' Her mood was already changing and he saw a flash of anger back in her eyes.

'Yes, I promise.' He dropped down into an armchair and hoped that would be the last time he would have to lie to Julia.

The woman he loved deserved better than that. He would have to see Laura, to talk about their obligations to their families.

The rain pounding on to the corrugated tin roof brought Laura slowly out of her sleep. She awoke with a strange nagging feeling in her stomach and searched her mind for anything she had to worry about. Nothing presented itself and the feeling left her. Instead of dragging herself from the warm, straw-filled mattress she turned over, curled up and enjoyed the snug feeling that had taken over, indulging in the first thoughts of the day.

She imagined herself enjoying the fresh air of Kent without the hardships. Richard's house was bound to have a guest room or two, a second bathroom. She tried to see Liz in her mind's eye, sitting at the same table as Richard. Liz and Bert together, in one of those spare rooms, soaking up some of the luxury. It would be good for Kay to have them there.

The sound of a car pulling on to the common snapped Laura out of her fantasy. Judging by the darkness, she guessed it must be somewhere around five a.m. The rustling sound of straw and garbled words from Kay caused Laura to lie still. She didn't want to wake her daughter so early on a Sunday morning.

'Is that our car, Mum?' Kay mumbled sleepily.

Laughing inwardly, Laura guessed that the noise of an engine had drifted into Kay's dreams. She carefully lifted herself so she could lean forward and look at her. She was right, Kay was sound asleep. For a few seconds she felt sad that she and her daughter would probably never sleep nose to toes again after this year.

The quiet closing of the car door outside evoked

a curiosity in Laura which she found slightly disturbing. Why would someone be pulling on to the common so early? Crawling carefully to the window, leaving a gap between her and Kay, she pulled herself up and peered out of the tiny window. Black clouds were drifting into the distance and the rain had dwindled to a fine shower.

The sight of the black police car filled her with horror. There were two plain-clothes officers and one in uniform, climbing out of the Wolseley. They were splitting up and going in different directions. A sudden wave of panic swept through her. The chickens! Surely the owner hadn't sent the police to search for his livestock?

The warm feeling she had been savouring for those few moments turned to dread. What would Richard think of her if he knew she had stolen property hidden away under the bed? She was no less a thief than those who had dragged the birds from their owner. A sudden short, sharp tapping on the wall from Liz's hut next door told Laura that her sister-in-law wanted a quiet word.

'What's going on?' Kay was half asleep.

'It's nothing, love. Go back to sleep. A car just pulled up, that's all.'

'I thought it was Sunday,' she sighed.

'It is, love. Just someone's weekend visitor, that's

all.' Laura was worrying more by the minute. She couldn't help feeling they were there to find something more valuable than a few dead chickens. She peered out of the window again and got a good look at one of the plain-clothes officers. 'I thought as much; it's not poultry they're after. They're from Bow Street station and I bet I know why they're here. Bangle watches and whisky. I'll kill your father!'

'Dad didn't pinch 'em, did he?' Kay was suddenly awake.

''Course he didn't. Just passed 'em on for someone, that's all. But that's enough. More than enough.' She climbed down from the bed and pulled her slacks on, then her wellington boots and finally her swagger coat to cover her half-dressed state.

'What yer gonna do?' Kay was sick with worry.

'Warn Liz for a start. She 'asn't taken that watch off since Bert bought it. Goes to bed in it!'

'But Mum . . .' Kay was close to tears. 'What if they catch yer?'

'No crime in 'aving an early cuppa with my sister-in-law. I only hope your father 'asn't kept any back, that's all.' She stroked Kay's hair back off her face. 'Stop worrying. They 'ave to get up early to catch the Armstrongs' out.'

'They did,' Kay murmured as she pulled herself

up from her bed and tried frantically to open the window.

'Come away from the window!' Laura hissed. 'You'll never shift it in any case, it's paint-bound.'

'I think one of 'em's coming over, and Aunt Liz is out there setting the fire!'

With trembling hands, Laura unbolted the door and pushed it open and was just about to call out to Liz, but one of the officers was almost at the fire with another following close behind. Without thinking, Laura stepped back into the hut and grabbed her own watch and threw it into a far corner under the bed.

'You gonna go out there, Mum?' Kay pulled the bedcovers back ready to climb out.

'No.' Laura's mind was going ten to the dozen. 'And you get right back down under those covers, Kay! If they come in 'ere, pretend you're asleep.'

'But what about Aunt Liz?' she cried.

'She won't want me out there yet. Knowing Liz, she'll be spinning them a convincing story and I might just throw her off track. I'll give it a couple more minutes.' She opened a narrow drawer in the small pine table and grabbed a packet of Weights. Striking a match she turned to Kay. 'My one and only vice,' she smiled.

'Can I 'ave one?'

Laura's jaw dropped; she could hardly believe her ears. 'That was meant to be a joke?'

'There's a first time for everything, Mum, and this seems like a good time to try it out.'

'Kay . . . ?' Laura was so upset and angry she could hardly speak. 'If I catch you smoking . . .'

'I was only kidding.' Kay was sorry she had given her mum something else to worry about. 'I'm surprised at you though. A bit of a dark 'orse on the quiet, ain't yer?' she grinned.

Deciding against the smoke, Laura began to get properly dressed; she would have a wash-down later.

Liz placed some firewood on to screwed-up newspaper while the two men stood over her. 'No sense in wasting hot ashes,' she said, making an excuse for being out so early. In truth she wanted to keep them out of the hut and away from the three chickens under her bed. Two of them were destined for London, a gift for Bert's sisters. 'This fire is all we've got to cook our joint on.' She lit the paper and within seconds the wood was crackling, sending sparks flying.

'That's a very nice piece of jewellery adorning your arm, Liz.' Babyface, as he was known in the East End, grinned at her. Liz slipped the handle of the kettle on to the hook which hung from the iron crosspole and pursed her lips, realizing too late that it wasn't chickens they were after. She couldn't believe how stupid she'd been, forgetting about the watch like that! She had been wearing it non-stop and it had almost become part of her. 'A little something you picked up cheap, was it? Or are you gonna tell me it fell off a lorry?' He was daring her not to come up with corny lies.

Liz smiled into his face. 'It's funny you should say that . . .'

'Oh, come on! You know better than that.'

'I found it lying on a pavement,' she sniffed. 'Not a mark on it neither.' She thrust her arm forward so he could get a closer look. 'And it keeps bloody good time 'an all.'

'Well,' grinned Babyface, 'let's hope that Georgie Smith keeps good time too, 'cos that's what he'll be getting, and lots of it.'

'Who?' Liz looked innocent.

'Come on, let's 'ave it over and done with. Then we can sit round your lovely fire and 'ave a cuppa.'

'I'll let you borrow it,' she reasoned, 'but I wanna receipt.'

'Yeah, all right. How's Bert?'

'Wake 'im up and ask, but don't mention his dick,' she chuckled while sliding the bangle watch over her hand. 'I s'pose your friend'll want a cup as well? And the other one, wherever he is?'

'I'd love one, thanks.' The young man smiled shyly at Liz, still shocked at the remark about her husband's private parts. He was obviously a new recruit.

'God, this thing's tight,' Liz said, forcing the watch over her knuckles. Then with a sudden good push, it flew off and into the fire.

'That wasn't clever, Liz.'

'No, it was bloody careless! I loved that little watch. First time in my life I've ever found anything, and I 'ave to go and lose it like that. Into the flames.' She was close to tears.

'Not to worry.' He dragged the blackened watch out with a twig and held it up. 'We're not looking for fingerprints. We've got enough to go on. And it's not your brother we're after. We know Jack's only a small-time fence. We need blokes like 'im around, they lead us to the source.' He walked away to the car carrying the twig and smoking watch.

'You won't forget my receipt!' she called after him. His laughter rang through the silent common.

'Kettle's boiling.' The younger inspector was hopeful.

'More than my life's worth, son.' She smiled

bravely. He had a nice face and a lot to learn. Covering the handle of the kettle with a thick pad, she lifted it and made her way to Laura's hut.

Once inside, she quickly put the kettle on the table and grabbed the back of a kitchen chair. Laura pushed another behind Liz and gently eased her down into it. Liz's pale face reminded Laura of the other times when her sister-in-law had those so-called heartburn attacks.

'I wouldn't mind a glass of water, Laura,' she managed to say in between the short, sharp pains.

'What's the police doing 'ere?' Bert appeared in the doorway, looking still half asleep.

Sipping her water, Liz kept her face turned away from Bert. He would see in an instant that she was in pain. 'They've come for Georgie Smith,' she said.

Bert screwed up his face and peered at Liz. 'You all right, mate? You look terrible . . . Liz?'

'I'm all right, Bert!'

'You sure?'

Pulling his attention away from Liz, Laura pushed a mug of tea into Bert's hand. 'I don't s'pose Jack's showed 'is face yet?'

'It's a bit early, Laura,' Bert said, always ready to defend his mate.

'We're up!' She sounded angry, and was, more

with herself than anyone else. She felt now that it had been the wrong decision, not going out to Liz when Kay told her to. Her sister-in-law could probably have done with a bit of moral support. Laura had got it wrong again.

'Listen to that,' Bert grinned, 'if Jack's own snoring don't wake 'im up, I'm sure nothing else will. No wonder you make 'im sleep in a 'ut by himself, Laura.' There was an awkward silence.

'They weren't interested in Jack,' she managed to say, as the pain eased off. 'George Smith's the man. You've gotta 'and it to 'im. First he nicks the stuff, then passes it on to someone else who passes it on to Jack who passes it back to Georgie who sells it on as if he's just another fence. That way he gets 'is original price plus a bit on top.'

'Didn't take you long to work that out, did it, Liz?' Laura chuckled, giving her sister-in-law a quick once-over. Liz looked a bit easier than she had a few minutes earlier but she was still far from well and Laura wondered whether she should go against her wishes and tell Bert or Jack about the attacks. She could see why Liz wouldn't want to worry Bert; he was a fusspot when it came to her welfare, and the pair of them were so close that Laura couldn't help wondering if Bert had twigged it and was trying not to look concerned for Liz's sake.

'I'm just gonna pay a visit to the throne, Liz. If Jack shows his face, tell him there's tea in the pot.' She would think about Liz and her state of health during her short walk to and from the lavatory.

It had been a bad start to what was usually the best day of the week – Sunday. The constant rain during the night had drenched the grass and some muddy patches were like mini-swamps, but now the sun was up and in full glory, with only a few wispy white clouds drifting across the light blue sky. This was Laura's favourite time of day, when hardly anyone was about and the only sounds came from the birds.

Carefully making her way through a gap in the hedge around the cottage, Laura heard the distant ringing of a bell from an ambulance; from what she could make out, it was heading in the direction of the farmhouse. She stood for a while until the ambulance had come to a stop but couldn't be sure of its destination. The tiny nagging worry that first woke her that morning was back and growing by the second. She felt a strong desire to make her way to the farmhouse, but her common sense stopped her. She had heard that young Brianny was going out with the parlourmaid, so she would ask him to call and find out what had happened. It would cost her half a crown but it would be worth it to put her mind at rest.

By the time Laura returned to her hut, Liz was looking slightly better and Jack had joined them. 'Was that an ambulance, Laura?' Liz asked.

'I think so, yeah.' She hoped the worry she felt inside didn't show in her voice. 'I'm not sure where it was headed, though.'

'Police car and ambulance in one morning. Not bad, eh?' Liz mused. 'Be the fire brigade next.'

Pulling a towel from the rail on the door, Laura wiped the splashes of mud from the backs of her legs, wondering if she might get a chance to see Brianny once the police had gone. Once again she felt Jack's eyes on her and felt embarrassed, not knowing quite how to handle the moment. They caught each other's eyes, but not a flicker of a smile passed between them.

Jack turned to Bert and grinned. 'How's your dick this morning?'

'As good as yours'll ever be.' He knew that it would take days to live it down so had his answer ready, knowing he would be asked the same question many times that day.

Liz glanced out of the hut, grinning from ear to ear. She thought it would be a bit much for poor old Bert if he caught her mocking him as well. 'Young Brianny's on 'is way over,' she said indifferently.

Brianny was in a thunderous mood. 'They've only

gone and nicked Dad, ain't they! You should be out there, Jack, sorting it! They're your fucking watches!'

'And the whisky?' Laura found herself speaking for Jack.

'Selling it on for a mate!' he snapped.

Liz pulled herself up from the chair, turned to Brianny and ran her hand through his hair. 'Listen cock; I know it's not nice seeing them cart your old man away, but they wouldn't 'ave come this far if they didn't 'ave enough on 'im. If you don't know exactly what's bin goin' on, wait till your dad finds time to tell yer. If you know, then take my advice and keep stum. He's probably covered 'is tracks well enough to get off.'

'Someone's grassed on 'im, Liz, ain't they?' The boy was close to tears.

'They've probably bin watching 'im for months, son,' Bert added.

'Yeah, well, that's all very well, Bert, but I still think Jack should be out 'ere, owning up. We was just doing 'im a favour, then this 'as to go an' 'appen. And we get caught with the effing lot!'

'Oi, oi, oi.' Jack was losing his temper. 'Watch your tongue in front of the ladies.' He glared at Brianny and then relaxed. 'Now then. If your old man's nicked, he's nicked. It's the risk you take. Now stop whining and get back there, and listen.'

Brianny wasn't going to be appeased so easily. 'What about the other cashmere jumper, then, eh? You know, the large size? How long d'yer want me to hang on to that for? Till she's 'ad the bastard?'

Caught off guard, Jack was lost for words but quickly recovered and moved closer to Brianny. 'Move yourself away from this 'ut before I give you a bloody good 'iding. And don't think I won't pull your trousers down to do it!'

Backing off, Brianny pushed his chin forward defiantly. 'You think you're King Shit, don't yer! Well there's someone else bin sitting on your throne! Ask your old woman who it is!' He turned on his heels and half-ran across the common, back to his hut.

Laura shifted nervously from one foot to the other.

'Oh, Gawd . . .' Liz broke the silence. 'They're taking Georgie away! Bleeders! Can't leave us alone.'

'Oh, do me a favour, Liz!' Jack yelled. 'He's bin slipping their net for as long as I can remember.' His anger arose more from Brianny's remark about Laura than anything else. It was the second time the news had been thrown at him in the past twenty-four hours and he didn't know how to deal with it. 'I'll go round there,' he said, more quietly, 'see Milly and calm young Brianny down while I'm at it. Poor little sod don't know what's hit 'im.' He half-turned his head and looked into Laura's guilty face. 'Wouldn't mind a bacon sandwich when I get back.' He walked slowly away, his head held not quite as high as usual.

'I dunno,' Liz murmured, 'we ain't bin up an hour and look at the muck that's hit the fan.'

'I think we've got some talking to do, Liz,' Laura said gravely.

'If it's anything to do with what Brianny said about Jack and the cashmere jumper, Laura, ask him yerself. I've 'ad enough.' She pulled herself up from her chair. 'I'm gonna lie down for a while.' The frown on her face said it all.

There was a strained atmosphere between Laura and Jack during the rest of the morning. Laura imagined that her husband's sulky mood was brought on by the fact that his little secret was out. She knew him well enough to see that the expression on his face when Brianny asked questions about Jack's bastard was more from guilt than anger. It shouldn't have affected her the way it had because her plans for the future, whether Richard was a part of them or not, hadn't included Jack. As far as she was concerned, once Kay was sixteen and mature enough to accept a break in the marriage, Laura was going to ask Jack whether he wanted to leave or if he would prefer her to find somewhere else to live.

Spooning the sizzling juice and spitting hot fat over her pot-roast chicken, Laura realized, after asking herself several times that morning, why she was feeling so low. Another woman was carrying Jack's child and it hurt. It hurt so much she couldn't think straight. Couldn't think of anything else but him holding a tiny baby boy. She wondered if things would have been different if she had turned to him after their tragedy instead of cutting herself off from love. He hadn't been the only one she screened herself from; her treasured Kay had received the same treatment as had her parents, her family and friends. She remembered how much she had wanted to scream at all of them to leave her alone until she could bear to face everyday living without her baby. She had needed time before she had dared to begin to feel again.

She placed the lid on the blue enamel casserole and wiped away her tears. There was no one to blame but herself. She had allowed too much time to pass by, nine years ago; she had lived in her imaginary bubble for so long that she couldn't pierce the thick, clear globe that she had made her prison. Not until Richard came along and made that first tiny slit which had turned into a skylight through which she had escaped from her sanctuary and back into the world; his world, a world of warmth and love.

'Smells good.' Jack's sudden intrusion into Laura's thoughts startled her.

'Let's hope the aroma doesn't reach the owner.' She spoke in a quiet tired voice.

'Could always invite him round for a taste.' Jack was trying his best to make conversation but still he managed to fuel her anger.

'Brianny Smith calmed down yet?' she asked deliberately.

'Yeah. He's all right. Slipped him a little treat. That put a smile on 'is face.' Jack grinned.

'Sounds like a bribe.'

'Leave off, Laura. Bribe! His old man's guilty and he knows it. I just wanted to stop him running around like a blue-arsed fly. Feel sorry for the poor little sod.'

Laura stood up and looked him straight in the eye. 'That's not what I meant!' A few seconds ticked by. 'Who's having your bastard, then?'

Drawing breath he looked away. 'Oh.' He sucked on his bottom lip. 'That.'

'Yes. That.'

He looked at her, tilting his head to one side. 'I didn't think you was interested in what I got up to.' His face was full of remorse but still she could feel nothing but anger.

Dragging her kitchen chair closer to the fire and away from where Jack was standing she sat down and pulled an old green baize shopping bag closer to her. 'Pass me that knife,' she snapped.

'Eh?' Jack's voice was suddenly full of worry. 'What for?'

'Peel these apples, what else?' She reached into the bag and pulled out a large cooking apple. 'So who's the cashmere for, then?' She snatched the knife from him and began to peel away the thick yellow-green skin.

'I was keeping 'em for Christmas . . . but now that Brianny's opened his big mouth, I might as well let you and Kay 'ave yours now.'

'I was talking about the large size!'

Jack took out his tobacco tin and placed a roll-up between his lips. 'It's for a friend,' he said, flicking back the top of his Zippo and lighting his cigarette.

Laura carved a bruise from the apple. 'The pregnant one?'

'Yes. The pregnant one,' he snapped: she was beginning to rattle him at last.

She cut the apple in quarters and dropped the pieces into a saucepanful of cold water. 'How long?'

'Three months.' Angry that she was forcing him to talk about it, he chewed at the inside of his cheek – a habit Laura used to try and get him to break.

'How long has it been going on?' She emphasized the word 'long'.

'Years. On and off.' He tried to sound casual about it; that was a mistake. She felt like punching him.

'Does it matter, for Christ's sake!'

'Yes!' Her heart was beating faster by the second and she could feel tears of anger welling up behind her eyes.

'Four years.' He emphasized the word 'four'.

'And were there any more before that?' She spat the words out.

'Yes! Several! And over a period of nine years!'

She threw the second apple down and glared at him. Then, slowly rising, she moved in. 'You slept with someone else before our baby had been gone twelve months? So much for your grieving! How could you make love to someone else while I was still in black?'

'Well, what did you expect me to do?' His eyes were full of fire and resentment. 'There wasn't much in the way of comfort coming from you at the time! What d'yer think I was made of – stone?'

Laura raised her right hand and moved in a little closer, her breathing showing every sign of uncontrolled fury.

'And you can stop pointing that knife . . .' He lowered his voice and backed off.

'I'm not just pointing it, Jack. It's aimed right at your heart!'

'Put it down, Laura,' he said reasonably, 'don't be a silly gel . . .'

She moved in closer.

'Back off, Laura . . . we don't want any accidents.'

'I don't need knives!' She hurled it to the ground. 'Not when I've got fists!' She pulled her right arm back and aimed it forward for all she was worth, her punch landing on his jaw.

'You swine!' she yelled, not caring that her tears were pouring down like a waterfall. 'You lying, cheating swine!' She punched his chest once, then twice, and again and again, cursing him while he just stood there and took it – almost as if it was what he wanted. 'I hate you!' she cried, 'I hate you! I hate you! I hate you!'

Inside her darkened hut, Liz lay on her bed waiting for the tight pains in her chest to ease. She could hear Laura crying and throwing abuse at Jack. She smiled weakly – at least they were talking again.

*   *   *

Early that evening, when it was time for Jack and Bert to make their way back to London, Laura slammed about in the hut, deliberately busying herself with chores which didn't necessarily need attending to. The last thing she wanted was to be outside, having to go through the motions of waving off her husband as if there were nothing wrong. She had done that many times before to keep up appearances, but those days were at an end and she didn't care how many people knew her marriage was over. She sprinkled Ajax on to the yellow Fablon which covered her small kitchen table and rubbed, not caring if she washed away the pattern of tiny white stars.

'I'll have to go, Laura, Bert's getting the 'ump.' How long Jack had been standing in the doorway was a mystery. She wished he could hear her thoughts. 'What d'yer want me to do, then?' He spoke as if the world and all its problems were on his shoulders.

'About what?'

'You know what I'm talking about.'

She stopped working on the table, keeping her back to him, and inhaled slowly. 'What do you expect me to say? Bring her round to meet the family?'

'I said I'd give Patsy an answer this week. What shall I tell 'er?'

'Do what you want.' Laura rubbed a dry cloth over the surface of the table, doing her best to keep control of her emotions. 'You've always done what you wanted in the past – why change now?'

He shrugged his shoulders and sighed. 'In other words you won't be sorry to see me go.' He was on the edge of tears.

'If you expect me to talk you out of it . . .'

'I'm asking you! Do you want me to go?'

She turned to look at him and slowly shook her head. 'It's just like you to try and corner me. Turn everything around as if I'm the one who's making this final move. God, you're crafty!'

A silence fell between them as they fought against their tears. The sound of Bert's impatient short sharp toots on the hooter helped in a strange way. Jack could vent his anger in another direction.

'For Christ's sake, Bert! Give us a couple of minutes will yer!' Jack turned back to Laura and lowered his voice. 'I'll come back next weekend. I want to tell Kay myself . . .' He was almost whispering.

'Do what you think best.' Laura could hear her voice cracking, she swallowed hard, forcing back her tears. There would be time enough for those once he was gone.

Jack slowly backed away, muttering distorted words of reassurance that things would turn out for the best in the end, and about what a useless husband he had been.

Once he was out of sight, Laura heard him call out to Liz, doing his best not to sound too choked. 'See you next week, Lizzie!' She heard the cab door slam and the lorry pull away. Dropping on to a chair she covered her face and sobbed.

Maybe Jack would get the son he had been pining for.

Eleven

Later that evening, just as the sun was setting, Liz relaxed on an easy chair outside her hut writing a letter to her son, David. This was the first time she had corresponded with him and she was surprised to find how easy it was. Why she was writing was another matter. She was suddenly missing her only child; she had found herself reminiscing about the early days when he was a little boy, enjoying it all over again. She had woken up that morning having dreamt about him, with an overwhelming desire to have him close. To hug him. To study his lovely face. She felt almost as if time was running out and that they should be together. Her mind was full of worry that he might be either ill or in some kind of trouble.

Liz also felt the need to talk to someone about Laura and Jack, having overheard their conversation earlier. Up until then, she had believed that they would patch things up and everything would go back to the way it was when the couple had been so much in love. It hadn't occurred to her that they would finalize things so quickly. She hadn't seen Laura since the men had left and could understand why her sister-in-law needed some time alone.

Liz was scribbling away when Kay appeared, looking flushed, with one hand gripping the gathered hem of her mauve-and-white floral cotton dress, forming a makeshift carrier for the apples she had just picked.

Arriving by her aunt's side, out of breath and looking decidedly anxious, Kay looked over her shoulder.

'What you looking so nervous about?' Liz asked.

'We got chased out of the orchard.' Kay tried to catch her breath. 'I kept hold of these though,' she grinned, 'for toffee-apples.'

Liz couldn't help smiling at her niece. 'What we gonna do with you, eh? One minute you're acting as if you've grown up too quick, and the next you're like a six-year-old. You shouldn't go round showing your legs off like that, Kay,' she carefully advised, wishing she didn't have to. If she had her way, Kay could act like a kid for as long as she wanted – it was other people and their narrow minds who were the problem.

'Aunt Liz! I've just bin chased out of the orchard! By one of Wright's men. He had a gun! And he nearly caught us . . .'

'Us?' Liz narrowed her eyes and watched Kay's face. She could read her niece like a book.

'Me and Terry,' she lied.

'Oh, yeah?' Liz raised her head slightly to watch as Mrs Brown made her way towards them. 'Looks like we've got company. Go and sling them bloody apples under my bed. Give me a few minutes with this dozy cow and then come back out. I wanna word with you, young lady.'

Sheepishly, Mrs Brown stood in front of Liz, her head bowed. 'I was wondering if you 'ad a minute . . . ?'

'What d'yer want, Mrs Brown?' After the rude behaviour of the woman and her family the evening before, Liz had no time for polite conversation.

'When you came over . . .' She looked exhausted and not far away from a nervous breakdown, 'I had to defend 'im. I daren't say a word against 'im. He'd kill me! I know it's not easy for people to understand, but when he's nice . . . when he's normal . . . he's loving and kind.'

'Yeah.' Liz couldn't help feeling sorry for the woman. 'And after the Lord Mayor's show comes the muck-cart. One of these days he's gonna do some real damage.' Liz pulled out her little blue tin. 'Look at yer! Skinny as a rake from worry.' She pinched some snuff between her thumb and forefinger and pushed it into each nostril. 'What d'yer want me to do? Have a word with our Jack or sort something out when we get back to London?' Liz could feel the pain in her chest again and wondered if there *was* a boiled sweet inside her which would never shift.

'I think he needs help.' Mrs Brown rubbed her forehead. 'Your Jack giving 'im an 'iding won't make things any better. Probably worse if anyfing.'

'All right. We'll sort something out with the Welfare when we get back.' Liz struggled against the tightening pain.

'They won't put 'im away, will they?'

'I doubt it. Now get back to your kids. They need your loving more than any of the others on this common.'

'You won't say anything to the others . . . ?'

Liz rolled her eyes and slowly shook her head. The woman should know better than that, but as far as Liz could see she was in no fit state to think clearly.

'Thanks,' Mrs Brown murmured and walked slowly away.

'What was all that about?' Kay asked, as she brought another chair out of Liz's hut and sat down.

'Never you mind.' Taking a long slow breath, Liz

began to feel easier. 'Now then miss – keep away from orchards and gypsies! And don't look at me like that. I wasn't born yesterday.'

'He's really nice, Aunt Liz.' Kay's voice was full of love.

'I didn't say he wasn't. I just don't like the way you go all moony-eyed when you see him. And if you do creep away when I'm not looking, keep both legs in one stocking.'

'Aunt Liz! What d'yer think I am?'

'It's not you I'm worrying about.' She smiled wryly, then rubbed her chest and winced in pain.

'You OK?' Kay looked with concern at her aunt.

''Course I am. Strong as an ox, me. Just wish this bloody pain would stop coming and going. Bit of rubbing with oil's what I need. That should do the trick.' Liz had no idea why she felt like shedding a tear for herself. Pity had never been her style.

The next few days dragged for Laura and she felt as if her old sparkle had gone forever. Not that she was brooding over Jack. She had dismissed him from her thoughts first thing on Monday morning, after she had spent the night shedding tears and remembering the way it used to be. Once her mind was back on Richard she longed to see him; there was so much to talk about. She couldn't think why, but he had positively avoided her on the hop fields and when she went to the cottage on Monday and Tuesday evening she had found it in darkness, not a glimmer of light had shone out from the small thatched dwelling. She supposed that his sudden absence was a way of preventing attention from any gossip that could cause problems and ruin any plans he was making. Still, she would have preferred it if he had at least made an effort to see her, if only to explain what he was doing. She hadn't been able to converse properly with anyone and ate only when she had to in order to stop Kay or Liz nagging her.

When Richard suddenly appeared on the hop fields not far from Laura's bin on Friday, she silently willed him to pay her some attention once he had finished speaking to his foreman. She wanted to go to him, ask where he had been. Without taking her eyes off him, she continued slowly picking the hops and humming the song 'Smoke Gets In Your Eyes'. When he did finally look her way, a brief half smile was all she received.

'You'll have to be tougher with them, Stanley.' Richard began to walk slowly away and out of Laura's vision. 'I'm getting complaints from the men working the kilns. They're having to spend far too much time cleaning out the leaves.' He stopped once he knew she could no longer see him.

'I guessed this would happen once they heard you were sacking them. I did warn you, Mr Richard.' Stanley spoke in a fatherly manner. 'You should have advised them when the letter went out. They needed time to get used to it.'

'Well, it's too late for all that now, Stanley,' he said stolidly, 'just see that those hops are clean when you measure. Don't take them if they're not. That should put a stop to it.'

'I hope you're right.' His foreman walked away, leaving Richard alone and wondering if he dare go back and speak to Laura. He decided against it.

Julia had been in pain since the accident and, having spent three days in hospital, she was now at home and resting. The blisters on her legs still looked angry: she made no secret of the fact that she was feeling down. He couldn't make a guess at how many times she had made him promise not to speak to Laura, always referring to her as 'the whore'.

Once Julia was feeling her old self with her confidence back, he would tell her of his intention to tell Laura face to face that it was over, instead of avoiding her. If Julia threw a tantrum then so be it. He had had enough. She had been right when she talked about their marriage being a sham and if he was really honest, it went back further than when he had fallen in love with Laura. His biggest regret now was that he had not forced himself to sit down with Julia and talk about it earlier, before mutual disrespect had set in. As far as he was concerned, they would continue to keep the marriage going until the twins were grown-up and living their own lives.

Although Richard was aching to see Laura and dreading the day when she would leave, he had to admit that he felt lighter inside now that he no longer had to live a lie.

He would make no promises, but he had every intention of contacting her later on in life and if she were free, maybe then they could live a decent, open life together. Until then they would have to face the fact that family commitments would keep them apart.

The sight of the Land-Rover driving slowly along the mud track towards him caused Richard to stare unbelievingly at his wife, who sat behind the wheel. How could she possibly drive when her legs were causing her so much pain? He stood rooted to the spot as she drew up beside him.

'Julia, have you gone mad?' He regretted the ill-chosen words as soon as they were out.

'Not quite, Richard, not quite,' she said coolly. 'The drive to Maidstone made a nice change. And I'm sure everyone will appreciate my good deed.' She threw the Land-Rover back into gear and drove further along the track. He turned away and headed for Stanley, who was speaking to one of the men driving a tractor.

Laura was enjoying a mug of tea when Liz arrived at her bin. She had spotted Julia arrive and was contemplating buying an ice-cream.

'Any more tea in that flask?' Liz perched herself on Laura's bin, keeping in the shade of the hop-bines.

'Help yourself,' Laura smiled. 'The weather forecast said it was gonna be hot, but this is ridiculous. I don't think we should be picking in this heat, Liz.'

Unscrewing the Thermos flask, Liz shook her head. 'Well, the measureman's out in it as well, Laura, so he knows what we're going through. I haven't heard his whistle telling us to leave off, though.' She poured some ready-made tea into her mug. 'Wright's around somewhere as well, so there's no excuse. All that man cares about is getting these hops on to the tractors and up the oast-house.'

'You don't give him any leeway, do you, Liz?'

'Nope,' she sniffed, 'I don't. Can't 'elp it. Don't trust the man.' She sipped her tea. 'Did he have anything to say last night, or wasn't he at the cottage – again?'

'What is it with you? You got a crystal ball under your bed, or what?'

'Don't need one. Not where you're concerned. Known yer too long.' She eyed her sister-in-law who looked just as sad as she had all week. 'We're family, Laura.'

Liz was fishing again. She wanted to know what was going on and Laura couldn't tell her. She was in the dark, too.

'D'yer think he's backing off?'

'No! He's being sensible. More than I can say for myself. Anyway, why don't you turn your mind to Jack, and the little nephew you might be gettin'?'

'Might be a girl.' Liz was treading on thin ice, goading Laura about a thing like that, but she thought it was worth taking the risk – anything to get her sister-in-law talking again.

'I see madam's back on the field again with her ice-creams,' Laura said, ignoring Liz's attempt to draw her into deeper conversation. 'I think I'll be first in the queue.' She tipped her tea away and tossed her empty mug into her bin to land on the pile of fresh green hops.

Liz stared after her, full of concern. Laura had been acting out of character all week but that was to be expected. Her marriage, after all, was on the line and as far as Liz was concerned, the one who had caused the rift, Laura's so-called lover, the cowardly Richard Wright, had slipped away into the shadows and would probably stay there until Laura was safely on her way back to London and out of his life.

Liz peered around the hop fields wondering if Kay was about. For some reason she felt the need for her company. All she saw was the other families, laughing, singing and picking the hops. The sound of happy children running through the tunnels of hops rang through her ears. She guessed that her niece was most likely to be with her boyfriend, the gypsy, and wondered if she should have mentioned him to Laura.

She picked the empty mug out of the bin and screwed it back on to the Thermos flask, deciding that even if she had spilled the beans about Kay's romance, Laura would have been too involved in her own problems to have taken in the possible consequences. Kay was at a vulnerable stage in her life and probably feeling a bit out of it. She had hardly been given the attention by her parents that a young teenager needed.

From where she sat, Liz could see Laura nearing the Land-Rover and wondered what the hell she was going to say to Julia Wright.

To take her mind off the family problems, Liz joined in with the chorus of singing as the pickers crooned to 'Silver Dollar'.

*   *   *

'Ah, Mrs Armstrong.' Julia tried to hide her feeling of triumph. 'I hardly expected you to be first in the queue,' she beamed, struggling to ignore the pain in her legs. She was still in the driver's seat, speaking to Laura through the open window. Glancing down at her pale lemon poplin skirt, double-checking that her ugly blisters could not be seen, she murmured, 'I don't know if my husband has had the courage to tell you yet, but your sordid little affair is over.' She smiled into Laura's beautiful face and felt nothing but hatred for this woman with her seductive eyes.

'Richard no longer requires your services. Picking by hand is history and so are you.' She felt a strong desire to push her long painted nails into Laura's face, claw into the flesh and scar her for life. 'Your intrusion into our marriage hasn't been too damaging. In fact, if anything, it's added a little spice. I have something to thank you for.' The spiteful expression on Julia's face was more damaging than any wound her nails could inflict.

She turned the key in the ignition, threw the gears into reverse and backed slowly away along the mud track, leaving Laura standing alone, staring after her, in shocked silence.

'Where's she bloody well going?' A woman's voice pierced the air. 'My kids are gasping for a lolly. Woman's a bleedin' nutcase!'

Laura walked slowly back towards her bin in a trancelike state, while others who had hoped for some flavoured ice to cool them down came together to moan about Julia Wright and the uncaring class she belonged to.

Liz hadn't taken her eyes off Laura and watched as she approached, wondering what had taken place. She was surprised when she walked straight past and away as if Liz wasn't there.

'Laura!' Liz quickly stood up, ready to go after her, when Milly arrived.

'You all right, Liz? You don't look so good.'

'Eh? Oh, it's you, Milly.' Liz inhaled slowly and sat down again. 'Never mind me, Mog. What about you?' She wanted to draw any attention away from Laura's behaviour. 'They shouldn't 'ave dragged your Georgie off like that.' She pulled a bine across the bin and began to pick the hops.

'It's 'is own fault, Liz. Not easy to hold my head up, though. I don't know why I should feel ashamed. I've never stolen a thing in my life. So I end up with someone like George.'

Liz shot her a warning look. 'Come on, Milly . . .'

'Yeah, I know what you're thinking,' she cut in, 'that I should stick by my man. Well, I shall. But I tell yer, my life'll be a lot easier with 'im inside.'

'That's just shock coming out. You don't mean it. But you'd best not say it to anyone else. They won't let you forget it.' Liz was trying not to let her mind wander back to Laura.

'Oh, don't worry. I won't give this lot anything to feed off. I do worry about my Brianny, though. Some example 'is father's set 'im.'

'Brianny's no different from most 'is age. Our kids don't get much going their way. Chucked out of school at fourteen and fifteen whether they're ready or not. Still, that's all gonna change, if we're to believe what we're told.' She felt a tightening in her chest again. 'Did you see where Laura went?'

Milly sat down on the edge of the bin and pulled a branch of hops off Liz's bine. It was unusual for anyone to pick into someone else's bin but since she was about to talk about Laura she felt it was the least she could do. It would also appease Liz, she hoped.

'I expect she's just gone for a breather,' Milly said carefully, 'but I did wanna 'ave a word about her, though.'

'You should know better than that, Milly,' Liz warned.

'Brianny blames Jack. Thinks he should have done something to stop them arresting his dad. He blew 'is top this morning when I took 'im his mug of tea. Ranted on like the devil was in 'im.'

'Go on then.' Liz rubbed her chest. 'What did he have to say?'

'Brianny reckons that Laura and Richard Wright . . .'

'Well, he's wrong!'

'Then he went on about Jack and what he's been up to . . .'

'We've got our fair share of troubles,' Liz sighed, 'I'll give you that.' She searched her pockets until she found her tin of snuff, then looked pleadingly at Milly. 'You won't say anything, will you, Milly?'

'I told yer, Liz, I'm feeding no one, but Brianny . . . well . . . I think he might. I'll do my best to stop 'im, you know I will. But if it should all come out, well, I just wanted you to know it'll be no fault of mine.'

Twelve

Laura walked through one field after another, over stiles, through gates and across a bridge. Once she arrived at a spot where she could not be seen from any direction, she dropped to the ground, lying flat with her face buried in her folded arms, and burst into tears. She allowed herself complete freedom, the strange loud noises escaping from her never seeming loud enough. Her body began to ache as she sobbed, howled, keened, one lament after another until she felt exhausted and completely drained of spirit and emotion.

As she slowly began to feel calmer, her body relaxed and she felt light enough to float up to the sky. She lay on the grassy bank, devoid of any feeling and enjoyed this new comforting sensation of being at one with her surroundings and herself. She silently thanked God for his being there.

Turning on to her side, Laura then curled up into

a ball the way she had done as a child when in bed at night, closed her eyes and enjoyed the warm sunshine on her back.

On the dot of three, when most pickers stopped for tea, Richard decided that enough was enough. His own short-sleeved shirt was soaked with perspiration. 'This is madness, Stanley.' Richard wiped his brow. 'The pickers will burn to a cinder in this heat. Blow the whistle. Tell them to take a couple of hours, before we have to drag the Red Cross in to one of them.'

'We'd best let them know at the oast-house. It'll put them back a couple of hours.' Stanley offered no resistance. He knew only too well that to push the workers would be folly.

'Send the tractor back with its half-load and get the driver to tell the foreman.' He gave Stanley a friendly punch to the shoulder. 'I should get your men out of this heat too, if I were you. Then get yourself off home for an hour or so. I shan't be going yet. I want to check the fields, see how the crop's bearing up.'

In a strange calm mood, Laura stood on the bridge, staring down at the river, wishing she could see her future in the reflection. She toyed with the idea of going to see Gypsy Rose, remembering the few words which had passed between them a couple of weeks back. Laura had felt so sure that Rose was referring to Richard when she said *You may be surprised who I see in your tea-leaves this year.*

It was an ambiguous remark, Laura told herself, but then what else could you expect from a fortune-teller?

Trailing her hand along the rail, she walked slowly across the bridge, wondering if her daughter was enjoying a swim somewhere further down the river. She tried to remember the last time she had gone in for a dip. It was a very long time ago, when Kay was four years old, just before Laura fell for baby John. Before then, the three of them, herself, Kay and Jack, would go regularly to the open-air swimming-pool every Sunday; to the lido in Victoria Park where they would take a picnic and sometimes meet Liz and Bert and their family. She realized then just how much had changed during the past years and wondered why she had allowed those happy, relaxed days to come to an abrupt end.

Feeling the burning sun on her shoulders, Laura tried to quicken her pace to avoid getting sunburnt but her body seemed to have a will of its own, as if it had gone into a lower gear. She felt as if she were part of a slow-motion film.

Pulling a gate shut behind her, she strolled back through a field and decided that she would head for Liz's bin and tell her that she was clocking off for the day. If Liz chose to join her, Laura would welcome it. She wanted to tell someone how much she and Richard loved each other. She could no longer keep it to herself, not now, not since that fleeting time spent in Julia's company. Julia. How she hated that name and that tormenting face.

Suddenly, the woman's words were swimming around inside her head; over and over again she could hear that smug voice telling her *He no longer requires your services . . . Your sordid little affair is over . . . It's added a little spice . . . He no longer requires your services . . . I have something to thank you for . . . He no longer requires your services . . .*

'It can't be true,' Laura murmured, 'she's making it up. I know she is.' She stopped in her tracks and began to breathe deeply, desperate to compose herself. 'Why does it hurt so much?' she cried. 'Why does it hurt so much?'

Standing there in the middle of a field, her eyes closed tight, she felt as if she were the only person in the world and realized that until then she had not truly known what it was to be lonely. She was suddenly aware of how much empty space

316

surrounded her and how infinite was the sky. She was craving for someone to put their arms around her, desperate for another person to touch her and say that it was all right. She needed someone to come along and walk her back to the hop fields and her friends.

The soft, distant sound of cattle lowing and running didn't seem part of her world. A different film. It wasn't until the gap between her and a herd of young cattle began rapidly to decrease and the soft thudding of feet on the hard-baked meadow became louder, that she turned her sluggish body and stared at the herd as it raced towards her. A cold sensation shot through her and she felt as if an electric wire were sending a million sparks through her flesh. Her legs were heavy and she felt as if it would need a crane to lift them. She tried telling herself to act fast; she ordered her legs to move, tried willing them but nothing happened. She was momentarily paralysed. There was a cloud of dust, the sickly humid smell of the animals and the terrifying din of a stampede.

Driving her legs forward, she found the instinct to run but the muscles in her legs felt as if they had turned to jelly and no matter how much she tried, it seemed impossible to move them across the tufts of grass and the cracked, baked earth.

'Don't run!' A voice bellowed out to her. 'Stand still!' it ordered. 'Dead still! They won't harm you!'

Covering her head with her arms, Laura obeyed the instruction, using every bit of her will to keep on her feet when all her body wanted was to drop to the ground. The stampeding feet were all about her and she could feel the heat of the bodies as they ran either side of her and eventually away. Then, as the noise came to an end, Laura opened her eyes to see the herd in a far corner of the field enjoying their fresh delivery of feed. Sinking to the ground, she covered her face and began to laugh at her own stupidity.

'I'm glad you kept your head.' Zacchi offered Laura his hand, 'I had a horrible feeling you might panic.'

She looked up at him. 'Panic?' she murmured. 'Me? No chance. I'm made of iron, Zacchi – or so everyone seems to think.'

'Would you like to sit for a while?'

'Yes. I would.' She wiped away a tear.

Sitting down beside her, Zacchi pulled at a tuft of grass, 'It's bulls you 'ave to worry about, not bullocks.' He tried to stop himself from chuckling. 'You're not the first it's happened to and I dare say you won't be the last.'

318

Not knowing whether to laugh or cry, Laura shook her head. 'I must've looked a right idiot. I'm glad you were in the right place at the right time, Zacchi. I would've run, you know. And then they wouldn't've been able to steer themselves around me . . . would they?'

'Probably not.'

'I can't tell you how pleased I am that you were out here.' She sounded choked.

'I . . . needed to be by myself,' he said carefully.

'You and me both.'

His deep blue eyes caught hers while they allowed a few seconds to tick by. 'I'm a good listener.' He smiled, showing his gleaming white teeth. 'Someone,' he added knowingly, 'is breaking your heart.'

'Well, you're certainly a chip off the old block. Gypsy Rose'd be proud. Don't read the cards as well, do yer?'

'I might.' He drew his knees up and leaned on them, giving her a sideways, cheeky look. 'I can see where Kay gets her looks from.'

'Oh, come on, Zacchi. She's as fair as I'm dark,' she laughed.

He playfully examined her long, dark wavy hair. 'The sun's brought a few blonde streaks out,' he teased.

'You reckon?' She smiled at his cheek. 'I can see why Kay's walking around like a lovesick puppy. Quite the little charmer you've turned out.'

'I was trying to picture Kay at home' – he gazed out at nothing – 'in her room; the colour of her walls . . . what ornaments she looked at before she turns out the lights.' He was away in a world of his own. 'I try to imagine her at school, at her desk.' Bringing himself sharply to, he chewed on a blade of grass. 'We Romanies teach ourselves mostly. Start with an Oxo box, then work our way through everything that has a name on it.' He became pensive again. 'I try to imagine her life back there, and mine on the road, without her.' His voice trailed off.

'Come on, Zacchi. Enough of this! We'd best get back.'

Pulling her up he caught the wistful look in her eye. 'Your secret will be safe with me, y'know.'

'Secrets are for keeping,' she said, ending it. They walked side by side in silence, each absorbed in their own thoughts.

As they reached the hop fields, Zacchi bade Laura farewell and made his way back to his people, turning just once to give her another brief show of his hand. There was a message in his final gesture and Laura picked up on it instantly. Not many words had passed between them but they each knew how the other was feeling – love being the strongest master.

It caught Laura off guard, finding the hop fields so quiet and deserted; she wondered if something bad had happened. Had she been her usual self, she would have known instantly that the whistle had been blown owing to the unbearable heat.

It felt strange being there alone. She sat on the edge of her bin and looked down at the yellow-green hops. There was a small branch which shouldn't have been in there. She picked it out and brushed it against her face and, without thinking, kissed one of the soft cones.

'You took your time.' Richard stepped out of a thick tunnel. 'I had almost given up.'

Laura could do no more than gaze up at him. She could feel the tears behind her eyes and her throat begin to dry. Her lips and face quivered and try as she might she could not stop the distortion of her features. She covered her face with both hands and managed to stop herself shedding a tear.

He stroked her hair and her neck. 'I saw you go.' His voice was low and sad. 'I've been waiting ever since. What did Julia say to you?'

She shook her head, 'I can't . . .' Her voice broke. 'I can't . . . talk, Richard . . .'

'You mustn't take too much notice of her. She's not . . . herself.'

Laura pulled her handkerchief out and turned away from him while she dried her eyes and composed herself. After taking deep breaths she finally managed to speak. 'Where is everyone?' she asked, knowing the answer.

'I've given them time off – for two reasons. It's far too hot to pick, and I wanted to see you alone. I had every intention of contriving it.'

Feeling better, Laura turned to face Richard. 'If you haven't got the courage to talk to me when the others are around . . .' She pressed the palm of her hand to her lips to stop herself from crying. 'You shouldn't have to creep about like a fugitive.'

'I know,' he murmured.

'I understand from your wife that you no longer require my services,' Laura said bitterly.

'She's spoken to you?'

'Oh, yes. Very much so.'

'She's . . . not feeling too well . . . there was an accident . . .'

'How could you let me go to that dark cottage

night after night?' Laura cut in. 'Do you have any idea what that made me feel like?'

'I had no choice,' he said miserably. 'She's been in hospital for a few days and since she's been out I haven't been able to move. She watches me all the time.' He wanted to explain to Laura about Julia's sometimes irrational behaviour but his wife had made him promise never to talk about it to anyone, not even his own family. She had always tried desperately hard and succeeded, as far as he knew, not to show any signs to the outside world, so what right did he have to blow her cover?

Laura sighed and waited. Waited for him to break it to her gently. It didn't take much to see what was coming, it was written all over his face. Julia had him where she wanted. Laura had been a fool to think that he would not choose his wife when it came right down to it. Liz had been right all along.

'I had better go. Before anyone sees us together.' She pulled her arm away from his hand but he was in no mood for her tantrums. He gripped her by both arms and stared into her face. 'Listen to me, you idiot! It's you I love. I can't do anything about it but that doesn't stop the pain.' His face became distorted. 'I love you so much, I can't think about anything else! I don't know what to do, Laura. I can't leave Julia – I can't leave the twins!'

'You mean you can't leave the farm!' she retorted.

'Of course I can't leave the farm, be reasonable!'

'What about Julia? Would she leave it?'

'I don't know. But if she did, she would take the children and I couldn't have that,' he sighed.

'You surprise me. You packed them off to boarding-school quick enough.'

'That's different, Laura, and you know it.' He placed his hand under her chin and lifted her face to meet his. 'Could you live without Kay?'

She pulled her face away. 'No.'

'Well, then?'

'It's a pity you didn't think about all this when you made your promises. It was you who said nothing would stop you from seeing me!'

'I know.' He sat down on the edge of the bin next to her. 'And I feel like saying it again.'

She felt sorry then, sorry she had been thinking only of herself and her feelings. 'Oh, Richard . . . what we gonna do?'

He smiled into her face. 'I don't know. I've been over it a thousand times and still – I don't know.'

Remembering the news he had delivered earlier

she took his hand and looked down at his wedding ring. 'What accident?' she asked.

'She scalded herself. I don't know how she managed to drive the Land-Rover today, or why she did it.'

'I do.' It was Laura's turn to smile. 'She wanted to put me in my place, and who can blame her? How did it happen?'

Richard stood up and slowly shook his head. 'Don't ask.' He turned back to her and offered his hand. 'Come on – let's go for a walk.'

'In broad daylight?' She couldn't believe her ears.

'Yes. In broad daylight. Smile today, for tomorrow we may cry,' he joked.

Laura shook her head. 'No. It would be reckless and you know it. We both have to be strong – and at the same time.'

He narrowed his eyes as he looked into her face, then reached out and pulled her close, holding her as tightly as he could. She stroked his hair as he let out a low cry.

'It's all right, Richard . . .' Her soothing voice only made matters worse. He buried his head deeper into her neck and began to kiss her until neither of them wanted to stop.

*   *   *

Laura was concerned when she got back to the huts to find Liz lying on her bed. She pulled back the curtain just enough to see her sister-in-law lying in the dark with only a thin streak of sunshine at the foot of her bed, from the small window.

'Liz? You asleep?' she whispered.

'Oh, it's you, Laura.' Liz sounded as if she had been crying.

'It's not like you to lie down during the day.' Laura's voice was full of worry.

'No, I know. Just having a bit of a doze, that's all. They can keep their Indian summers . . . too much for me.' She winced with pain and pushed her hand to her chest.

'Liz, you look terrible! It can't just be the heat.'

Carefully pulling herself up, Liz plumped up her pillows and sank back into them. 'It's as if a needle's being pushed right through my heart. Bloody things. If it's not one pain going through it's another. I don't know why I'm so tired . . .'

Laura cupped a hand over Liz's and looked into her drawn face. 'Why don't we get someone to give you a lift into Yalding? See a doctor?'

'No. I'll wait till we get back to London. Dr Brunnberg'll know what it is. He'll give me something.'

'But that's at least two weeks away.'

Liz slipped down on to her back again. 'We'll see. If it don't wear off by the weekend, I'll get Bert to run me into town.'

'Please, Liz.' Laura tried her best but knew in her heart that it was useless trying to persuade her stubborn sister-in-law. 'Let me go and phone the Red Cross. Give 'em something to do,' she joked.

'Don't push me, Laura.' Liz's grave voice was firm. 'I want to wait for Bert. I don't wanna see a strange doctor if my Bert's not 'ere.'

Laura swallowed hard. 'All right,' she managed, 'but no more picking today . . . or in the morning, right?'

'Yeah, all right, Mog. The men'll be 'ere tomorrow, won't they? I forgot it was Friday already.' She gave Laura a little pat on the arm. 'I took a couple of aspirins – they'll start to work soon. Stop worrying.'

Leaving Liz to rest for a while, Laura unlocked her hut door and decided to have a short afternoon nap. Not feeling in the best of spirits herself, she carried a mug of steaming Horlicks to her bed and settled herself into the comfortable nook she had made using her pillows and Kay's. Filled with a sick worry, she wasn't sure if it was due to Liz

327

being ill or the dawning of the end of her and Richard.

With the door wide open and the dividing curtain hooked back, she could enjoy the rays of the sun which poured into the living-area while making the most of the shade. She watched the comings and goings of the other hop-pickers and enjoyed the distant sound of a wireless. The afternoon play was on and although she couldn't hear well enough to follow the story, still the muted sounds of voices was somehow comforting. It was strange not to hear the children playing outside but they would, Laura imagined, either be in the river cooling off, or being kept out of the scorching sun by their mothers.

'Oh, now you really are living up to your name!' Kay beamed as she walked into the hut. 'Queen of the hop fields or the Queen of Sheba? Which d'yer prefer?'

'Cheeky cow.' Laura perked up at the sight of her rosy-cheeked daughter standing there without a care in the world. 'And where you been, miss? Haven't seen you since lunch-time.'

Pouring some cream soda into a glass, Kay turned deliberately so that Laura couldn't see her blushing. 'I've been blackberrying with Terry.' That was the truth, she had; but only for an hour after she had spent time with Zacchi. 'His mum's gonna make two summer puddings, one for us.'

'That's nice.' Laura waited to see if Kay was going to elaborate on how her time had been spent.

'And before that, I learned how to make a peg basket,' she said carefully.

'Oh, yeah? And who showed you?' As if Laura didn't know.

'Gypsy Rose.'

'You were honoured. First time I've known that to 'appen.' She waited for a bit more information.

'I've not been invited inside a wagon yet.' Kay lifted the glass to her parched lips and swallowed the lukewarm soda.

'You'll be lucky. There's a line, Kay, and you 'ave to know when to toe it.'

'I know.' A silence hung in the air as mother and child wondered if their line had just been reached. Kay decided it had.

'Where's Aunt Liz?' she asked.

'Having a lie down. I don't like the look of her, Kay. And I'm worried about her so-called indigestion.'

'She knows it's much worse than that . . .' Kay threw Laura a look of recrimination. 'And I think we've let it go on too long. I think we should call a doctor, while she's in the mood.'

'What d'yer mean? In the mood? Am I missing something?' Laura suddenly felt as if she was in the dark. 'What's she told yer?'

'If she's lying down, Mum, that means she's scared and wants a doctor!' Kay snapped impatiently. 'She won't ask – you should know that.'

Swinging her legs off the bed, Laura sat on the edge and leaned her head to one side to catch Kay's face. 'You're angry with me?'

'Yeah, I am a bit.' Kay swallowed and then took a deep breath, turning away from her mother's searching eyes. 'My Aunt Liz's not been well all week and all you could do was mope about like an old misery.'

Laura pressed her lips together and nodded. 'Well, you certainly know how to hit home.' She waited for a response but Kay busied herself spreading some raspberry jam on to a slice of bread, choking back her tears.

'What d'yer think we should do?'

'Send for a doctor!' Kay barked.

Suddenly filled with urgency, Laura pushed her feet into her sandals and grabbed her hairbrush. 'I hope you're overreacting, Kay, that's all.' She brushed her hair back off her face and pushed a couple of combs in. 'I'll borrow Milly's push-bike and go down to the phone box.'

'No!' Kay said, alarmed. 'I'll go . . . you stay and look after Aunt Liz.' She lowered her voice. 'I can't go in there, Mum. I can't bear to see her in pain and trying to cover it for my sake.'

'You're only a kid, Kay – they might not . . .'

'I'm fifteen!' Kay snapped. 'Stop treating me like a child!'

Laura was taken aback, as if she was seeing a new Kay. She narrowed her eyes and focused on that innocent freckled face. It looked the same. She was taller, shapelier this year . . . Suddenly it dawned on Laura that she hadn't really sat down and talked to Kay in a very long time.

'And anyway,' Kay said more quietly, trying to mend the rift, 'it won't be the phone box I'll head for. I'm gonna go to the post office – send a telegram to Uncle Bert. I think he should come down after work.'

'That's goin' a bit far, surely? Your dad and Uncle Bert'll be here tomorrow afternoon in any case.' Try as she might, Laura couldn't hide the worry in her voice.

'I can't explain it, Mum. I just know we should do what we can to make Aunt Liz . . .' Her voice cracked and she had to take a long deep breath. 'I don't care if she's not that ill. Something's wrong and she needs Uncle Bert!' The crack in Kay's voice was not unlike Jack's when he was feeling emotional and on the brink of unshed tears.

'All right, love.' Laura kissed Kay on the cheek and hugged her. 'You go, and I'll sit with your Aunt Liz.'

'What should I put in the telegram?' Kay asked, looking like a child again.

Thinking on her feet, Laura shrugged her shoulders: '"Liz not well. Calling a doctor. Come now".'

A brief silence hung in the air as the gravity of this sad turn of events crept into their personal world. 'Yeah . . .' Kay murmured, 'that should get it across.'

'But what if your Uncle Bert rushes off and 'as an accident? You know what a worrier he is.'

'That's a risk we'll have to take. Anyway, Dad'll keep him on an even keel.'

Overwhelmed by her daughter's mature thinking, Laura felt relieved that there was someone else to help carry her burdens and make decisions.

'Take those two half-crowns off the shelf, that should be plenty. Bloody GPO! We should 'ave 'ad our phone by now.'

Kay squeezed Laura's arm. 'Don't worry, Mum. At least we've gone into action at last.'

Laura sat on the edge of the bed and watched Kay striding out with determination towards Milly's hut and realized that her little girl was fast becoming a lovely young woman. She also realized just how much she loved her, and could see what a wrench it would be for Richard to lose the twins. And there was no doubt that Julia would do her best to keep them from him. Opening a narrow drawer, Laura withdrew her packet of five Weights. She would have a cigarette before she went in to see Liz. As she blew out the smoke a shadow fell across the doorway. 'Hallo, Laura, how's Liz?' It was Milly, and Laura was surprised how pleased she was to see her.

'I'm not sure, Milly, to tell the truth. I'm just giving 'er five minutes before I pop in to check. I take it you saw Kay?'

'Yeah. Poor little cow – she looks worried sick. I got Brianny to pump up the bike tyres for 'er. He even offered to go down the post office but she wasn't gonna 'ave that.'

'They can say what they like about us, eh? But they'd 'ave to go a long way to find a closer-knit group. I really appreciate you coming over.' Laura was choked and didn't mind showing it.

'You'd do the same for me, mate. And you know' – Milly studied her nails to avoid eye contact with Laura – 'if you need to talk about anything else . . .'

'Oh, don't tempt me!'

'Well, you know what they say . . . a trouble shared is a trouble halved,' Milly smiled.

'Yeah . . . but to be honest with you, Milly, I'm more upset about Liz than . . . well, you know . . .' Laura smiled at her. 'I don't know how you know but you do, don't you?' She stubbed her cigarette out in the ashtray. 'I'll be all right – in a decade or two . . .'

'Well, you know where I am.'

'Thanks. I might well take you up on it. Not that you 'aven't got enough on your plate, eh?'

'Well there you are; maybe I need your company as much as you need mine,' Milly said as she turned away. 'Let me know if Liz needs anything. Brianny's always on hand. Do the lazy little sod good to have to do a good deed!'

Laura gave a show of her hand, 'I'll remember that!' she called out as she left her hut on her way to see Liz.

Tiptoeing inside, Laura crept up to the curtain and gently lifted it, to see that Liz was awake and obviously pleased to see her. 'Fancy a cuppa?'

'No, Mog. A glass of water would be nice, though.'

Pouring water from the enamel jug, Laura broached the subject of a doctor, and to her surprise Liz made no sounds of protest.

'Whatever you think, Laura. I'm too worn out to argue,' she said.

With one arm across her sister-in-law's back, Laura helped her up into a sitting position and put the glass of water to Liz's lips.

'It's for the best, Liz. You'd 'ave done the same if it was me lying in that bed, you know you would. Bert'll get the telegram by the time he gets in from work, so you can bet your bottom dollar he'll be down tonight with Jack.'

'What telegram?'

Laura gave her a guilty smile. 'I'm sorry, Liz, but it was Kay's idea and there was no stopping 'er. She wants her Uncle Bert . . . and 'er dad to be 'ere. She's worried for yer, that's all.'

Liz started to chuckle at the thought of Bert getting a telegram – then she winced in pain. 'Oh, Gawd . . .' she cried softly.

'Oh, Liz, I wish I could take the pain away.'

'It'll pass,' she managed to say, 'bloody hearts – if it's not one kind of pain going through, it's another.'

'I wish you'd 'ave told me how bad it had been, Liz.'

'I thought you 'ad enough on your plate. What with everyone dipping their cornets into other people's ice-cream.'

It was a direct insult for Laura, but she couldn't help chuckling and neither could Liz. Pain or no pain.

When Bert got home from the dock that afternoon just after five his next door neighbour, Iris, was waiting for him. 'It's a telegram, Bert,' she said gravely, 'from Tonbridge.'

Bert read the words over and over, he couldn't believe it. 'It's Liz!' he yelled to Iris who was already in the scullery brewing him some tea, 'she's ill!'

'Let me fry you up some bacon and eggs, Bert. You can't drive all that way on an empty stomach!' Iris insisted.

'Tea and biscuits'll do fine!' Bert said. 'I'll 'ave to pick our Jack up from . . .' He just managed to stop himself in time. No sense in letting the world know that he had another woman. He hoped his brother-in-law wouldn't 'ave taken Patsy out for a drink by the time he got there.

'Drink this, love.' Iris smiled warmly, passing him a cup of strong tea.

'I knew she wasn't hundred per cent . . . but

would she admit it when I asked?' He placed his cup on the coffee-table and stared into the woman's eyes. 'It doesn't even say what's wrong with 'er, Iris! It could be anything!'

'Listen. If it was that bad, they would 'ave called an ambulance, not a doctor, right? It's probably a bit of nervous reaction from Laura. You know how thick those two are.'

'Yeah,' he said thoughtfully, 'could be that our Lizzie don't know she's sent for me. She would 'ave put a stop to it all right . . . that is, if she's not . . . I'll 'ave to go!' He jumped up and grabbed his overcoat and cap. 'Sorry about the tea, Iris. You drink it. And turn the lights off and . . .'

'Yeah, yeah, go on. Get going. No sense in trying to stop yer.'

Bert raced down the passage, 'Thanks, Iris!'

'And take your time!' she yelled after him. 'Better to get there late than not get there at all!' She heard the door slam shut behind him. 'Poor old Liz,' she murmured. She knew her neighbour well enough to know that if Liz was admitting she was ill, it had to be serious.

'Yeah, well, you've not exactly helped, 'ave yer!' Bert barked, as he and Jack travelled through the

Blackwall Tunnel. 'You've been piling your troubles on a bit lately!'

'I know,' Jack said quietly.

'Well just don't worry Liz with all your problems this time, that's all!'

'What d'yer think I am, Bert – made of stone?' Jack said miserably.

'I know . . . I know . . .'

'Anyway,' Jack cut in, 'my problems are on a train right now, to Leicester. Patsy's moving in with 'er mother. Gonna stay there till she's 'ad the baby. Then she's gonna decide whether to have it adopted . . . or keep it.'

'You mean she's given you the elbow?' Bert said with a touch of ridicule in his voice.

'Mutual agreement.' Jack ignored his brother-in-law's goading. 'We thought it best to give each other a bit of time to get used to the new . . . predicament. She wants to see 'ow I get on, fending for myself.'

'What d'yer mean, fending for yerself? Laura wouldn't kick you out.'

'She won't get the chance. I've packed all my stuff up ready to go. Found a bedsit just round the corner from you.'

'Oh, yeah? Well don't expect Liz to wash, cook and scrub for yer!'

'It's a bit small.' Jack was losing his patience with Bert but he kept his cool, knowing the man was under strain. 'It'll do for the time being, till I find something with a bit more space.'

'It all sounds too complicated for me . . .'

'You've gotta know when to walk away, Bert,' Jack cut in. 'No point staying where you're not wanted. At least this way I might salvage something from the mess. Our Kay'll see I've not left 'er mum to live with someone else. She can come and visit me. I'll get a put-you-up for 'er.'

Jack pulled his tobacco tin from his pocket and took out two roll-ups. 'It's a weird feeling, I tell yer. It's all come to an end . . . over and done with. No more Laura.'

He lit both cigarettes and offered one to Bert's mouth. 'Probably for the best,' he lied.

Bert drove on in silence, worrying about Liz and feeling choked about Jack and Laura. He never dreamt that something like this, a break-up, could ever happen in their family. He still couldn't believe it.

'How did you get on with the petition?' Bert decided to make conversation to take his mind off his worries.

'Didn't wanna know, did they? All over the bloody dockyard I went with me clipboard. They're

339

all saving up to take their women to the Isle of Sheppey next year. Chalets 'ave taken over from 'uts!'

'Can't blame 'em. It's what our Liz wants.'

'Running hot and cold water, proper Calor gas stoves, electricity; just like – home.' He emphasized the word 'home'. 'All that'll be missing is the tallyman.'

'Sounds all right to me,' Bert said.

'You won't be saying that in a few years' time, Bert! You'll be more bloody nostalgic for hop-picking than any of us!' Bert's complacency was beginning to get to him.

'Anyway,' Jack continued, 'I'm still not finished with Richard Wright. I might still get my way. Don't see why he should get away scot-free. Not telling us before! He knew what he was doing, all right. I'd like to punch his nose through to the other side of 'is effing 'ead!'

'Goin' a bit far, innit?' Bert was quite enjoying the banter now.

'You reckon? Ha! Just give me the man on a dark night.' Jack was seething and he was finding it difficult to hide his anger.

Raising an eyebrow, Bert half smiled. 'You sure it's not more than the machines that's bugging yer?'

340

Wild Hops

'Keep your eyes on the road, will yer, Bert. Your fucking driving leaves a lot to be desired as it is.' Jack ended the conversation, but his mind was racing. Bert's deliberately searching question confirmed that his brother-in-law knew more than he had let on about Laura and Richard Wright. That figured. Liz would have told him. The question now in the forefront of Jack's mind was how long had it been going on, and, more importantly, how long had Liz and Bert known?

Jack cast his mind back to the previous season and the one before that, and before that. Suddenly he seemed to have instant recall; the way Laura always wore a new dress on the first day of the picking season; her hair always brushed and looking lovely; make-up always on. He had been a fool not to have realized then that she was happier in Kent than she had been in London! He smiled inwardly at his stupidity, thinking she was celibate. He had heard that ignorance was bliss and maybe it had been, but wasn't knowledge supposed to be better? One thing he knew for certain, the way he was feeling inside was far from healthy. There was a sick, heavy feeling in his guts which seemed to be moving to his chest and he didn't like it. He didn't like it one bit.

'You should 'ave said something, Bert.' Jack's

voice gave him away, he was deeply hurt and very jealous.

'I only heard about it last weekend and you was in such a bad mood on the way home, I thought Laura'd told yer.' Bert knew exactly what Jack was talking about.

They travelled along the country lanes in silence, the sides of the lorry brushing against the hedgerows. Jack believed his brother-in-law. He had no reason to lie and in any case he wouldn't, not Bert.

'I don't s'pose you know how long . . .'

'No, Jack, I don't,' Bert interrupted, 'and that's the truth.'

Jack began to chuckle and shake his head. 'What a dark horse she's turned out to be, eh? Cow.'

'Can you blame 'er?' Bert asked carefully. 'Be truthful.'

'Blame 'er? I can't even give 'er a right 'ander can I? That's what really gets me. I haven't got the right to 'ave a go at my own wife for . . . sleeping with someone else.'

'You wouldn't hit 'er, Jack, would yer?' Bert couldn't believe that.

'You know what I mean! 'Course I wouldn't! It's just a . . . you know, terminology. I might 'ave strangled 'er, though – if it hadn't been for Patsy.'

'And the rest.'

'Yeah, yeah, yeah . . . and the rest.' There was anger in Jack's voice. 'There 'aven't been that many women, Bert . . . I'm not a complete bastard, you know.' His voice trailed off.

'You gonna say anything to Laura?'

'No. No, I'm not gonna say anything. It's none of my business really. What she does is 'er affair. She's got her sights set high, I'll say that for 'er. Richard Wright!' Jack laughed. 'He must 'ave got the right wind up when I turned up on 'is doorstep!'

Bert could see the funny side of it too. Once the men started to think about it, they laughed on and off for the rest of the journey.

Watching from her hut doorway, Laura almost jumped out of her skin when Bert's lorry pulled in through the gateway. 'They're here, Kay!' she yelled excitedly, and ran out to meet the men.

'Oh, Bert . . . thank God you got here safely,' Laura cried, not caring now about tears flowing down her cheeks.

'How is she?' Bert slammed the cab door behind him and waited, hoping the news wasn't bad.

'Pretty sick, Bert.' Laura could hardly speak. 'Trust Liz' – she smiled through her tears – 'not only her heart but pleurisy as well.'

343

Bert leaned on the side of his lorry, speechless and shaking his head, trying to take it in.

'What d'yer mean, Laura? What's wrong with her heart?' Jack demanded.

'Angina . . . whatever that is when it's at home. And as for pleurisy, it's one step away from pneumonia. I should know, Dad got it once, when I was a kid.'

'Fuck me . . .' was all Jack could manage. 'I didn't think it would be this bad, Laura.' Jack joined Bert and leaned up against the lorry, next to him.

'Well, aren't you gonna go in and see her, then? She must know you're here.' Had the situation not been so serious she would have allowed herself to laugh at the two strong dockers who looked as if they were about to pass out.

'You telling me she's in the hut?'

'Yes, Jack, I am.'

'She's not in hospital, then?' Bert found his voice at last.

'No. The doctor's been. Told her off for leaving it so long; gave her pills and medicine and said she's to go to her own doctor when she's back in London.' Laura's voice took on a different tone then. 'The pains in the heart were a warning, Bert. She's gonna have to take it a lot easier from now on. The pleurisy's got to be nursed. She's allowed out of bed but not until the dampness of these mornings has passed. She can be out of bed around midday. But no more picking!' Laura enjoyed giving the orders – it felt good to be positive and in charge of the situation.

'Oh, Bert . . .' Liz wailed, squeezing his hand, 'you don't know 'ow pleased I am to see you. You're a sight for sore eyes, all right.'

'You frightened the life out of me, Liz. I couldn't get down 'ere quick enough. Can I get you anything? A cup of tea?'

Liz smiled and shook her head slowly. 'No thanks, love; get Laura to make you one though.'

'I can't understand why the doctor didn't send you away, Liz.'

'Thanks,' she chuckled weakly.

'You know what I mean.'

'It was a warning, Bert, not a full-blown heart attack. He's given me some pills and reckons providing I take things easy I can get up tomorrow and . . .'

'That's enough of that, Liz!' Bert cut in, 'Laura'll tell you when you can and can't get up.'

'He said I could have an hour at the pub with you all on Saturday night . . .'

Bert patted her hand. 'We'll see about that when

345

the time comes. Jack's waiting to come in, he's worried sick.'

'Tch. All this fuss! Both losing work!'

'You don't think we give a toss about that, do yer? You're all that matters.' He swept her fringe back off her face. 'I stopped on the way, got you some jellied eels.'

Liz tried not to laugh at him, it was a sweet thought but jellied eels were the last thing she could face. 'Thanks, love. I'll eat 'em later on, eh?' she said, wincing with pain. Knowing how upset Bert would be, she tried to cover up her revulsion but the best actress in the world would have been forgiven for fluffing her lines right then. 'I'm so pleased you're here, love . . .' she murmured and closed her eyes, then added, 'I'm not asleep love. You can talk to me . . .'

Getting a grip on himself, Bert looked away from her pained face. 'Tch. Fancy you getting angina, eh . . . ? You can sit with Iris's old man when we get back and exchange pains and pills.'

'Yeah, that's right, that's what he's got,' Liz murmured, keeping her eyes closed and resting, 'don't look any the worse for it, does he? Thank God.'

'Shall I let your baby brother pop in for a minute then? Or d'yer wanna sleep?' Bert asked.

'Yeah, 'course he can come in. And Bert . . . thanks for coming, love. You didn't mind Laura sending you the telegram, did yer?'

Standing by the door he smiled and shook his head. 'If you put feed in a trough, what do the cattle do?'

Liz smiled to herself. 'Ask Laura,' she said, remembering the reported event of that morning.

There was a strange, quiet mood in the Armstrong family during that Friday evening after the men arrived. Laura, Jack, Kay, Liz and Bert each would happily have sat down to talk, any combination of the five would have made interesting conversation, but as so often happens when there is a problem within a family, no one knew where to begin. From Jack, who was moody and made no effort to hide it, there came short verbal snipes directed at Laura; he was obviously spoiling for a fight and wanting to clear the air.

Laura attended to her duties, cooking for all of them, tidying the huts and taking care that Liz took her medication and rested. She hardly said a word to anyone and seemed to float from one place to another in a zombie-like state. A quiet Yes or No was all she gave in reply to any of Jack's inane remarks. Had she known that he had discovered the truth about her and Richard, she would have taken more notice of his probing.

Instead of the usual jokes and banter around the fire when they would have sat up till late, joining in with the camp-fire songs, they were happy to have an early night, except Kay, who sat with Zacchi's family outside the wagons, by their fire, absorbed in the travellers' tales.

It was Jack who was up first the next morning, outside and lighting a fire. Laura could have been knocked down with a feather when he tapped on her door and asked for a kettle of water and enough provisions for all their breakfasts.

Settling himself by the fire, Jack tossed rashers of bacon into the sizzling fat and gave the pan a quick shake. He couldn't shift the nagging worry he had over his sister. Liz may well have been given good advice and excellent medicine, but as far as he was concerned she looked like death, and only time would tell if she really was strong enough to pull through and get back to her old self. She wasn't, after all, getting any younger. It hadn't ever crossed his mind that she might die before him and the thought of it left him cold. She had been like a mother to him, as well as the best sister anyone could wish for. Gazing around the common, he wondered if the news about the end of hop-picking had had anything to do with her going down so quickly like that.

Most of the pickers were up and about and wrapped in their woollies protecting themselves against the chilly morning air. The sun was beginning to climb to its full glory and Jack reckoned it wouldn't be long before everyone would be peeling off their outer clothes.

Glancing around him, he caught sight of Mrs Brown as she pulled her hut door shut behind her. Wrapping her coat around her thin body she walked slowly across the common in Jack's direction, heading for the lavatories. He narrowed his eyes and studied the pathetic figure who appeared to be limping as she passed him by without so much as a nod, looking as if she were in another world. He saw the bruise on her face and the swollen, closed eye.

He remembered the cries from the Browns' hut the previous week and Liz telling him about the brute Brown. Jack's temper instantly rose and he wanted to go over and shake the life out of the coward.

'That smells nice, Jack mate,' Bert said, arriving by his side. 'Nothing like the smell of fried bacon to get the taste buds going.'

'Did you see that?' Jack's face was hard with anger.

'Eh?' Bert was slow off the mark. He hadn't been awake that long.

'The poor cow who just passed!'

'No . . . ?' He yawned. 'Who you talking about, Jack?'

'Brown's bin knocking 'is missus about again.'

'Oh, right.' Bert scratched his head and yawned again. 'It's 'ardly anything new, is it? They're always at it, them two.'

'You make me fucking wild sometimes, Bert, my life, you do.' Jack turned the bacon over. 'How comes I'm always the last to know about these things, eh?'

'Oh shut up, Jack. It's too early for all that.'

'Yeah? Well, it's not too early for me to give that excuse for a man a good hiding! Watch the bacon.'

Bert grabbed Jack's arm. 'Don't.' He looked Jack straight in the eye. 'That's not the way.'

'No?' Jack grinned sardonically.

'No! We'll discuss it properly after breakfast and decide the best way to sort him out. Which will not be your way.' Bert pulled his braces up over his shoulders and half turned away. 'I'll cut and butter the bread.'

Jack pursed his lips and kept his eyes fixed on Bert. 'All right, 'ave it your way. But after breakfast and no later!'

Bert cocked his head to one side. 'There's four little ones over there, Jack. You want them to see their dad get a bashing?'

'All right, all right!' Jack was irritated by Bert's good sense. 'And 'ave a quick shave, will yer? Look like a bloody tramp!'

Bert couldn't help laughing at Jack, who had always been a bad loser. 'Wouldn't mind a bit of that bacon!' he grinned.

'I'm doing enough for all of us,' Jack said. 'How's Liz?'

Bert stretched and yawned. 'Says she feels a lot better. Got a night's sleep; s'pose that's something. Wants me to go out and pick this morning.'

'She'll only nag if you don't,' Jack mused, while turning the bacon.

'True. Wouldn't mind as it 'appens. My fingers are picking-happy!'

'We can take it in turns to pop back and see how she is.' Jack cracked an egg on the side of another frying pan. 'Set the table up then, Bert, and get that bread buttered! We're in for a feast.'

While the Armstrong family tucked into eggs, bacon and tomatoes, the Wrights nibbled on toast and marmalade. The atmosphere around their table was tense. Julia had caught the faint waft of Laura's perfume on Richard and had made him confess that he had seen her.

No matter how well he lied, insisting that it was a chance meeting and had lasted no more than a few minutes, she refused point-blank to believe him.

'I think it's time for a confrontation,' Julia said, wiping the corner of her mouth with her napkin. 'Knowing the way those people's minds work they wouldn't want to come here – they'll want a neutral venue. The White Horse should do.'

'That's out of the question and you know it. And besides, there would be no point. It's over and done with.'

'You think so?' She smiled mischievously. 'Not in my book. The way I see it, it's another beginning.'

'I'm not with you.' Richard was determined to play it down.

'The whore's husband must be told that his wife is leaving him. And you must tell him why. Simple.'

'There's no question of Laura leaving her family. I told you, it's over!'

'I think lunch-time would be best. When it's quiet . . .'

'Will you shut up, woman!' He banged his fist down on the table. 'I've had enough!'

Julia stood up and pushed her chair under the table with vengeance. 'Well I haven't! Not yet.'

Richard pushed his hands through his hair and his breathing became erratic.

'I want you out of this house by the end of the week!' she yelled. 'And I don't want you to come anywhere near me while you are packing up ready to clear out. You can tell your family what you like. You can live where you like. In the cottage if you must.' She placed the palms of her hands down on the table, leaned forward and spoke into his face. 'I want you out of my life.'

He suddenly found the turn of events amusing. She was giving him his freedom, at a price of course, but she was giving it to him.

'I need time to think about this . . .'

'No! No more time to think. If you don't arrange a meeting with her husband, I shall.' Julia's mind was obviously made up.

'Fine.' Richard forced a smile. 'You go ahead. Make whatever arrangements you like. But don't expect me to be part of it. I have work to do.' He made for the door, hoping that would be an end of it.

'Coward!' she screamed. 'Dreamer!' Filled with frustration, Julia picked up a dining-chair, raised it above her head and brought it down on the floor;

raised it again, smashed it, raised it and smashed it, until the mahogany chair was a pile of broken wood and ripped velvet.

Standing in the doorway, shocked at the scene, Janet the maid could do nothing but stare in horror. Unfortunately for her, Julia looked up. 'How long have you been standing there?' she screeched, before hurling a piece of the broken chair across the room, just missing Janet's head.

Grabbing Julia's arm from behind, Richard pulled the chair from her. 'I think some strong tea would be in order, Janet,' he said, keeping a tight grip on his wife.

Settling Julia on the sofa, Richard went into the kitchen to reassure Janet. 'I'm sorry about that,' he said, embarrassed.

'But sorry isn't really enough, is it, Mr Richard? Sorry won't make your wife better.' She was angry and didn't care that he knew.

'I've spent three happy years here' – she poured tea into three cups – 'and Mrs Wright has never treated me the way she has these past two weeks.' She kept her back to him. 'And it's all your fault.'

Richard couldn't believe his ears, even the maid was getting at him. 'I don't think . . .'

'I don't care what you think! Jealousy's a terrible thing. You've got to make her believe you love her. You owe her that . . . she's not as strong as . . .' Her voice trailed off.

Feeling drained, Richard dropped into a kitchen chair. 'I suppose you're right,' he said slowly, 'I am the stronger of the two . . .'

'Only just!' She shot him a look, picked up the tray and marched towards the door. 'Now come and drink this tea and spend a bit of time with your wife!'

Bemused by Janet's sudden display, he followed her into the sitting room and sat on the arm of a sofa while she handed Julia a cup of tea. 'I have a feeling I'm not the most popular man in the world,' he mused.

'I heard all of that,' Julia said quietly. 'Thank you, Janet. I can't tell you how much I appreciate your loyalty.'

'It's not loyalty in my book, ma'am – it's fondness. I know you were ready to kill me just now when I had done nothing wrong, but I want you to know that I do like you.' Janet swallowed back her tears. 'And I love my work. I hope you won't feel you have to let me go because of it. As far as I am concerned, it didn't happen.'

Julia looked from Janet to Richard. 'Well – I've

heard of blessings in disguise . . . It seems I've got a friend as well as an excellent maid.'

'Which according to my mother, ma'am, is how it should be.' Janet sipped her tea. 'I haven't been as trustworthy as I should have been. I let my boyfriend come into your home without asking permission. He was hidden away in my room and we did things . . . we didn't ought to.'

Julia raised an eyebrow and tried not to laugh. She caught Richard's eye and could see that he too was struggling to keep a straight face. 'I think we can forgive you for that, Janet,' she managed to say.

'But it might be worth asking us first . . . should the occasion arise in the future . . .'

'I realize that now, sir.'

'Good.' Julia stood up. 'Um . . . I think I'll take my tea into the library, Janet, if you don't mind . . .'

'No, ma'am, that's only right and proper.'

'Yes, I er, I think I'll join you,' said Richard.

Once inside the panelled room with the door shut and their cups safely on the table, Julia and Richard giggled at their maid's surprising intervention in their lives.

Liz enjoyed being pampered; waited on hand and foot, having her breakfast in bed while the others sat round her pine table just outside the hut. 'You should cook more often, Jack! This is lovely!' she called through the open doorway.

'I've always cooked the breakfast, Lizzie. Ask Laura!' Jack's retort came flying back. 'Of course, she only tells you what I *don't* do!'

'Don't need to!' Liz said. 'I know you from old . . . my lazy little brother!'

Jack appeared in the doorway. 'You're loving this, ain't yer?'

'Makes a bloody change!'

Jack sat on the edge of her bed and sipped his tea. 'Just saw that poor cow, Mrs Brown. One eye looks like 'er belly button and she's got a bruise as big as a mushroom.'

'Bastard,' Liz murmured.

'I wanted to go over and see 'im but Bert stopped me.'

'And so he should. I'm gonna report Brown to the Welfare when I get back.'

'So you don't think I should . . .'

'No!' Liz cut in, 'he's such an artful sod he'll put you in the wrong.'

'Well, we'll see.' He watched Liz as she picked at her food disinterestedly. 'You won't get up, Liz, will yer, while we're on the hop fields and can't keep an eye on you?'

'No . . . I know when I'm beaten.' She handed him her plate and slid down under her covers. 'Besides, I've got to get my strength back for the pub tonight. And before you say anything, Jack, I'm going. I don't wanna miss out on those final get-togethers . . .'

'Fair enough,' Jack sniffed, 'at least there's a bit more colour in your face this morning . . . not as much as Mrs Brown's though,' he grinned.

Liz closed her eyes and yawned. 'You're not gonna leave it be, are yer?'

'Don't know what you mean,' he said with mock innocence.

'Wotcher, Jack!' Brianny stood in the doorway.

'You're up early, boy.' Jack wondered what he wanted.

'Well, I didn't get any worms, Jack – but I did get this.' Cupping his hand around the silver pocket watch so that only Jack could see it, he sniffed proudly, 'What d'yer think of that then, eh? Antique that is.'

'Yeah, and white-hot from the Wrights' place, no doubt?'

'I can just see you with this when you're in that three-piece whistle. I've put an order in for a silver fob-chain an' all.'

Jack sucked his teeth, leaned back in his chair and

peered at Brianny for a few silent seconds. 'You've gotta get yourself back into that place before that's missed.'

'Leave off!' Brianny chortled. 'You gone mad, or what?'

'I'm telling yer to put it back!'

'No way! What d'yer take . . .'

'Brianny!' Jack broke in, 'I'm 'aving real trouble not giving you a clip round the ear. Look at my face.' Brianny peered back at him, a scared look in his eyes.

'They'll 'ave you for this. You'll get time. Right? You're walking into their hands, you silly bastard!' Jack's eyes were blazing with fury. 'And for Christ's sake don't get caught putting it back!'

'It's a bit strong, innit Jack?' Brianny was worried – very worried.

'Yes! You've done a silly thing and now you're gonna 'ave to work ten times as hard undoing it.' He sounded grave. 'I s'pose it all seemed so simple – pop into a room and take just one thing, which they're bound not to miss, right?'

'Yeah,' Brianny murmured, 'what's wrong with that?'

'What's wrong with it? That lot don't miss a trick! They'd scrape mould off cheese rather than throw it away. Richard Wright probably goes round checking his possessions every night! It's 'opping time, Brian! They expect! They wait!'

Jack drew breath and slowly shook his head again. 'You've walked into it,' he said more quietly.

'You'll be all right, love,' Liz said, turning over on her side to ease the pain, 'that skinny body of yours'll be able to slip in the farmhouse when its dark.'

'Yeah, well, trouble is, I've 'ad a row with Janet, you know, the maid.' He pushed one shoulder back, a nervous habit. 'So I doubt if she'll open the side door for me tonight, or tomorrow come to that.'

Jack sighed heavily. 'What am I gonna do with you, eh?' He thought about it for a while and then held his hand out. 'Give us it, I'll see what I can do. If anything 'appens, keep your mouth shut as to who took it in the first place.'

'But it was me! I took it!' Brianny was confused.

'I said – keep your mouth shut! There's only three people who know that; you, me and Liz. Now then, tell me exactly where the room is. The one where this belongs.'

Once Janet had cleared the kitchen and attended to her other duties, she tapped on the door of the library where Julia was reading the Sunday papers, and entered. 'I was wondering, ma'am, if I could please have an hour off? I've an errand to attend to. I'll make the time up this afternoon.'

'An errand, Janet?' Julia smiled. 'That sounds rather mysterious.'

'It's a personal matter I need to sort out, ma'am.'

Julia looked over the top of her reading glasses. 'There's nothing wrong, is there? You haven't got yourself into trouble with that boyfriend of yours?'

'No, Ma'am. Actually I wanted to tell him that I shan't be seeing him again.'

'Oh, I see. Very well, Janet. But don't be too long.' Julia flicked her newspaper and disappeared behind it again.

Once outside, Janet walked with determination towards the common. She was furious with Brianny and ready to give him a piece of her mind. If Mr Richard were to notice that a watch from his prize collection was missing, she probably would be dismissed on the spot.

As she approached the wide entrance, Janet began to lose her confidence. She imagined a hostile mob of hoodlums ganging up on her. She hadn't been to the huts before; it was a strict rule of Julia's that staff keep their distance from the pickers.

Finding most of the huts locked and the place fairly deserted gave Janet time to adjust to her surroundings. It all looked quite civilized and welcoming and she wondered why she had been afraid. She quickly realized that everyone except a few were already on the hop fields and she had no choice but to go in search of Brianny.

After asking one of the pickers where his mother's bin was and ignoring the wisecracks about a possible shotgun wedding Janet made her way to field three and found Milly, who took an instant liking to her. 'You won't find Brianny picking 'ops, love – not if he can 'elp it,' she said. 'He's only five minutes away, though. Just take the quickest route to the river.'

'He's not swimming already?' Janet smiled back at Milly.

'Fishing, love, fishing. Can't keep 'im away.'

'Oh, right. I'll see if I can find him, then.'

'Yeah. You do that. And get 'im to fetch you round tomorrow for Sunday tea. I'll show you some pictures of when he was little.'

'Thanks.' Janet suddenly felt shy.

Seeing Brianny's red hair, she stepped up her pace and tried to feel angry again. Meeting his mother had taken the edge off her temper and she knew that could be her ruin. This new boyfriend

362

had a way with him. He could get her round his little finger, no trouble.

'I've been looking everywhere for you!' she snapped.

Brianny spun his head round to face her and a broad smile spread across his face. 'Come to make up, 'ave yer?'

'No I have not! I still think you're wrong about the upper classes but that's not why I'm here. Silver pocket watch?' she said, hoping he wouldn't deny it and waste time.

'Shhh . . . keep your voice down!' Brianny stood up and looked embarrassed. He sighed and shook his head. 'I dunno what came over me. It's me mum's birthday next week and I'm skint. I thought I might be able to sell it.' He pushed his hands in his pockets and hung his head in mock shame. 'I couldn't do it, though. I felt as if I'd really let you down.'

'Where is it, Brianny? I've got to get it back before it's missed!'

'I went to see my uncle this morning and confessed. He took it away from me.'

'Oh, yeah? And pigs might fly!' Her cheeks flushed with anger. 'I should have known you'd pull something like this. You've sold it, haven't you?' she yelled.

'It's the truth! My life! I'll take you to 'im, if you like, and he'll give it back.'

'You're a liar! You sold it, and now that you know I've found you out you're gonna get it back!'

Brianny could see over Janet's shoulder that Jack was making his way towards them and couldn't think quickly enough for the next best thing to say so he tried a bit of romance. Moving in close he cupped Janet's face. 'Look, don't go and upset yourself over a silly watch . . .'

She pulled away and pushed his arm from her. 'You're nothing but a common thief, like your so-called uncle!' she yelled.

'Oi, oi, oi!' Jack's loud voice boomed. 'Less of that, young lady,' he said more quietly as he arrived. He grabbed her right hand and pushed the watch into her palm. 'I was going to return it myself, but since you're here . . .'

'You followed me from the hop field!' she snapped.

'That's right, I did. I knew the minute I saw you why you were here. You don't 'ave to do this for Brianny. I'm prepared to take it myself and admit that he stole it. I expect they'll call the police but it'll be good for 'im. A few nights inside a cell should teach him a lesson. Then when he gets back to London, he'll have the Old Bailey to face.' Jack hoped she wouldn't call his bluff.

'Well . . . I suppose he did see he'd done wrong
. . .' She began to weaken. 'And if it came out, I
would lose my job straight away!' She turned to
Brianny. 'How could you do that to me? I trusted
you. You could have got me into so much trouble.
My parents would have killed me.'

For the first time in his life, Brianny looked
ashamed of himself. 'Yeah, I know. I'm sorry,'
he said, surprising Jack.

Janet slipped the watch into her pocket. 'If you
knew how much this is worth . . .'

'Yeah?' Brianny couldn't resist showing sudden
interest.

Missing the point, Janet smiled at him. 'Shall I
see you later, by the oak tree?'

'Yeah. By the oak tree.'

Janet turned and walked quickly away.

'Uncle?' Jack grinned at Brianny.

Brianny scratched his cheek, 'Well, I suppose you
are in a way. I've known you long enough.'

'That's right, you 'ave.' Jack was moved by the
sincerity in the lad's voice. 'So you won't mind if
I keep my eye on you then, till yer dad gets out?'

'When you can see me, Jack.' Brianny grinned
cheekily. 'When you can see me.'

'I'll tell you what,' Jack said casually, 'you don't
grab that rod, you'll lose it.'

365

Brianny spun around to see that he had well and truly got a bite. He grabbed the rod and, with a little advice from Jack, reeled in a struggling pike.

When Janet arrived back at the farmhouse, Richard and Julia were waiting for her. She could tell by their expressions that they had something on their minds and she had a feeling she knew what it was. Pretending not to notice their stern faces, she rushed by, excusing herself for a couple of minutes, saying she would be down directly.

Once upstairs she slipped into the silver-room and placed the watch on the window-sill, so that it was just hidden by the drawn curtains, and unrolled the green baize. She quickly scanned the room, to check nothing else was missing, before she left.

'Janet, we'd like a word,' Julia said frostily, 'please come into the library.'

Once they were seated, Janet smiled inwardly. She knew what was coming and was pleased that she had been driven to go in search of Brianny that very morning. Fate, she decided, had a way of seeing right done.

'Mr Richard has something to ask you.'

Janet looked innocently at Richard. 'Yes, sir?'

Richard cleared his throat. 'I er . . . I just noticed, my collection of antique pocket watches . . .'

'Oh, Lord!' Janet's hand flew to her mouth. 'I had intended to polish them, I even made a start, this morning in fact, just before . . .' She was alluding to Julia's outburst and the smashing of the chair.

'No, no, Janet. I'm not concerned about that. I know you have a lot to do and . . . and besides they don't look that dull . . .' He was floundering and could feel Julia's piercing eyes willing him to get to the point. 'It would appear,' he said, 'that one of the pocket watches . . . is missing.'

Janet sat back in her chair and looked thoughtful. 'Missing? I don't see how that can be. They were there earlier . . . just a couple of hours ago.'

'You said you had some business to attend to, Janet. With this boyfriend of yours. The one, presumably, who you allowed into this house without our consent.' Julia suddenly seemed very cold and distant.

'Not business, ma'am. It was more personal than that, and as a matter of fact, we've made up.' Janet was almost enjoying the scenario; had she not noticed that watch missing, it would have been a very different scene. She would by now have been reduced to a quivering wreck.

'That's as may be, but—'

'I feel as if I'm on trial!' Janet cut in with a sham protest.

367

'No, Janet, of course not!' Richard was feeling extremely uncomfortable. 'We just wondered if you . . .'

'May I see the collection?'

'Good idea.' Julia strode out of the library looking very much in charge.

Richard gave Janet a comforting, apologetic look and stood aside, allowing her to pass.

Marching into the silver-room, Julia stood by the collection with her arms folded. The gap where a watch should have been spoke for itself.

'It can't be far,' Janet said, 'it's the one I first picked up when I was starting to lay them out for polishing. Normally I would have laid it on the polishing cloth but when I heard the racket from below . . .'

'Yes, all right Janet!' Julia snapped, 'but where is the watch?'

'On the window-sill, ma'am. I put it there before I rushed down to see . . .'

'Where on the window-sill?' Julia did not wish to be reminded of her earlier outburst.

Janet walked to the window and pointed. 'Right here, ma'am,' she said, trying not to sound smug. She picked up the watch. 'I don't know how you could have missed it.'

*   *   *

On her way back to the huts to check on Liz, Laura caught up with Terry's mother who looked down in the dumps. 'Cheer up, Nell; it may never 'appen.'

'It already has, Laura, that's the trouble.' She pushed her hand into her apron pocket and pulled out a crumpled piece of paper. 'My Terry left this on the table this morning.' She handed the note to Laura. 'I 'aven't shown it to no one else. Didn't take it too seriously at first, then I got to thinking while I was picking the hops . . .' She sighed heavily and rubbed her eyes. 'Just as well 'is father's not around to see it. He'd have tried shaking it out of the boy. You know what men are like.'

Walking slowly by Nell's side, Laura read the note.

I'm sorry Mum, but I think this is for the best.
I'll write and let you know where I end up.
I love you.
Terry.

Laura looked into Nell's troubled face. 'Shake what out of 'im, Nell?' she asked carefully.

'Oh, come on, Laura, you know full well.' There was a short pause while Laura waited. She couldn't commiserate until she knew for sure. It would have been embarrassing for both of them if she had got it wrong.

'My Terry's not like other boys . . .' Her voice trailed off.

'Not all lads are toughies.'

'The boy's a—' She stopped, took a breath. 'Terry's a—' She stopped again and bit her lip. She couldn't say the word.

'Has he said so?'

'Yeah. Last night. In bed. Told me outright.' She leaned against a hut wall. 'He's all I've got. He's everything.' She looked into Laura's face. 'I'm scared. I'm scared of what he might do.'

Laura took Nell by the arm and held her hand tight. 'Come on. I'll walk you back to your hut and we'll see what we can sort out. He couldn't 'ave got far. We'll send Bert out in his lorry to catch 'im up.'

'No. He'd die if he thought I'd told the men.'

Looking across to Nell's hut, Laura's face opened into a beautiful smile. 'Bless 'is little luminous socks,' she laughed. Sitting crosslegged outside the locked hut was Terry, his bulging bag next to him. When he saw his mother, he beamed, stood up and waved. 'Go on,' Laura smiled, 'he won't want me around. But don't be too soft with 'im! Yell if you have to; but get it through his thick skull

370

that we love him no matter what! And tell 'im I know, right?'

Nell bit her bottom lip. 'You think I should?'

'Yes! Get it out from under the mat, for God's sake! Anyone'd think he was the Ripper!' Laura brushed a kiss across Nell's cheek. 'There are thousands like Terry, Nell. He won't be alone. Don't try to change 'im, eh?' she said tenderly.

'I wouldn't want 'im any different,' Nell grinned.

'That's the spirit! And make sure he knows it!'

Half-walking, half-running, Nell left Laura standing there wondering why God made everyone so very different when he expected them all to get on together in one small world.

'God, I'm bored, Laura!' Liz was already getting back on form. 'Hope you've managed to collect me some True Love paperbacks?' She plumped her pillows and sank into them.

Laura tossed two paperbacks on to Liz's bed. 'Kay and Jack 'ave skived off already, so I 'ave as well. Don't see why I should pick when that lazy sod can't be bothered.' She poured herself a glass of lemonade. 'Walked away without a by your leave!'

'Where'd he go?'

'I don't know and I don't care! I'm not his keeper, thank God.'

'What about lover-boy? Any more light been thrown on 'is antics?'

Laura couldn't help laughing at Liz. 'Look at you; weak as a kitten, but your brain's still going non-stop . . .'

'The day my brain goes, Laura, is the day I'll lay me down to—'

'Yeah, all right, Liz!' Laura cut in sharply. She didn't even want Liz to mention the word. Picking up the white enamel bucket, she poured water into Liz's blackened kettle. 'That nutcase of a wife's been keeping her strings round Richard's neck all right.' Laura reached for a box of matches on the shelf.

'You know what, Liz,' she said thoughtfully, 'I don't think there's anything wrong with Julia Wright . . . up there, I mean.' She tapped the side of her head. 'She's only on tranquillizers for God's sake; how many people do we know that take pills, eh? Uppers, downers . . .' She struck a match and lit the Primus stove. 'She bloody well uses it to get her way, that's all. And everyone falls for it. Even Fran thinks she's got a split personality. Well, if she thinks I'm giving up that easily, she's got another think coming!'

'What's that supposed to mean?' Liz mumbled, her face half buried in her pillow.

Laura sat on the edge of Liz's bed. 'She paid me a visit; I'm gonna return it.'

'No you're not, don't be daft.'

'She's really got to me this time.' Laura remembered Julia's spiteful words. *He no longer requires your services . . .*

'This world's like a fucking madhouse,' Jack said, lighting his roll-up.

'How long 'ave you been in that doorway?' Laura snapped.

'I've just got 'ere,' Jack said innocently, in his little-boy tone. He wasn't going to let her know he had heard everything. Why should he? 'I've just saved young Brianny's neck. Don't suppose I'll get any thanks for it.' He was good at changing the subject – always had been.

'Do me a favour, you two,' Liz quietly moaned, 'piss off and let me 'ave a doze . . .'

'I was just gonna make you a fresh cup of tea!'

'Later Laura . . . later. I'm tired . . .'

'All right. I'll look in on you in half an hour. Just in case you're "bored stiff" again.'

Flicking her long hair off her face, Laura stood proudly, waiting for Jack to stand aside and let her pass. She was furious with Liz for using her wiles to pair them up in that way.

'After you,' Jack teased, and improvised a gentle-manly gesture as he stood aside. 'If there was a puddle I would gladly . . .' He started to chuckle as she marched away, ignoring his sarcasm.

'And get back to that field the pair of yer . . .' Liz mumbled to herself, 'leaving Bert all on 'is own!' She sighed and drifted off into a light drug-induced sleep.

Jack stood behind Laura as she turned the key in the padlock. 'What d'you want?' she asked curtly.

'Cup of tea and a talk,' he said casually.

She turned and glared at him. 'No, and no!'

'Stop throwing tantrums – you're too old for all that, now.'

'All right,' she said, composing herself, 'please go away, I do not want your company. Better?' She pulled the door open and went inside, daring him to follow her.

'I only wanna talk, Laura.'

'Well go and find someone else to fill in your spare time.' She slammed her flask down on to the small table. 'I'm sorry, Jack, but I do mean it. I don't wanna be in your company unless I 'ave to.'

Her voice had taken on a different tone, one he didn't recognize. It didn't sound like the old Laura, and he suddenly realized that somewhere along the

374

way, she really had changed. 'You mean we can't be friends – not even for Kay's sake?' He was using Kay again.

'No. It's all or nothing.' She found herself offering an ultimatum when she had already moved on from that.

Jack was quick to pick up on it. 'You mean we should think about—'

'No!' she snapped, then lowered her voice. 'No, I don't. I was just, emphasizing . . .' She turned away, embarrassed.

'Nothing?' he asked miserably.

'That's right. Nothing.' She spoke in a quiet voice. 'We did have everything, once. But now there's nothing.'

'Fair enough,' he managed to say and turned away from her.

Laura watched as he walked towards the hop fields. He looked sad, and somehow she felt he would be shedding a tear and, to her own surprise, it left her cold. She felt nothing. She had already cried him out of her system. All she wanted to do now was think about Richard and the best way to deal with Julia Wright. She had been humiliated a second time and she was not going to let Julia get away scot-free.

*   *   *

'I expect you'll be glad to see the back of that lot, eh, Mr Wright?' There was a touch of bitterness in the bartender's voice as he shouted to be heard above the sound coming from the public bar. 'Brewery won't be too happy about it, mind you. We rely on the hop-pickers' trade.'

The man was in the middle of delivering his rehearsed speech and Richard knew it. There was more to come, from him and from one or two other landlords who would be feeling miffed. He consoled himself that things would settle down in a couple of months and until then he would have to take what was coming. He swallowed his beer without saying a word, hoping the bartender would serve his noisy, demanding customers in the other bar.

'You're not going to be too popular,' the man grinned. 'That lot in there are out for blood, if you ask me.'

Richard finished his beer. 'That's absolute nonsense and you know it. They're out for no such thing. In fact' – he pushed his empty glass forward – 'if I were you I would serve them pretty quick; otherwise it could well be you they'll lynch.' He leaned forward and narrowed his eyes. 'Can you imagine the reaction if you had to tell them you had no beer? Think about it. No hops – no beer.'

The barman stared blankly back at Richard.

'Half that lot wouldn't want to come back next year,' Richard said. 'Our numbers were nearly a third down this year. Several of the huts are empty. Thank your lucky stars that we can afford the bloody machines!' He picked up his car keys and stormed out.

'He's in a black mood tonight,' one of the locals said with a wry smile.

'Yeah . . . he's got a point though,' the bartender said thoughtfully, 'he certainly has got a point.'

Richard turned the key in the ignition, wishing he hadn't bothered to go into the White Horse tonight. He was sick of the same old conversation. Anyone would think he had invented the machines himself. Sometimes he wished he could pack a bag and walk away from the lot of them. Catch a train to the farthest corner of the earth where he knew no one.

Pulling slowly out of the car park and into the lane, he noticed a torch shining in the distance and made a mental note to take care when he passed, in case it was a drunk who just might walk out in front of him. He stayed in second gear, feeling in no hurry to go home and face Julia and the kind of mood she might be in now. She was fine when he left, but there was no telling. He approached the pedestrian with caution and was mildly surprised to see he was being waved down, and even more surprised on arrival to see that it was Laura's daughter who was shining her torch into his car.

'I'm sorry to stop you, Mr Wright. I wondered if you could give me a lift back as far as your farmhouse. It's darker out here than I thought.'

Without hesitation, Richard reached across and opened the passenger door. 'I really don't think you should be strolling along dark lanes at this hour . . .'

Kay climbed in and pulled the door shut behind her. 'I didn't realize how dark it was tonight. I've walked back on my own before.'

'Have you, now?'

'My torch battery seems to be going,' Kay continued, trying to ignore his disapproving tone.

'It can be pretty black along these lanes once you get away from the lights of the White Horse,' Richard continued, determined to drive home his word of warning.

'I know. I don't think I'll do it again.'

Kay was telling him what she knew he wanted to hear, simply to end it. Richard recognized a little of her mother coming out and wished he could talk openly about Laura. He allowed himself the pleasure of imagining the three of them in the car, as a family, and drove along in silence until they reached the farmhouse.

'You should be safe now,' he smiled. 'The lights from the cottages will see you back.'

Kay nodded and smiled shyly. 'Thanks, Mr Wright.'

'Pleasure.'

She climbed out of the car and looked back at him, and as their eyes met he could tell instinctively that Kay knew. She shut the car door behind her and walked slowly away.

Richard watched as she disappeared along the lane, quite unaware of the perilous situation he had placed himself in.

Julia was in her bathrobe by the fire, sipping cognac. She looked genuinely pleased to see him.

'How any parent can allow a girl of fifteen to be out alone at night beats me.' He told her he had given Kay a lift; he had decided to tell Julia before another web of lies had to be woven in order to cover up. Her perception of late had been pretty good and he felt sure she would have picked up something from his manner had he not said anything.

'They have a completely different way of looking at things, Richard,' she said casually, 'it can't just be ignorance.'

Grateful that she was in a calm mood, he poured

himself a drink and joined her. 'Maybe you're right,' he said.

'And you,' she snapped, 'shouldn't be giving fifteen-year-olds a lift! Especially not that particular one!'

Richard dropped his head back and sighed.

'Thank goodness they'll soon be out of our lives.' She lit a cigarette, blew the smoke towards him and smiled. 'Then perhaps we can start to live again.'

'Yes, let's hope so,' he said, resigned to it, miserable at the thought of spending his life without the woman he loved and with someone he could hardly face waking up to.

Thirteen

The lively mood had spread into the private bar as some of the pickers found their way in and socialized with the locals, managing to bring everyone together in a matter of minutes. Jack had insisted that Liz sat in the only armchair, in a corner with her feet up. Smokers were not allowed too close to her and he had borrowed a nice soft cushion and propped it behind her head. She had told him to stop fussing, but was more than relieved that he was looking after her. She wasn't feeling as good as she had let on.

Once he was satisfied that she was OK, Jack started to enjoy himself in his favourite pub, that is until he realized that Kay, after two, maybe three Babychams had gone back to the huts without them.

'Dark as a fox's mouth out there!' He directed his anger at Laura, but she kept her head turned away while he ranted on.

'Lettin' 'er go back in the dark!' Jack barked. 'Only 'ope her torch battery don't pack up, that's all. Pitch-bloody-black!'

'It's not all that bright in here either, all this smoke. And you shouldn't 'ave let her have those Babychams. She's only fifteen!'

Liz grinned at the pair of them and then, timing it perfectly, with the piano-player taking a breather, she started to sing quietly: *What Do You Want To Make Those Eyes At Me For.*

Kay had made it safely back to the common and met up with Zacchi, who had been waiting for her. After arranging a secret rendezvous they met again across the river and walked hand in hand until they came to a freshly built haystack.

Clambering to the top, Zacchi reached out for Kay's hand and tried to pull her up. They were both laughing so much it seemed an impossible task.

'Farmer'd go mad if he saw us,' Kay giggled, 'spoiling his lovely neat haystack.'

'Grip my hand and stop messing about.'

'I can't climb right to the top, Zacchi! It's all right for you with your long legs.'

'Come on, you've done it enough in the past, I bet! I can just imagine you and Terry when you were little.'

Kay grabbed his hand and allowed him to pull
her up to the very top. Once there, they dropped
down and stretched out. Kay was still laughing and
trying to get her breath back.

'This is it.' Zacchi gazed up at the star spangled
sky. 'This is the place. Away from everyone. Our
little piece of heaven. Just us, and the stars.'

'And the moon,' Kay added.

'And the moon,' he agreed.

Quietening down, Kay stroked Zacchi's hand.
'This reminds me of Christmas. A bit of snow
and we'd 'ave a nativity scene. All that's missing
is the baby Jesus.'

'Well.' Zacchi smiled, turning on his side and
kissing her cheek lightly. 'We could always do
something about that.'

'I walked into that one, didn't I?'

'Want me to propose, do you?'

'Don't be daft. All I want from you is a cuddle.'
She became pensive for a while. Zacchi waited, he
was used to her and liked it when she went off into
her private world.

'My mum and dad used to cuddle me all the
time,' she said finally, 'until a big solid icicle came
crashing through the ceiling, when my baby brother
died . . . they froze. Still,' she said more brightly,
'I've got you now . . . for a little while longer.'

383

They lay there, silently enjoying their time alone, listening to the occasional owl and a dog barking in the distance.

'This is something special, you know. What we've got,' Zacchi said thoughtfully.

'I know. And it's scary.' Kay sat up and wrapped her arms around her knees. 'It's all right now. We've got every day. But what happens when it's time to go?'

Zacchi reached across and pulled her back down. 'You must have been reading my mind,' he said in a deep voice, before kissing her full on the mouth.

Jack leaned on the bar in the White Horse, soaking up the atmosphere and enjoying the colourful scene. The sounds of people talking and laughing reverberated around the smoky room. The hubbub was reaching a crescendo. He wondered if the pickers had finally realized that their social gatherings would now be few and were making the most of things. There was a special relationship between hop-pickers; the way they lived on the common, sharing basic facilities, time, problems . . .

The happy banter, the intimate conversations and patchy group singing created the loudest, most excited buzz the bartender had heard in the saloon. 'Can't hear myself think,' he told Jack happily.

'You will soon, mate. You will soon. Be as dead as a doornail in 'ere once we've gone – never to return.' Jack downed the rest of his beer in one go and passed over the empty glass.

'Don't remind me!' The barman shook his head slowly as he pulled Jack another pint. 'We'll miss you – that's for sure.'

Catching sight of Brown by the door, shoving his wife outside, made Jack's blood boil. 'What's that spiteful bastard up to now?'

'Don't get involved, Jack. It's not worth it.' The bartender had seen many domestic arguments in his lifetime.

'Keep my beer for me,' Jack said, throwing back his shoulders and turning towards the door.

Once outside in the cool night air, Jack watched as Brown ordered his skinny wife and kids home.

'Ain't they got a torch?' he asked casually, trying to keep his cool.

'Torch?' Brown grinned, showing his gappy stained teeth. 'What the fuck she wanna torch for? The moon's out, en' it?'

Jack grabbed him by the arm. 'I couldn't help noticing that swollen eye. How'd she get that?'

Pulling his arm away sharply, Brown peered at Jack through his bleary eyes. 'She fell over. Why?'

'Fell over, eh? Sure she wasn't pushed?'

Brown shook his head slowly and grinned. 'She been telling porkies agen? Tch. Women!' He grabbed the brass handle and pulled the pub door open. 'Got nuffing better to do, 'ave they?'

'Your bullying days are over, Brown.'

Brown's skinny body shook with thin laughter. 'I'll buy you a pint – come on.'

Jack's hand was on the man's collar before he could wipe the grin from his face. He dragged him in close, eyeball to eyeball. 'I would 'ave done this a long time ago if I had known what you been up to, you yellow streak of . . .' He let go his grip. 'I don't know why I'm talking to you!' He pulled back his right arm and threw his fist forward to land one almighty punch on Brown's face, which forced him to the ground.

'Get up!' Jack yelled. 'Get up!'

He grabbed Brown by the lapels of his jacket and lifted him into the air before throwing him into the nearby lane. Within seconds he was at the man again, dragging him back up the lane by his leg and back on to the grass outside the pub. Again, he lifted him into the air with one hand and slapped him hard across the face with the other, once, twice, three times, until Brown looked like a limp rag doll.

Trying to regain his breath and his temper, Jack stood over him as he lay moaning on the grass. 'Now . . . if you so much as shout at that poor cow again . . . I'll break a bone – right?'

He waited for a response but the man just keeled over, trying to get away. Jack dropped to his knees, pushed his face close up to Brown's and grabbed him by his greasy hair. 'Did you hear what I said?'

'I 'eard . . . I 'eard . . .'

'Good. Because I mean it. And don't think I won't find out, I will!'

Leaving the coward lying in fresh duck shit, Jack stormed back into the bar, picked up his beer and swallowed it as if he had been chewing on chalk. The barman raised an eyebrow and waited, but Jack turned his attention to Laura and Liz who were enjoying a singsong with the others.

'Last orders, please!' The barman's voice rang out above the din, taking Jack by surprise.

'Right in my bloody ear!'

The bartender grinned. 'Shouldn't ignore me, should you? I've been waiting to hear what happened out there.'

'Yeah? Well keep your mind on what's happening in 'ere instead.' Jack winked at him and made his way towards the women.

'What d'yer want to drink, ladies?' His voice was drowned by the others so he moved closer and picked up on the conversation.

'Yeah, but it's so dark out there, Laura . . .'

'Stop worrying, Liz. She'll be all right.'

'Who you talking about now?' Jack asked.

'Kay,' Laura said, 'who else?'

'She 'ad someone with 'er, didn't she?' There was a pause in the conversation while Laura and Liz looked sheepishly at each other. 'You mean to tell me you let her walk back down that dark lane by 'erself?'

'If you 'adn't been so busy flirting with the women you would 'ave noticed and done something about it!'

'What's wrong with you, Laura?' he yelled.

'Oh, give it a rest you two . . .' Liz pleaded. 'It's not the first time she's skived off on 'er own . . . and I doubt it'll be the last.'

Time had slipped by quickly for Kay, who was in a world of her own, enjoying the heavy petting. As Zacchi moved his hand across her breasts, she offered no resistance. Although a message of warning flashed through her mind, Kay's body seemed to have taken on a will of its own and was responding to Zacchi's touch.

Taking her by surprise, he stopped and looked into Kay's face, his dark blue eyes full of questions. Maybe Zacchi was going to call a halt? Didn't want to go any further in case he couldn't stop? Whatever he was thinking, the one thing she wanted was for him to go on. She had left her world behind and was experiencing the sensuous pleasure she had read about in her paperbacks.

Kay gazed into Zacchi's eyes, unable to control her heavy erratic breathing as his hands moved slowly up her legs. Her soft moaning fused with his red-blooded sighs. He kissed her again, holding back no more. Whatever he did was welcomed. Kay had left the world of right and wrong. She was somewhere else now, and it was heavenly.

It wasn't until she felt him unbuckling his leather belt that Kay came down from those heady heights and felt the cold air on her naked thighs.

'Zacchi, not that . . .' she murmured.

'It's all right. I won't hurt you, I promise.' His breathing felt like fire on her neck.

'No Zacchi! . . .' She was unconvincing, wanting him as much as he wanted her.

'Just relax,' he whispered.

'It's not that I don't want to . . .' It felt as if her body was melting as he touched her.

'I love you, Kay. I love you so much . . .' His voice was shaky and sounded different.

'We've go to stop, Zac. We've gone too far . . .'

He kissed her long and passionately until she ached for more, but still somewhere inside a voice sent out that old warning. She pulled her face away from his. 'I need a bit more time,' she moaned, wanting the delicious feeling to go on for ever.

'We don't have that much time, Kay.' His breathing was at fever pitch. 'I'll be able to stop if you want me to. If it hurts. I promise.' He eased himself on top of her and slowly pushed her legs apart with his, pressing his hard body against her naked flesh. 'I won't hurt you,' he said soothingly.

'No, Zacchi!' The alarm bells were louder now. 'No! This is wrong! We've got to stop!'

'You want me as much as I want you . . . It's love Kay, that's all it is. We want to be as close as we can . . .'

'No!' She began to push him off. 'No, Zacchi . . . not this, not yet, I'm not ready . . .'

'I love you, Kay . . .'

She could tell he wasn't listening to her, he was still in that other world where she herself had been a few seconds before.

Realizing she would have to act quickly, she drew a breath and spoke sharply: 'Stop it, right now!'

Taken aback by her sudden mood swing, Zacchi looked puzzled. His eyes showed the merest hint of anger. 'Well, why come here in the first place then?'

'Because I wanted us to be on our own, Zac, but . . .'

'Stop fighting it, Kay. You're driving me mad. Please . . . please let me.'

'We've got to get back before we're missed.' Her voice held guilt and anxiety. 'It's late!'

'One more kiss?' He smiled, hoping to win her back.

'No, Zacchi. I want to go.'

'Well, I'm not letting you,' he teased, grabbing her arms and holding them a little too tightly for her liking.

'Zacchi? Let me *go* . . .'

'No.' He tightened his grip and moved back on top, bringing his face close to hers. 'Stop teasing me, you little minx.' He was smiling but there was a different tone in his voice and it scared Kay.

'Stop it, Zacchi! Get off!' She could hear him laughing playfully as he pinned her down. 'I – said – get – off!' She eased one leg up and began to push and kick him off.

With a mixture of anger and passion, Zacchi

straddled her, sat up and pulled at her blouse, causing it to tear. 'You've teased me for the last time!'

Scared and vulnerable, Kay thought the worst of herself for allowing them to get into this situation. Zacchi was acting out of character. He was different.

'Please don't,' she whispered, her voice almost lost, 'please Zacchi?' The tears trickled down her cheeks as she gazed helplessly up at him.

Seeing her tears, Zacchi stopped. 'Kay! What am I doing?' He threw himself off her and fell back on the haystack. 'Go! Go!' he moaned.

Crying and pulling her underwear back on she scrambled away, half slipping, half climbing down the haystack until she lost her footing and tumbled the rest of the way, falling down until she crashed to the ground, hitting one side of her face on landing. She lay there waiting for Zacchi. She could hear him calling her, saying he was sorry, begging her to forgive him.

'It's all right,' she repeated over and over, trembling from head to toe, 'it wasn't your fault . . .'

Turning-out time at the White Horse was a noisy affair. The publican was having a hard time convincing the Londoners that he really did want to lock up and go to bed. But gradually, one by one, the high-spirited crowd left and headed back to the common, either on foot, swaying from side to side, or by car, depending on their good fortune. Liz was given the front seat of an old shooting-brake belonging to one of the pickers. 'I 'ope you're in a fit state to drive a sick woman,' she told the driver in a drunken, slurring voice which caused laughter all round.

Those who hadn't gone to the pub, or had returned earlier, were sitting by their camp-fires in small groups waiting for the others who would no doubt be bringing back a crate of beer. The night was hardly ended. Terry saw Bert's lorry arrive and made his way over, promising his mother he wouldn't be out too late. He was glad she hadn't told him not to try beer, for once. He felt like getting drunk with the rest of the men.

'Where's Kay?' he asked Laura as she stood by her hut. 'I've been waiting ages for 'er.'

'What d'yer mean, where is she? Kay must 'ave got back well over an hour ago, if not two.'

'Well I ain't seen 'er and nor 'as anyone else.'

Laura sobered up instantly while Liz pulled out her little blue tin. 'Oh, Gawd . . . Jack'll 'ave a field day over this,' she said, knowing how much her brother loved to be right.

'I saw Kay,' a child's voice murmured, 'she got in a car.'

Laura stared down at little Mandy Brown. 'What did you say?' she demanded.

'I saw her . . . it wasn't my fault. I thought she knew him,' Mandy cried. 'I was sitting on the step, with my crisps and lemonade, a car stopped and she got in.'

A stunned silence fell as they looked down at the frail girl who stood rubbing her tired eyes. Liz eased herself down on to a chair by the camp-fire and gently pulled Mandy to her. 'Now then love,' she said, 'you mustn't go saying things like that. You'll worry poor old Liz.'

Mandy looked frightened. 'But she did get in a car. I saw 'er. She told me she was coming back 'ere, then she went down the lane and the car drove up next to 'er and she talked to the man and then she got in. I saw it!' The girl was crying now. 'I'm not telling lies,' she said, 'honest I'm not.'

'It's all right, Mog . . . it's all right.' Liz cuddled Mandy and rocked her. 'Liz knows you wouldn't fib about a thing like that.' She looked into Laura's ashen face – her expression spoke volumes.

'Someone's taken our Kay . . .' she murmured, 'someone's taken our Kay! Jack! Jack!' Laura's screams echoed round the common.

Word went round like lightning, and it wasn't long before the men had gathered to organize a search, having sent a sober man to the farmhouse to give a firsthand report to Richard Wright. For some reason, they felt duty-bound to tell him what had happened to one of his picker's children.

Liz had found it all a bit too much and had taken to her bed, with Bert sitting by her side until she slipped into welcomed sleep.

The women gathered around Laura and in their quiet way gave her the support she needed. She sat by the fire, staring into the flames, shaking from head to toe.

'Someone get her a brandy,' Milly whispered, 'to stop the shaking and get her to talk. She's harbouring shock.' Before they could carry out her instructions, Laura lifted her head and let out a rousing cry. 'Jack! Where's our Kay?' she howled. 'Where is she?'

Jack didn't know how to answer. There was no ducking out of this one. It was bad news about the car, and he knew it.

Zacchi cradled Kay in his arms and rocked her like a baby. 'I'm sorry Kay,' he pleaded, 'I'm really sorry . . .'

'Shhh . . . it's all right . . . I'm all right.' She felt his tears on her face.

'Please don't hate me. Please, please don't hate me.'

'I could never hate you, Zacchi. I love you. I love you so much, I can't bear the thought of a day going by without you being there.'

'I should have know better than to bring you out here. It's my fault. It's all my fault,' he cried, not caring that young men weren't supposed to.

Pulling a handkerchief from her cardigan sleeve, she lovingly wiped the tears from his face and smiled. 'What we gonna do, Zac?'

'I don't know!' He took her handkerchief and blew his nose, which made her laugh. 'Sorry,' he grinned, 'I shouldn't have done that.'

''Course you should. But you can wash it!' She started to laugh and cry at the same time. They fell backwards, laughing. 'We'll have to be careful,' Kay said, 'we'll have to make sure we don't get into a situation like that again.' She was silent for a moment, then she said, 'I don't s'pose I've got the right to ask you, Zacchi, but . . .'

'But what?'

'Have you ever . . . ?'

'Yes, you have got the right to ask. And yes, I have. Does it make any difference?'

'No. I feel jealous, that's all. But I'll tell you something.'

He waited, wondering what was coming.

'That was the first time I've let someone touch me . . . and it's left me wanting more. Does that mean I'm a—?'

'Hardly,' he laughed. 'Come on, let's get back before you're missed.' He took her hand and pulled her up. Wrapped in each other's arms, they walked slowly towards the bridge.

'It is natural, Kay. What we wanted to do.'

'So I shouldn't feel guilty?'

'No.' He stroked her hair. 'And stop worrying; we can wait. We can wait until we're ready to jump the broomstick.'

They walked on in silence, absorbing what he had just said. In his roundabout way, Zacchi had just asked her to marry him.

'And we don't want a local bobby on a bike, neither!' Jack was giving orders while pushing Laura away. She clung on to his arm, begging him to go now, to stop organizing things; to run; to find her Kay.

'Four of you go with Bert and split up once you get to the river!' Jack yelled. 'I'll take the others and we'll comb the hop fields and lanes.'

Kay could hear her dad yelling as she and Zacchi approached the common. 'Zacchi, listen!' she hissed.

'Check the ditches! Check everything!'

'Oh, God . . . what's going on?' Kay groaned. 'We'd best split up, Zacchi. You go round the back way. Go on! I'll see you tomorrow!'

Zacchi was reluctant. 'But your blouse, Kay? And your face – it's swelling on one side!'

'I'll be all right. Just *go*!'

Kay quickened her pace, realizing what was going on. Her dad was organizing a search-party and she was in deep trouble.

'Jack!' Laura cried out, 'Jack, it's Kay!'

Spinning around he saw Kay approach. 'What does she think she's playing at? Where 'ave you been, you little cow!' he yelled. 'And don't stand there like a lemon, come over 'ere!'

Laura felt faint, but willed herself to stay upright. 'Jack . . . she's limping,' she managed to say.

Jack could see her torn blouse and swollen face. 'Who did that to you?' he demanded. 'What d'yer wanna get in a car for? Where's your sense?'

Kay stood motionless; she was dumbstruck. What could she say?

'Jack, stop it! Leave her. Where's your sense?' It was Laura's turn to cry now. 'Leave her be.' She gripped Bert's arm for support while Jack grabbed Kay by the shoulders.

'What sort of a car was it? What colour? What did he look like? Was it someone you knew?' Jack was beside himself. 'Who did this to you?' His voice resounded around the common, bounced off of the tin huts, echoed through Laura's brain.

'Leave her be, Jack . . .' was all Laura could manage as she gently guided Kay towards their hut.

'Nothing terrible happened, Dad!' Kay called back. 'It was just an accident, that's all.'

Jack moved in again and stood in front of the hut doorway, blocking their path. 'Who was it?' he demanded in a voice that neither Kay nor Laura had heard before. It scared them both.

'I don't wanna talk about it, Dad.' Kay bit her bottom lip. 'Please don't make me . . .' She turned into her mother's arms. 'Tell Dad to leave off, Mum, please.'

Laura shot Jack a look and he backed off. 'All right . . . all right; I'll take a walk to cool off, down to the phone box . . . tell the police she's turned up . . .' He walked away, keeping his eyes down; he wanted no one to see what he was feeling.

While Laura bathed Kay's face, Bert poured milk into the small red enamel saucepan for cocoa. He was keeping a low profile, only there in case they needed him.

'D'yer wanna talk about it, love?' Laura asked, not really knowing how she would cope if Kay said Yes. Speculation of what she might have been through was haunting the place – the thoughts were so horrible that no one could put them into words.

The silence told Bert that it was time he was out of the way. He put the saucepan of milk on the Primus stove and turned the gas up until the low blue flame flickered with yellow, then left to check up on Liz.

Laura soothed Kay with soft words of comfort and the warm milky drink before tucking her between clean white sheets on their straw bed. She was ready to strip down herself and climb in when there was a soft tapping on the hut door. Laura opened it to Mrs Brown and young Mandy.

'Can we come in? Mandy's got something she wants to tell yer.'

Laura sighed loudly, this was the last person in the world she wanted to see. 'Can't it wait till the morning?'

'I think it's best she tells you and no one else.'

'Come in then.' Laura made no secret of the fact that she was tired.

Closing the door behind them, Mrs Brown urged

Mandy forward. 'Go on Mand, there's a good girl.'

The frightened child with tear-stained cheeks swallowed hard. 'I know whose car it was,' she said hurriedly, wanting to get it over and done with.

Kay pulled the curtain back and glared at Mandy. 'No you don't! It was dark! She couldn't have seen!'

'Yes I did! It was Mr Wright's car. I saw him come out of the pub, get in his car and then stop. I saw it!'

The tension in that small room could have been cut with a knife.

'That's all we've come to say, Laura. She won't mention it again. I just thought you should know.' Silence consumed the tiny hut.

'One good turn deserves another,' she finally added.

'What good turn?' Laura was grateful for the chance to change the topic of conversation.

'Your Jack. He did me and my kids the biggest favour tonight when he gave my old man an 'iding. I've never seen 'im look sheepish before. It made me realize . . . he's just as weak as . . . in a way. I don't know why, but I'm not so scared of 'im now.'

'That's good, Mrs Brown. Jack did right.' Laura wanted her out of the hut.

'He won't be lashing out at us no more, 'cos I'll be in there with a rolling-pin if I 'ave to.' A smile spread across her face and Laura could see a different look in her eyes; one of hope.

'Come on, Mandy. It's bedtime. And don't worry, Laura. She won't say a word.' The woman left, dragging Mandy behind her.

Laura turned to Kay. 'Well?'

'I don't wanna talk about it.'

'Don't do this to me, Kay . . . tell me what happened.'

From the tone of Laura's voice, Kay realized it would be cruel not to say something. 'All right.' She raised her eyebrows and bit her bottom lip. 'He did give me a lift. I asked him for one. But he dropped me at the farmhouse. I walked back from there. I met up with Zacchi. We had an argument, it broke into a fight.'

Laura felt the tension fall from her. How could she have thought anything else? How could she for even one second have imagined that Richard could have hurt Kay? Guilt flooded through her and she hated herself for jumping to such terrible conclusions. Richard was the gentlest man she had ever met. He wouldn't harm a fly. His face filled her mind but was suddenly overshadowed by Jack. What if he got to hear about Richard giving Kay a lift?

Trying to hide her fear, Laura spoke as casually to Kay as she could, with her mind racing.

'What, exactly, were you having to fight for, Kay?'

'It's not like you think. Things got a bit out of hand, that's all. It was my fault as much as his.'

'Yeah? Tell that to your father.'

'No! No, Mum. You know we can't tell him! There'd be murders between their men and ours. Please don't tell him, please!'

Laura lit a cigarette. 'And what do you think they'll do to Richard Wright? Because that's who they'll think did this. He was seen picking you up!'

'They don't have to know!'

'Oh, come on, Kay! Mrs Brown might keep quiet tonight, but it'll be all round the common first thing! She only has to tell the secret to one of 'em and that's all it'll take!'

'We can't let Dad know about Zacchi! We can't! There'll be a fight and it'll be my fault!'

It was Julia who had opened the door the second time to a messenger from the common, and all within thirty minutes. The first was to say that the Armstrong girl was missing and had been seen accepting a lift, and the second to say she had turned up. Neither of these messages had been given to Richard, who was fast asleep in bed. Julia would have woken him but she was so annoyed with the first that she needed time to think. Her husband had managed at last to threaten their good name.

The second message having put her mind at ease, she found herself smiling as she sipped her cognac. She wondered how best to use the drama to torment Richard.

She had smoked one Sobranie after another and by the time Richard appeared in the doorway the library had a blue smoke-blanket drifting through it.

'What's the matter now?' He sounded rather impatient as well as ill-tempered. He hated to have his sleep broken.

'I thought you were asleep,' Julia purred.

'I was. The smell of those cigarettes has filled the house. It smells foul in the hall.'

'Really. Well come and sit down and I'll tell you why I've been chain-smoking.'

'I'd rather not,' he sighed. 'Perhaps if you opened a window?'

'We've had a visit,' she said, pouring herself

some more brandy. She would tell him about the first but not the second. 'One of the pickers.'

There was a deliberate silence from Julia while Richard waited for her to explain. She thought it would do him good to wonder who had called and why.

Dropping into an armchair, he looked at her wearily. 'What's happened now?'

'I've been trying to think of a way to solve our little problem but I fear there isn't one. The Armstrong girl is missing,' she lied. 'One of the rabble's offspring saw her get into a car outside the White Horse. They are presuming that whoever it was gave her a lift has seduced her and left her for dead in some ditch.' She smiled gracefully at him. 'Murder is on their minds.'

'Well, surely you told them it was me?'

'No Richard, I did not.' As Julia had predicted, he was thinking like a cretin again. 'My guess was that you would. Which is precisely why I didn't wake you.'

Agitated by her smug tone, he stood and began to pace the floor. 'We must tell them. Of course we must.'

Julia squashed her cigarette-end into the ruby glass ashtray. 'I may not be filled with adoration and loyalty right now, but I would prefer not to see my husband swinging from a tree. What would the neighbours think?' She spoke with calm precision. 'You, my love, will be prime suspect. It won't be long before they find their way here; for the second time,' she said, thoroughly enjoying her role as leading lady.

'You think they'll come here, at this time of night?'

'She was seen getting into your car.'

'Yes! But I dropped her off just outside! They wouldn't think that I . . . oh, God, yes, I see what you mean.' He remembered vividly the mood of the pickers that night when he popped into the White Horse, the angry looks. After a night's drinking they could easily forget how well he had treated them in the past.

'There's nothing we can do but sit tight. If they call, you must hide while I phone for the police. They'll lynch you first and ask questions later.'

Richard dropped back into the armchair, stared into the fire and scratched his neck, a nervous habit which he only did when he was truly worried. Apart from anything else, what must Laura be going through? He knew how much Kay meant to her; had begun to mean to him. Part of him wanted to go out and help the men search but he knew that would hardly be wise. Maybe he should take a walk along the lane, check the ditches?

Julia read his mind in a flash. 'Yes, I expect your whore must be feeling quite guilty. But I do think it would be unwise of you to rush gallantly to her rescue,' she grinned.

He looked from the fire to her face. 'I think I'll go back to bed,' he murmured.

'I don't think you should. It's safer here. No danger of us falling asleep. I'll make some strong coffee. We'll need to be alert.' Lighting another cigarette, she made for the door. 'It's going to be a long night,' she mused and left him alone to worry.

As the clock in the drawing-room struck one, it made a faint but welcoming sound for Richard. It reminded him so much of his late father of whom he had been very fond and whose advice he had always welcomed. What would he say now, Richard wondered.

The house had taken on a strange silence; even the Siamese cats were quiet; not asleep, just curled up in their baskets, watching their master.

The creaking of the door as it slowly opened made Richard jump, more because his father had been on his mind than anything else.

'Is anything wrong, Mr Richard?' Janet asked.

'Goodness, Janet, you made me jump! You look wide awake! Can't you sleep?' He smiled broadly at her, pleased to have another person around him.

'I did manage to go off after the second call, sir, but then I heard you down here, talking.'

'What do you mean, Janet, the second call?'

'When the man came to say that the Armstrong girl had turned up, sir.' Janet knew exactly what she was doing, why she was there. She had deliberately put her ear to the floorboards and heard everything.

The two of them looked at each other, an understanding between them. 'I appreciate that, Janet, thank you.' This piece of news really was a blow. Julia had been deliberately lying. 'I think it might be best if you were to go back to bed.'

Janet looked into his face and smiled; he could see both fear and pity in her eyes, which moved him.

Once she had gone, Julia arrived with a tray. 'If that girl thinks she can roam around in her nightclothes—'

'She came down to see if we needed her. Thought that the comings and goings might have woken us and we couldn't get back to sleep.' He spoke in a short sharp tone. 'She would have dressed had we needed her to make some tea or . . . something.'

'How considerate,' Julia said sarcastically. 'I do hope you've not been fucking her too, Richard?'

Richard stared motionless at her. He noticed the smug, twisted expression. 'Julia, you can't mean that?'

'Oh, for goodness' sake, Richard! Where's your sense of humour?'

Tired of trying to work her out, Richard slumped back in his chair and decided not to bother telling her that he knew Kay had been found. He would drink his tea and go to bed.

Lying awake in her bed, Kay had given up trying to force sleep. Dawn was beginning to break and the sound of a cockerel in the distance was a comfort. Soon she would hear people moving about outside. The thought of what the day held in store, though, tore her apart. Questions she could not answer would be thrown at her and if her mother was right about Mandy Brown spilling the beans about the car . . .

After a long time of trying hard to lie still and not disturb her mother, Kay decided it would be best if she got up there and then and waited for the Browns to emerge. She could have a quiet word with Mandy.

Pulling her legs carefully from beneath the sheets,

she slipped out of bed without waking Laura and pulled on her coat and wellingtons. She didn't want to risk making any noise by getting dressed properly.

Inching the door open, she managed to leave and close it behind her without making a sound other than the tiny click of the latch. Once outside in the chilly air, her idea seemed like a bad one. The place was deserted and she felt isolated, and the reality of the web spun the night before hit her. She knew her dad well enough to realize that he would want answers. Her face had swelled up even more during the night and was now beginning to throb.

Looking across to the gypsy camp, Kay wished she could slip into one of the wagons and hide away from all the trouble. She walked slowly away from the huts towards the river, her step quickening as she went until she was running. She had no thoughts on where she might stop and if it were possible she would just keep going, hitching a lift once she was on a main road, and travel to the farthest tip of England, where no one knew her or cared about her bruised face.

Laura was in a deep sleep and a soft tapping on her door mingled with her dreams. She awoke with a start and listened. The tapping continued. She peered at her wrist-watch; it was a couple of minutes before seven a.m. She moved quickly out of the bed, half asleep, and opened the door to Jack who looked drawn and dark around the eyes.

'How's Kay?'

'It's not even seven o'clock, Jack!' She spoke in a low whisper, moving aside to let him in. 'She's still asleep!'

'I've been worried, Laura! I can't 'elp it!' he whispered back.

'Sunday! The only chance for a lie-in!'

Laura closed the door quietly behind him while Jack lit the oil-lamp.

'Keep it turned down low!' she urged. 'I don't wanna wake Kay.'

Jack dropped on to a kitchen chair and ran his hands through his hair. 'I 'aven't slept a wink,' he sighed, 'tossing and turning all night, wondering what she must 'ave gone through. I thought you might 'ave been having the same problem.'

'We'd best go outside so we don't wake 'er.' Laura pulled her coat on and a thick scarf.

'Yeah.' He looked up at her. 'It's really creased me up, y'know.'

'Outside, Jack!' Laura tried to sound sympathetic but she had too much on her mind.

'All right if I take a peep?'

'No, Jack. Leave her be. She's soundo.'

411

'Just look at her, Laura, that's all. I won't wake 'er.'

'Oh, go on then! But be it on your 'ead if you disturb 'er. You know she likes 'er sleep.'

Jack tiptoed forward and carefully lifted a corner of the curtain, and then pulled it back sharply almost bringing it down. 'What're you playing at, Laura!' he snapped; raising his voice, he turned on her: 'What's going on?'

'Shush, Jack! What's wrong with you?'

'She's not there!' he yelled.

Laura gripped the edge of the curtain and pulled it down, sending the supporting hooks flying.

'I can't take this,' Laura said faintly, 'I can't . . .' There was a plea for help in her voice but Jack missed it.

'Where the fuck is she?' His eyes were wide and angry.

'I don't know!' Laura yelled at him. 'I don't know, I don't know, I don't *know*!' She clenched her fists until her nails dug into the palms of her hands.

'All right, all right!' He lowered his voice, trying to pacify her. 'No need to panic. She's probably gone for an early morning stroll. It must 'ave been early as well; I've been out there nearly half an hour wondering whether to come in. I know I'm not . . .'

412

'I'll find her! Little cow!' Laura tried to push his tall broad body out of her way. 'She's gone too far this time!'

Jack stood his ground. 'You can't go out like that, Laura,' he reasoned, 'get yourself dressed properly first. I'll wait outside.'

Laura pulled her coat off and threw it on the bed. 'I'm sick of her moods and swings.' She pulled furiously at her nightdress, almost ripping it from her body. 'Stop gawking! You've seen my body enough times before!'

Jack turned away, it had been years since he had seen her naked.

'I don't know what she thinks she's playing at. But I've had enough. Pass me those slacks!'

Jack tried his best to avert his eyes. 'Oh, yeah, right.' He kept his back to her and passed the garment over.

'Socks. Top drawer.' Her orders were flying at him, she had no time to be coy. 'Red jumper, behind you.'

Once dressed, Laura paused for a breather. She gripped the back of a chair and composed herself. 'Where are we supposed to look first?' She spoke more to herself than to Jack.

'Liz reckons she spends most of 'er time by that river.'

'You can cover the hop fields,' she said, not listening to Jack. 'If I see our Kay floating . . .' She bit her lip and tried not to cry.

'Come on, Laura. You're overdoing it a bit. She's gone out for a walk, that's all!'

'Yeah? Well, maybe she's not walking but running, Jack? Christ knows she's got reason to!'

'What's that supposed to mean?'

There was nothing Laura would have liked more than to tell him everything. About Zacchi. About Richard. About Jack neglecting his daughter all those years. Everything.

'You don't know what her mood swings are like,' she said quietly, 'but how could you, when your thoughts are always somewhere else?'

Jack couldn't help smiling at her nerve. As if she had been such an angel! He had to admit it, though; he quite liked it that she was still feeling jealous. 'Is this the time to go through all that again?'

If Liz had seen Laura and Jack walking side by side on the desolate common it would have done more for her heart than any pills could, but she was fast asleep in spite of Bert's snoring.

'You reckon we should have given Liz a knock?' Jack tried making conversation.

'Don't be stupid. She's not exactly a picture of health right now.'

'True. We haven't helped much, 'ave we?'

'If Kay's back in the hut before we are, I'll kill 'er for this.' Laura was determined not to get into conversation with him. Hate was still in her heart for the man she had given her love to; the man who had betrayed her; slept with another woman long before she had taken a lover.

Once by the river they split up. It made sense to do so and they were now feeling extremely uncomfortable, silent in each other's company. They agreed to keep looking for Kay until an hour was up, then they would meet back there, by the bridge.

Liz was up when they got back, sitting on the edge of her bed enjoying a cup of tea. 'What's up now?' she asked, seeing the look of anguish on Laura's face.

'Madam's decided to go wandering off again. Can't see 'er anywhere,' Laura said. 'She's been out since the crack of dawn.'

'How do we know that?' Jack said worriedly. 'She could 'ave been out all night for all we know.'

'I know, because I was awake all night too. Dropped off somewhere around half past four.'

'Don't know what you're gettin' all stewed up about. Nothing wrong with an early-morning stroll,

is there?' Liz sipped her tea. 'What d'yer reckon
. . . she's topped herself?' Liz grinned.

'That's not funny, Liz!'

'Dozy pair! Kay's got more sense than the two
of you put together. Don't suppose she could
sleep neither.' Liz was determined to remain calm.
Someone had to. 'I take it you've had a good look
along by the river?'

'First place we went.' Jack sounded tired.

'Well, there you are then. She didn't chuck
herself in there, did she? And you tell me any
other way she's gonna end it all?'

'I suppose you're right, Liz,' Jack said.

'So what are we supposed to do then, Liz, sit
'ere and wait?'

'That's right, Laura. Now you're being sensible.
Pour yourselves a drop of that tea. Be able to stand
your spoon up in it. Do you both the world of good,
that will. Meanwhile, I'm climbing back into my
straw bed in case you all forget I need looking
after,' she said cheekily, then added, 'it's a funny
age, fifteen . . . I wouldn't wanna be there again.'

As expected, it didn't take long for the news that
Kay was missing again to go through the common.
Laura was so embarrassed and drained she stayed
inside her hut, and told any interested party that Kay

was not missing but had gone out for a walk. Terry was the only one she invited in. She found herself comforting him, when what she really needed was someone to reassure her.

'She's a bit mixed up, Terry, that's all.' Laura wished she was right and that Kay hadn't done anything silly. 'That's what love does to you,' she said thoughtfully.

'She 'as been acting differently this year,' he said with a touch of spite, 'seemed really moody when you first got 'ere. She wasn't all that friendly.'

That remark made Laura's hackles rise. Kay had told her how Terry and his mother had responded to her on that first day.

'I can't see how you make that out, Terry. Kay was as bright as anything when we arrived; it was after she'd been round to your hut that she sank.'

'Why?' Terry sounded genuine enough. His sad cow-eyes looked questioningly at her. 'What did I do?'

'You rejected her.' Laura didn't want to hurt his feelings, but right was right and she felt he should know. 'You made it painfully clear, as far as I could make out, that you wanted to spend your time with Ray. And your mum was no different.'

Terry blushed and started to push one thumbnail

under the other, a reason to keep his face down: 'Yeah . . . but that was only the first day.'

'I know. The only reason I'm saying it is because you mustn't blame Kay for the way you felt. It's not fair.'

Terry still wouldn't look at her as he made for the door. 'I'm gonna check the river again.'

Laura watched him walk away and, although she felt sorry for him, there was a part of her that felt lighter. In defending Kay, she had realized that she and Jack were just as guilty as Terry. They had been so wrapped up in their own affairs that Kay's feelings had probably been pushed to one side.

Thinking back to that first night when she went off to see Richard, when Kay wanted her to stay and play cards, she was filled with regret and guilt. Her daughter might be fifteen but really, that was no age. She was still a baby who wanted her mum . . . and probably her dad too.

'She's gonna feel my hand on the back of her legs when she does turn up!' Jack suddenly appeared in the doorway. 'Little cow.'

'You haven't laid a finger on her before, Jack – why start now?' Laura said, tired of this show of anger. He was worried, so why couldn't he admit it?

'I think there's more to last night than you're telling me, Laura. Fell over?'

Now he was easing the blame over to her. He could be artful when he put his mind to it.

'I think I'll go and have a little chat with young Mandy Brown. See if she can remember anything about that car.'

Laura felt rage suddenly grip her. 'Oh, leave it be, Jack! Go and look for your daughter instead of standing thinking about what you might do!'

'I've looked everywhere! Searched the fucking place!'

'And don't use that language in front of me!'

'Oh, and you never swear, I s'pose?' he snapped back.

'Not in front of you, no!'

'Well, what bloody difference does that make?'

'Quite a lot, actually!'

'Like what?'

'Oh, fuck off!' she yelled at the top of her voice.

Jack sucked hard on his top lip, trying his best not to laugh at her. 'Wouldn't mind a cup of tea,' he said, pushing his luck for the sheer fun of it.

Terry wandered back towards the river and common, having looked in the small copse where, as children, he and Kay used to play. He walked through the potato field and made his way to the wooden bridge. Once on it, he leaned on the handrail and peered along the river as far as his eye could see, and just as if a magician had tapped his wand, Kay appeared from behind a thick clump of bulrushes. She was paddling on the edge of the river.

Relief swept through him and then anger. 'Kay!' he yelled. 'Kay!'

She began to walk towards him, kicking the water as she came.

'They all think she's dead,' one of the pickers' boys said, 'chucked 'erself in the river in the night.' He sounded disappointed. 'Me and my mate 'ad a bet who'd find 'er floating down the river first.'

Ignoring the ten-year-old, Terry called out again: 'They're organizing a search-party, y'know!'

'You found me easy enough, Terry, why couldn't Mum or Dad?' she called back flatly, a far-away look in her eyes.

'Someone tried to murder 'er, didn't they?' the young boy asked hopefully.

'Because I know how much you love the river, you silly cow!'

'And they don't?'

'They don't know your favourite spots like I do!'

'No, that's right. And you know why? Because they never come for a swim with me, or watch me swim! They never bother to ask where I go or what I do. And please don't tell me it's not true, Terry, because it is.'

'Come out of there, Kay! You're getting your coat soaking wet!'

Slipping her arms out of the sleeves, she tossed her coat on to the bank and if Terry had been more perceptive, he would have realized that she was asking for help. The coat was a lure to bring him down from the bridge and on to the bank, closer to her.

'She ain't all there . . .' The boy shook his head all-knowingly. 'She's definitely got a bit missing up top.'

Kay didn't particularly want to stay in the cold water, and she didn't particularly want to get out. What she needed was someone to drag her out screaming. Someone who could make her feel angry. It was as if her spirit had decided to step out of her body for a while, leaving her numb. She couldn't even cry.

She didn't even mind now about the drama she had caused. So what if they went for Richard Wright? So what if there was a bit of a punch-up between the gypsies and her lot?

'You're acting like a sodding four-year-old!' Terry's voice was filled with anger.

An outraged angler shook his fist at them. 'Can't you keep your voices down? I'm trying to fish!'

'Oh, shut up!' Terry surprised himself, answering back so boldly.

'And what about your Aunt Liz, Kay? You know she's not well!'

'Go and tell 'er I'm OK, then!'

The veins on Terry's neck looked ready to burst. 'Tell 'er yourself!'

'Will you shut up!' The angler stood up, gripping his rod as if it were a whip, and looked threatening.

'I need to swim, Terry. That's all. I just need to swim.'

'With your nightdress on?'

'I need something to keep me warm. It's freezing cold in here.'

'Well, get out then!'

Kay lowered herself into the water, turned on to her back and began to move her feet up and down. It felt wonderful. Freezing cold water on her body with the warm sun on her face.

Poor Terry. She knew he was in a dilemma. 'I'm not going back yet, Tel.' She spoke reassuringly, hoping to calm him. 'I'm sick of the lot of them.

Why don't you come in? I'll teach you to swim. Come on!'

'If I don't go back, Kay, and tell them you're all right, they'll call the police again!'

This time Kay did not answer him. An excruciating pain gripped her left leg as it went into cramp. Her scream pierced the morning, infuriating the angler.

'Bloody cockneys!' he fumed. 'I'll get Mr Wright to ban you from swimming in this river!'

Unable to swim properly, Kay had to use her arms in order to keep up, but the pain worsened and she instinctively grabbed her leg. Crying out as she went under, her mouth filled with water. She let go of her leg and forced the water back with her arms as she pushed herself up to the surface. The pain struck again and she went under, this time going down deeper with her eyes open, the river looked dark and murky. She felt the bed under her right leg and pushed against the soft mud, propelling herself upwards, using her arms and right leg for all they were worth.

As she surfaced, Kay spurted the water out and took in air, treading water and calling out for help.

'Stop messing about, Kay!'

She could hear Terry's voice but before she was

able to answer, the water was covering her again and she went down. Again she kicked against the slimy river-bed and pushed herself up, using her arms, but they were beginning to tire and the pain was now creeping through her right leg, too.

She managed to come up for air again and used every bit of strength and will-power to stay up. 'Terry! Get help! I've got cramp!' she screamed before going under.

Terry was off the bridge now, on the bank and screaming out to Kay to be serious.

'She mucking about or what?' The boy sounded frightened now.

'No,' Terry cried, 'I don't think so.'

The pair of them stood there waiting for her to reappear and were relieved when she did.

'Help me, Terry . . .' Kay managed to say. 'Get help!' she murmured before disappearing into the dark green river.

'She's drowning!' the boy said. 'She's gonna die!'

'Go back!' Terry screamed hysterically. 'Go back to the common! Run! Go! Get someone!' Terry pushed the boy forward once then twice. 'Move, will yer?' he cried. 'Move!'

Terry watched as the shocked boy turned and ran for all he was worth towards the common. Turning to the angler, he screamed for him to help. 'Please, fisherman! Please help! She's drowning!'

'Noisy bloody cockneys! You'll not swim here again – I promise you that!'

'Please! Please! I can't swim! She's drowning and I can't swim!'

Kay still hadn't surfaced. 'She's got cramp!' he screamed. 'She's got cramp and I can't swim. Please,' he begged, 'please! We won't make a noise again, I promise! Please get her out of there!'

'Jack, we 'ave to do something. We can't leave it any longer.' Laura was sick with worry.

'I know that! I never thought I'd be calling on the Old Bill for their help . . .' he murmured. 'Makes you look at things a bit differently, don't it? If Babyface from Bow station was to turn up now I think I'd make a fool of myself.' His voice had the familiar crack in it. 'It's bloody right what they say, eh? Never know what's gonna come and kick you in the guts.

'Gawd knows what this is doing to Liz,' he said, deliberately avoiding eye contact with Laura. He knew she was going through it but didn't know how to comfort her any more. If he tried and she rejected his feeble attempts, he would break down and he couldn't afford to do that, not right then.

The small boy sent by Terry ran through the common towards Laura's hut, yelling and shouting as he went.

'What now?' Liz murmured to Bert as he was plumping up her pillows and straightening her sheets.

'She's dead! She's dead!' The words pierced the quiet that had spread through the entire common. A nervous hush settled as they began to absorb his words. 'Drowned!' he screamed, 'drowned!'

'Who? Who?' someone yelled.

'The fisherman won't pull her out, so she's dead!' The boy was hysterical and full of panic as he approached Laura's hut.

Jack stepped forward and caught the boy as he ran, and lifted him into the air. 'Who's in the river?' he demanded. 'Who?'

'Kay! She's been drowned!'

Laura didn't wait to hear any more; she was running, and crying. 'Wait for me, Jack!' she screamed as Jack raced by. Even though he ignored her words and ran on, she yelled after him. 'No, don't stop! Keep going – I'll catch up!'

'The second bridge, Laura!' A desperate voice followed her. 'She's by the second bridge!'

'Oh Bert!' Liz cried, 'hold me . . . hold me tight!'

Bert pulled Liz close to him; he rocked her, rubbed her back and cradled her head against his chest so she wouldn't see his tears and his distorted face.

Laura tried to run faster, half stumbling, half running and pushing aside anyone who got in her way. It was her Kay the boy was talking about; her baby, and he was saying she was dead. 'Dear God, please don't let it be Kay; don't let it be Kay,' she said over and over until she arrived at the river where a small crowd had already gathered. 'Jack!' she screamed, 'Jack, where are you?'

Jack was swearing, cursing and hitting out at the four men who held him back.

'They're doing all they can, Laura,' someone said, 'the fisherman's giving her artificial respiration.'

Laura froze. Why were those men barring Jack's way? Why was everyone looking at her like that? 'No!' she screamed. 'No! Not my baby! Not my Kay!'

'She kept going under . . .' Terry sobbed. 'I would 'ave gone in but I can't swim . . . she put her arms out to me and I couldn't go in!'

Laura stared at Terry. What was he saying? What was happening? Her brain wasn't functioning; everything was floating, and there was a strange buzzing sound in her head . . . thousands of tiny stars were shooting through a white blanket of light . . . her legs ached and throbbed as if they couldn't take the weight of her slim body.

Grateful for the two pairs of arms that gripped her and held her up, Laura allowed her head to be pushed forward while she repeatedly filled and expelled the air from her lungs. She could hear Jack's desperate voice somewhere in the distance.

'That's my girl! Let me through, you bastards!' Jack was behaving like a caged tiger that had just had its cub stolen. 'That's my daughter!' he sobbed.

'Get away, please!' The angler was working on Kay with speed and expertise. 'Leave me! All of you! Stand back!'

The small crowd obeyed and a silence spread as the circle of friends moved back and watched anxiously. Jack pulled away from the men and dropped to his knees as close to Kay as he could get.

Laura knelt beside him. 'Jack, come away. He knows what he's doing.' She looked into his face. 'He knows what he's doing . . .' she repeated, praying to God that she was right.

'How do we know that, Laura? Eh? How do we know?'

Slowly shaking her head she murmured, 'It's all

we've got.' She felt sorry for him. The only other time she had seen him really cry was when his dog died, way back in the past, before they were married.

'It's not gonna 'appen again, is it?' His tear-filled eyes looked pleadingly at her. 'He wouldn't do that to us again. Not twice, not our Kay as well. Not our Kay. He wouldn't! No! Not two babies, that would be cruel . . . that would be mean.'

Laura slipped her arm around his shoulders. 'Shush, Jack . . . shush,' was all she could manage.

'I'm sorry, Laura. I'm really sorry.'

'Try to calm down, Jack . . . people are listening.'

'I'll make it up to 'er.' He pulled his blue and white handkerchief out of his pocket and blew his nose. 'I've let 'er down, I know that, missed out on her growing up. I was there though, wasn't I? I never left 'ome. I was there. I remember when she passed her eleven-plus.' He suddenly stopped. 'Why didn't she go to grammar school? That was daft, wasn't it? How come she never went?'

'We'll talk about it later, Jack.'

'He won't take her, will he? He won't take our Kay?'

Laura closed her eyes and pressed her lips together, willing herself not to break down.

'She's being sick!' The shrill voice of a child pierced through the air and a loud cheer went up.

The angler continued to pummel Kay's back until he was sure he had cleared everything from her lungs. He waved his arms at the small crowd, instructing them to be quiet and move away. Then he turned to Laura and Jack. 'Come on,' he smiled, 'I think she'll want to see you.'

Kay opened her eyes to the sky and thought how beautiful it was. So much space . . . space without anyone or anything to clutter it. She thought how nice it would be to live up there instead of on the ground with all the noise and clumsy bodies. She could smell her mother next to her. She was holding her hand. She could hear her dad. Why was he crying?

'I want to live with the angels,' Kay tried to say, 'up there – with the people you can't see.'

'It's all right, baby. You're OK now . . . you're safe.'

Her mum was crying too; her voice sounded as if it were coming through a tunnel.

'I'm here . . . and so is your dad.'

'Dad?' Kay wanted to ask why he was crying.

'We can all go there,' she said instead, her voice sounding strange to her own ears, as if she were speaking in slow motion; 'but not together. We have to wait until there's a space . . .'

'*That's enough now,*' the comforting voice floated through to her, '*be quiet.*'

Kay allowed the soft light to move through her body and into her head. It was as if a warm golden liquid was flowing gently through her body and soul. She closed her eyes.

'What's happened?' Laura began to panic. 'What's happened?' She grabbed the rescuer by his arm and glared maniacally into his eyes.

The angler patted Laura's hand and smiled. 'She'll be all right. She's breathing properly now. Put her to bed, let her rest. She'll live.'

'I don't know what to say to you, mate. Words? There ain't any; not that I can think of, anyway.'

'I was going to suggest you carry her back but I think your missus might need supporting . . .'

Jack swung around to see Laura holding her head and swaying unsteadily; springing forward, he gripped her by the arms.

'I'll take Kay, Jack,' one of the men said, 'you see to Laura.'

Terry stepped forward and held out his arms. 'Let me, Frank,' he said, 'let me carry Kay.'

Frank smiled affectionately at Terry and shook his head. 'She's a dead weight, Terry, son.'

'Help her into my arms then. I'll manage. Please, Frank?' There was determination in his voice. 'Please?'

'All right, mate,' Frank conceded, 'but I'll walk by your side, just in case you need me. Fair enough?'

'Yeah, that's fair enough.'

Jack watched nervously as Terry held his daughter in his arms but Frank's reassuring wink put him at ease. He turned his attention back to his wife. 'Blimey, Laura. You're trembling . . .'

'Bit of shock, that's all,' the fisherman said, 'strong tea and a drop of brandy and she'll be all right.'

Scooping Laura up in his strong arms, Jack looked at her pale face and felt waves of remorse. 'You're still as light as a feather,' he smiled, 'light as a feather . . . and shaking like a leaf.'

'I can't stop trembling, Jack,' Laura managed, 'why can't I stop trembling?'

He pulled her to him as close as possible and carried her back towards the huts. 'You'll be all right once we've got you snuggled down on your straw bed.'

'Take me home, Jack,' she whispered. 'Take me home . . . back to Stepney.'

Jack swallowed hard. He was too choked for words.

Liz and Bert waited as first Kay, then Laura were carried across the common towards them. News had reached them that Kay was alive but nothing had been said about Laura and when they saw Jack carrying her they could only surmise that it had all been too much for her.

'Fetch Kay into my hut, Terry. I think we should let her mum and dad have a bit of time by themselves,' Liz said.

As Terry and Frank eased Kay on to Liz's bed they were relieved to see Kay half open her eyes. 'Terry . . .' she murmured. 'What happened?'

'You got cramp, in the river, you silly cow!' He smiled into her pale face. 'Scared the life out of me.'

'How did I get here?' She sounded exhausted but it was the same old Kay, had to know everything.

'The fisherman pulled you out.'

'The fisherman?' she murmured, and closed her eyes. 'I've got to sleep, Tel . . . I don't know

433

what's going on . . .' Her hushed voice soon gave out.

Slipping a pill under her tongue, Liz washed it down with a glass of water. 'Thanks, boys,' she said, giving them each a squeeze, a kiss on the cheek and a gentle shove out of the door. She wanted to have her niece to herself, not to question her, not even to talk, just to be there in the same tiny room.

'Janet, I've called you in here because I think there are a few things we should discuss.' Richard sounded serious, and the weak smile he put on did not fool his astute maid. 'I don't want you to feel as if I'm going behind your mistress's back while she's out riding, but—'

'It's all right, Mr Richard. You don't have to explain yourself. I do know my place and you have every right—'

'Please, Janet!' He smiled fondly at her. 'We can forget all that status business for the moment.' He shrugged, slightly embarrassed. 'I just wanted to talk to you.'

Janet looked questioningly at her employer. She had no idea what was on his mind and couldn't even guess.

'You've played quite an important part in this family over the past week or so.' He lit his pipe

434

and sat down. 'You know quite a bit about us and that can't be wiped out.'

'It won't go any further, sir, if that's what you think.'

'No, that isn't what I think. I know you better than that. I think we can assume that you realize the full extent of our . . . problems?' He glanced sideways at her, checking her reaction. She seemed fairly cool and calm. 'You've probably gathered that my wife has been taking tranquillizers for several years . . . bad nerves, that sort of thing, and she's probably slightly addicted by now.' He looked into Janet's earnest face. 'Am I making sense?'

'I can't help overhearing some things, sir. And if I am allowed an opinion . . . ?'

'I think we've already established that,' Richard smiled.

'Tranquillizers aside, bad nerves aside, it's my opinion that your wife can be viciously jealous . . . Apart from that sir, she can be very generous. I like her.'

'Quite.' He took a deep breath and sighed. 'The thing is, even though we . . . well . . . we're not exactly what you might call a perfect match, we have to, I have to, make our marriage work. For the sake of the twins.'

'That sounds fair, Mr Richard, but—'

'No please – let me speak,' he interruped her again. 'You must have gleaned from all this that I am in love with another woman.'

The sudden confession threw Janet. She looked quite shocked at his having spoken to her about his personal life. Her eyes darted from him to her hands and then back again. He could see from the expression on her face that her quick brain was going ten to the dozen. It was probably sinking in that there wasn't anyone else Richard could talk it over with. She smiled at him, flattered and moved that he was being so honest.

'If you can call it love?' she said carefully.

'Oh, yes; believe me, Janet – I do know the difference.' Feeling emotional, Richard sat down again. 'Obviously, an end has to be put to all of that . . .' he said, covering his face. Then, almost as if he had a new burst of energy, he made a conscious effort to compose himself. Clearing his throat, he started to rap his fingers on the arm of his chair. 'So,' his voice was suddenly full of determination, 'I am going to use every bit of my will to set things straight, but . . .' he paused, leaned forward and reached out for Janet's young working hands. He looked at them admiringly and then let his eyes wander up to her face. 'I need to know you'll be around; not just for me, but for

Julia. She's going to need moral support, too. I'm afraid you've become part of our lives now . . . and I really would miss you if you were to go. We both would.'

'I don't understand . . .' Janet made no attempt to remove her hands from his. 'I haven't said that I'm leaving.'

'I know you haven't . . .' He smiled knowingly. 'But that young man of yours – won't you be tempted to follow him to London? Won't he be asking you to do just that? You'll be twenty-two next month, and I'm not daft enough to think that an engagement either to him or some other lad won't be on the cards.'

Janet smiled shyly and slipped her hands from his. 'I didn't think it was that obvious, the way I feel about Brianny . . .'

Richard leaned back in his chair. 'Apparently, Janet,' he smiled, 'we can't hide love.'

'So what is it you want from me; a promise not to choose my boyfriend if he should ask . . .'

'No. I want your honest opinion about this young man of yours.'

Janet's eyes clouded over, full of concern.

'I shall need a few extra hands to help with the machines when they arrive. They can't operate by themselves.'

'You mean – Brianny?' Her eyes lit up and a grin spread across her flushed cheeks.

'Yes, I do, but . . . I have to be certain he's someone to be trusted. You know the rumours we hear about the East End of London and all the thieves . . .'

'I'm sure he'd be all right, sir!' she exclaimed excitedly. 'I *know* he would!'

'I could give the cottage over to him . . . he might have to share with another hand—'

Janet leapt to her feet. 'That would be wonderful! Really, really wonderful!'

Richard chuckled and nodded. 'I'll speak to his mother tomorrow. I'll be taking a risk. You must have heard about his father and the police?'

'You'd be giving him a chance, Mr Richard! A real opportunity to break away from all that!'

'Yes, I know. Well, perhaps you had best get on with your chores and I'll keep you informed.'

Janet made for the door, then turned back to him. 'Thank you, Mr Richard. You won't regret it!'

'I hope you're right. Oh, and Janet, I would rather you didn't say anything to him until I've finalized it.'

'Of course, sir!' Her hand flew to her mouth as she tried to stop herself giggling.

438

Feeling lighter inside, Richard knew he had taken the first small step. At least someone's wish was being granted. He couldn't help thinking that he would be a lot happier, though, if it were his own.

Fourteen

With Kay sleeping soundly, Laura attended to the Sunday pot-roast while Jack sat next to her, prodding the fire with a twig.

'Think she'll be all right?' Jack asked, his voice having taken on a softer tone with Laura.

'Will be. After a sleep.'

'Just as well that fisherman was there.'

'I don't wanna think about it, Jack. She's alive and well and we've been spared another tragedy. That's all that matters.'

'Is it?' He was probing and knew by her expression that she realized it. He waited for Laura to advance the conversation but she gave her attention to the golden lamb-joint sizzling in the pan. 'What a life, eh?'

'It's only what you make it, Jack,' she said non-committally.

'Yeah. Not very nice when it crumbles before

you though, is it? I just heard whose car she got in.'

Laura carefully laid the long-handled fork across the pan and leaned back in her chair.

'I said, I know whose car she got in.' Jack was determined to have it out once and for all.

'Richard gave her a lift as far as his farmhouse because she asked him to. She met up with someone else after that. They were messing about and she fell over.'

'What, and I'm s'posed to believe that, am I?'

'Believe what you like, I don't care. It's over and done with.'

'So I've got no cause to punch Wright in the face, then?' It was a loaded question and Laura knew it.

'Oh, leave me alone, Jack, please.'

'Is that what you want?'

She gave him a look to shut him up.

'I dunno . . .' Jack sighed. 'I dunno what happened to us, Laura, those years back . . . I've been a silly bastard, risked everything. I would like to make it up to yer, though.'

'It's a bit late for that. We can't just turn it around as if it never happened.' Her voice dropped to a murmur. 'Everyone knows our business.'

'Down 'ere in Kent they do, yeah, but not back in Stepney.'

442

'Anyway, not much of a compliment for me, is it? I can't be second best; it's not in my nature.'

'Don't talk daft. You know that's never been the case.'

'How can you say that?' Laura picked up her three-pronged fork again and jabbed at the roast lamb. 'She's dumped you, hasn't she. You only want me because you know you're hopeless on your own!'

'She didn't dump me. When it came down to it, when I was really up against the wall, I couldn't – I couldn't bear the thought of us breaking up. And then when I heard about Wright I was . . . jealous.'

'Oh, don't give me that! You? Jealous?'

'Yeah . . . jealous! The word don't even cover what I felt. I was gutted.'

Laura tossed the fork on to the parched grass. Jack wouldn't take his eyes off her. He was waiting. Waiting to see if there was a spark left. He watched as she pushed her hand through her long, lustrous hair. She looked lovely. He couldn't understand why he had neglected her for so long. He wanted to take her in his arms again, hold her close, feel her soft flesh against his and smell that perfume she always wore.

'Can't we give it a try, Laura? See if we can get it back . . .'

'I can't turn love on and off just like that, Jack. You're not the only one with emotions. It wasn't just sex with me and Richard.'

Jack drew back at the very mention of the man's name. The very thought of him making love to Laura cut him to the quick. Trying to hide his feelings but get to the truth, he grinned cheekily at her. 'Hasn't asked you to leave me, 'as he?'

'If we do try again,' Laura said, ignoring the question, 'what about this baby of yours?'

He threw his head back and sighed. 'I don't know. I can't undo what's happened. I can't promise not to wanna see it . . . I know it's a lot to ask.'

'Too right it is.' She thought about it for a while. 'It'll be Kay's half-brother or -sister; I suppose she's got every right to—' Laura covered her face. 'How could you do this, Jack? Didn't you ever think about me and how I would feel? You knew I wanted another baby to make up for the one I lost.' She looked at him through those hazel-green eyes which were filling up with tears. 'Didn't you even consider what it would do to me?'

'I swear to God, Laura, I was careful. I never wanted it to happen. But Patsy did. She wanted to be a mother. You can't blame 'er for that.'

'So it's her fault, then? Is that what you're saying?'

'Yes. She set it up. And she's not sorry. Said she would do it again.'

Laura bit her bottom lip. 'What a mess.'

'Will it help you to know that I love you as much now as I ever did? More if anything. And that's the truth – may God strike me dead.'

'Why? Why, Jack? Why do you love me?'

He narrowed his eyes, a puzzled expression hung on his face; how could she even ask that? 'Why? You're asking me why?'

'Yes, Jack, I am!'

'I dunno . . . I just do. From your toes up to your silly 'ead. Fancy asking me a thing like that! I'm not a bloody poet, am I?'

'No. You can say that again!' Laura kept a straight face.

'What about . . . you know . . . was he . . . "more romantic"?'

'There's gonna be some changes,' she said firmly. 'You have got a lot of making up to do. You want me back? Well, you're gonna 'ave to work for it. You're gonna have to court me again. Just like you did in the first place. Remember? Hours you hung about outside our green gate with a box of Dairy Milk under your arm.'

Jack started to remember, and laughed. 'Nothing wrong with your memory, is there?'

'No. And I want it all over again: dinner out at Lyon's Corner House, flowers, pictures on a Saturday night, chocolate-covered Brazils . . .'

'What about me,' he grinned, 'what do I get?'

'We'll just 'ave to wait and see, won't we?'

He nodded, only too happy to see the old sparkle back in her eyes. 'Fair enough,' he said, 'it's a deal. A one-sided deal but there we are; you'll never change, will yer?' he teased.

'I wish you were staying to the end of the season, Kay. It won't be the same without you.'

'Come and see me as soon as you get back to London, right?'

'You don't 'ave to go, you know. If you want you can stay with me and Mum in our hut.'

It hadn't occurred to Kay that she could stay on. That her family could go back without her. But would they? 'Terry, that's the best idea you've 'ad since I've known yer.'

It wasn't the hop-picking that was tempting her, or the place. She was ready to go back to Stepney and pick up with her best friend, Lorraine. She had much to tell her. Zacchi was the only reason she would stay and, fast as the thoughts were flying through her mind, that was the one that hit home: Zacchi. She knew her mum and dad would never leave her there in the hands of the handsome gypsy.

'Come and see me when you get back,' Kay said, hugging Terry.

'They reckon we've only got about ten more days of picking left in any case . . .' Terry spoke to himself more than to Kay.

'Do me a favour, Tel? I'm going over to see Zacchi. If Mum or Dad ask where I am, just say I'm doing the rounds, saying Cheerio to everyone and letting them know I'm OK.'

'Yeah, go on then. And don't go roaming off again!'

'More than I dare do,' Kay laughed and walked towards the gypsy camp.

'Bet I know where madam's off to,' Liz said.

'Saying her goodbyes,' Terry offered, knowing full well that Liz knew exactly who she was going to see.

'You had a bit of a shock earlier, love, didn't yer?' Liz cupped Terry's face and smiled. 'Cheer up then, she's not going on no wagon-trail. Not while I'm around to spill the beans. You'll see 'er back in London.'

'You gonna leave these half empty packets, Liz?' Bert called from the hut doorway.

'Don't I always? Give the little ones something to

find. Half a box of Bisto's like finding treasure to them, even if they do chuck it away.'

'What about all the straw from the beds?'

'Leave it in the hut! I'm sure Richard Wright'll find a use for it!'

'And the curtain? You won't be needing that any more.'

The curtain. The thick red hopping curtain. It had seen her through a good ten years of picking and was still in good condition. But Bert was right – she wouldn't be needing it any more. Strolling over to her hut, she ran her hand over the door, touched the wooden shelves Bert had fixed up for her some years back. She could feel Bert looking at her.

'You know what,' he said, 'I wouldn't mind buying a little caravan for two.'

Liz beamed. 'Yeah,' she said, 'that'd be lovely, Bert.'

'I'll be there, Kay. I'll find you. It might not be till next year, but . . .'

'Write to me, Zacchi,' Kay said with a plea in her voice.

He stroked the side of her face, pulled her close and kissed her lightly on the mouth. ''Course I will.'

'Bye, Zac.'

'Bye.'

Kay pulled away, smiled and nodded to his family and turned towards her Uncle Bert's waiting lorry. As she walked slowly away from Zacchi his voice followed her: 'Don't look back, Kay!'

She obeyed his instructions, respected them. It was an old gypsy saying. *Never look back . . .*

Arriving at the lorry she came face to face with Laura. 'Mum . . . it feels as if there's a big hole in my chest . . . it hurts, but there's no pain. Have you ever felt anything like that?'

Laura smiled. 'Yeah, I have. Come on! Get yourself on to that lorry and let's get back to London. There's a life back there as well, you know.'

Liz strolled away from her hut and joined Laura and Kay. 'That's it, then?' She looked around her, choked.

'You sure you're strong enough for this journey, Liz?'

'I'm ready for it, Laura. I think we all are.' She sat on the floor of her and Bert's lorry and swung her legs up.

'Liz! I'm getting an eyeful 'ere!' Laura laughed.

'Clean and well paid for, Mog.' She remembered Kay saying the same when they were at the start of their journey in Stepney. Pulling herself up she held out her hand to Kay. 'Come on – up you come.'

'You women do take your time . . .' Jack arrived and looked keen to get on the road. 'Ready Laura?' Without giving her time to answer he swept her up on to the back of the lorry and then made a business of securing the chains and bolting up the tailboard.

'You OK?'

'Yeah, I'm OK, Jack.' A certain smile and a look of promise passed between them.'

'Good. It's back to the old smoke, then!' Jack turned to Terry who was looking a bit down in the mouth. 'See yer, Terry, mate. Look forward to you filling us in about the last week or so that we'll miss . . . and the last day, of course. Perhaps Wright'll give you a sending-off party, eh?'

Hearing Richard being referred to by Jack in that way put Laura's back up. She glared at her husband and he returned the reprimanding look with a wink and a grin which, annoying as it was, made her laugh.

She hoped that Jack had done as she asked earlier and told Bert to take the longest route so she wouldn't have to see Richard's farmhouse. She had slipped away earlier, boldly walked to his door and was relieved when he had appeared in the doorway and not Julia or her maid.

It hadn't been quite as Laura had expected; no tears, no gripping pains in the chest, no promises.

She had explained why she had to leave early, using Liz's health as the main reason and Richard, as far as she could tell, had already begun to withdraw, wanting to get the parting over with, out of the way. It was an awkward moment for them both.

Waving to the rest of the pickers who were there to see them off, Jack strode to the front of the lorry to join the ever-impatient Bert. As he climbed into the cab he couldn't help noticing Milly by her hut door. She looked a right cracker in that red and white spotted dress. 'See yer, Milly!'

'Not if I see you first, Jack!' She laughed and waved.

They started to pull away from the huts to fond farewells, tears and laughter as they waved goodbye. Approaching that familiar gateway and knowing it would be for the last time, neither Laura nor Liz could stop themselves shedding a private tear.

'All part of life's rich tapestry, Mum,' Kay said, trailing her hand across the shoulders of Laura's maroon velvet-trimmed jacket which she had bought in Hammond's and was wearing for the very first time.

Laura and Liz enjoyed that. Their Kay had grown up fast in just a couple of weeks.

'I expect you'll be pining for that handsome gypsy

of yours,' Liz teased. 'Look at 'im – face as long as a kite.'

There was a sudden lurch as the lorry braked. 'Oh God, what now?' Liz moaned.

They waited for Jack to appear – but it was Milly's red face that grinned up at them. She had been running and was out of breath. 'You forgot to pull your last bine to take back with yer!' Using all her strength she threw the bine with its plump yellow-green hops into the back of the lorry. 'Gotta 'ave something to remind yer!' she laughed, 'I pulled 'em out of the hedgerow!'

Carefully pulling the wild hops into the lorry, Laura draped them across a tea chest. 'Thanks, Milly, you're an angel!'

Milly leaned across the tailboard and stretched her hand up to Laura and as they clasped fingers, she grinned and winked at her. 'He's a right cracker, Laura. Look after 'im.'

'Yeah, I suppose you're right . . . but he's still a sod when it comes to a pretty face!' She grinned and winked back at her bubbly friend. 'Don't forget to pop in and see me when you get back to London!' Laura called out as the lorry moved off.

'You're on! So long as Jack's in!' Milly's high-pitched, contagious laughter started the others off and changed what would have been a sadder parting.

The three faces of Laura, Kay and Liz laughing after all their traumas was something they could each remember.

As the lorry disappeared through the gateway, Zacchi stood apart from everyone, away from the happy banter. Making his vow, he smiled to himself. He would somehow make his way to London. He would find Kay.